D0374935

THE KING OF THE CATS

The King of the Cats
and Other Feline Fairy Tales

EDITED BY

JOHN RICHARD STEPHENS

Faber and Faber

BOSTON • LONDON

The author wishes to express his appreciation to Martha and Jim Goodwin, Scott Stephens, Mollie Seibert, Danny Schutt, Bill and Norene Hilden, Doug and Shirley Strong, Frank and Marybeth DiVito, Marty Goeller, and to his agent, Charlotte Cecil Raymond.

Library of Congress Cataloging-in-Publication Data

Stephens, John Richard.
  The king of the cats : and other feline fairy tales / John Richard Stephens.
      p.   cm.
  ISBN 0-571-19827-9
  1. Cats—Folklore.   2. Fairy tales.   I. Title.
GR725.S74   1993
398.24'52974428—dc20   93-14354
                                                                CIP

Interior cat drawing by Arthur Rackham from his *Mother Goose, The Old Nursery Rhymes,* 1913

Jacket design by Lorna Stovall
Printed in the United States of America

This book is dedicated to

Joyce Dianne Whiteaker

and the newly discovered
members of my family

CONTENTS

LESSER KNOWN CAT FAIRY TALES

PREFACE

I WAS RAISED with cats and have always enjoyed their company, but it wasn't until I was conducting the research on my first book, *The Enchanted Cat,* that I first became interested in cat fairy tales. *The Enchanted Cat*—which is about the mysterious and magical aspects of cats as they appear in art, history, literature, and folklore—does contain a chapter on cat fairy tales, but there is very little overlap between the two books. Although I collected many cat fairy tales while researching *The Enchanted Cat,* I wasn't able to include them in that book because of lack of space. At the time, I was a bit disappointed that I had to leave out some of the best stories.

It wasn't until I uncovered many more of these fairy tales while I was researching *Mysterious Cat Stories*—a short story anthology—that I suddenly realized that if they were gathered together, all these fairy tales would make a fascinating book.

Once I set out searching specifically for cat fairy tales, I was able to assemble enough material to fill two or three volumes. It was interesting trying to track down the more obscure tales through the often oblique references I ran across. My search led me through many old and dusty volumes before I found what I was after. I also had dozens of long out of print books shipped to me from all over the country. There was even one story that I discovered during my travels through Scotland while I was researching an as yet unpublished book. Though I found a lot of worthless material, every once in a while I discovered a nugget of gold.

Sorting through the pile of stories I amassed, I selected the most interesting tales and the best, most representative versions of the popular tales for inclusion in this book. I also did my best to include stories from all over the world. Unlike most fairy tale collections, I have also placed an emphasis on accuracy. I have not altered the stories in any way, with the minor exception of standardizing and modernizing the spelling and punctuation. Typographical errors and a few problems with translation were also corrected to make the stories easier to read and understand.

I hope you enjoy this enchanting collection of feline fairy tales as much as I have.

INTRODUCTION

The Magic in Cats' Eyes

THERE IS something magical about cats. They can be completely self-sufficient—when no one is willing to take care of them, they have the ability to survive just about anywhere—and yet cats love to live with us and are affectionate, loving companions. They are swift and silent. They are sleek and graceful. They seem to glide rather than walk. When they fall, they always land on their feet. They can see at night just as well as they can by day. They have sudden tremendous bursts of energy, but spend most of the day lying around taking catnaps and watching the world go by. All of them are a bit erratic and unpredictable. French author Colette summed it all up nicely when she said, "There are no ordinary cats."

Throughout history, cats were associated with things magical and supernatural. They were sacred gods of the Pharaohs and the devoted familiars of witches. They were thought to be possessors of secret powers and abilities, such as that of second sight. The idea that cats can see ghosts and spirits is found all over the world. This belief stems from the cat's ability to see at night much better than we can and may date all the way back to the ancient Egyptians. They believed cats stored sunlight in their eyes and used it to see at night. The inspiration for this was probably the strange appearance of the cat's eyes. The pupils are just a narrow line in daylight, but the way they reflect light gives them the appearance of two glowing moons in the darkness. The Chinese believed cats' ability to see in the dark enabled them to ward off evil spirits at night; the Europeans came to the opposite conclusion, thinking cats were working with and warning these spirits, so they could scramble into hiding when humans drew near.

It is a common belief around the world that cats can understand human conversation, and some say they can also speak when they want to.

Some have even thought cats can communicate with the gods, taking messages to them and relaying back their desires.

People have also thought that some cats are not really cats at all. In the Middle East, it was said that genii would take on the form of cats. Japanese vampires were thought to prefer this form to that of bats. It was thought in Scotland and Ireland that cats were actually fairies in disguise. In Europe, witches were often said to turn themselves into cats. On the other hand, some people believed that witches were actually cats in disguise.

Cats were thought to be able to control the weather and the tides. They were thought to listen in on conversations and watch people doing things in secret, and then report these things to witches, fairies, or to other cats. And they were thought to reward those who were kind to them and bring a disastrous end to those who did them wrong. Although few people still believe any of this, even today cats are still seen as mysterious, magical creatures.

Perhaps it is this quality which accounts for their appearance in so many fairy tales. There are very few fairy tales featuring the other most common pet—the dog. In fact, there are probably more fairy tales about cats than there are about any other animal (with the exception of mythical beasts, such as the dragon). This book is an extensive collection of these cat fairy tales. Since fairy tales are stories full of magic and enchantment, they seem perfectly suited for such a creature as the cat.

Fairy tales are windows to a fantastic and wonderful realm. It is therefore quite appropriate that the eyes of cats were once thought to be magical windows to the domain of the fairies. It was said that the fairy kings would look out through the cat's eyes and watch what people in our human world were doing. This was how the fairy kings kept track of what people were up to. As proof of this, those who believed would point to the fact that cats are always watching people very closely, noticing everything we do. They seem to be aware of us even when they are asleep.

Interestingly enough, these windows were said to work both ways. They allowed the fairy kings to see out, but they also allowed people to see in. According to this belief, if you look very deeply into your cat's eyes, you will be able see the strangely illuminated world of the fairies.

Well-Known
Cat Fairy Tales

The Eleventh Night, The First Fable

One of the earliest versions of "Puss in Boots" was written by Giovanni Francesco Straparola (c. 1480–1558). This story is from Le piacevoli notti (The Pleasurable Nights), *which was published in Venice in two parts—the first in 1550 and the second in 1553. The framework of this book was taken from* The Decameron, *the fourteenth-century classic where 100 tales are told by ten people over ten days while they try to escape the plague by hiding out in the gardens and villas above the city. In* The Pleasurable Nights, *the people are hiding in a palace in Venice from political enemies and the stories are told over thirteen nights. This book contains what may be the first appearance of fairy tales in Italian literature. The most famous story from this book is its version of "Puss in Boots," although the star of the story has not yet taken to wearing boots. This story appears to have originated in India, with a jackal in the leading role. It has since spread throughout the world. Although versions featuring cats seem to be the most common, there are versions with dogs, foxes, rabbits, monkeys, and gazelles. Many people have taken exception to the morality of this story in which a con-artist cat achieves riches for his undeserving master. Despite this, "Puss in Boots" has become one of the world's most popular fairy tales.*

The shadowy night, nursing mother of the world's fatigues, had already fallen, and the wearied beasts and birds had gone to rest, when the gentle and amiable company of dames and cavaliers, putting aside all somber thoughts, took themselves to the accustomed meeting-place. Then, after the damsels had danced diverse measures according to the rule of the assemblage, the vase was brought forth, and out of it, by chance, was first drawn the name of Fiordiana . . .

And then, in order to begin at once the story-telling for the evening, the Signora bade Fiordiana to commence, and the latter, having made her due salutation, told the story which follows:

It is no rare event, beloved ladies, to see a rich man brought to extreme poverty, or to find one who from absolute poverty has mounted to high estate. And this last-named fortune happened to a poor young man of whom I have heard tell, who from being little better than a beggar attained the full dignity of a king.

There was once in Bohemia a very poor lady named Soriana, who had three sons: one was called Dusolino, the other Tesifone, and the third Constantine the Lucky. She owned nothing valuable in the world but three things: a kneading-trough, a rolling-board, and a cat. When Soriana, laden with years, came to die, she made her last testament, and left to Dusolino, her eldest son, the kneading-trough, to Tesifone the rolling-board, and to Constantine the cat.

When the mother was dead and buried, the neighbors, as they had need, borrowed now the kneading-trough, now the rolling-board; and because they knew that the owners were very poor, they made them a cake, which Dusolino and Tesifone ate, giving none to Constantine, the youngest brother. And if Constantine asked them for anything, they told him to go to his cat, which would get it for him. Wherefore poor Constantine and his cat suffered greatly.

Now the cat, which was a fairy in disguise, moved to compassion for Constantine and angry at the two brothers who treated him so cruelly, said: "Constantine, do not be downcast, for I will provide for your support and my own." And leaving the house, the cat went out into the fields and, pretending to sleep, caught a hare that passed and killed it.

Thence, going to the royal palace and seeing some of the courtiers, the cat said that she wished to speak with the king, who, when he heard that a cat wished to speak to him, had her shown into his presence and asked her what she wished. The cat replied that her master, Constantine, had sent him a hare which he had caught. The king accepted the gift, and asked who this Constantine was. The cat replied that he was a man who had no superior in goodness, beauty, and power. Wherefore the king treated the cat very well, giving her to eat and drink bountifully.

When the cat had satisfied her hunger, she slyly filled with her paw (unseen by any one) the bag that hung at her side, and taking leave of the king, carried it to Constantine. When the brothers saw the food over which Constantine exulted, they asked him to share it with them; but he refused, rendering them tit for tat. On which account there arose between them great envy, that continually gnawed their hearts.

Now Constantine, although handsome in his face, nevertheless, from the privation he had suffered, was covered with scabs and scurf, which caused him great annoyance. But going with his cat to the river, she licked him carefully from head to foot, and combed his hair, and in a few days he was entirely cured.

The cat (as we said above) continued to carry gifts to the royal palace, and thus supported her master. But after a time she wearied of running up and down so much, and feared that she would annoy the king's courtiers; so she said to her master: "Sir, if you will do what I order, I will make you rich in a short time."

"How?" said her master.

The cat replied: "Come with me, and do not ask any more, for I am ready to enrich you."

So they went together to the stream, which was near the royal palace, and the cat stripped her master, and with his agreement threw him into the river, and then began to cry out in a loud voice: "Help! help! Messer Constantine is drowning." The king hearing this, and remembering that he had often received presents from him, sent his people at once to aid him.

When Messer Constantine was taken out of the water and dressed in fine clothes, he was taken to the king, who received him cordially, and asked him why he had been thrown into the river. Constantine could not answer on account of his agitation; but the cat, which was always at his side, said: "Know, O king, that some robbers learned from spies that my master was loaded with jewels, which he was coming to present to you. They robbed him of all, and threw him into the river, thinking to kill him, but thanks to these gentlemen he has escaped from death."

The king, hearing this, ordered that he should be well cared for; and seeing that he was handsome, and knowing him to be wealthy, he concluded to give him Elisetta, his daughter, for a wife, endowing her with jewels and most beautiful garments.

After the wedding festivities had been ended, the king had ten mules loaded with money, and five with costly apparel, and sent his daughter to her husband's home, accompanied by a great retinue. Constantine, seeing that he had become so wealthy and honored, did not know where to lead his wife, and took counsel with his cat, which said: "Do not fear, my master, for we shall provide for everything."

So they all set out gaily on horseback, and the cat ran hastily before them; and having left the company some distance behind, met some horsemen, to whom she said: "What are you doing here, wretched men? Depart quickly, for a large band of people are coming, and will take you prisoners. They are near by: you can hear the noise of the neighing horses."

The horsemen said in terror: "What must we do, then?"

The cat replied: "Do this—if you are asked whose horsemen you are, answer boldly, Messer Constantine's, and you will not be molested."

Then the cat went on, and found a large flock of sheep, and did the same with their owners, and said the same thing to all those whom she found in the road. The people who were escorting Elisetta asked the horsemen: "Whose knights are you," and "whose are so many fine flocks?" and all with one accord replied: "Messer Constantine's." Then those who accompanied the bride said: "So then, Messer Constantine, we are beginning to enter your territory." And he nodded his head, and replied in like manner to all that he was asked. Wherefore the company judged him to be very wealthy.

At last the cat came to a very fine castle, and found there but few servants, to whom she said: "What are you doing, good men; do you not perceive the destruction which is impending?"

"What?" asked the servants.

"Before an hour passes, a host of soldiers will come here and cut you to pieces. Do you not hear the horses neighing? Do you not see the dust in the air? If you do not wish to perish, take my advice and you will be saved. If any one asks you whose this castle is, say, Messer Constantine's."

So they did; and when the noble company reached the handsome castle they asked the keepers whose it was, and all answered boldly Messer Constantine the Lucky's. Then they entered, and were honorably entertained.

Now the lord of that place was Signor Valentino, a brave soldier, who, a short time before, had left the castle to bring home the wife he had lately married; and to his misfortune, before he reached the place where his wife was he was overtaken on the way by a sudden and fatal accident, from which he straightway died, and Constantine remained master of the castle.

Before long, Morando, King of Bohemia, died, and the people elected for their king Constantine the Lucky because he was the husband of Elisetta, the dead king's daughter, to whom the kingdom fell by right of succession. And so Constantine, from being poor and a beggar, remained Lord and King, and lived a long time with his Elisetta, leaving children by her to succeed him in the kingdom.

The fable told by Fiordiana gave great pleasure to all the company.

FRANCE

Puss in Boots

Charles Perrault (1628–1703) originally published "Le Chat Botté (Puss in Boots)" in his book Histoires ou contes du temps passé (Histories and Stories of Past Times) *in 1697. Perrault's version appears to be based on that of Straparola. Even though a version by Giambattista Basile—which appears later in this book—had already been published in Italy (in 1634), it is very unlikely that Perrault was aware of it since Basile's version had not been translated into French and Straparola's had. This conclusion is supported by the similarities between Perrault's and Straparola's tales and their differences from Basile's. Perrault's "Puss in Boots" is the most famous version of this fairy tale, and it is also the first in which the hero wears boots. This is the most famous of all cat fairy tales.*

There was once upon a time a miller, who left no more estate to the three children that he had, who were all boys, but his mill, his ass, and his cat. The partition was soon made. Neither the clerk nor attorney were sent for; they would soon have eaten up all the poor inheritance. The eldest had the mill, the second the ass, and the youngest nothing but the cat.

The poor young fellow was quite comfortless at having so poor a lot. "My brothers," said he, "may get their living very handsomely, by joining their stocks together; but for my part, when I have eaten up my cat, and made me a muff of his skin, I must die with hunger."

The cat, who heard all this but acted as if he hadn't, said to him with a grave and serious air, "Do not thus afflict yourself, my good master, you have nothing else to do but to give me a bag and have a pair of boots made for me, that I may scamper through the dirt and the brambles, and you shall see that you are not as bad off as you imagine."

Though the cat's master did not build very much upon what he said, he had often seen him play a great many cunning tricks to catch rats and mice; as when he used to hang by his feet, or hide himself in the meal, and make as if he was dead;[1] so that he did not altogether despair of his affording him some help in his miserable condition. When the cat had what he asked for, he booted himself very gallantly; and putting his bag about his neck, he held the two strings of it in his two fore-paws, and went into a warren where there was a great number of rabbits. He put bran and sow-thistle into his bag, and stretching himself out at length, as if he had been dead, he waited for some young rabbits, not yet acquainted with the deceits of the world, to come and rummage his bag for what he had put into it.

He had scarcely laid down when he had what he wanted —a silly rash young rabbit jumped into his bag, and Mr. Puss drawing immediately the strings, took him and killed him without mercy. Proud of his prey, he went with it to the palace, and asked to speak with the king. He was shown up stairs into his majesty's apartment, and said to him, "I have brought you, Sir, a rabbit of the warren which my master, my Lord Marquis of Carabas" (for that was the title he was pleased to give his master) "has commanded me to make Your Honor a present of it from him."

"Tell your master," said the king, "that I thank him, and he does me a great deal of pleasure."

Another time he went and hid himself amongst the corn, holding still his bag open; and when he saw a brace of partridges run into it, he drew the strings, and took them. He went and made a present of these to the king, as he had done before of the rabbit.

The king in like manner received the partridges with a great deal of pleasure, and ordered him some money for drink. The cat continued after this manner for two or three months, to carry, from time to time, game of his master's taking to the king. One day above the rest, when he knew for certain that the king was to take the air along the river with his daughter, the most beautiful princess in the world, he said to his master, "If you will follow my advice, your fortune is made. You don't have to do anything, but go and wash yourself in the river as I will show you, and leave the rest to me."

The Marquis of Carabas did what the cat advised him to, without

---

[1] These refer to cats in the fables of Jean de La Fontaine.

knowing why or wherefore. While he was washing, the king passed by, and the cat began to cry out as loud as he could, "Help! Help! My Lord Marquis of Carabas is going to be drowned."

At this noise the king put his head out of the window of his coach, and finding it was the cat who had brought him so often so much good game, he commanded his guards to run immediately to the assistance of the Marquis of Carabas.

While they were drawing the poor marquis out of the river, the cat came up to the coach, and told the king that while his master was washing, there came by some robbers, who went off with his clothes, though he had cried out "Thieves!" several times, as loud as he could. (Actually this cunning rogue of a cat had hidden them under a great stone.)

The king immediately commanded the officers of his wardrobe to go and fetch one of his best suits of clothes for the Lord Marquis of Carabas. The king caressed him after a very extraordinary manner and, as the fine clothes he had given him set off his good appearance (for he was well made, and very handsome in his person), the king's daughter took a secret inclination to him. The Marquis of Carabas had no sooner cast two or three respectful and somewhat tender glances, but she fell in love with him to distraction.

The king made him come into the coach, and take part of the airing. The cat, quite ravished to see his design succeed, marched on before, and meeting with some countrymen, who were mowing a meadow, he said to them, "Good people, you that mow, if you do not tell the king that the meadow you mow belongs to my Lord Marquis of Carabas, you shall be chopped as small as herbs for the pot."

The king did not fail asking of the mowers whom the meadow they were mowing belonged to. "To my Lord Marquis of Carabas," said they all together; for the cat's threats had made them terribly afraid. "You see, Sir," said the Marquis, "this is a meadow which never fails to yield a plentiful harvest every year."

The Master-Cat, who went still on before, met with some reapers, and said to them, "Good people, you that reap, if you do not tell the king that all this corn belongs to the Lord Marquis of Carabas, you shall be chopped as small as herbs for the pot."

The king, who passed by a moment after, asked to whom all that corn which he then saw belonged to. "To my Lord Marquis of Carabas," said the reapers, and the king was very well pleased with it, as well as the marquis, whom he congratulated thereupon.

The Master-Cat, who went always before, said the same words to all that he met, and the king was astonished at the vast estates of my Lord Marquis of Carabas. The Master-Cat came at last to a stately castle, the master of which was an ogre, the richest that ever was known; for all the land that the King had then gone over belonged to this castle. The cat—who had taken care to inform himself who this ogre was and what he could do—asked to speak with him, saying he would not pass so near his castle without having the honor of paying his respects to him.

The ogre received him as civilly as an ogre could do, and made him sit down.

"I have been assured," said the cat, "that you have the power of changing yourself into all sorts of creatures you have a mind to; you can, for example, transform yourself into a lion, an elephant, and the like."

"This is true," said the ogre very briskly, "and to convince you, you shall see me now a lion."

The cat was so much frightened to see a lion stand before him, that he immediately jumped up on the gutters. (But not without a great deal of trouble and danger because of his boots, which were of no use to him at all in walking upon the tiles.)

Some time after, when the cat saw that he had taken his natural form, he came down, and owned he had been very much frightened. "I have also been informed—," said the cat, "though I don't know whether to believe it or not—that you also have the power to take on the shape of the smallest animals; for example, to change yourself into a rat or a mouse. I must tell to you, I take this to be impossible."

"Impossible!" said the ogre, "You shall see that presently." And at the same time changed himself into a mouse that began to run about the floor. The cat no sooner perceived this, but he jumped on him, and ate him up.

The king, in the meantime, saw this fine castle of the ogre's as he passed and decided to come into it. The cat—who heard the noise of the coach running over the draw-bridge—ran out and said to the king, "Your Majesty is welcome to this castle of my Lord Marquis of Carabas."

"What?" said the king, "My Lord Marquis, does this castle also belong to you? There can be nothing finer than this court, and all these stately buildings that surround it. Let's go into it, if you please."

The marquis gave his hand to the princess, and followed the king, who went up first. They came into a great hall where they found a magnificent meal which the ogre had prepared for his friends, who were to come to see him that very day, but dared not enter, knowing the king was there. The king was quite charmed with the good qualities of my Lord Marquis of Carabas—as was his daughter, who had fallen extremely in love with him—and seeing the vast estate he possessed, said to him (after having drunk five or six glasses), "it will be owing to yourself only, my Lord Marquis, if you are not my son-in-law."

The marquis, making several low bows, accepted the honor the king conferred upon him and married the princess that same day. The cat became a great lord and never ran after mice again, except for his entertainment.

Gagliuso

This version of "Puss in Boots" was actually written over half a century before Perrault's but, since Perrault's version is so similar to Straparola's and this version continues the story, I have decided to place it after. "Gagliuso" was written by Giambattista Basile (1575–1632), who was also known as Giovanni Batiste Basile and Gian Alesio Abbattutis. Basile grew up on the island of Crete and studied at the university in Venice. He became a well-known court poet while serving as an administrator for several dukes and princes in Italy. His sister and her daughter were two of the most famous Italian singers of that time and he often wrote songs for them, as well as musical plays. "Gagliuso" is from The Pentameron, *which was published in Naples in 1634. It was the first great collection of folktales in Europe and had considerable influence on later fairy tales. Originally titled* Lo Cunto de li Cunte (The Tale of Tales), *the title was changed to* Il Pentamerone (The Five Days) *in imitation of* Il Decamerone (The Ten Days), *the fourteenth-century Italian masterpiece mentioned in the introduction to "The Eleventh Night." Once again the tales are presented as if they were told over a series of days. Although "Gagliuso"—which means "young one" in Italian—is very similar to "Puss in Boots," the ending of this story is quite different.*

It was time that Paola should begin her story, paying from her lips the golden coins of good words, and in this manner she discharged her debt:

Ingratitude is a rusty nail, which, nailed to the bark of a tree, causes the tree to wither and die. It is a broken sink, which soaks up all troubles and afflictions. It is a spider's web, which falling in the pot of friendship, makes it lose its scent and flavor, as is seen daily, and as you will hear in this story which I will relate.

There once lived in the city of Naples a miserly old man, thin, and tall, and ragged, and tattered, and withered, and wrinkled, so that he went

13

about as nearly naked as a flea. And as he had reached the time when the sacks of life are shaken, he called to his side Oraziello and Pippo his two sons, and said to them, "I have been sent for to pay the debt that we all owe to Nature, and believe me, O my sons, that I would feel most happy to exit from this world of trouble, this hovel of travail, but for the thought that I leave you, grown tall and strong as Santa Clara and the five roads of Melito, without a single coat to your backs, like a barber's basin; sharp as a drilling sergeant, and dry as a plum-pit. Your net worth is not even as much as a fly could carry tied at its foot; and if we were to run a hundred miles, you would not drop a mite. All this because my ill-luck brought me all my life on the dung heap; but as you can see, thus you may paint me. As you know, I have done many things; and many times I have crossed myself and went to bed without cinnamon to my wine.

"Notwithstanding all this, I desire to leave you at my death with a sign of my love; therefore, you Oraziello, who are my first born, take that sieve which you see hanging upon the wall, with which you may gain the wherewithal to keep life in you. And you Pippo, who are the youngest, take the cat, and may both of you remember your father." And so having ended his way, he wept with bitter weeping, and his sons wept with him, and straightway he spoke again, and said, "Adieu, it's night," and died.

Now after Oraziello had him laid out and buried for charity, he took the sieve and went about sifting to gain a livelihood: and the more he sifted the more he gained. Pippo, taking the cat with him, said, "Now see, what heritage has my father left me? I have nothing to eat, and I will have to think for two. What a heritage is mine! Who ever heard of such a gift? Far better had he left me nothing."

But the cat, hearing this complaining, said to him, "Your lamenting is needless, for you are more fortunate than your brother. You just do not know your own good fortune, for I shall enrich you. Now I shall set to work." On hearing this, Pippo thanked the cat, and ran his hand down her back three or four times, placed himself in her charge. The cat felt great compassion for the sad hearted Gagliuso.

Every morning when the sun fished the shadows of the night with his bait of light and gold, the cat made her way to the sea-shore at Chiaja, and watched for an opportunity of catching a large gold fish. As soon as she caught one, she would take it to the king, saying, "My Lord Gagliuso, a slave of your highness and a loyal liege, sends this fish with his humble greetings, saying, 'To a great lord small is the gift.'"

The king—with the happy expression he generally wore to those who brought him presents—answered the cat, "Say to this lord, that I don't know, that I thank him." Another time the cat would run to some marshy ground where the hunters had let fall some pheasants, or wild ducks, or partridges and take them to the king in the same manner. For many a day she continued doing this, till one morning the king said to her, "I feel myself under deep obligation to this your lord Gagliuso, and I should like to make his acquaintance so that I may thank him for his offerings and, as proof of my gratitude, do something for him in exchange."

Answered the cat, "It is the desire of my lord Gagliuso to lay down his life for the good of your realm and your crown, so tomorrow morning without fail—when the sun shall have set fire to the ricks of straw in the fields —he shall stand before you to pay homage."

Now when the morning came, the cat came to the king and said, "O my lord, the lord Gagliuso sends you greetings, and would you excuse him for not coming this morning, as last night some of his attendants took to their heels, carrying with them all my master's wardrobe, and have left him without even a shirt to his back." On hearing this, the king sent to his master of the robes, and ordered that he should send at once some of his own clothes for the lord Gagliuso.

In two hours' time Gagliuso came to the palace, guided by the cat, and when he stood in the royal presence, the king thanked and complimented him, and made him sit by his side. He then led him to the banquet-hall, where the tables were spread with dainties, and while they ate, Gagliuso turned round, and said to the cat, "O my cat, I pray you watch over my tattered clothes, that they should not be stolen." The cat replied, "Be silent, hold your tongue, and speak not of these beggarly objects," and to the king, who desired to know what he wanted, the cat answered that he longed for a small lemon. The king immediately sent to the garden for a basketful.

Shortly after, Gagliuso returned to the same music about those few rags. The cat told him again to shut his mouth and the king again inquired what he wanted. The cat quickly gave another excuse to remedy the vileness and meanness of Gagliuso.

After they finished eating and had chatted upon various subjects, Gagliuso begged leave to retire. The cat remained with the king, describing to him the prowess, ability, and just judgment of Gagliuso, and above all his great riches, being master of estates near Rome, in the Campagna, and in Lombardy.[1] She added that he deserved to marry a king's daughter. The king inquired as to the extent of his holdings and the cat answered that no account could be kept of the goods, and properties, and houses, and estates of this very rich lord, and it was unknown how much he possessed. But if the king would send forth some of his officers to inquire beyond his kingdom they might have an idea of what he was worth, for no one was so rich as Gagliuso.

The king at once sent for some of his most trusty followers, and bade them inquire concerning him, and they departed taking the cat with them as a guide, and she, excusing herself, saying that she would order some food, went before them, and no sooner were they outside the kingdom than she ran on ahead. As she met many flocks of sheep, and cows, and horses, and pigs, she would say to the shepherds and keepers, "Ho there, keep your brains clear, as a company of robbers is scouring the country. If you wish to escape unharmed, and that respect should be shown to your homes and belongings, when they come by, say that all you hold belongs to the lord Gagliuso, and then no harm shall come to you." She continued doing this with all the farms she came to, so that wherever the king's messengers went they found a general accord of music and all things fell into the same reply—that they belonged to the lord Gagliuso. Finally tiring of asking questions, they returned to the king and told him wonders upon wonders of the great riches of this lord.

On hearing this, the king promised a good present to the cat, if she would manage to bring about this marriage. The cat, pretending to go and come backwards and forwards, at last concluded the marriage. Gagliuso came to court and the king gave him a rich dowry with his daughter in marriage. After a month of high festivities and joy and enjoyance, Gagliuso told the king that he desired to take his bride to his estates. The king gave him leave, accompanied him part of the way, and then bade them adieu. Gagliuso continued his journey to Lombardy, where by puss's advice he bought some lands and a palace and at once became a baron.

Now Gagliuso, finding himself in so much opulence, thanked the cat with deepest gratitude, saying that he owed her his life, and his happiness, and his greatness, since more good had been brought about by the craft of a cat than by the genius and wit of his father; therefore she could bid and

1 Campagna is the plain around Rome and Lombardy is one of the major regions in northern Italy with Milan as its capital.

forbid and do whatsoever she chose with his life and his goods; promising faithfully that even if she died in an hundred years, he would have her embalmed, and enclosed in a golden urn, and kept in his room, so as to have ever before his eyes the memory of all her benefits. The cat, hearing this boast, thought she would put it to the test, and three days after, she pretended death, and lay stretched out at full length in the garden. Seeing this, the wife of Gagliuso cried, "O my husband, a great misfortune has happened! The cat is dead!"

Gagliuso answered, "May every evil go with her, better she than ourselves."

"What shall we do with her?" the wife asked.

"Take hold of one leg, and throw her out of the window," he replied.

The cat, hearing in what way his gratitude was to be shown when least she expected it, cried out, "These are the thanks I get for the lice I have cleaned from your neck? This is your gratitude for ridding you of your rags? This is the reward for my spider-like industry in lifting you up from the dust? Beggar! Clothes-tearer! You were in rags, tattered, and torn, and full of lice. You villain! You scoundrel! Such is the reward of those that wash the ass's head. Accursed be all the good I have done for you, for you do not even deserve that I should spit down your throat! A fine golden urn have you prepared for me; a beautiful grave you have consigned me to! I went and served you, worked and sweated, to receive such a reward. O wretched is he that puts the pot to the fire in hopes that another may fill it. That sage spoke well who said, 'Whoever goes to bed an ass, an ass rises again,' and 'Whoever does most expects least.' But good words and bad deeds deceive the wise and the foolish."

When she finished, she jumped up and took to her heels. Although Gagliuso, with sweet talk and omelette in mouth, tried to smooth down her ruffled fur, it was no use. The cat refused to come back. She continued running and, without turning her head, kept saying,

"God guard you from the rich man who has become poor,
And from a beggarly clown made rich by fate."

Beware the Cat

(Excerpt)

Beware the Cat *was written in 1553 by William Baldwin (c. 1518–1563?).*
As the earliest original piece of long prose fiction written in the English lan-
guage, scholars give it the distinction of being the very first English "novel."
Although it is difficult to read and practically unknown outside scholarly cir-
cles, it is a fascinating book. Our interest in it here is that it contains what is
possibly the earliest version of what has come to be known as "The King of the
Cats," a story which has been told over and over with countless variations all
the way down to the present day. The story appears to have originated in Ire-
land. According to an old Irish legend, there was a cat named Írusan who
ruled over all cats. He was as big as an ox and lived in a cave at Knowth in
Meath, Ireland. Robert Graves believed that this legend supported his theory
that there was once a cat cult in Ireland. It is unknown whether or not this
legend was the basis for Baldwin's tale. Still, that he set this portion of his story
in Ireland supports the theory that it originated there. Interestingly enough,
you will see that "The King of the Cats" is only half of the story. The other part
appears to be the inspiration for other folktales. Beware the Cat *also contains*
what may be the earliest use of the name "Grimalkin," which has come to
refer to cats as witches' familiars or to cats in general. This may be where
Shakespeare got the name, which is used by the witches in Macbeth *(c. 1606).*

Wherefore on a time as I was sitting by the fire with certain of the
house: I told them what a noise and what a wawling[1] the cats had made
there the night before from ten o'clock till one, so that neither I could
sleep nor study for them; and by means of this introduction we fell in

---

[1] Caterwauling.

communication of cats. And some affirming, as I do now (but I was against it then), that they had understanding, for confirmation whereof one of the servants told this story.

"There was in my country," quoth he, "a man" (the fellow was born in Staffordshire) "that had a young cat which he had brought up of a kitling, and would nightly dally and play with it; and on a time as he rode through Kank wood[2] about certain business, a cat (as he thought) leaped out of a bush before him and called him twice or thrice by his name. But because he made none answer nor spake (for he was so afraid that he could not), she spake to him plainly twice or thrice these words following: 'Commend me unto Titton Tatton and to Puss thy Catton, and tell her that Grimalkin is dead.' This done she went her way, and the man went forward about his business. And after that he was returned home. In an evening sitting by the fire with his wife and his household he told of his adventure in the wood, and when he had told them all the cat's message, his cat, which had harkened unto the tale, looked upon him sadly, and at the last said, 'And is Grimalkin dead? Then farewell dame.' And therewith went her way and was never seen after."

When this tale was done, another of the company, which had been in Ireland, asked this fellow when this thing which he had told happened. He answered that he could not tell well, howbeit, as he conjectured, not past forty years, for his mother knew both the man and the woman which ought the cat that the message was sent unto.

"Sure," quoth the other, "then it may well be; for about that same time, as I heard, a like thing happened in Ireland where, if I conjecture not amiss, Grimalkin of whom you spake was slain."

"Yea sir," quoth I, "I pray you how so?"

"I will tell you, Master Streamer," quoth he, "that which was told me in Ireland, and which I have till now so little credited, that I was ashamed to report it. But hearing that I hear now, and calling to mind my own experience when it was, I do so little misdoubt it that I think I never told, nor you ever heard, a more likely tale.

"While I was in Ireland, in the time that Mac Murrough and all the rest of the wild lords were the King's enemies, what time also mortal war was between the Fitz Harrises and the Prior and Convent of the Abbey of Tintern, who counted them the King's friends and subjects, whose neigh-

---

[2] Now called Cannock.

bor was Cahir Mac Art, a wild Irishman then the King's enemy and one which daily made inroads into the county of Wexford and burned such towns and carried away all such cattle as he might come by, by means whereof all the country from Clonmines to Ross became a waste wilderness and is scarce recovered until this day. In this time, I say, as I was on a night at Cosher with one of Fitz Harris' churls, we fell in talk (as we have done now) of strange adventures, and of cats. And there, among other things, the churl (for so they call all farmers and husbandmen) told me as you shall hear.

"There was, not seven years past, a kern[3] of John Butler's dwelling in the fassock[4] of Bantry called Patrick Apore, who minding to make a prey in the night upon Cahir Mac Art, his master's enemy, got him with his boy (for so they call their horse-keepers be they never so old knaves) into his country, and in the night time entered into a town of two houses, and brake in and slew the people, and then took such cattle as they found, which was a cow and a sheep, and departed therewith homeward. But doubting they should be pursued (the cur dogs made such a shrill barking), he got him into a church, thinking to lurk there till midnight was past, for there he was sure that no man would suspect or seek him—for the wild Irishmen have had churches in such reverence (till our men taught them the contrary) that they neither would, nor durst, either rob ought thence or hurt any man that took the churchyard for sanctuary, no, though he had killed his father.

"And while this kern was in the church he thought it best to dine, for he had eaten little that day. Wherefore he made his boy go gather sticks, and strake fire with his feres,[5] and made a fire in the church, and killed the sheep, and after the Irish fashion laid it thereupon and roasted it. But when it was ready, and that he thought to eat it, there came in a cat and set her by him, and said in Irish, 'Shane foel,' which is, 'give me some meat.' He, amazed at this, gave her the quarter that was in his hand, which immediately she did eat up, and asked more till she had consumed all the sheep; and, like a cormorant not satisfied therewith, asked still for more. Wherefore they supposed it were the Devil, and therefore thinking it wisdom to please him, killed the cow which they had stolen, and when they

[3] A foot-soldier.
[4] Grasslands.
[5] The means for lighting a fire.

had flayed it gave the cat a quarter, which she immediately devoured. Then they gave her two other quarters; and in the meanwhile, after their country fashion, they did cut a piece of the hide and pricked it upon four stakes which they set about the fire, and therein they sod a piece of the cow for themselves, and with the rest of the hide they made each of them laps[6] to wear about their feet like brogues,[7] both to keep their feet from hurt all the next day, and also to serve for meat the next night, if they could get none other, by broiling them upon coals.

"By this time the cat had eaten three quarters and called for more. Wherefore they gave her that which was a-seething; and doubting lest, when she had eaten that, she would eat them too because they had no more for her, they got them out of the church and the kern took his horse and away he rode as fast as he could hie.[8] When he was a mile or two from the church the moon began to shine, and his boy espied the cat upon his master's horse behind him and told him. Whereupon the kern took his dart, and turning his face toward her, flang it and struck her through with it. But immediately there came to her such a sight of cats that, after long fight with them, his boy was killed and eaten up, and he himself, as good and as swift as his horse was, had much to do to escape.

"When he was come home and had put off his harness (which was a corslet of mail made like a shirt, and his skull covered over with gilt leather and crested with otterskin), all weary and hungry he set him down by his wife and told her his adventure, which, when a kitling which his wife kept, scarce half a year old, had heard, up she started and said, 'Hast thou killed Grimalkin!' And therewith she plunged in his face, and with her teeth took him by the throat, and ere that she could be plucked away, she had strangled him. This the churl told me now about thirty-three winters past; and it was done, as he and diverse other creditable men informed me, not seven years before. Whereupon I gather that this Grimalkin was it which the cat in Kank wood sent news of unto the cat which we heard of even now."

[6] Leather coverings for shoes that could later be eaten when no other food was available.
[7] Shoes with a decorative flap on top.
[8] Go.

SCOTLAND

Sir Walter Scott's Cat

This account was written by Washington Irving (1783–1859), best known for his short stories "Rip Van Winkle" and "The Legend of Sleepy Hollow." His essay "Abbotsford," from which this account is taken, is a description of his 1817 visit to Sir Walter Scott's mansion of the same name in Scotland. Although it was written in 1817, it was not published until 1835. Sir Walter Scott (1771–1832) was the author of Ivanhoe *and the story-poem* The Lady of the Lake. *Scott's intimate knowledge of Scottish folklore is reflected throughout his writings.*

Among the other important and privileged members of the household who figured in attendance at the dinner, was a large gray cat, who, I observed, was regaled from time to time with titbits from the table. This sage grimalkin was a favorite of both master and mistress, and slept at night in their room; and Scott laughingly observed, that one of the least wise parts of their establishment was, that the window was left open at night for puss to go in and out. The cat assumed a kind of ascendancy among the quadrupeds—sitting in state in Scott's arm-chair, and occasionally stationing himself on a chair beside the door, as if to review his subjects as they passed, giving each dog a cuff beside the ears as he went by. This clapper-clawing was always taken in good part; it appeared to be, in fact, a mere act of sovereignty on the part of grimalkin, to remind the others of their vassalage; which they acknowledged by the most perfect acquiescence. A general harmony prevailed between sovereign and subjects, and they would all sleep together in the sunshine . . .

The evening passed away delightfully in this quaint-looking apartment, half study, half drawing-room. Scott read several passages from the old romance of Arthur, with a fine deep sonorous voice, and a gravity of tone that seemed to suit the antiquated, black-letter volume. It was a rich treat to hear such a work, read by such a person, and in such place; and his appearance as he sat reading, in a large armed chair, with his favorite hound Maida at his feet, and surrounded by books and relics, and border trophies, would have formed an admirable and most characteristic picture.

While Scott was reading, the sage grimalkin already mentioned had taken his seat in a chair beside the fire, and remained with fixed eye and grave demeanor, as if listening to the reader. I observed to Scott that his cat seemed to have a black-letter taste in literature.

"Ah," said he, "these cats are a very mysterious kind of folk. There is always more passing in their minds than we are aware of. It comes no doubt from their being so familiar with witches and warlocks." He went on to tell a little story about a gude man who was returning to his cottage one night, when, in a lonely out-of-the-way place, he met with a funeral procession of cats all in mourning, bearing one of their race to the grave in a coffin covered with a black velvet pall. The worthy man, astonished and half frightened at so strange a pageant, hastened home and told what he had seen to his wife and children. Scarce had he finished, when a great black cat that sat beside the fire raised himself up, exclaimed "Then I am king of the cats!" and vanished up the chimney. The funeral seen by the gude man was one of the cat dynasty.

"Our grimalkin here," added Scott, "sometimes reminds me of the story, by the airs of sovereignty which he assumes; and I am apt to treat him with respect from the idea that he may be a great prince incog., and may some time or other come to the throne."

ENGLAND

The King of the Cats

This story has become a very common folktale and there are many different versions of it around. This version, published in the late nineteenth century in the British Folk-Lore Journal, *is representative of these.*

Many years ago, long before shooting in Scotland was a fashion as it is now, two young men spent the autumn in the very far north, living in a lodge far from other houses, with an old woman to cook for them. Her cat and their own dogs formed all the rest of the household.

One afternoon the elder of the two young men said he would not go out, and the younger one went alone, to follow the path of the previous day's sport looking for missing birds, and intending to return home before the early sunset. However, he did not do so, and the elder man became very uneasy as he watched and waited in vain till long after their usual supper-time. At last the young man returned, wet and exhausted, nor did he explain his unusual lateness until, after supper, they were seated by the fire with their pipes, the dogs lying at their feet, and the old woman's black cat sitting gravely with half-shut eyes on the hearth between them. Then the young man began as follows:

"You must be wondering what made me so late. I have had a curious adventure today. I hardly know what to say about it. I went, as I told you I should, along our yesterday's route. A mountain fog came on just as I was about to turn homewards, and I completely lost my way. I wandered about for a long time, not knowing where I was, till at last I saw a light, and made for it, hoping to get help. As I came near it, it disappeared, and I found myself close to a large old oak tree. I climbed into the branches the better to look for the light, and, behold! it was beneath me, inside the hollow trunk of the tree. I seemed to be looking down into a church, where a funeral was in the act of taking place. I heard singing, and saw a coffin,

24

surrounded by torches, all carried by—But I know you won't believe me if I tell you!"

His friend eagerly begged him to go on, and laid down his pipe to listen. The dogs were sleeping quietly, but the cat was sitting up apparently listening as attentively as the man, and both young men involuntarily turned their eyes towards him. "Yes," proceeded the absentee, "it is perfectly true. The coffin and the torches were both borne by cats, and upon the coffin were marked a crown and scepter!" He got no further; the cat started up shrieking: "By Jove! old Peter's dead! and I'm the King, o' the Cats!" rushed up the chimney and was seen no more.

ENGLAND

The History of Whittington

This version of the famous Dick Whittington story was included in Andrew Lang's The Blue Fairy Book, *which was published in 1889. This story existed in Europe as far back as the thirteenth century. It became attached to Sir Richard Whittington (c. 1358–1423) by the end of the fifteenth century. The real Dick Whittington was from an aristocratic British family. When he was thirteen, his parents sent him from their home in Pauntley, Gloucestershire, to become an apprentice textile merchant in London. He was very successful and amassed quite a fortune. As is mentioned in this version of the fairy tale, he did marry an Alice Fitz-Warren and became the Lord Mayor of London three times. During his third term, he entertained King Henry V and his queen. It is said that during this visit, as a gift to the king, he burned £60,000 worth of bonds (a tremendous fortune in that day) from the king on the fire.*

Dick Whittington was a very little boy when his father and mother died; so little indeed, that he never knew them, nor the place where he was born. He strolled about the country as ragged as a colt, till he met with a wagoner who was going to London, and who gave him leave to walk all the way by the side of his wagon without paying anything for his passage. This pleased little Whittington very much, as he wanted to see London sadly, for he had heard that the streets were paved with gold, and he was willing to get a bushel of it; but how great was his disappointment, poor boy! when he saw the streets covered with dirt instead of gold, and found himself in a strange place, without a friend, without food, and without money.

Though the wagoner was so charitable as to let him walk up by the side of the wagon for nothing, he took care not to know him when he came to town, and the poor boy was, in a little time, so cold and so hungry that he wished himself in a good kitchen and by a warm fire in the country.

In this distress he asked charity of several people, and one of them bid

26

him, "Go to work for an idle rogue." "That I will," says Whittington, "with all my heart; I will work for you if you will let me."

The man, who thought this savored of wit and impertinence (though the poor lad intended only to show his readiness to work), gave him a blow with a stick which broke his head so that the blood ran down. In this situation, and fainting for want of food, he laid himself down at the door of one Mr. Fitzwarren, a merchant, where the cook saw him, and, being an ill-natured hussy, ordered him to go about his business or she would scald him. At this time Mr. Fitzwarren came from the Exchange, and began also to scold at the poor boy, bidding him to go to work.

Whittington answered that he should be glad to work if anybody would employ him, and that he should be able if he could get some victuals to eat, for he had had nothing for three days, and he was a poor country boy, and knew nobody, and nobody would employ him.

He then endeavored to get up, but he was so very weak that he fell down again, which excited so much compassion in the merchant that he ordered the servants to take him in and give him some meat and drink, and let him help the cook to do any dirty work that she had to set him about. People are too apt to reproach those who beg with being idle, but give themselves no concern to put them in the way of getting business to do, or considering whether they are able to do it, which is not charity.

But we return to Whittington, who would have lived happy in this worthy family had he not been bumped about by the cross cook, who must be always roasting or basting, and when the spit was idle employed her hands upon poor Whittington! At last Miss Alice, his master's daughter, was informed of it, and then she took compassion on the poor boy, and made the servants treat him kindly.

Besides the crossness of the cook, Whittington had another difficulty to get over before he could be happy. He had, by order of his master, a flock-bed placed for him in a garret, where there was a number of rats and mice that often ran over the poor boy's nose and disturbed him in his sleep. After some time, however, a gentleman who came to his master's house gave Whittington a penny for brushing his shoes. This he put into his pocket, being determined to lay it out to the best advantage; and the next day, seeing a woman in the street with a cat under her arm, he ran up to know the price of it. The woman (as the cat was a good mouser) asked a deal of money for it, but on Whittington's telling her he had but a penny in the world, and that he wanted a cat sadly, she let him have it.

This cat Whittington concealed in the garret, for fear she should be beat about by his mortal enemy the cook, and here she soon killed or frightened away the rats and mice, so that the poor boy could now sleep as sound as a top.

Soon after this the merchant, who had a ship ready to sail, called for his servants, as his custom was, in order that each of them might venture something to try their luck;[1] and whatever they sent was to pay neither freight nor custom, for he thought justly that God Almighty would bless him the more for his readiness to let the poor partake of his fortune.

All the servants appeared but poor Whittington, who, having neither money nor goods, could not think of sending anything to try his luck; but his good friend Miss Alice, thinking his poverty kept him away, ordered him to be called.

She then offered to lay down something for him, but the merchant told his daughter that would not do, it must be something of his own. Upon which poor Whittington said he had nothing but a cat which he bought for a penny that was given him. "Fetch thy cat, boy," said the merchant, "and send her." Whittington brought poor puss and delivered her to the captain, with tears in his eyes, for he said he should now be disturbed by the rats and mice as much as ever. All the company laughed at the adventure but Miss Alice, who pitied the poor boy, and gave him something to buy another cat.

While puss was beating the billows at sea, poor Whittington was severely beaten at home by his tyrannical mistress the cook, who used him so cruelly, and made such game of him for sending his cat to sea, that at last the poor boy determined to run away from his place, and, having packed up the few things he had, he set out very early in the morning on All-Hallows day. He traveled as far as Holloway, and there sat down on a stone to consider what course he should take; but while he was thus ruminating, Bow bells, of which there were only six, began to ring; and he thought their sounds addressed him in this manner:

> Turn again, Whittington,
> Thrice Lord Mayor of London."

"Lord Mayor of London!" said he to himself; "what would not one

---

1 The merchant allows each member of his household to send any item to be sold in a foreign country with that person receiving all proceeds from the sale.

endure to be Lord Mayor of London, and ride in such a fine coach? Well, I'll go back again, and bear all the pummeling and ill-usage of Cicely rather than miss the opportunity of being Lord Mayor!" So home he went, and happily got into the house and about his business before Mrs. Cicely made her appearance.

We must now follow Miss Puss to the coast of Africa. How perilous are voyages at sea, how uncertain the winds and the waves, and how many accidents attend a naval life!

The ship which had the cat on board was long beaten at sea, and at last, by contrary winds, driven on a part of the coast of Barbary which was inhabited by Moors unknown to the English. These people received our countrymen with civility, and therefore the captain, in order to trade with them, showed them the patterns of the goods he had on board, and sent some of them to the King of the country, who was so well pleased that he sent for the captain and the factor to his palace, which was about a mile from the sea. Here they were placed, according to the custom of the country, on rich carpets, flowered with gold and silver; and the King and Queen being seated at the upper end of the room, dinner was brought in, which consisted of many dishes; but no sooner were the dishes put down but an amazing number of rats and mice came from all quarters, and devoured all the meat in an instant.

The factor, in surprise, turned round to the nobles and asked if these vermin were not offensive. "Oh! yes," said they, "very offensive; and the King would give half his treasure to be freed of them, for they not only destroy his dinner, as you see, but they assault him in his chamber, and even in bed, so that he is obliged to be watched while he is sleeping, for fear of them."

The factor jumped for joy; he remembered poor Whittington and his cat, and told the King he had a creature on board the ship that would dispatch all these vermin immediately. The King's heart heaved so high at the joy which this news gave him that his turban dropped off his head. "Bring this creature to me," said he; "vermin are dreadful in a court, and if she will perform what you say I will load your ship with gold and jewels in exchange for her." The factor, who knew his business, took this opportunity to set forth the merits of Miss Puss. He told his Majesty that it would be inconvenient to part with her, as, when she was gone, the rats and mice might destroy the goods in the ship—but to oblige his Majesty he would fetch her. "Run, run," said the Queen; "I am impatient to see the dear creature."

Away flew the factor, while another dinner was providing, and returned with the cat just as the rats and mice were devouring that also. He immediately put down Miss Puss, who killed a great number of them.

The King rejoiced greatly to see his old enemies destroyed by so small a creature, and the Queen was highly pleased, and desired the cat might be brought near that she might look at her. Upon which the factor called "Pussy, pussy, pussy!" and she came to him. He then presented her to the Queen, who started back, and was afraid to touch a creature who had made such a havoc among the rats and mice; however, when the factor stroked the cat and called "Pussy, pussy!" the Queen also touched her and cried "Putty, putty!" for she had not learned English.

He then put her down on the Queen's lap, where she, purring, played with her Majesty's hand, and then sang herself to sleep.

The King having seen the exploits of Miss Puss, and being informed that her kittens would stock the whole country, bargained with the captain and factor for the whole ship's cargo, and then gave them ten times as much for the cat as all the rest amounted to. On which, taking leave of their Majesties and other great personages at court, they sailed with a fair wind for England, whither we must now attend them.

The morn had scarcely dawned when Mr. Fitzwarren arose to count over the cash and settle the business for that day. He had just entered the counting-house, and seated himself at the desk, when somebody came, tap, tap, at the door. "Who's there?" said Mr. Fitzwarren. "A friend," answered the other. "What friend can come at this unseasonable time?" "A real friend is never unseasonable," answered the other, "I come to bring you good news of your ship *Unicorn*." The merchant bustled up in such a hurry that he forgot his gout, instantly opened the door, and who should be seen waiting but the captain and factor, with a cabinet of jewels, and a bill of lading, for which the merchant lifted up his eyes and thanked heaven for sending him such a prosperous voyage. Then they told him the adventures of the cat, and showed him the cabinet of jewels which they had brought for Mr. Whittington. Upon which he cried out with great earnestness, but not in the most poetical manner:

> "Go, send him in, and tell him of his fame,
> And call him Mr. Whittington by name."

It is not our business to animadvert upon these lines; we are not Critics, but historians. It is sufficient for us that they are the words of Mr. Fitzwarren; and though it is beside our purpose, and perhaps not in our power to prove him a good poet, we shall soon convince the reader that he was a good man, which was a much better character; for when some who were present told him that this treasure was too much for such a poor boy as Whittington, he said; "God forbid that I should deprive him of a penny; it is his own, and he shall have it to a farthing." He then ordered Mr. Whittington in, who was at this time cleaning the kitchen and would have excused himself from going into the counting-house, saying the room was swept and his shoes were dirty and full of hob-nails. The merchant, however, made him come in, and ordered a chair to be set for him. Upon which, thinking they intended to make sport of him, as had been too often the case in the kitchen, he besought his master not to mock a poor simple fellow who intended them no harm, but let him go about his business. The merchant, taking him by the hand, said: "Indeed, Mr. Whittington, I am in earnest with you, and sent for you to congratulate you on your great success. Your cat has procured you more money than I am worth in the world, and may you long enjoy it and be happy!"

At length, being shown the treasure, and convinced by them that all of it belonged to him, he fell upon his knees and thanked the Almighty for his providential care of such a poor and miserable creature. He then laid all the treasure at his master's feet, who refused to take any part of it, but told him he heartily rejoiced at his prosperity, and hoped the wealth he had acquired would be a comfort to him, and would make him happy. He then applied to his mistress, and to his good friend Miss Alice, who refused to take any part of the money, but told him she heartily rejoiced at his good success, and wished him all imaginable felicity. He then gratified the captain, factor, and the ship's crew for the care they had taken of his cargo. He likewise distributed presents to all the servants in the house, not forgetting even his old enemy the cook, though she little deserved it.

After this Mr. Fitzwarren advised Mr. Whittington to send for the necessary people and dress himself like a gentleman, and made him the offer of his house to live in till he could provide himself with a better.

Now it came to pass when Mr. Whittington's face was washed, his hair curled, and he dressed in a rich suit of clothes, that he turned out a genteel young fellow; and, as wealth contributes much to give a man confidence, he in a little time dropped that sheepish behavior which was principally occasioned by a depression of spirits, and soon grew a sprightly and good companion, insomuch that Miss Alice, who had formerly pitied him, now fell in love with him.

When her father perceived they had this good liking for each other he proposed a match between them, to which both parties cheerfully consented, and the Lord Mayor, Court of Aldermen, Sheriffs, the Company of Stationers, the Royal Academy of Arts, and a number of eminent merchants attended the ceremony, and were elegantly treated at an entertainment made for that purpose.

History further relates that they lived very happy, had several children, and died at a good old age. Mr. Whittington served Sheriff of London and was three times Lord Mayor. In the last year of his mayoralty he entertained King Henry V and his Queen, after his conquest of France, upon which occasion the King, in consideration of Whittington's merit, said: "Never had prince such a subject"; which being told to Whittington at the table, he replied: "Never had subject such a king." His Majesty, out of respect to his good character, conferred the honor of knighthood on him soon after.

Sir Richard many years before his death constantly fed a great number of poor citizens, built a church and a college to it, with a yearly allowance for poor scholars, and near it erected a hospital.

He also built Newgate for criminals, and gave liberally to St. Bartholomew's Hospital and other public charities.

A version of this story in an old English chapbook adds, "The figure of Sir Richard Whittington with his cat in his arms, carved in stone, was to be seen till the year 1780 over the archway of the old prison at Newgate, that stood across Newgate Street." Today there is a monument to Whittington's cat on Highgate Hill in London, the spot where Whittington is said to have heard the bells ring out their prophecy.

The Origin of Venice

The Chronicle of Albert contains what is probably the oldest surviving European version of the "Whittington" story. Albert—the abbot of the convent of St. Mary at Stade, near Hamburg—wrote his book in about 1256. This was close to a hundred years before Sir Richard Whittington was born. In his chronicle, which extends from Creation to the year 1256, Albert places this story under the year 1175 and says that it occured in Italy.

At this time the Venetians had a dispute with the Emperor. Now Venice is a city in the Adriatic Sea—an island, not indeed by nature, but made by art; and it thus began. King Attila, besieging Aquilina, put its inhabitants to flight, who coming to the place where Venice now is, heaped up there an island, and named it Venice, *á venalitate vel venatione.* There dwelt there in the beginning two fellow-citizens, the one rich, the other poor. The rich man went to trade, and he asked his comrade for merchandise. "I have nothing," said the poor man, "but two cats." The rich man took them with him, and he came by chance to a land where the whole place was devastated by mice. He sold the cats for a great deal of money, and having purchased very many things for his comrade, he brought them to him.

The Genoese Merchant

It is interesting that The Chronicle of Albert *(the source for "The Origin of Venice") appears to point to Italy as Albert's source for the "Whittington" story because there is a version which has survived in Italy for many centuries, only this one has a different ending. Probably the oldest of the Italian "Whittingtons" is the one written about Piovano (which means "parson") Arlotto, who was born in 1396 and died in 1483. It is interesting to note that he was born at about the same time that Sir Richard Whittington first became Lord Mayor of London. It is also interesting to note that the Italian version is still being told today with very little difference from this one. The modern versions still contain their unique ending. Here is the story as it was told about Piovano Arlotto shortly after his death almost 500 years ago.*

A priest, who was somewhat akin to the parson, having gone in the Florentine galleys, and finding in Flanders tennis-balls at a low price, bought three great casks full of them, without consulting the parson or any one else. He laid out all the money he had; and thinking he had made a capital hit, told it with great glee to the parson, who, being a prudent man, would not blame the thing, since it was done, but told him that when they should be returned to Florence, he would tell him the story of the cats of the Genoese merchant. When the galleys returned to the port of Pisa, the priest began to sell his balls there; and then he sold them at Florence, and with less than half a cask he supplied all the shops for several years; and having no hope of getting them off in five-and-twenty years, even though he should sell them ever so cheap, he went to the parson Arlotto, lamenting that he had not acted by his advice. The parson then said to him, "I will tell you the story of the cats."

There was a lucky Genoese merchant, who, as he was at sea, was carried by fortune to a very distant island, where there had never been any Chris-

tian; and a great king reigned there, who, when he heard of the ship, wondered much, and having spoken with the owner one morning, invited him
to dinner: and when they sat down to table, a wand was put into the hands
of each, and of the merchant among the rest, at which he wondered greatly; and when the bread and the other meats were set on the table, more
than a thousand mice presented themselves with great noise, so that if
they would defend the victuals, it was necessary to employ the wands.

The Genoese was astonished at all this, and he asked whence this great
multitude of mice came. He was told that the whole island was full of
them, and that if it were not for that curse, there would not be a happier
realm than it; for all the precious things of the world grew there, and were
found there, such as gold, silver, metals of every kind, wheat, wine, corn of
every sort, fruits, wax, silk, and every good thing that the earth produces;
but that these animals destroyed everything; and it was necessary to keep
the bread, the clothes, and all other things hung in the air, from those
hooks in the roofs. Then said the merchant, "Your Majesty has had me to
dine with you this morning, and I will take the liberty to return of myself
tomorrow." And going back to the ship, he put next morning a cat in his
sleeve, and returned to the city: and when they sat down at the table with
those same wands in their hands, and the bread and victuals came, the
mice ran in hundreds as usual; and then the captain opened his sleeve, and
the cat in an instant jumped among the mice with such dexterity and
ferocity, that in a little time she killed more than a hundred of them, and
all the rest fled away in terror. The agility and ferocity of so small an animal appeared a wonderful thing to the king and all the bystanders; and he
asked particularly where she was bred, what she fed on, and how long she
lived. The captain told him all, and added, "Sire, I will present Your
Majesty with two pair of these cats, which, if they are taken proper care of,
will fill the whole kingdom with cats in a few years." He sent for them to
the ship, and gave them to the king, who thought this a gift which could
not be compensated. So having consulted with his barons, and reckoning
that he had brought the salvation of the whole kingdom, he gave him,
between gold, silver, and jewels, the value of more than 200,000 ducats.

The merchant, thus grown rich, returned to Genoa, where in a few
days the fame of his good fortune spread, and several thought of trying
their luck by going to that country, though it was such a way off and the
voyage dangerous, and taking thither the same kind of animals. There was
among them one of a lofty mind, who resolved to take thither other mer-

chandise than cats, though he was advised against it by the first; and he brought with him to present to the king garments of brocade, of gold, of silver, furniture for beds, for horses, and other things, and various sweetmeats, and presents of great value, to the amount of more than 10,000 crowns.

The king joyfully accepted the rich present; and after several banquets and caresses, he consulted with his wise men what he should give the merchant in return. One said one thing, and one another. The king thought everything else of little worth; and being liberal and great-minded, he resolved to give him part of the most valuable things he had; and he presented him with one of those cats, as a thing most precious. The unlucky merchant returned to Genoa in very ill humor. And so I say to you, that as you would not act by my advice, you bought, out of thirst of gain, what you did not understand, and you never will get back one half of your money.

The Island of Kais

There is evidence that the "Whittington" story existed outside of Europe at an early date. It is unknown whether the story originated in Europe and went elsewhere or vice versa. The following version comes to us from Persia (now Iran). The Persian historian Abdulláh, the son of Fazlulláh—who wrote under the name of Wásif (which means "the Describer")—included the story in Events of Ages and Fates of Cities, *which he wrote in 1299—almost sixty years prior to Sir Richard Whittington's birth. The ending of this version contains little of the moralism that is so prevalent in the European versions.*

Kais, the eldest son of a man named Kaiser, having spent the whole of his patrimony at Siráf, and disdaining to seek for service in a place where he had lived in opulence, passed over to an island (from him called Kais) opposite to the city with his two brothers in a small skiff, and left his widowed mother behind, helpless and forlorn. The brothers built a dwelling with the branches and leaves of trees, and supported life with dates and other fruits, the produce of the island. It was customary for the masters and captains of ships to ask the poorest people for some gift when they were setting out on a trading voyage, which they disposed of to the best advantage at the port to which they were bound; and if the trip proved prosperous, and they ever returned, they repaid the amount of the gift or venture, with the profit upon it, and a present besides, proportionate to the good luck with which, in their opinion, the prayers of the poor had blessed their concerns. It so happened that the captain of a vessel bound to India from Siráf applied for a gift to the poor old widow of Kaiser, who gave him the only property which the extravagance of her sons had left her—a Persian cat. The captain, a kind-hearted man, received the old lady's present gratefully, although he did not consider it as the best kind of venture for a foreign port. Heaven had ordained otherwise. After the ship had anchored at an Indian port, the captain waited on the Sovereign with costly presents, as is usual, who received him graciously, and invited him to dinner in a kind hospitable manner. With some surprise he perceived that every dish at table was guarded by a servant with a rod in his hand; but his curiosity about the cause of this strange appearance was shortly satisfied without asking any questions, for on looking about he perceived hundreds of mice running on all sides, and ready to devour the viands, whenever the vigilance of the domestics ceased for a moment. He immediately thought of the old woman's cat, and on the following day brought it in a cage to the palace. The mice appeared as usual, and the cat played her part amongst them to the astonishment and admiration of the monarch and his courtiers. The slaughter was immense. The captain presented the cat to his Majesty, mentioned the case of the old lady, and the motive for bringing so strange, but, as it turned out, so acceptable a freight with him, on which the king, happy at his delivery from the plague of mice, not only rewarded the captain with splendid presents, but loaded his ship with precious articles of merchandise, the produce of his kingdom, to be given to the mistress of the cat, with male and female slaves, money, and jewels. When the vessel returned to Siráf, the old lady came down to the landing-place to ask about the fate of her cat, when, to her great joy and astonishment, the honest and worthy captain related to her the fortunate result of her venture, and put her in possession of her newly-acquired wealth. She immediately sent for her son Kais and his brothers to share her opulence; but as they had collected a large settlement in their island, she was soon persuaded by them to accompany them to it, where, by means of her riches, they formed more extensive connections, purchased more ships, and traded largely with India and Arabia. When Kais and his friends had sufficiently added to their wealth by commerce, they by a signal act of treachery having murdered the crews of twelve ships from Omán and India, then at anchor there, seized the ships and property in them. With this addition to their fleet they commenced a series of outrageous acts as pirates, and successfully resisted every attempt of the neighboring states to suppress their wicked practices. Every year added to their power and wealth, and at length a King was elected to the chief government of the island of Kais. This monarchy lasted for nearly two hundred years, until the reign of Atábeg Abubaker, A.H. 628 (A.D. 1230), when the descendants of Kais were reduced to vassalage to the court of Persia.

NORWAY

The Honest Penny

This much more recent version of the "Whittington" story originally appeared in Peter Christen Asbjörnsen's Norske Folke-Eventyr (Norwegian Folk-Tales), *which was published in 1871. It was translated by Sir George W. Dasent for his* Tales from the Fjeld, *which was published in 1874. It is interesting, not only because the cat becomes part of a con game, but because the cat also appears to possess supernatural powers.*

Once on a time there was a poor woman who lived in a tumble-down hut far away in the wood. Little had she to eat, and nothing at all to burn, and so she sent a little boy she had out into the wood to gather fuel. He ran and jumped, and jumped and ran, to keep himself warm, for it was a cold gray autumn day, and every time he found a bough or a root for his billet, he had to beat his arms across his breast, for his fists were as red as the cranberries over which he walked, for it was very cold. So when he had got his billet of wood and was off home, he came upon a clearing of stumps on the hillside, and there he saw a white crooked stone.

"Ah! you poor old stone," said the boy; "how white and wan you are! I'll be bound you are frozen to death;" and with that he took off his jacket and laid it on the stone. So when he got home with his billet of wood his mother asked what it all meant that he walked about in wintry weather in his shirt-sleeves. Then he told her how he had seen an old crooked stone which was all white and wan for frost, and how he had given it his jacket.

"What a fool you are!" said his mother; "do you think a stone can freeze? But even if it froze till it shook again, know this—every one is nearest to his own self. It costs quite enough to get clothes to your back, without your going and hanging them on stones in the clearings;" and as she said that, she hunted the boy out of the house to fetch his jacket.

39

So when he came where the stone stood, lo! it had turned itself and lifted itself up on one side from the ground. "Yes! yes! this is since you got the jacket, poor old thing," said the boy.

But when he looked a little closer at the stone, he saw a money-box, full of bright silver, under it.

"This is stolen money, no doubt," thought the boy; "no one puts money, come by honestly, under a stone away in the wood."

So he took the money-box and bore it down to a tarn hard by and threw the whole hoard into the tarn; but one silver penny-piece floated on the top of the water.

"Ah! ah! that is honest," said the lad; "for what is honest never sinks."

So he took the silver penny and went home with it and his jacket. Then he told his mother how it had all happened, how the stone had turned itself, and how he had found a money-box full of silver money, which he had thrown out into the tarn because it was stolen money, and how one silver penny floated on the top.

"That I took," said the boy, "because it was honest."

"You are a born fool," said his mother, for she was very angry; "were naught else honest than what floats on water, there wouldn't be much honesty in the world. And even though the money were stolen ten times over, still you had found it; and I tell you again what I told you before, every one is nearest to his own self. Had you only taken that money we might have lived well and happy all our days. But a ne'er-do-weel thou art, and a ne'er-do-weel thou wilt be, and now I won't drag on any longer toiling and moiling for thee. Be off with thee into the world and earn thine own bread."

So the lad had to go out into the wide world, and he went both far and long seeking a place. But wherever he came, folk thought him too little and weak, and said they could put him to no use. At last he came to a merchant, and there he got leave to be in the kitchen and carry in wood and water for the cook. Well, after he had been there a long time, the merchant had to make a journey into foreign lands, and so he asked all his servants what he should buy and bring home for each of them. So, when all had said what they would have, the turn came to the scullion too, who brought in wood and water for the cook. Then he held out his penny.

"Well, what shall I buy with this?" asked the merchant; "there won't be much time lost over this bargain."

"Buy what I can get for it. It is honest, that I know," said the lad.

That his master gave his word to do, and so he sailed away.

So when the merchant had unladed his ship and laded her again in foreign lands, and bought what he had promised his servants to buy, he came down to his ship, and was just going to shove off from the wharf. Then all at once it came into his head that the scullion had sent out a silver penny with him, that he might buy something for him.

"Must I go all the way back to the town for the sake of a silver penny? One would then have small gain in taking such a beggar into one's house," thought the merchant.

Just then an old wife came walking by with a bag at her back.

"What have you got in your bag, mother?" asked the merchant.

"Oh! nothing else than a cat. I can't afford to feed it any longer, so I thought I would throw it into the sea, and make away with it," answered the woman.

Then the merchant said to himself, "Didn't the lad say I was to buy what I could get for his penny?" So he asked the old wife if she would take four farthings for her cat. Yes! the goody was not slow to say "done," and so the bargain was soon struck.

Now when the merchant had sailed a bit, fearful weather fell on him, and such a storm, there was nothing for it but to drive and drive till he did not know whither he was going. At last he came to a land on which he had never set foot before, and so up he went into the town.

At the inn where he turned in, the board was laid with a rod for each man who sat at it. The merchant thought it very strange, for he couldn't at all make out what they were to do with all these rods; but he sat him down, and thought he would watch well what the others did, and do like them. Well! as soon as the meat was set on the board, he saw well enough what the rods meant; for out swarmed mice in thousands, and each one who sat at the board had to take to his rod and flog and flap about him, and naught else could be heard than one cut of the rod harder than the one which went before it. Sometimes they whipped one another in the face, and just gave themselves time to say, "Beg pardon," and then at it again.

"Hard work to dine in this land!" said the merchant. "But don't folk keep cats here?"

"Cats?" they all asked, for they did not know what cats were.

So the merchant sent and fetched the cat he had bought for the scullion, and as soon as the cat got on the table, off ran the mice to their holes, and folks had never in the memory of man had such rest at their meat.

Then they begged and prayed the merchant to sell them the cat, and at last, after a long, long time, he promised to let them have it; but he would have a hundred dollars for it; and that sum they gave and thanks besides.

So the merchant sailed off again; but he had scarce got good sea-room before he saw the cat sitting up at the mainmast head, and all at once again came foul weather and a storm worse than the first, and he drove and drove till he got to a country where he had never been before. The merchant went up to an inn, and here, too, the board was spread with rods; but they were much bigger and longer than the first. And, to tell the truth, they had need to be; for here the mice were many more, and every mouse was twice as big as those he had before seen.

So he sold the cat again, and this time he got two hundred dollars for it, and that without any haggling.

So when he had sailed away from that land and got a bit out at sea, there sat Grimalkin again at the masthead; and the bad weather began at once again, and the end of it was, he was again driven to a land where he had never been before.

He went ashore, Up to the town, and turned into an inn. There, too, the board was laid with rods, but every rod was an ell and a half long, and as thick as a small broom; and the folk said that to sit at meat was the hardest trial they had, for there were thousands of big ugly rats, so that it was only with sore toil and trouble one could get a morsel into one's mouth, 'twas such hard work to keep off the rats. So the cat had to be fetched up from the ship once more, and then folks got their food in peace. Then they all begged and prayed the merchant, for heaven's sake, to sell them his cat. For a long time he said "No;" but at last he gave his word to take three hundred dollars for it.

That sum they paid down at once, and thanked him and blessed him for it into the bargain.

Now, when the merchant got out to sea, he fell a-thinking how much the lad had made out of the penny he had sent out with him.

"Yes, yes, some of the money he shall have," said the merchant to himself, "but not all. Me it is that he has to thank for the cat I bought; and besides, every man is nearest to his own self."

But as soon as ever the merchant thought this, such a storm and gale arose that every one thought the ship must founder. So the merchant saw there was no help for it, and he had to vow that the lad should have every penny; and no sooner had he vowed this vow, than the weather turned good, and he got a snoring breeze fair for home.

So, when he got to land, he gave the lad the six hundred dollars, and his daughter besides; for now the little scullion was just as rich as his master, the merchant, and even richer; and, after that, the lad lived all his days in mirth and jollity; and he sent for his mother, and treated her as well as or better than he treated himself; "for," said the lad, "I don't think; that every one is nearest to his own self."

ICELAND

The Cottager and His Cat

This version of "Dick Whittington and His Cat" is from Isländische Märchen (Icelandic Fairy Tales), *which was published in the late nineteenth century. You will notice that some significant changes have been made to the story.*

Once upon a time there lived an old man and his wife in a dirty, tumble-down cottage, not very far from the splendid palace where the king and queen dwelt. In spite of the wretched state of the hut, which many people declared was too bad even for a pig to live in, the old man was very rich, for he was a great miser, and lucky besides, and would often go without food all day sooner than change one of his beloved gold pieces.

But after a while he found that he had starved himself once too often. He fell ill, and had no strength to get well again, and in a few days he died, leaving his wife and one son behind him.

The night following his death, the son dreamed that an unknown man appeared to him and said: "Listen to me; your father is dead and your mother will soon die, and all their riches will belong to you. Half of his wealth is ill-gotten, and this you must give back to the poor from whom he squeezed it. The other half you must throw into the sea. Watch, however, as the money sinks into the water, and if anything should swim, catch it and keep it, even if it is nothing more than a bit of paper."

Then the man vanished, and the youth awoke.

The remembrance of his dream troubled him greatly. He did not want to part with the riches that his father had left him, for he had known all his life what it was to be cold and hungry, and now he had hoped for a little comfort and pleasure. Still, he was honest and good-hearted, and if his father had come wrongfully by his wealth he felt he could never enjoy it, and at last he made up his mind to do as he had been bidden. He found

44

out who were the people who were poorest in the village, and spent half of his money in helping them, and the other half he put in his pocket. From a rock that jutted right out into the sea he flung it in. In a moment it was out of sight, and no man could have told the spot where it had sunk, except for a tiny scrap of paper floating on the water. He stretched down carefully and managed to reach it, and on opening it found six shillings wrapped inside. This was now all the money he had in the world.

The young man stood and looked at it thoughtfully. "Well, I can't do much with this," he said to himself; but, after all, six shillings were better than nothing, and he wrapped them up again and slipped them into his coat.

He worked in his garden for the next few weeks, and he and his mother contrived to live on the fruit and vegetables he got out of it, and then she too died suddenly. The poor fellow felt very sad when he had laid her in her grave, and with a heavy heart he wandered into the forest, not knowing where he was going. By-and-by he began to get hungry, and seeing a small hut in front of him, he knocked at the door and asked if they could give him some milk. The old woman who opened it begged him to come in, adding kindly that if he wanted a night's lodging he might have it without its costing him anything.

Two women and three men were at supper when he entered, and silently made room for him to sit down by them. When he had eaten he began to look about him, and was surprised to see an animal sitting by the fire different from anything he had ever noticed before. It was gray in color, and not very big; but its eyes were large and very bright, and it seemed to be singing in an odd way, quite unlike any animal in the forest. "What is the name of that strange little creature?" asked he. And they answered, "We call it a cat."

"I should like to buy it—if it is not too dear," said the young man, "it would be company for me." And they told him that he might have it for six shillings, if he cared to give so much. The young man took out his precious bit of paper, handed them the six shillings, and the next morning bade them farewell, with the cat lying snugly in his cloak.

For the whole day they wandered through meadows and forests, till in the evening they reached a house. The young fellow knocked at the door and asked the old man who opened it if he could rest there that night, adding that he had no money to pay for it. "Then I must give it to you," answered the man, and led him into a room where two women and two men were sitting at supper. One of the women was the old man's wife, the other his daughter. He placed the cat on the mantel-shelf, and they all crowded round to examine this strange beast, and the cat rubbed itself against them, and held out its paw, and sang to them; and the women were delighted, and gave it everything that a cat could eat, and a great deal more besides.

After hearing the youth's story, and how he had nothing in the world left him except his cat, the old man advised him to go to the palace, which was only a few miles distant, and take counsel of the king, who was kind to everyone, and would certainly be his friend. The young man thanked him, and said he would gladly take his advice; and early next morning he set out for the royal palace.

He sent a message to the king to beg for an audience, and received a reply that he was to go into the great hall, where he would find his Majesty.

The king was at dinner with his court when the young man entered, and he signed to him to come near. The youth bowed low, and then gazed in surprise at the crowd of creatures who were running about the floor, and even on the table itself. Indeed, they were so bold that they snatched pieces of food from the king's own plate, and if he drove them away, tried to bite his hands, so that he could not eat his food, and his courtiers fared no better.

"What sort of animals are these?" asked the youth of one of the ladies sitting near him.

"They are called rats," answered the king, who had overheard the question, "and for years we have tried some way of putting an end to them, but it is impossible. They come into our very beds."

At this moment something was seen flying through the air. The cat was on the table, and with two or three shakes a number of rats were lying dead round him. Then a great scuffling of feet was heard, and in a few minutes the hall was clear.

For some minutes the king and his courtiers only looked at each other in astonishment. "What kind of animal is that which can work magic of this sort?" asked he. And the young man told him that it was called a cat, and that he had bought it for six shillings.

And the king answered: "Because of the luck you have brought me, in freeing my palace from the plague which has tormented me for many years, I will give you the choice of two things. Either you shall be my

Prime Minister, or else you shall marry my daughter and reign after me. Say, which shall it be?"

"The princess and the kingdom," said the young man.

And so it was.

Although the "Whittington" stories vary considerably, it is possible they contain an element of truth. The ancient Egyptians considered cats to be so valuable that they made it illegal to export them. The Europeans, who only had skunks and weasels for pest control, continually tried to talk the Egyptians out of a few cats, but to no avail. Eventually, around 1500 B.C., the Greeks were able to steal a few dozen and they soon began to trade them to the Romans, Gauls, and Celts. It is said that the Spanish conquistador Diego de Almagro (c. 1475–1538) gave 600 pieces of eight for the first cat that was brought to South America. It is also reported that two cats who were taken to Cuyabá, Brazil, to combat a plague of rats were sold for a pound of gold. Their kittens were each sold for thirty pieces of eight and the price gradually fell as the cats became more plentiful.

GERMANY

The Bremen Town Musicians

The next three stories come from the Brothers Grimm. Jakob (1785–1863) and Wilhelm (1786–1859) Grimm lived together in harmony their entire lives, even after Wilhelm married in 1825. Both were professors at the University of Berlin and they were the first to compile folktales in a scholarly manner. Their book Die Kinder- und Hausmärchen (Children's and Household Fairy Tales) *was published in two volumes in 1812 and 1815. Many of the stories they collected themselves from peasants of Hesse. Wilhelm expanded and revised the folktales in later editions of this book, turning many of them into literary fairy tales.*

There was once an ass whose master had made him carry sacks to the mill for many a long year, but whose strength began at last to fail, so that each day as it came, found him less capable of work. Then his master began to think of turning him out, but the ass, guessing that something was in the wind that boded him no good, ran away, taking the road to Bremen; for there he thought he might get an engagement as town musician.

When he had gone a little way he found a hound lying by the side of the road panting, as if he had run a long way. "Now, Holdfast, what are you so out of breath about?" said the ass.

"Oh dear!" said the dog, "now I am old, I get weaker every day, and can do no good in the hunt, so, as my master was going to have me killed, I have made my escape; but now how am I to gain a living?"

"I will tell you what," said the ass, "I am going to Bremen to become town musician. You may as well go with me, and take up music too. I can play the lute, and you can beat the drum." And the dog consented, and they walked on together.

It was not long before they came to a cat sitting in the road, looking as dismal as three wet days. "Now then, what is the matter with you, old shaver?" said the ass.

"I should like to know who would be cheerful when his neck is in danger?" answered the cat. "Now that I am old my teeth are getting blunt, and I would rather sit by the oven and purr than run about after mice, and my mistress wanted to drown me, so I took myself off; but good advice is scarce, and I do not know what is to become of me."

"Go with us to Bremen," said the ass, "and become town musician. You understand serenading." The cat thought well of the idea, and went with them accordingly.

After that the three travelers passed by a yard, and a cock was perched on the gate crowing with all his might. "Your cries are enough to pierce bone and marrow," said the ass, "what is the matter?"

I have foretold good weather for Lady-day,[1] so that all the shirts may be washed and dried; and now on Sunday morning company is coming, and the mistress has told the cook that I must be made into soup, and this evening my neck is to be wrung, so that I am crowing with all my might while I can."

"You had much better go with us, rooster," said the ass. "We are going to Bremen. At any rate that will be better than dying. You have a powerful voice, and when we are all performing together it will have a very good effect." So the cock consented, and they went on all four together.

But Bremen was too far off to be reached in one day, and towards evening they came to a wood, where they determined to pass the night. The ass and the dog lay down under a large tree; the cat got up among the branches; and the cock flew up to the top, as that was the safest place for him. Before he went to sleep he looked all round him to the four points of the compass, and perceived in the distance a little light shining, and he called out to his companions that there must be a house not far off, as he could see a light, so the ass said, "We had better get up and go there, for these are uncomfortable quarters." The dog began to fancy a few bones, not quite bare, would do him good. And they all set off in the direction of the light, and it grew larger and brighter, until at last it led them to a rob-

[1] A festival commemorating Gabriel's announcement to Mary that she was going to have a baby. Lady-day is celebrated on March 25.

ber's house, all lighted up. The ass, being the biggest, went up to the window, and looked in.

"Well, what do you see?" asked the dog. "What do I see?" answered the ass; "here is a table set out with splendid eatables and drinkables, and robbers sitting at it and making themselves very comfortable." "That would just suit us," said the cock. "Yes, indeed, I wish we were there," said the ass.

Then they consulted together how it should be managed so as to get the robbers out of the house, and at last they hit on a plan. The ass was to place his fore-feet on the window sill, the dog was to get on the ass's back, the cat on the top of the dog, and lastly, the cock was to fly up and perch on the cat's head. When that was done, at a given signal they all began to perform their music. The ass brayed, the dog barked, the cat mewed, and the cock crowed; then they burst through into the room, breaking all the panes of glass. The robbers fled at the dreadful sound; they thought it was some goblin, and fled to the wood in the utmost terror. Then the four companions sat down to table, made free with the remains of the meal, and feasted as if they had been hungry for a month. And when they had finished they put out the lights, and each sought out a sleeping-place to suit his nature and habits. The ass laid himself down outside on the dunghill, the dog behind the door, the cat on the hearth by the warm ashes, and the cock settled himself in the cock loft; and as they were all tired with their long journey they soon fell fast asleep.

When midnight drew near, and the robbers from afar saw that no light was burning, and that everything appeared quiet, their captain said to them that he thought that they had run away without reason, telling one of them to go and reconnoiter. So one of them went, and found everything quite quiet. He went into the kitchen to strike a light, and taking the glowing fiery eyes of the cat for burning coals, he held a match to them in order to kindle it. But the cat, not seeing the joke, flew into his face, spitting and scratching. Then he cried out in terror, and ran to get out at the back door, but the dog, who was lying there, ran at him and bit his leg; and as he was rushing through the yard by the dunghill the ass struck out and gave him a great kick with his hind foot; and the cock, who had been wakened with the noise, and felt quite brisk, cried out, "Cock-a-doodle-doo!"

Then the robber got back as well as he could to his captain, and said, "Oh dear! in that house there is a gruesome witch, and I felt her breath and her long nails in my face; and by the door there stands a man who stabbed me in the leg with a knife; and in the yard there lies a black specter, who beat me with his wooden club; and above, upon the roof, there sits the justice, who cried, 'Bring that rogue here!' And so I ran away from the place as fast as I could."

From that time forward the robbers never ventured to that house, and the four Bremen town musicians found themselves so well off where they were, that there they stayed. And the person who last related this tale is still living, as you see.

GERMANY

The Poor Miller's Boy
and the Cat

This story by the Brothers Grimm is similar to "The White Cat," which appears later in this book.

There once lived an old miller who had neither wife nor child, and three apprentices served under him. As they had been with him several years, one day he said to them, "I am old, and want to sit in the chimney-corner; go out, and whichsoever of you brings me the best horse home, to him will I give the mill, and in return for it he shall take care of me till my death." The third of the boys was, however, the drudge, who was looked on as foolish by the others; they begrudged the mill to him, and afterwards he would not have it. Then all three went out together, and when they came to the village, the two said to stupid Hans, "You may just as well stay here; as long as you live thou will never get a horse."

Hans, however, went with them, and when it was night they came to a cave in which they lay down to sleep. The two sharp ones waited until Hans had fallen asleep, then they got up, and went away leaving him where he was. And they thought they had done a very clever thing, but it was certain to turn out ill for them. When the sun arose, and Hans woke up, he was lying in a deep cavern. He looked around on every side and exclaimed, "Oh, heavens, where am I?" Then he got up and clambered out of the cave, went into the forest, and thought, "Here I am quite alone and deserted, how shall I obtain a horse now?"

While he was thus walking full of thought, he met a small tabby cat which said quite kindly, "Hans, where are you going?" "Alas, you cannot help me." "I well know your desire," said the cat. "You wish to have a beautiful horse. Come with me, and be my faithful servant for seven years long, and then I will give you one more beautiful than any you have ever seen in your whole life." "Well, this is a wonderful cat!" thought Hans, "but I am determined to see if she is telling the truth."

So she took him with her into her enchanted castle, where there were nothing but cats who were her servants. They leapt nimbly upstairs and downstairs, and were merry and happy. In the evening when they sat down to dinner, three of them had to make music. One played the bassoon, the other the fiddle, and the third put the trumpet to his lips, and blew out his cheeks as much as he possibly could. When they had dined, the table was carried away, and the cat said, "Now, Hans, come and dance with me." "No," said he, "I won't dance with a pussy-cat. I have never done that yet." "Then take him to bed," said she to the cats. So one of them lighted him to his bed-room, one pulled his shoes off, one his stockings, and at last one of them blew out the candle.

Next morning they returned and helped him out of bed, one put his stockings on for him, one tied his garters, one brought his shoes, one washed him, and one dried his face with her tail. "That feels very soft!" said Hans. He, however, had to serve the cat, and chop some wood every day, and to do that he had an ax of silver, and the wedge and saw were of silver and the mallet of copper. So he chopped the wood small; stayed there in the house and had good meat and drink but never saw any one but the tabby cat and her servants.

Once she said to him, "Go and mow my meadow, and dry the grass," and gave him a scythe of silver, and a whetstone of gold, but bade him deliver them up again carefully. So Hans went thither, and did what he was bidden, and when he had finished the work he carried the scythe, whetstone, and hay to the house, and asked if it was not yet time for her to give him his reward. "No," said the cat, "you must first do something more for me of the same kind. There is timber of silver, carpenter's ax, square, and everything that is needful, all of silver; with these build me a small house." Then Hans built the small house, and said that he had now done everything, and still he had no horse. Nevertheless, the seven years had gone by with him as if they were six months.

The cat asked him if he would like to see her horses? "Yes," said Hans. Then she opened the door of the small house, and when she had opened it, there stood twelve horses—such horses, so bright and shining, that his heart rejoiced at the sight of them. She gave him to eat and to drink and said, "Go home, I will not give you your horse away with you; but in three days' time I will follow you and bring it." So Hans set out, and she showed him the way to the mill.

She had, however, never once given him a new coat, and he had been obliged to keep on his dirty old smock-frock, which he had brought with him, and which during the seven years had every where become too small for him.

When he reached home, the two other apprentices were there again as well, and each of them certainly had brought a horse with him, but one of them was a blind one, and the other lame. They asked Hans where his horse was. "It will follow me in three days' time." Then they laughed and said, "Indeed, stupid Hans, where will you get a horse? It will be a fine one!" Hans went into the parlor, but the miller said he should not sit down to table, for he was so ragged and torn, that they would all be ashamed of him if any one came in. So they gave him a mouthful of food outside, and at night, when they went to rest, the two others would not let him have a bed, and at last he was forced to creep into the goose-house, and lie down on a little hard straw. In the morning when he awoke, the three days had passed, and a coach came with six horses and they shone so bright that it was delightful to see them! And a servant brought a seventh as well, which was for the poor miller's boy.

A magnificent princess alighted from the coach and went into the mill, and this princess was the little tabby cat whom poor Hans had served for seven years. She asked the miller where the miller's boy and drudge was? Then the miller said, "We cannot have him here in the mill, for he is so ragged; he is lying in the goose-house. Then the king's daughter said that they were to bring him immediately, so they brought him out, and he had to hold his little smock-frock together to cover himself. The servants unpacked splendid garments, and washed him and dressed him, and when that was done, no King could have looked more handsome. Then the maiden desired to see the horses which the other apprentices had brought home with them, and one of them was blind and the other lame.

So she ordered the servant to bring the seventh horse, and when the miller saw it, he said that such a horse as that had never yet entered his yard. "And that is for the third miller's boy," said she. "Then he must have the mill," said the miller, but the king's daughter said that the horse was there, and that he was to keep his mill as well, and took her faithful Hans and set him in the coach, and drove away with him.

They first drove to the little house which he had built with the silver tools, and behold it was a great castle, and everything inside it was of silver and gold; and then she married him, and he was rich, so rich that he had enough for all the rest of his life. After this, let no one ever say that any one who is silly can never become a person of importance.

The Three Children of Fortune

This story by the Brothers Grimm is a somewhat twisted version of "Dick Whittington and His Cat."

Once upon a time a father sent for his three sons. He gave to the eldest a cock, to the second a scythe, and to the third a cat.

"I am now old," said he, "my end is approaching, and I would like to provide for you before I die. Money I have none, and what I now give you seems of but little worth. Yet it rests with yourselves to turn my gifts to good account. Go to a country where what you have is as yet unknown, and your fortune is made."

After the death of the father, the eldest set out with his cock. But wherever he went, in every town he saw from afar off a cock sitting upon the church steeple, and turning round with the wind. In the villages he always heard plenty of them crowing, and his bird was therefore nothing new; so there did not seem much chance of his making his fortune. At length it happened that he came to an island where the people who lived there had never heard of a cock, and knew not even how to reckon the time. They knew, indeed, if it were morning or evening; but at night, if they lay awake, they had no means of knowing how time went.

"Behold," said he to them, "what a noble animal this is! How like a knight he is! He carries a bright red crest upon his head, and spurs upon his heels; he crows three times every night, at stated hours, and at the third time the sun is about to rise. But this is not all. Sometimes he screams in broad daylight, and then you must take warning, for the weather is surely about to change."

This pleased the natives mightily. They kept awake one whole night, and heard to their great joy how gloriously the cock called the hour, at two, four, and six o'clock. Then they asked him whether the bird was to be sold, and how much he would sell it for. "About as much gold as an ass can carry," said he. "A very fair price for such an animal," they cried with one voice, and agreed to give him what he asked.

When he returned home with his wealth, his brothers wondered greatly; and the second said, "I will now set forth likewise, and see if I can turn my scythe to as good an account." There did not seem, however, much likelihood of this; for go where he would, he was met by peasants who had as good a scythe on their shoulders as he had. At last, as good luck would have it, he came to an island where the people had never heard of a scythe. There, as soon as the corn was ripe, they went into the fields and pulled it up with their hands, but this was very hard work, and a great deal of it was lost. The man then set to work with his scythe, and mowed down their whole crop so quickly that the people stood staring open-mouthed with wonder. They were willing to give him what he asked for such a marvelous thing; but he only took a horse laden with as much gold as it could carry.

Now the third brother had a great longing to go and see what he could make of his cat. So he set out. At first it happened to him as it had to the others; so long as he kept upon the main land, he met with no success. There were plenty of cats everywhere, indeed too many, so that the young ones were for the most part, as soon as they came into the world, drowned in the water. At last he passed over to an island, where, as it chanced most luckily for him, nobody had ever seen a cat, and they were overrun with mice to such a degree that the little wretches danced upon the tables and chairs, whether the master of the house were at home or not. The people complained loudly of this grievance; the King himself knew not how to rid himself of them in his palace. In every corner mice were squeaking, and they gnawed everything that their teeth could lay hold of. Here was a fine field for Puss. She soon began her chase, and had cleared two rooms in the twinkling of an eye. Then the people besought their King to buy the wonderful animal for the good of the public, at any price. The King willingly gave what was asked—a mule laden with gold and jewels. And thus the third brother returned home with a richer prize than either of the others.

Meantime the cat feasted away upon the mice in the royal palace, and devoured so many that they were no longer in any great numbers. At length, quite spent and tired with her work, she became extremely thirsty; so she stood still, drew up her head, and cried, "Miau, miau!"

The King gathered together all his subjects when they heard this strange cry, and many ran shrieking in a great fright out of the palace. But the King held a council below as to what was best to be done; and it was at length fixed to send a herald to the cat, to warn her to leave the castle forthwith, or that force would be used to remove her. "For," said the counselors, "we would far more willingly put up with the mice (since we are used to that evil), than get rid of them at the risk of our lives." A page accordingly went, and asked the cat, whether she were willing to quit the castle. But Puss, whose thirst became every moment more and more pressing, answered nothing but "Miau! Miau!" which the page interpreted to mean "No! No!" and therefore carried this answer to the King.

"Well," said the counselors, "then we must try what force will do." So the guns were planted, and the palace was fired upon from all sides. When the fire reached the room where the cat was, she sprang out of the window and ran away. But the besiegers did not see her, and went on firing until the whole palace was burnt to the ground.

The White Cat

This story was written during the seventeenth century in France, when fairy tales were a very popular form of fiction. Writing other kinds of fiction had pretty much come to a halt out of fear of the royal censors, who were the Inquisitors of that time. The fairy tale was one of the few safe forms of fiction. Countess Marie-Catherine d'Aulnoy (1649–1705) became one of the most popular writers of fairy tales during this period. Born to a wealthy family in Normandy, she married a middle-aged count when she was sixteen. One of her closest friends was publicly beheaded because she had murdered her husband. This event may have had an influence on d'Aulnoy when she decided to rid herself of her husband. Four years into her marriage, the countess and her mother, along with their two lovers, falsely accused her husband of treason and he was thrown in prison. The plot was revealed when the conscience of one of the lovers caused him to admit the charges were trumped up. The count narrowly escaped losing his head and the countess and her mother fled into exile for fifteen years. They were allowed to return to France in 1685 after performing secret services for the government. She formed a literary salon in Paris and took up writing. Her first book of fairy tales came out in 1697 and contained "Serpent vert (Green Serpent)," upon which "Beauty and the Beast" was based. Her most famous story, "La Chatte Blanche (The White Cat)," comes from her second book of fairy tales, titled Les Contes nouvelles ou les fées à la mode (New Tales, or the Fancy of Fairies), *which was published in 1698. The story has since been abbreviated and rewritten for countless children's books. Here is her original fairy tale.*

Once upon a time there was a king who had three brave and handsome sons. He was afraid they might become anxious to reign during his lifetime. There were even some whispers in circulation that they sought to make partisans with a view of depriving him of his kingdom. The king felt he was growing old; but his mental capacity being undiminished, he had no fancy for vacating in their favor a place he filled so worthily. He thought, therefore, that the best way to live in peace was by amusing them with promises which he could always elude the performance of. He called them into his closet,[1] and after having spoken very kindly to them he added, "You will agree with me, my dear children, that my great age forbids my applying myself to the business of the state with so much assiduity as formerly. I fear my subjects may suffer from this circumstance. I wish to transfer my crown to one of you; but to deserve such a gift, it is only right that you should, on your own, seek to please me. Now, as I contemplate retiring into the country, it appears to me that a pretty, faithful, and intelligent little dog would be an excellent companion for me. So in lieu of preferring my eldest to my youngest son, I declare to you, that whichever of you three shall bring me the handsomest little dog shall forthwith become my heir."

The princes were exceedingly surprised at the inclination the king expressed for a little dog; but the two youngest saw they might find their account in it, and accepted with pleasure the commission to go in search of one. The eldest was too timid or too respectful to urge his own right. They took leave of the king, who distributed amongst them money and jewels, adding that the following year, without fail, on the same day and hour they would return and bring him their little dogs.

Before setting out, they repaired to a castle within a league of the city, assembled therein their most intimate friends, and gave splendid banquets, at which the three brothers pledged to each other an eternal friendship, and declared that they would act in the affair in question without jealousy or mortification, and that the successful candidate would always be ready to share his fortune with the others. At length they departed, agreeing to meet on their return at the same castle, and from there to proceed together to the king. They declined having any followers, and changed their names that they might not be known.

Each took a different road. The two eldest met with many adventures, but I shall only recount those of the youngest. He was well-mannered, of a gay and joyous temperament, had an admirable head, a noble figure, regular features, fine teeth, was very skillful in all exercise that became a

---

[1] This probably refers to the king's private rooms.

prince, sang agreeably, touched the lute and the theorbo[2] with a delicacy that charmed every one; could paint; in one word, was highly accomplished; and as to his courage, it amounted to intrepidity.

Scarcely a day passed that he did not buy dogs, big or little: greyhounds, mastiffs, bloodhounds, pointers, spaniels, water-dogs, lapdogs; the instant he found one handsomer than the other, he let the first go to keep the new purchase; for it would have been impossible for him to lead about by himself thirty or forty thousand dogs, and he persevered in his determination to have neither gentlemen, nor valets de chamber, nor pages in his train. He continued his journey without having any fixed point to proceed to, when night, accompanied with thunder and rain, surprised him in a forest through which he was no longer able to trace a path.

He took the first he could find, and after having walked a long way, he saw a glimmer of light, which convinced him that there was some habitation near him in which he might find shelter till the morning. Guided by the light, he came to the gate of the most magnificent castle that could ever be imagined. This gate was of gold covered with carbuncles,[3] the pure and vivid light of which illuminated all the neighborhood. It was this light which the prince had perceived at a great distance. The walls were of transparent porcelain of several colors, on which were represented the histories of all the fairies from the beginning of the world to that day. The famous adventures of Peau d'Ane, Finette, the Orange-tree, Gracieuse, the Sleeping Beauty in the Wood, Green Serpent, and a hundred others,[4] were not forgotten. He was delighted to meet amongst them, with Prince Sprite; for he was his uncle, according to the fashion of Brittany.[5] The rain and storm prevented his staying longer on a spot where he was being wetted to the skin; besides which he could not see anything beyond where the light of the carbuncles extended to.

He returned to the golden gate. He saw a kid's foot attached to a chain of diamonds. He admired all this magnificence, and the security in which the owners of the castle appeared to live. "For, after all," said he, "what is to prevent thieves from coming and cutting down this chain and pulling the carbuncles off the gate? They would enrich themselves for ever."

---

[2] A bass lute.
[3] Red gemstones.
[4] These are stories by Countess d'Aulnoy, except for "*Peau d'Ane* (Donkey Skin)" and "Sleeping Beauty," which are by Charles Perrault.
[5] A distant relative who is called an "uncle."

He pulled the kid's foot, and immediately heard a bell ring, which seemed by its sound to be of gold or silver; a moment after, the gate was opened without his perceiving anything except a dozen hands in the air, each of which held a torch. He was so astonished that he hesitated to advance; when he felt other hands which pushed him forwards with gentle violence. He moved on, therefore, with some distrust, and at all risks, keeping his hand on the hilt of his sword; but on entering a antechamber entirely encrusted with porphyry[6] and lapis lazuli,[7] he heard two enchanting voices which sang these words:

> "Start not at the hands you see,
> Nor fear in this delightful place
> Naught, except a lovely face
> If from love your heart would flee."

He could not believe that he was invited so graciously for the purpose of eventually injuring him; so that, feeling himself pushed towards a large gate of coral, which opened directly that he approached it, he entered a salon of mother-of-pearl, and afterwards passed through several apartments variously ornamented, and so rich with paintings and jewels, that he was perfectly enchanted with them. Thousands and thousands of lights, from the vaulted roof of the salon down to the floor, illuminated a portion of the other apartments, which were also filled with chandeliers, girandoles,[8] and stages covered with wax-candles; in fact, the magnificence was so great that it was not easy to imagine the possibility of it.

After having passed through sixty rooms, the hands that conducted him stopped him. He saw a large easy-chair moving by itself towards the fireplace. At the same moment the fire was lighted, and the hands, which appeared to him very handsome, white, small, plump, and well-shaped, began to undress him; for he was wet through, as I have already told you, and they were afraid he would catch cold. They presented him, still without his seeing any one, with a shirt as fine as if it was for a wedding-day, and a morning gown of some rich stuff shot with gold, and embroidered with little emeralds in ciphers. The bodiless hands moved a table close to him on which his toilet was set out. Nothing could be more magnificent.

[6] A purplish-red rock found in Egypt.
[7] Sapphires, which are deep blue.
[8] Ornate brackets for candelabra.

They combed him with a lightness and a skill which was very agreeable to him. Finally, they dressed him again, but not in his own clothes; they brought him others much richer. He observed with silent wonder all that took place, and occasionally felt some slight alarm, which he could not altogether conquer.

After they had powdered, curled, perfumed, adorned, attired, and made him look handsomer than Adonis, the hands led him into a hall superbly gilt and furnished; around it were represented the stories of all the most famous cats. Rodilardus hung by the heels in *The Council of Rats, Puss in Boots, Marquis of Carabas, The Writing Cat, The Cat That Became a Woman, Witches in the Shape of Cats*, their Sabbat, and all its ceremonies.[9] In short, nothing was ever more curious than these paintings.

The cloth was laid, and there were two covers, each accompanied by its golden cadenas.[10] The buffet astonished him, by the quantity of cups upon it of rock crystal and a thousand rare stones. The prince could not imagine for whom the two covers were placed, when he saw several cats take their places in a small orchestra, fitted up expressly for them. One held a music-book, the notes in which were of the most extraordinary kind; another a roll of paper to beat time with; and the rest had little guitars.

Suddenly each began to mew in a different tone, and to scratch the strings of their guitars with their claws. It was the strangest music that had ever been heard. The prince would have thought himself in the infernal regions if he had not found the palace too marvelously beautiful to permit him to fall into such an error; but he stopped his ears and laughed heartily at the sight of the various postures and grimaces of these novel musicians.

He was meditating on the different things that had already happened to him in the castle, when he saw a little figure enter the hall, scarcely a cubit in height. This poppet was covered with a long black crepe veil. Two cats preceded it dressed in deep mourning and wearing cloaks and swords; a numerous train of cats followed, some carrying rat-traps full of rats, and others mice in cages.

The prince could not recover from his astonishment; he knew not what to think. The black figure approached, and lifting its veil he perceived the most beautiful white cat that ever was or ever will be. She had a

[9] Most of these refer to tales by Perrault and fables of Jean de La Fontaine.
[10] An ornate box containing eating utensils of an important person. These boxes were often locked so the utensils could not be poisoned.

very youthful and very melancholy air, and commenced a mewing so soft and sweet, that it went straight to the heart. "Son of a king," said she to the prince, "you are welcome; my mewing majesty beholds you with pleasure." "Madam cat," said the prince, "it is very generous of you to receive me with so much attention: but you do not appear to me to be an ordinary little animal. The gift you have of speech, and the superb castle you inhabit, are sufficient evidence to the contrary." "Son of a king," rejoined the white cat, "I pray thee cease to pay me compliments. I am plain in my language and my manners; but I have a kind heart. Come," continued she, "let them serve supper and bid the concert cease; for the prince does not understand what they are singing." "And are they then singing any words, madam?" inquired he. "Undoubtedly," she answered; "we have poets here of considerable talent, and if you remain amongst us some little time, you will be convinced of the fact." "It is only for you to say so and to be believed," replied the prince politely; "but I must also consider you, madam, a cat of a very rare description."

The supper was served up. It was placed on the table by the hands of invisible bodies. First, there were two soups, one of pigeons and the other of very fat mice. The sight of the latter prevented the prince from touching the former, believing that the same cook had concocted both; but the little cat, who guessed from the face he made what was passing in his mind, assured him that their meals had been cooked separately, and that he might eat what was set before him with the perfect assurance that there were neither rats nor mice in it.

The prince did not wait to be told twice, feeling satisfied that the pretty little cat had no wish to deceive him. He observed that she had on her paw a miniature set in a bracelet. This surprised him. He begged her to show it to him; supposing it to be that of Master Minagrobis.[11] He was astonished to find it the portrait of a young man so handsome that it was almost incredible nature could have formed such a being, and who resembled himself so greatly that he could not have been better painted. The white cat sighed, and becoming still more melancholy, she observed a profound silence. The prince saw clearly that there was something extraordinary connected with the portrait, but did not venture to ask any questions, for fear of displeasing the cat or afflicting her. He entertained

[11] A cat's name derived from the fables and stories by the French writers Jean de La Fontaine and François Rabelais.

her with the relation of all the news he was in possession of, and found her intimately acquainted with the various interests of princes and other things passing in the world. After supper the white cat invited her guest to enter a salon, in which there was a theater, wherein twelve cats and twelve monkeys danced a ballet. One party was dressed as Moors, the other as Chinese. It is easy to imagine the leaps and capers they executed; and every now and then they gave each other a scratch or two. Thus finished the evening. The white cat said "Good night" to her guest; the hands who had been his conductors so far, took hold of him again and led him into an apartment quite different from any he had seen. It was not so magnificent as it was elegant. The hangings were all of butterflies' wings; the various colors of which formed a thousand different flowers. There were also the feathers of exceedingly rare birds, and which, perhaps, have never been seen elsewhere. The bed-furniture was of gauze, tied up with a thousand bows of ribbon. There were large mirrors from the ceiling to the floor, with frames of chased gold, representing a thousand little cupids.

The prince went to bed without saying a word, for there were no means of talking with the hands that waited upon him; he slept little, and was awakened by a confused noise. The hands immediately lifted him out of bed, and dressed him in a hunting habit. He looked into the courtyard of the castle, and perceived more than five hundred cats, some of whom led greyhounds in the slips, others were blowing the horn. It was a grand feast-day. White cat was going to hunt, and wished the prince to accompany her. The officious hands presented him with a wooden horse, which went full gallop and kept up the pace wonderfully. He made some objection to mounting it, saying that it wanted but little to make him a knight-errant like Don Quixote; but his resistance was useless; they placed him on the wooden horse. The housings and saddle of it were embroidered with gold and diamonds. White cat rode a monkey, the handsomest and proudest that had ever been seen. She had thrown off her long veil, and wore a dragoon's cap, which made her look so bold that she frightened all the mice in the neighborhood. Never was there a more agreeable hunting party. The cats outran the rabbits and hares, and as fast as they caught them white cat had the curée[12] made in her presence, and a thousand skillful feats were performed, to the great gratification of the whole company.

---

[12] A hunting term referring to the rewarding of hounds or hawks with a portion of prey.

The birds, on their part, were by no means safe, for the kittens climbed the trees, and the great monkey carried white cat up even to the nests of the eagles, to place at her mercy their little highnesses the eaglets.

The hunt being over, the white cat took a horn, about the length of one's finger, but which gave out a tone so clear and loud that it was easily heard ten leagues off. As soon as she had sounded two or three flourishes, she was surrounded by all the cats in the country. Some appeared in the air, riding in chariots; others came in boats by water; in short, so many were never seen together before. They were nearly all dressed in different fashions, and, attended by this splendid train, she returned to the castle, requesting the prince to accompany her. He was perfectly willing to do so, notwithstanding that so much caterwauling smacked a little of a witch's festival, and that the talking cat astonished him beyond all the rest.

As soon as she reached home, she put on her great black veil. She supped with the prince, who was hungry, and did justice to the good cheer. They brought him some liqueurs, which he sipped with much satisfaction, and they immediately effaced all recollection of the little dog he was to find for the king. He no longer thought of anything but mewing with white cat, that is to say, remaining her kind and faithful companion. He passed his days in agreeable amusements, sometimes fishing, sometimes hunting. After which there were ballets, carousals, and a thousand other things which entertained him exceedingly. Even the beautiful cat herself frequently composed verses and sonnets so full of passionate tenderness that it seemed as if she had a susceptible heart, and that no one could speak as she did without being in love. But her secretary, who was an old cat, wrote such a vile scrawl, that, although her works have been preserved, it is impossible to read them.

The prince had forgotten even the land of his birth. The hands, of which I have spoken, continued to wait upon him. He regretted sometimes that he was not a cat, to pass his whole life in such excellent company. "Alas," he said to white cat, "how wretched it will make me to leave you! I love you so dearly! Either become a woman, or make me a cat." She was amused by his wish, and returned him some mysterious answers, out of which he could scarcely make anything. A year flies away quickly when one has neither care nor pain, when one is merry and in good health. White cat knew the time at which the prince was bound to return, and as he thought no more of it, she reminded him. "Do you know," said she, "that you only have three days left to look for the little dog that the king your father wishes for, and that your brothers have already found several very beautiful?" The prince's memory returned to him, and, astonished at his negligence, "What secret spell," he exclaimed, "could have made me forget a thing, the most important to me in the world? My honor and my fortune are staked upon it. Where shall I find such a dog as will win a kingdom for me, and a horse swift enough to perform such a journey in so short a time?" He began to be very anxious and sorrowful.

White cat said to him, with much sweetness, "Son of a king, do not distress yourself, I am your friend. You may yet remain here one day longer; and, although it is five hundred leagues from this to your country, the good wooden horse will carry you there in less than twelve hours." "I thank you, beautiful cat," said the prince; "but it is not sufficient for me merely to return to my father; I must take him a little dog." "Hold," said white cat, "here is an acorn which contains one more beautiful than the dog-star." "Oh, madam cat," cried the prince, "your majesty jests with me." "Put the acorn to your ear," she replied, "and you will hear it bark." He obeyed her, and immediately the little dog went "bow, wow," which transported the prince with delight, for such a dog as could be contained in an acorn was certain to be very diminutive indeed.

He was going to open the acorn, so eager was he to see the dog, but white cat told him that it might catch cold on the journey, and it would be better for him to wait till he was in the presence of his royal father. He thanked her a thousand times, and took a most tender leave of her. "I assure you," he added, "that the days I have passed with you have flown so quickly, that I regret in some measure leaving you behind me; and although you are a sovereign here, and all the cats that compose your court possess much more wit and gallantry than ours, I do not hesitate to invite you to come with me." The cat replied to this invitation only by a deep sigh.

They parted: the prince was the first to reach the castle where he had appointed to meet his brothers. They arrived shortly after him, and were surprised to see a wooden horse in the courtyard which curveted with more grace than any one sees in the riding schools.

The prince came forward to receive them, they embraced several times, and recounted their travels to each other; but our prince kept his principal adventures a secret from his brothers, and showed them an ugly turn-spit,[13] observing that he thought it so beautiful that he had selected it for presentation to the king. Notwithstanding the friendship that existed between the brothers, the two eldest felt a secret joy at the bad taste of their younger brother. Being seated at table, they trod on each other's toes, by way of signifying that they had not much to fear on that account.

The next morning they set out together in the same coach. The king's two eldest sons carried in baskets some little dogs, so beautiful and deli-cate that one could scarcely venture to touch them. The youngest son car-ried the poor turnspit, which was so filthy that nobody could bear the sight of it. As soon as they set foot in the palace, everybody surrounded them to welcome them back to court. They entered the king's apartment. He was puzzled in whose favor to decide, for the little dogs which were presented to him by the two eldest were so nearly equal to each other in beauty; and they had already begun to dispute the right of succession, when their younger brother reconciled them by taking out of his pocket the acorn which the white cat had given him. He opened it immediately, and then everybody beheld a little dog lying upon cotton. It passed through a ring without touching any part of it. The prince placed it on the floor, and it began directly to dance a saraband[14] with the castanets as lightly as the most celebrated Spanish dancer. It was of a thousand differ-ent colors; its hair and its ears swept the ground. The king was dumb-founded, for it was impossible to find a word to say against the beauty of Toutou. Nevertheless, he was by no means inclined to resign his crown. The smallest fleur-de-lis[15] in its circle was dearer to him than all the dogs in the universe. He told his children, therefore, that he was gratified by the trouble they had taken; but that they had succeeded so well in fulfilling the first request he had made to them, that he should test their ability again before he performed his promise. He therefore gave them a year to travel over land and sea, in quest of a piece of cloth so fine that it would pass through the eye of a needle used to make Venetian point-lace with. They were all three exceedingly chagrined to be obliged to go upon a new voyage of discovery. The two princes, whose dogs were less beautiful than that of the youngest, consented. Each took his own way, without so many

[13] A small dog with a long body and short legs used to run a treadmill that turned a spit.
[14] A Spanish dance.
[15] A coat of arms of the French royal family.

professions of friendship as before, for the turnspit had rather cooled their ardor.

Our prince remounted his wooden horse, and without wishing to find other assistance than he might hope for from the friendship of white cat, he set out at full speed, and returned to the castle where he had been so kindly received by her. He found all the doors open. The windows, the roofs, the towers, and the walls were all illuminated by a hundred thousand lamps, which produced a wonderful effect. The hands which had waited so well upon him advanced to meet him, and took the bridle of the excellent wooden horse, which they led to the stable, while the prince entered white cat's apartments.

She was lying in a little basket on a very neat mattress of white satin. She was in her morning cap, and seemed low-spirited, but when she perceived the prince she cut a thousand capers, and played as many gambols to testify her delight to him. "Whatever reason I had to hope you would return," said she to him, "I confess, son of a king, that I dared not flatter myself by indulging in it, and I am generally so unfortunate in matters that concern me that this is an agreeable surprise." The grateful prince caressed her a thousand times. He recounted to her the success of his journey, which she knew perhaps better than he did, and that the king wanted a piece of cloth which could pass through the eye of a needle; that in truth he believed it was impossible to find such a thing, but that he had not hesitated to make the attempt, relying implicitly upon her friendship and assistance. White cat, assuming a more serious air, told him it was a matter that demanded consideration; that, fortunately, there were some cats in her castle who spun exceedingly well; that she would put a claw to it herself, and forward the work as much as possible, so that he might rest contented without going further in search of what he would more readily find in her castle than in any other place in the world.

The hands appeared, bearing torches, and the prince, following them with white cat, entered a magnificent gallery running along the side of a large river, on which there was an astonishing display of fireworks. Four cats were to be burnt there, that had been tried and sentenced in due form. They were accused of having eaten the roast meat provided for the white cat's supper, her cheese, her milk, and even of having conspired against her life with Martafax and L'Hermite, two famous rats of that country, and held as such by La Fontaine, a very faithful historian: but with all that, it was well known there was a great deal of cabal in the mat-

ter, and that the majority of the witnesses had been tampered with. However this might be, the prince obtained their pardon. The fireworks did no
injury to any one, and never yet were seen such splendid sky-rockets.

After this, a very nice supper was served, which gave the prince more
gratification than the fireworks, for he was very hungry, and the wooden
horse had brought him at such a pace that he had never ridden so hard
before in his life. The following days were passed like those that had preceded them, in a thousand various entertainments with which the ingen-
ious white cat regaled her guest. Our prince is probably the first mortal
who ever found so much amusement amongst cats, without any other
society.

It is true that white cat was possessed of agreeable, sweet, and almost
universal talent. She was wiser than a cat is allowed to be. The prince was
sometimes astonished at her knowledge. "No," said he, "it is not natural
for you to possess all these wonderful qualities I discover in you. If you
love me, charming pussy, explain to me by what miracle you are enabled
to think and speak so perfectly, that you might be elected a member of the
most famous Academy of Arts and Sciences?" "Cease to question me, son
of a king," said she to him; "I am not allowed to answer; and you may
carry your conjectures as far as you will without my contradicting you. Let
it suffice that I have always a velvet paw for you, and that I take an affectionate interest in all that concerns you."

The second year slipped away as insensibly as the first. The prince
could scarcely think of anything that the diligent hands did not instantly
provide him with, whether books, jewels, pictures, antique medals; in
short, he had but to say I want a certain gem that is in the cabinet of the
Great Mogul or of the King of Persia, or such a statue in Corinth or any
part of Greece, and he saw it instantly before him, without knowing how
it came or who brought it. This was not without its charms, and as a relax-
ation, it is sometimes very agreeable to see one's self the possessor of the
finest treasures in the world.

White cat, who was ever watchful for the prince's welfare, warned him
that the hour of departure was approaching, that he might make himself
easy about the piece of cloth which he required, and that she had made a
most wonderful one for him. She added, that it was her intention, this
time, to furnish him with an equipage worthy of his birth; and, without
waiting for his reply, she compelled him to look into the great courtyard
of the castle. He saw in it an open carriage of gold, enameled flame-color,

with a thousand gallant devices, which satisfied the mind as much as the eye. It was drawn by twelve horses as white as snow, four-and-four abreast, their harness being of flame-colored velvet embroidered with diamonds and plated with gold. The carriage was lined to match, and a hundred coaches, each with eight horses, filled with noblemen of high bearing, very superbly attired, followed the carriage. There was also an escort of a thousand body-guards, whose uniforms were so covered with embroidery that you could not see the stuff they were made of. It was a remarkable feature of this cavalcade that the portrait of white cat was to be observed in every part of it, either in the devices on the carriage or on the uniforms of the body-guard, or attached by a ribbon to the doublets of those who formed the train, as if it were a new order with which she had decorated them.

"Go," said she to the prince, "go and appear at the court of the king, your father, in such sumptuous state that your magnificence may make an impression upon him and prevent his again refusing to bestow on you the crown you deserve. Here is a walnut. Crack it but in his presence, and you will find in it the piece of cloth you have asked me for." "Amiable white cat," said he to her, "I protest to you that I am so penetrated by your bounties, that if you would consent, I should prefer passing my life here with you to all the grandeur which I have reason to expect elsewhere." "Son of a king," replied she, "I am convinced of the kindness of your heart. It is a rare article amongst princes. They would be loved by everybody, yet not love any one themselves. But you are proof that the rule has its exception. I give you credit for the affection you display for a little white cat that after all is good for nothing but to catch mice." The prince kissed her paw and departed. We should have some difficulty in believing the speed with which he traveled if we were not already aware of the way in which the wooden horse had carried him in less than two days a distance of five hundred leagues from the castle; so that, impelled by the same power, these other steeds traveled so swiftly that they were only four-and-twenty hours on the road, stopping nowhere till they reached the king's palace, to which the two elder brothers had already repaired, and, not seeing their youngest, congratulated themselves on his negligence, and whispered to each other, "Here's a piece of good luck! He is either dead or very ill. He will not be our rival in the important business which is about to be decided." They immediately displayed their cloths, which were, in truth, so fine that they could pass them through the eye of a large needle, but not through that of a small one; and the king, very glad of this pretext for refusal, produced the needle he had previously selected, and which the magistrates, by his order, had brought out of the City Treasury, wherein it had been carefully kept in the meanwhile.

There was much murmuring at this objection. The friends of the princes, and particularly those of the eldest, for his cloth was of the finest texture, protested that it was a downright piece of chicanery, in which there was equal ingenuity and Normanism.[16] The king's parasites contended that he was only bound by the conditions he had proposed. At length, to settle the matter, a fine flourish was heard of trumpets, kettledrums, and hautboys: it announced the arrival of our prince in all his pomp and paraphernalia. The king and his two other sons were all equally astonished at such great magnificence.

After the prince had respectfully saluted his father and embraced his brothers, he took out of a box covered with rubies the walnut, which he cracked, expecting to find in it the boasted piece of cloth; but in lieu of it there was a hazel nut. He cracked that also, and was surprised to see in it a cherry-pit. Everybody looked at one another, and the king laughed in his sleeve, and jeered at the notion of his son being credulous enough to believe he could bring a whole piece of cloth in a walnut; but why should he not have believed it, when he had already given him a little dog that had come out of an acorn? He therefore cracked the cherry-pit, which was filled with its kernel. A great murmur then arose in the apartment. Nothing was heard but the opinion that the young prince had been duped in this adventure. He made no answer to the jokes of the courtiers; he opened the kernel and found in it a grain of wheat, and in the grain of wheat a millet seed. Ah! in truth he began to doubt, and muttered between his teeth, "White cat, white cat, you have fooled me!" At that moment he felt a cat's claw upon his hand, which gave him such a scratch that the blood came. He did not know whether this scratch was given to encourage or to dishearten him; nevertheless, he opened the millet seed, and great was the astonishment of the whole company when he drew out of it a piece of cloth four hundred ells in length, so wonderfully wrought, that all the birds, beasts, and fishes were seen in their natural colors, with the trees, fruits, and plants of the earth; the rocks, curiosities, and shells of the ocean; the sun, the moon, the great and lesser stars and planets of the

[16] During this period, the people of Normandy were considered to be devious and untrustworthy by the rest of France.

sky. There were also the portraits of all the kings and other sovereigns at that time reigning in the world, with those of their wives, of their mistresses, of their children, and of all their subjects, not forgetting the tiniest little urchin—every one, in his particular class of life, accurately represented, and dressed in the habit of his country.

When the king saw this piece of cloth, he became as pale as the prince had become red with confusion at having been so long finding it. The needle was produced, and the prince passed and re-passed the cloth through the eye of it six times. The king and the two eldest princes looked on in sullen silence, except when the beauty and curiosity of the cloth forced them occasionally to acknowledge there was nothing that could be compared to it in the universe.

The king heaved a deep sigh, and, turning towards his children, "Nothing," said he, "could give me so much consolation in my old age as observing the deference paid by you to my wishes. I am therefore desirous to put your obedience to a new test. Go and travel for another year, and he who, at the end of it, brings back with him the most beautiful maiden, shall marry her, and be crowned king on his wedding-day. It is, besides, necessary that my successor should marry, and I swear, I pledge my honor, that I will no longer defer bestowing the reward I have promised."

All the injustice of this proceeding fell upon our prince. The little dog and the piece of cloth were worth ten kingdoms rather than one, but he was so well bred that he would not dispute the will of his father, and without hesitation he re-entered his carriage. All his train followed him, and he took the road back to his dear white cat. She knew the day and the moment he would arrive. All the way was strewn with flowers; thousands of vases of perfume smoked on all sides, and particularly within the castle. White cat was seated on a Persian carpet, under a pavilion of cloth of gold, in a gallery, from whence she could see him approach. He was received by the hands that had always attended upon him. All the cats climbed up into the gutters to welcome him with a desperate squalling.

"So, son of a king," said white cat to him, "you have returned once more without the crown." "Madam," he replied, "your bounties placed me in a position to gain it; but I am convinced that it would have given the king more pain to part with it than I could have received pleasure from its possession." "No matter," said she, "you must neglect nothing to deserve it. I will assist you in this matter, and as you are bound to take back with you a beautiful maid to your father's court, I will find one for you who shall gain you the prize. In the meanwhile let us be merry. I have ordered naval combat between my cats and the terrible rats of this country. My cats will, perhaps, be a little embarrassed, for they are afraid of the water; but otherwise they would have had too much the advantage, and one ought, as much as possible, to equalize matters." The prince admired the prudence of madam puss. He praised her exceedingly, and accompanied her to a terrace which overlooked the sea.

The ships in which the cats were embarked were large pieces of cork on which they sailed conveniently enough. The rats had joined together several egg-shells, and of these their navy consisted. The battle was cruelly obstinate. The rats flung themselves into the water, and swam much better than the cats, so that they were victors and vanquished alternately twenty times; but Minagrobis, admiral of the feline fleet, reduced the rattish race to the greatest despair. He devoured the general of their forces, an old rat of great experience, who had been round the world three times, in capital ships, in which he was neither captain nor common sailor, but simply a flatterer.

White cat would not permit the utter destruction of all these poor unfortunate creatures. She was an acute politician, and calculated that if there were no more rats or mice left in the country, her subjects would live in a state of idleness, which might become highly prejudicial to her.

The prince passed this year as he had the two preceding, that is to say, in hunting, fishing, or chess, at which white cat played exceedingly well. He could not help occasionally questioning her anew as to the miraculous power by which she was enabled to speak. He asked her whether she was a fairy, or whether she had been transformed into a cat; but as she never said anything but what she chose, she also never made answers that were not perfectly agreeable to her, and consequently her replies consisted of a number of little words which signified nothing particular, so that he clearly perceived she was not inclined to make him a partaker of her secret.

Nothing runs away faster than time passed without trouble or sorrow, and if the cat had not been careful to remember the day when it was necessary the prince should return to court, it is certain that he would have absolutely forgotten it. She informed him on the evening preceding it that it only depended on himself to take home with him one of the most beautiful princesses in the world; that the hour to destroy the fatal work of the fairies had at length arrived, and for that purpose he must resolve to cut off her head and her tail, and fling them quickly into the fire. "I!"

exclaimed the prince, "Blanchette! My love! I be so barbarous as to kill you! Ah! you would doubtless try my heart; but rest assured that it is incapable of forgetting the love and gratitude it owes you." "No, son of a king," continued she, "I do not suspect you of ingratitude. I know your worth. It is neither you nor I who in this affair can control our destiny. Do as I bid you. We shall both begin to be happy, and, on the faith of a cat of reputation and honor, you will acknowledge that I am truly your friend."

The tears came several times into the eyes of the young prince, at the mere thought of being obliged to cut off the head of his little kitten, so pretty and so amiable. He continued to say all the most tender things that he could think of, in order to induce her to spare him such a trial. She persisted in replying that she desired to die by his hand, and that it was the only means of preventing his brothers obtaining the crown. In a word, she pressed him so earnestly, that all in a tremble he drew his sword, and, with a faltering hand, cut off the head and tail of his dearly-beloved cat. The next moment he beheld the most charming transformation that can be imagined. The body of white cat increased in size and changed suddenly into that of a young maiden—one that cannot be described; there has never been any so perfect. Her eyes enraptured all hearts, and her sweetness held them captive. Her form was majestic, her carriage noble and modest, her spirit gentle, her manners engaging; in fact, she exceeded everything that was most amiable.

The prince, at her sight, was so struck with surprise, and that surprise was so agreeable, that he fancied himself enchanted. He could not speak, nor open his eyes wide enough to look at her. Tongue-tied, he was unable to express his astonishment; but it was still greater when he saw an extraordinary number of lords and ladies enter the apartment, who, each having his or her cat's skin flung over the shoulders, advanced, and threw themselves at the feet of their queen, and testified their delight at beholding her restored to her natural form. She received them with marks of affection that sufficiently indicated the goodness of her heart, and after passing a short time in the circle, she desired them to leave her alone with the prince, to whom she spoke as follows:

"Think not, my lord, that I have been always a cat, nor that my birth is an obscure one in the eyes of men. My father was king of six kingdoms; he loved my mother tenderly, and allowed her full liberty to do whatever she liked. Her ruling passion was traveling, and shortly before I was born she undertook a journey to a certain mountain of which she had heard a most surprising account. Whilst on her road thither she was told that near the spot she was then passing there was an old fairy castle, the most beautiful in the world; at least, so it was believed to be, from a tradition concerning it; for as no one entered it, they could not form an opinion; but they knew for certain that the fairies had in their garden the finest, the most delicious and most delicate fruit that was ever eaten.

"The queen, my mother, immediately took such a violent fancy to taste it, that she turned her steps towards the castle. She arrived at the gate of that superb edifice, which blazed with gold and azure on all sides: but she knocked in vain. Nobody appeared to answer her; it seemed as if everybody in the castle was dead. Her desire was increased by the difficulty. She sent for ladders in order that her attendants might get over the garden walls, and they would have succeeded in doing so if the said walls had not visibly increased in height though no one was seen to work at them. They lengthened the ladders by tying two or three together, but they broke under the weight of those who mounted them, and who either lamed or killed themselves.

"The queen was in despair. She saw the great trees laden with fruit which looked delicious. She was determined to eat some, or die. She therefore had some very splendid tents pitched before the castle, and remained there six weeks with all her court. She neither slept nor ate; she sighed unceasingly; she talked of nothing but the fruit of the inaccessible garden. At length she fell dangerously ill, without any one soever being able to find the least remedy for her complaint, for the inexorable fairies had never so much as even appeared since she had established herself in front of the castle. All her officers afflicted themselves exceedingly. Nothing was to be heard but sobs and sighs, while the dying queen kept asking for fruit from her attendants, but cared for none except that which was denied her.

"One night, having felt a little drowsy, she saw on reopening her eyes, a little old woman, ugly and decrepit, seated in an arm-chair at the head of her bed. She was surprised that her women had suffered a stranger to come so near her, when the old woman said to her, 'We think your majesty very obstinate in persisting in your desire to eat of our fruit: but since your precious life depends upon it, my sisters and I consent to give you as much as you can carry away, as well as what you may eat upon the spot, provided you will give us something in exchange.' 'Ah! my good mother,' exclaimed the queen; 'speak! I will give you my kingdoms, my heart, my soul! I cannot purchase such fruit at too high a price.' 'We wish,' said the fairy, 'for the daughter that you are about to bring into the world. As soon as she is born, we will come and fetch her: she will be brought up amongst us. There are no virtues, no charms, no accomplishments, with which we will not endow her. In a word, she will be our child; we will make her happy: but observe, that your majesty will see her no more until she is married. If this proposal is agreeable to you, I will cure you instantly, and lead you into our orchard. Notwithstanding that it is night, you will be able to see well enough to pick whatever fruit you may fancy. If what I have said does not please you, good-night, queen; I am going to bed.'

"'Hard as the condition may be which you impose upon me,' replied the queen, 'I will accept it sooner than die, for I am satisfied I could not live another day, and my infant would therefore perish with me. Cure me, wise fairy,' continued she, 'and delay not a moment my enjoyment of the privilege you have promised to grant me.'

"The fairy touched her with a little golden wand, saying, 'Let your majesty be free from all the ills that confine you to this bed!' It seemed immediately to the queen as if some one were divesting her of a heavy and stiff robe which had oppressed her, and that some portions of it clung to her still. This was apparently in the places most affected by her disorder. She sent for all her ladies, and told them with a smiling countenance, that she was quite well, that she was going to get up, and that at length the gates, so well bolted and barred, of the fairy palace, would be opened for her to enter and eat the fine fruit, and take away with her as much as she liked.

"There was not one of her ladies who did not believe the queen to be delirious, and that her mind was at that moment running on the fruit she had so much wished for, so that instead of answering her, they began to weep, and went and woke all the physicians, that they might come and see the state her majesty was in.

"This delay exasperated the queen. She ordered them to bring her clothes to her directly. They refused. She flew in a passion, and became scarlet with rage. They attributed it to the effect of fever: but the physicians having arrived, after feeling her pulse and going through the usual ceremonies, could not deny that she was in perfect health. Her women, who perceived the error into which their zeal had betrayed them, endeavored to atone for it by dressing her as quickly as possible. Each of them asked her majesty's pardon; peace was restored, and the queen hastened to follow the old fairy, who was still waiting for her.

"She entered the palace, which required no addition to make it the most beautiful place in the world.

"You will easily believe it, my lord," added queen white cat, "when I tell you it was that in which we are at present: two other fairies, a little younger than the one who conducted my mother, received her at the gate, and welcomed her very graciously. She begged they would lead her directly into the garden, and to those trellises where she would find the best fruit. 'It is all equally good,' said they to her, 'and if it were not that you desired to have the pleasure of picking it yourself, we have only to call the fruit we wish for, and it would come to us here.' 'I implore you, ladies,' said the queen, 'to satisfy me by so extraordinary a sight.' The eldest fairy put her finger into her mouth and whistled three times, then cried, 'Apricots, peaches, nectarines, brunions,[17] cherries, plums, pears, bigareaus,[18] melons, muscatel grapes, apples, oranges, lemons, gooseberries, strawberries, raspberries, come at my call!' 'But,' said the queen, 'all the fruit you have summoned is not to be found at the same season.' 'In our orchard,' they replied, 'we have all the fruits of the earth, always ripe, always excellent, and they never spoil or rot.'

"Meanwhile the fruit came rolling in over the floor pell-mell, but without being bruised or dirtied; so that the queen, impatient to satisfy her longing, threw herself upon it, and took the first that came to hand, devouring rather than eating it.

"After having partly satisfied her appetite, she begged the fairies to let her proceed to the trellises, that she might have the pleasure of choosing the fruit on the tree, and then gathering it. 'We give you free permission,' said they, 'but remember the promise you have made us, you will not be allowed to recall it!' 'I am convinced,' said she, 'that you live so well here, and this palace appears to me so handsome, that if I did not love the king my husband dearly, I should propose to remain here with you as well as my daughter; you need have no fear, therefore, of my retracting my word.'

"The fairies, perfectly satisfied, opened all their gardens and enclosures to her; she remained in them three days and three nights without wishing to go out again; so delicious did she find them. She gathered fruit to take

---

[17] A type of peach.
[18] A type of heart-shaped cherry.

home with her, and as it would not spoil, she had four thousand mules laden with it. The fairies, in addition to the fruit, gave her golden baskets of the most exquisite make to put it in, and many rarities of exceeding value. They promised her that I should be educated like a princess, that they would make me perfection, and choose a husband for me; that she should receive notice of the nuptials, and that they hoped for her presence at them.

"The king was enraptured at the return of the queen. All the court testified its delight to her. There were nothing but balls, masquerades, runnings at the ring, and banquets, at which the queen's fruit was served as a delicious treat. The king ate of it in preference to anything that could be presented to him. He knew not of the bargain the queen had made with the fairies, and often asked her into what country she had traveled to find such good things.

"At one time she told him they were found on an almost inaccessible mountain; at another she said they grew in some valleys; and at others, again, in a garden or in a great forest. The king was surprised at so many contradictions. He questioned those who had accompanied her: but she had so strictly forbidden them to tell any one of her adventure, that they dared not speak of it. At length the queen, becoming uneasy respecting her promise to the fairies, as the time approached for her confinement, fell into an alarming melancholy. She sighed eternally, and looked daily worse and worse. The king grew anxious; he pressed the queen to reveal to him the cause of her sadness, and after a great deal of trouble she informed him of all that had passed between her and the fairies, and how she had promised to give them the daughter she was about to bring into the world. 'What!' said the king, 'we have no children, you know how much I desire to have some, and for the sake of eating two or three apples you are capable of having given away your daughter? You can have no affection for me!' Thereupon he overwhelmed her with a thousand reproaches, which were almost the death of my poor mother; but that did not satisfy him, he had her locked up in a tower, and surrounded it with soldiers to prevent her having communication with anybody in the world except the officers of her household, and of these he changed such as had been with her at the fairy castle.

"The misunderstanding between the king and the queen threw the whole court into infinite consternation. Everybody changed their fine clothes for such as were more suitable to the general sorrow. The king, on his part, appeared inexorable. He never saw his wife, and as soon as I was born he had me brought into the palace to be nursed, while she remained a most unhappy prisoner. The fairies knew all that took place; they became irritated, they would have me, they looked upon me as their property and my detention as a theft.

"Before they sought for a vengeance proportionate to their vexation, they sent a grand embassy to the king to warn him to set the queen at liberty, to restore her to his favor, and to beg him also to deliver me up to their ambassadors, in order that I might be nursed and brought up by the fairies. The ambassadors were so little and so deformed (for they were hideous dwarfs) that they had not the power of persuading the king to comply with their request. He refused bluntly, and if they had not taken their departure instantly something worse might have happened to them. When the fairies heard of my father's conduct, they were indignant to the greatest degree, and after having desolated his six kingdoms by the infliction of every ill they could think of, they let loose a terrific dragon that poisoned the air wherever he passed, devouring man and child, and killed all the trees and plants he breathed on.

"The king was in the deepest despair. He consulted all the wise men in his dominions as to what he ought to do to protect his subjects from the misfortunes with which he saw them overwhelmed. They advised him to seek throughout the world for the best physicians and the most excellent remedies; and, on the other hand, to offer a free pardon to all malefactors under sentence of death who would undertake to fight the dragon. The king, approving this advice, acted upon it directly; but without success, for the mortality continued, and the dragon devoured all who attacked him: so that at last the king had recourse to a fairy who had been his friend from his earliest infancy. She was very old, and scarcely ever left her bed. He went to see her, and reproached her a thousand times over for permitting fate to persecute him without coming to his assistance. 'What would you have me do?' said she. 'You have irritated my sisters. They are as powerful as I am, and we rarely act against one another. Try to appease them by giving up your daughter to them. The little princess belongs to them by right. You have put the queen into prison. What has that amiable woman done to you that you should treat her so severely? Make up your mind to redeem her pledge to the fairies; I assure you you will be greatly rewarded for it.'

"The king my father loved me dearly; but seeing no other mode of saving his kingdoms and delivering himself from the fatal dragon, he told his friend he would take her advice; that he was willing to give me up to the fairies, as she had assured him that I should be cherished and treated as a princess of my rank ought to be; that he would also take the queen back to court, and that she had only to name the person to whom he should confide the task of carrying me to the fairy castle. 'You must take her,' she said, 'in her cradle, to the top of the mountain of flowers. You may even remain in its vicinity, if you please, to witness the entertainment that will take place there.' The king told her that in the course of a week he would proceed there with the queen, and begged she would give notice to her sister fairies of his intention, that they might make whatever arrangements they considered necessary.

"As soon as he returned to the palace he sent for the queen, and received her with as much affection and distinction as he had exhibited haste and anger in her imprisonment. She was so wasted and depressed that he would scarcely have recognized her had not his heart assured him she was the same person he had formerly loved so tenderly. He implored her, with tears in his eyes, to forget the misery he had caused her, assuring her it was the last she should ever experience on his account. She replied that she had brought it upon herself by her imprudence in promising her daughter to the fairies, and if anything could plead in her favor it was only the condition to which she was reduced. The king then informed her that he had determined to place me in the hands of the fairies. The queen, in her turn, opposed this intention. It seemed as if some fatality attended the affair, and that I was doomed to be always a subject of dissension between my father and mother. After she had groaned and wept for a considerable time without obtaining her object (for the king saw too clearly the fatal consequences of hesitating, and our subjects continued to perish as if they were answerable for the faults of our family), she consented to all he desired, and every preparation was made for the ceremony.

"I was placed in a cradle of mother-of-pearl, ornamented with everything art could imagine that was most elegant. It was hung round with garlands and festoons of flowers, composed of jewels, the different colors of which reflected the rays of the sun with such dazzling splendor that you could scarcely look at them. The magnificence of my clothing surpassed, if it could be possible, that of the cradle. All the bands of my swaddling clothes were formed of large pearls. Four-and-twenty princesses of the

blood-royal carried me on a sort of very light litter. Their dresses were all
different, but they were not allowed to wear any color but white, in token
of my innocence. All the court accompanied me according to the order of
precedence.

"While we were ascending the mountain a melodious symphony was
heard more and more distinctly. At length the fairies appeared to the
number of thirty-six. They had invited their friends to accompany them.
Each was seated in a pearly shell, larger than that in which Venus arose out
of the ocean. Sea-horses, that seemed rather awkward in getting over the
ground, drew these pearly cars, the occupants more sumptuous in appearance than the greatest queens in the universe, but at the same time exces-
sively old and ugly. They carried olive branches, to signify to the king that
his submission had found favor with them; and when I was presented to
them, their caresses were so extraordinary, that it seemed as if they had no
object in living, except to make me happy. The dragon they had made the
instrument of their vengeance on my father followed them in chains of
diamonds. They took me in their arms, kissed me a thousand times,
endowed me with various qualifications, and then began to dance the fairy
brawl.[19] It is a very lively dance, and you would scarcely believe how well
these old ladies jumped and capered. After this, the dragon that had
devoured so many people crawled forward. The three fairies to whom my
mother had promised me seated themselves on it, placed my cradle
between them, and striking the dragon with a wand, it immediately
spread its great scaly wings, finer than gauze, and glittering with all sorts of
extraordinary colors, and in this way they returned to their castle. My
mother, on seeing me in the air, upon this terrible dragon, could not help
screaming loudly. The king consoled her with the assurance his friend the
old fairy had given him that no accident would happen to me, and that I
should be taken as much care of as if I had remained in his own palace.
She was pacified by this assurance, though she felt much distressed at the
idea of being separated from me for so long a time, and having only herself to blame for it; for if she had not insisted on eating the fruit of that
garden, I should have been brought up in my father's dominions, and
never have suffered the misfortunes which I have still to relate to you.

"Know then, son of a king, that my guardians had built a tower,
expressly for my habitation, in which there were a thousand beautiful

---

[19] Balls were usually opened with this dance.

apartments suitable for each season of the year, magnificent furniture, and amusing books; but without a door, so that it could only be entered by the windows, which were placed prodigiously high. On the top of the tower was a beautiful garden, ornamented with flowers, fountains, and green arbors, where you might be cool in the hottest of the dog-days. In this place I was brought up by the fairies with a care even beyond all they had promised the queen. My dresses were made in the highest fashion, and so magnificent that any one to see me would have thought it was my wedding day. I was taught everything befitting my age and my rank. I did not give them much trouble, for there were few things I did not learn with the greatest ease. My docility was very agreeable to them, and as I had never seen any other persons, I might have lived there in perfect tranquillity all the rest of my life.

"They always came to see me, mounted on the terrible dragon I have already spoken of. They never talked to me about the king or the queen. They called me their daughter, and I believed myself to be so. Nobody lived with me in the tower, but a parrot and a little dog, which they had given me to amuse me; for the creatures were endowed with reason, and spoke admirably.

"On one side of the tower was a hollow way, full of deep ruts and trees which choked up the road, so that I had not seen anyone pass by since I had been shut up there. But one day that I was at the window, talking with my parrot and my dog, I heard a noise; I looked all about, and perceived a young cavalier who had stopped to listen to our conversation. I had never seen a young man before but in a painting. I was not sorry that an unlooked-for accident had afforded me this opportunity; so that, not dreaming of the danger that attends the gratification of contemplating a charming object, I came forward to gaze upon him, and the more I looked at him the more was I delighted. He made me a profound bow, fixed his eyes on me, and appeared greatly embarrassed to find some way of conversing with me, for my window was very high, and he feared being overheard, for he knew well enough that I was in the fairies' castle.

"The night came suddenly upon us, or, to speak more correctly, it came without our perceiving it; he blew his horn twice or thrice, and entertained me with a few flourishes upon it, and then took his departure without my being able to ascertain which way he went—so dark was the night. I remained very thoughtful; I no longer felt the same pleasure in talking to my parrot and my dog that I had been wont to do. They said the prettiest things in the world to me, for fairy creatures are very witty; but my mind was preoccupied, and I was too artless to conceal it. Perroquet remarked it. He was a shrewd bird; he betrayed no sign of what was running in his head.

"I did not fail being up as soon as it was light. I ran to my window, and was most agreeably surprised to perceive the young knight at the foot of the tower. He was magnificently attired. I flattered myself it was partly on my account, and I was not mistaken. He addressed me through a sort of speaking trumpet, by the aid of which he informed me, that having been up to that time insensible to the charms of all the beauties he had seen, he suddenly felt himself so strongly smitten by mine, that he could not imagine it was possible for him to live without seeing me every day of his life. I was mightily pleased with this compliment, and very much vexed that I did not dare reply to it, for I should have been compelled to bawl with all my might, and still run the risk of being better heard by the fairies than by him. I threw him some flowers I had in my hand, which he received as a signal favor, kissing them several times, and thanking me. He then asked me if I should approve of his coming every day at the same hour under my windows, and if so, to throw him something else. I had a turquoise ring on my finger, which I pulled off instantly, and flung to him in all haste, making signs to him to decamp as quickly as possible, for I heard on the other side of the tower the fairy Violente, who was mounting her dragon to bring me my breakfast.

"The first words she uttered on entering my apartment were, 'I smell the voice of a man here. Search, dragon!' Oh, what a state was I in! I was sinking with fear that the monster would fly out at the opposite window, and follow the cavalier, for whom I already felt deeply interested. 'Indeed, my good mamma,' said I (for the old fairy would have me call her so), 'you are jesting, surely, when you say you smell the voice of a man. Is it possible to smell a voice? And if so, what mortal would be rash enough to venture climbing this tower?' 'What you say is true, daughter,' replied she; 'I am delighted to hear you argue so nicely, and I fancy it is the hatred I have of all men that makes me sometimes imagine they are near me.' She gave me my breakfast and my spindle. 'When you have breakfasted do not forget to spin,' said she, 'for you did nothing yesterday, and my sisters will be angry with you.' In fact, I had been so occupied with the stranger that I had found it quite impossible to spin.

"As soon as the fairy was gone, I flung away my spindle with a little rebellious air, and ascended the terrace to look out as far as I could. I had an excellent telescope; there was nothing to interrupt the view. I looked in every direction, and discovered my cavalier on the summit of a mountain. He was reposing beneath a rich pavilion of cloth of gold, and surrounded by a very numerous court. I felt satisfied he was the son of some king who reigned in the vicinity of the fairies' palace. As I feared that if he returned to the tower he would be discovered by the terrible dragon, I went and fetched my parrot, and told him to fly to that mountain, where he would find the person who had spoken to me, and beg him in my name never to come again, as I was alarmed at the vigilance of my guardians, and the probability of their doing him some mischief. Perroquet executed his commission like a parrot of sense. The courtiers were all surprised to see him come flying at full speed, perch upon their master's shoulder and whisper in his ear. The king (for such he proved to be) was both delighted and troubled by this message. My anxiety on his account was flattering to his heart; but the many difficulties there were in the way of his speaking with me, distressed without being able to dissuade him from the attempt to make himself agreeable to me. He asked Perroquet a hundred questions, and Perroquet asked him as many in return, for he was naturally inquisitive. The king gave him a ring to bring me in return for my turquoise. It was a turquoise also; but much finer than mine, and cut in the shape of a heart, and surrounded with diamonds. 'It is fit,' said he to the parrot, 'that I should treat you as an ambassador. I therefore present you with my portrait. Show it to no one but your charming mistress.' He tied the miniature under the bird's wing, who brought the ring to me in his beak.

"I awaited the return of my little green courier with an impatience I had never known before. He told me that the personage to whom I had sent him was a great king; that he had been most kindly received by him, and that I might rest assured he only lived for my sake; that, notwithstanding there was much danger in coming to the foot of the tower, he was resolved to brave everything sooner than renounce the pleasure of seeing me. These tidings perplexed me sadly, and I began to weep. Perroquet and my little dog Toutou did their best to console me, for they loved me tenderly; and then Perroquet gave me the king's ring, and showed me his portrait. I confess I had never been so delighted as I was by being thus enabled to contemplate closely the image of him I had only seen at a dis-

tance. He appeared to me much more charming than I had supposed. A
hundred ideas rushed into my mind, some agreeable, some distressing,
and gave an expression of great anxiety to my features. The fairies who
came to see me perceived it. They observed to each other that I was no
doubt tired of my dull life, and that it was time for them to find a husband
for me of fairy race. They named several, and fixed at last upon little King
Migonnet, whose kingdom was about five hundred leagues off; but that
was a trifle. Perroquet overheard this fine council. He flew to give me an
account of it, and said to me, 'Ah, how I pity you, my dear mistress, if you
should become the queen of Migonnet! He is a monkey that would fright-
en you! I am sorry to say so; but in truth, the king who loves you would
not condescend to have him for his footman!' 'Have you seen him, Perroquet?' 'I believe so, indeed!' continued the bird; 'I was brought up on the
same branch with him.' 'How! On a branch!' I exclaimed. 'Yes,' said he,
'he has feet like an eagle.'

"Such an account as this afflicted me extremely. I gazed on the charming portrait of the young king. I felt sure he had only bestowed it on Perroquet to give me the opportunity of seeing it, and when I compared it
with the description of Migonnet, I felt I had nothing more to hope for in
life, and I resolved to die rather than marry the latter.

"I had no sleep all night. Perroquet and Toutou talked matters over
with me. I dozed a little towards daybreak, and as my dog had a good nose
he smelt that the king was at the foot of the tower. He woke Perroquet; 'I
will lay a wager,' said he, 'the king is below.' Perroquet replied, 'Hold your
peace, babbler; because your own eyes and ears are almost always open,
you envy the repose of others.' 'But bet something, then,' insisted the
good Toutou; 'I am sure he is there.' 'And I am sure he is not there,'
replied Perroquet. 'Have I not forbidden him to come here in my mistress's name?' 'Oh! you are truly amusing, with your forbiddings,'
exclaimed my dog; 'a man in love consults only his heart;' and therewith
he began to pull Perroquet by the wings so roughly that he made him
angry. The noise they both made woke me; they acquainted me with the
cause of it. I ran, or rather flew, to my window. I saw the king, who
extended his arms towards me, and said through his trumpet that he could
no longer live without me; that he implored me to find means to escape
from my tower, or to enable him to enter it. That he called all the gods
and all the elements to witness that he would marry me immediately, and
that I should be one of the greatest queens in the world.

"I ordered Perroquet to go and tell him that what he desired appeared to me an impossibility; but, nevertheless, relying on the word he had pledged to me, and the oath he had taken, I would endeavor to accomplish his wishes. That I conjured him not to come every day, as he might at length be observed, and that the fairies would have no mercy upon him.

"He retired full of joy at the hope I had flattered him with, and I found myself in the greatest embarrassment when I began to reflect on the promise I had made to him. How was I to escape from that tower in which there were no doors? And to have no one to help me but Perroquet and Toutou! I, so young, so inexperienced, so timid! I resolved therefore not to make an attempt I could never succeed in, and I sent word to that effect by Perroquet to the king. He was at first about to kill himself before the bird's eyes; but at length he charged him to persuade me either to come and witness his death or to bring him some comfort. 'Sire,' exclaimed my feathered ambassador, 'my mistress is sufficiently willing: she only lacks the power.'

"When the bird repeated to me all that had passed, I felt more wretched than ever. The fairy Violente came to see me. She found me with my eyes red and swollen; she observed that I had been crying, and said that unless I told her the cause she would burn me alive: her threats were always terrible. I replied, trembling, that I was tired of spinning, and that I wanted to make some little nets to catch the young birds that came and pecked the fruit in my garden. 'You shall cry no longer for that, daughter,' said she, 'I will bring you as much twine as you need;' and in truth I received it that very evening; but she advised me to think less of working than of attending to my personal appearance, as King Migonnet was shortly expected. I shuddered at those fatal tidings, and made no reply.

"As soon as she was gone, I began to make two or three pieces of net; but my object was to construct a rope ladder, which I succeeded in doing very well, though I had never seen one. The fairy, in fact, did not furnish me with as much twine as I wanted, and continually said to me, 'Why, daughter, your work is like that of Penelope; it never progresses, and yet you are still asking for more material.' 'Oh, my good mamma,' I replied, 'it is easy for you to talk. Don't you see that I am very awkward at my work, and burn a great deal of it. Are you afraid I shall ruin you in pack thread?' My air of simplicity amused her, though she was a very ill-tempered and cruel creature.

"I sent Perroquet to tell the king to come on a certain evening under the window of the tower, where he would find the ladder, and that he would learn the rest when he arrived. In fact, I fastened it as securely as possible, being determined to make my escape with him; but the moment he saw it, without waiting for me to descend, he mounted it eagerly, and jumped into my apartment just as I was preparing everything for my flight.

"The sight of him delighted me so much that I forgot the peril in which we were placed. He renewed all his vows, and implored me not to delay becoming his wife. We took Perroquet and Toutou as witnesses of our marriage. Never was a wedding between two persons of such exalted rank celebrated with less publicity or noise, and never were two hearts so perfectly happy as ours.

"Day had not dawned when the king left me. I had related to him the dreadful intention of the fairies to marry me to little Migonnet. I described to him his person, which horrified him as much as it had me. The hours seemed long years to me after the king's departure. I ran to the window, and followed him with my eyes, notwithstanding the darkness; but what was my astonishment at seeing in the air a fiery chariot drawn by winged salamanders, whose flight was so rapid the eye could scarcely follow them. The chariot was escorted by several soldiers mounted on ostriches. I had not time enough to distinguish who the ugly creature was thus posting through the sky, but I readily imagined that it must be either a fairy or an enchanter.

"Shortly afterwards, the fairy Violente entered my apartment. 'I bring you good news,' said she to me. 'Your lover has arrived within these few hours; prepare to receive him. Here are dresses and jewels for you!' 'And who has told you,' I exclaimed, 'that I desire to be married? It is very far from my intention. Send King Migonnet away again, I will not add a pin to my dress; let him think me handsome or ugly, I am not going to be his.' 'Hey day! Hey day!' rejoined the fairy, 'here's a little rebel! Here's a head without any brains in it! I am not to be trifled with, and I warn you—' 'What will you do to me?' cried I, reddening at the names she had called me; 'Can I be more miserably situated than I am already in this tower, with only a dog and a parrot, and seeing several times a day the horrible form of a dreadful dragon!' 'Hah, you ungrateful little wretch,' said the fairy, 'do you deserve so much care and pains as we have taken with you? I have too often told my sisters we should reap a sorry reward for it.' She departed to seek them; she related to them our quarrel; they were as much surprised at it as she was.

"Perroquet and Toutou remonstrated with me, and assured me, that if I continued refractory, they foresaw that I should suffer some terrible misfortunes. I felt so proud of possessing the heart of a great king that I despised the fairies and the advice of my poor little companions. I did not dress myself, and I took pleasure in combing my hair the wrong way, in order that Migonnet might think me ugly. Our interview took place on the terrace. He came in his fiery chariot. Never since dwarfs have existed has there been seen one so diminutive. He walked upon his eagle's feet and on his knees at the same time, for he had no bones in his legs, so that he was obliged to support himself on a pair of diamond crutches. His royal mantle was only half an ell long, and yet more than a third of it dragged on the ground. His head was as large as a peck measure, and his nose was so big, that a dozen birds sat upon it, whose warbling entertained him. He had such a bushy beard that canary-birds made their nests in it; and his ears rose a cubit higher than his head; but they were not very perceptible, in consequence of the high-pointed crown that he wore to make him appear taller. The flames of his chariot roasted the fruit, scorched the flowers, and dried up the fountains in my garden. He approached with open arms to embrace me. I held myself bolt upright, and his principal equerry was compelled to lift him; but as soon as he was brought near me, I fled into my apartment, and fastened the door and the windows, so that Migonnet returned to the fairies highly incensed against me.

"They begged his pardon a thousand times for my rudeness, and to appease him, for he was much to be feared, they determined to bring him into my chamber at night, while I slept, to tie me hand and foot, and place me in his fiery chariot, to be taken away by him. Having decided on this plan, they scarcely said a cross word to me about my rude behavior to him, but merely advised me to think of making amends for it. Perroquet and Toutou were astonished at such great kindness. 'Do you know, mistress,' said my dog, 'my heart misgives me. My lady fairies are strange personages, and particularly Violente.' 'I laughed at these fears, and awaited my dear husband's arrival with the greatest anxiety. He was too impatient to see me to keep me long waiting. I threw him the rope-ladder, fully resolved to fly with him. He mounted it lightly, and said such tender things to me, that I dare not even now recall them to mind.

"While we were conversing together as calmly as if we had been in his own palace, the windows of my room were suddenly burst in. The fairies entered upon their terrible dragon. Migonnet followed them in his fiery chariot, attended by all his guards on their ostriches. The king fearlessly drew his sword, and only thought of saving me from the most dreadful fate that ever awaited mortal; for, in short, must I speak it, my lord, those barbarous creatures urged their dragon upon him, which devoured him before my eyes.

"Distracted at his fate and my own, I flung myself into the jaws of the horrible monster, hoping he would swallow me, as he had already swallowed all I loved in the world. He was equally willing to do so; but the fairies, still more cruel than the dragon, would not permit it. 'She must be reserved,' they cried, 'for more protracted agony; a speedy death is too mild a punishment for this unworthy creature!' They touched me, and I immediately found myself assuming the form of a white cat. They conducted me to this superb palace, which belonged to my father.[20] They transformed all the lords and ladies of the kingdom into cats, left only the hands visible of the rest of his court, and reduced me to the deplorable condition in which you found me, after informing me of my birth, the death of my father and mother, and that I could only be released from my cat-like form by a prince who should perfectly resemble the husband they had deprived me of. It is you, my lord, who bear that resemblance," continued she: "you have the same features, the same air, the same voice. I was struck by it the moment I saw you. I was aware of all that has happened, and I am equally so of all that will happen. My troubles are about to end." "And mine, lovely queen," said the prince, flinging himself at her feet "how long are they to last?" "I already love you more than my life, my lord," said the queen; "you must return to your father; we will ascertain his sentiments respecting me, and whether he will consent to what you desire."

She went out of the castle, the prince gave her his hand; she got into a chariot with him. It was much more magnificent than those she had previously provided for him. The rest of the equipage corresponded with it to such an extent that the horses were all shod with emeralds, the nails being diamonds; such a thing has perhaps never been seen except on that occa-

---

[20] This appears to be an oversight. The white cat previously told the prince that this castle was identical with the fairy castle.

sion. I shall not repeat the agreeable conversation that took place between the queen and the prince on their journey. If her beauty was matchless, her mind was no less so, and the young prince was equally perfect, so that they interchanged all sorts of charming ideas.

When they reached the neighborhood of the castle, in which the prince was to meet his two elder brothers, the queen entered a little rock of crystal, the points of which were ornamented with gold and rubies. It was completely surrounded by curtains, in order that no one should see it, and carried by some very handsome young men superbly attired. The prince remained in the chariot. He perceived his brothers walking with two princesses, who were exceedingly beautiful. As soon as they recognized him, they advanced to receive him, and inquired if he had brought a lady with him. He replied that he had been so unfortunate throughout his journey as to have met with none but very ugly ones, and that the only rarity he had brought back with him was a little white cat. They began to laugh at his simplicity. "A cat!" they exclaimed; "are you afraid the mice will eat up our palace?" The prince admitted that he had been rather unwise in selecting such a present for his father; and thereupon they each took their road to the city.

The elder princes rode with their princesses in open carriages, all of gold and azure. Their horses' heads were adorned with plumes of feathers. Nothing could be more brilliant than this cavalcade. Our young prince followed them, and behind him came the crystal rock, which everybody gazed at with wonder.

The courtiers hastened to inform the king that the three princes were coming. "Do they bring with them beautiful ladies?" asked the king. "It is impossible to find any that could surpass them," was the answer, which appeared to displease him. The two princes eagerly ascended the palace stairs with their wonderful princesses. The king received them graciously, and could not decide which deserved the prize. He looked at his youngest son, and said to him, "Have you returned alone this time?" "Your majesty will perceive in this rock a little white cat," replied the prince, "that mews so sweetly, and has such velvet paws, you will be delighted with it." The king smiled, and went to open the rock himself; but as soon as he approached it, the queen, by means of a spring, made it fly in pieces, and appeared like the sun after it had been some time hidden in the clouds. Her fair hair fell in loose ringlets over her shoulders down to her very feet; she was crowned with flowers; her gown was of thin white gauze lined with rose-colored taffeta. She rose, and made a profound courtesy to the king, who could not resist exclaiming in the excess of his admiration, "Behold the incomparable beauty who deserves the crown!"

"My liege," said she to him, "I come not to deprive you of a throne you fill so worthily. I was born the heiress to six kingdoms; permit me to offer one to you, and to give one to each of your eldest sons. I ask of you no other recompense than your friendship and this young prince for my husband. Three kingdoms will be quite enough for us." The king and all the court joined in shouts of joy and astonishment. The marriage was celebrated immediately, as well as those of the other two princes, and the court consequently passed several months in entertainments and pleasures of every description. Finally, each couple departed to reign over their own dominions. The beautiful white cat immortalized herself in hers, as much by her goodness and liberality as by her rare talent and beauty.

> "The youthful prince was fortunate to find
> Beneath a cat's skin an illustrious fair
> Worthy of adoration, and inclined
> The throne, her friendship won for him, to share.

> "By two enchanting eyes, on conquest bent,
> The willing heart is easily subdued;
> And still more power to the charm is lent,
> When love's soft flame is fanned by gratitude.

> "Shall I in silence pass that parent o'er,
> Who for her folly paid so dear a price;
> And for some tempting fruit—as Eve before—
> The welfare of her race could sacrifice?

> "Mothers, beware! nor like that selfish queen,
> Venture to cloud a lovely daughter's lot
> To gratify some appetite as mean,
> Detest such conduct: imitate it not."

JAPAN

The Boy Who Drew Cats

Lafcadio Hearn (1850–1904) is famous for his many books on Japan. Born in Greece, he grew up in Greece, Ireland, England, Wales, and France. He spent the first half of his adult life in the United States and the latter half living in Japan, where he became a Buddhist and a Japanese citizen, adopting the name Yakumo Koizumi. This story is from Hearn's Japanese Fairy Tales, *which was published in 1902. It was also published as an illustrated children's book several decades later.*

A long, long time ago, in a small country village in Japan, there lived a poor farmer and his wife, who were very good people. They had a number of children, and found it very hard to feed them all. The elder son was strong enough when only fourteen years old to help his father; and the little girls learned to help their mother almost as soon as they could walk.

But the youngest child, a little boy, did not seem to be fit for hard work. He was very clever—cleverer than all his brothers and sisters; but he was quite weak and small, and people said he could never grow very big. So his parents thought it would be better for him to become a priest than to become a farmer. They took him with them to the village temple one day, and asked the good old priest who lived there if he would have their little boy for his acolyte, and teach him all that a priest ought to know.

The old man spoke kindly to the lad, and asked him some hard questions. So clever were the answers that the priest agreed to take the little fellow into the temple as an acolyte, and to educate him for the priesthood.

The boy learned quickly what the old priest taught him, and was very obedient in most things. But he had one fault. He liked to draw cats dur-

93

ing study-hours, and to draw cats even where cats ought not to have been drawn at all.

Whenever he found himself alone, he drew cats. He drew them on the margins of the priest's books, and on all the screens of the temple, and on the walls, and on the pillars. Several times the priest told him this was not right; but he did not stop drawing cats. He drew them because he could not really help it. He had what is called "the genius of an artist," and just for that reason he was not quite fit to be an acolyte—a good acolyte should study books.

One day after he had drawn some very clever pictures of cats upon a paper screen, the old priest said to him severely: "My boy, you must go away from this temple at once. You will never make a good priest, but perhaps you will become a great artist. Now let me give you a last piece of advice, and be sure you never forget it. *Avoid large places at night—keep to small!*"

The boy did not know what the priest meant by saying, *"Avoid large places—keep to small."* He thought and thought while he was tying up his little bundle of clothes to go away but he could not understand those words, and he was afraid to speak to the priest any more, except to say good-by.

He left the temple very sorrowfully, and began to wonder what he should do. If he went straight home he felt sure his father would punish him for having been disobedient to the priest: so he was afraid to go home. All at once he remembered that at the next village, twelve miles away, there was a very big temple. He had heard there were several priests at that temple; and he made up his mind to go to them and ask them to take him for their acolyte.

Now that big temple was closed up but the boy did not know this fact. The reason it had been closed up was that a goblin had frightened the priests away, and had taken possession of the place. Some brave warriors had afterward gone to the temple at night to kill the goblin; but they had never been seen alive again. Nobody had ever told these things to the boy, so he walked all the way to the village hoping to be kindly treated by the priests.

When he got to the village it was already dark, and all the people were in bed; but he saw the big temple on a hill at the other end of the principal street, and he saw there was a light in the temple. People who tell the story say the goblin used to make that light in order to tempt lonely travelers to ask for shelter. The boy went at once to the temple, and knocked. There was no sound inside. He knocked and knocked again; but still nobody came. At last he pushed gently at the door, and was quite glad to find that it had not been fastened. So he went in, and saw a lamp burning—but no priest.

He thought some priest would be sure to come very soon, and he sat down and waited. Then he noticed that everything in the temple was gray with dust, and thickly spun over with cobwebs. So he thought to himself that the priests would certainly like to have an acolyte, to keep the place clean. He wondered why they had allowed everything to get so dusty. What most pleased him, however, were some big white screens, good to paint cats upon. Though he was tired, he looked at once for a writing-box, and found one, and ground some ink, and began to paint cats.

He painted a great many cats upon the screens; and then he began to feel very, very sleepy. He was just on the point of lying down to sleep beside one of the screens, when he suddenly remembered the words, *"Avoid large places—keep to small!"*

The temple was very large; he was all alone; and as he thought of these words—though he could not quite understand them—he began to feel for the first time a little afraid; and he resolved to look for a *small place* in which to sleep. He found a little cabinet, with a sliding door, and went into it, and shut himself up. Then he lay down and fell fast asleep.

Very late in the night he was awakened by a most terrible noise, a noise of fighting and screaming. It was so dreadful that he was afraid even to look through a chink of the little cabinet: he lay very still, holding his breath for fright.

The light that had been in the temple went out; but the awful sounds continued, and became more awful, and all the temple shook. After a long time silence came; but the boy was still afraid to move. He did not move until the light of the morning sun shone into the cabinet through the chinks of the little door.

Then he got out of his hiding-place very cautiously, and looked about. The first thing he saw was that all the floor of the temple was covered with blood. And then he saw, lying dead in the middle of it, an enormous, monstrous rat—a goblin-rat—bigger than a cow!

But who or what could have killed it? There was no man or other creature to be seen. Suddenly the boy observed that the mouths of all the cats he had drawn the night before were red and wet with blood. Then he knew that the goblin had been killed by the cats which he had drawn. And then also, for the first time, he understood why the wise old priest had said to him, *"Avoid large places at night—keep to small."*

Afterward that boy became a very famous artist. Some of the cats which he drew are still shown to travelers in Japan.

The Cat That Walked by Himself

This story by Rudyard Kipling originally appeared in 1902 and was included in his Just So Stories, *which was published in 1912. Kipling (1865–1936) was born in Bombay, the son of a clergyman. He returned to India as a journalist in 1882 and stayed for eight years before moving back to England. His stories and poems of India made him famous. He was the author of* Kim, The Jungle Book, Captains Courageous, Puck of Pook's Hill, *and* Rewards and Fairies. *He also wrote the short story "The Man Who Would be King" and the poem "Gunga Din," both of which were made into movies. In 1907 he was awarded the Nobel Prize for Literature. "The Cat That Walked by Himself" is similar to the ancient animal fables, many of which originated in India. Some fairy tales, such as "Puss in Boots," were originally fables. This story contains elements of both fables and fairy tales.*

Hear and attend and listen; for this befell and behappened became was, O my Best Beloved, when the Tame animals were wild. The Dog was wild, and the Horse was wild, and the Cow was wild, and the Sheep was wild, and the Pig was wild—as wild as wild could be—and they walked in the Wet Wild Woods by their wild lones. But the wildest of all the wild animals was the Cat. He walked by himself, and all places were alike to him.

Of course the Man was wild too. He was dreadfully wild. He didn't even begin to be tame till he met the Woman, and she told him that she did not like living in his wild ways. She picked out a nice dry Cave, instead of a heap of wet leaves, to lie down in; and she strewed clean sand on the floor; and she lit a nice fire of wood at the back of the Cave; and she hung a dried wild-horse skin, tail-down, across the opening of the Cave; and she said, "Wipe your feet, dear, when you come in, and now we'll keep house."

That night, Best Beloved, they ate wild sheep roasted on the hot stones, and flavored with wild garlic and wild pepper; and wild duck stuffed with wild rice and wild fenugreek and wild coriander; and marrow-bones of wild oxen; and wild cherries, and wild grenadillas. Then the Man went to sleep in front of the fire ever so happy; but the Woman sat up, combing her hair. She took the bone of the shoulder of mutton—the big fat blade-bone—and she looked at the wonderful marks on it, and she threw more wood on the fire, and she made a Magic. She made the First Singing Magic in the world.

Out in the Wet Wild Woods all the wild animals gathered together where they could see the light of the fire a long way off, and they wondered what it meant.

Then Wild Horse stamped with his wild foot and said, "O my Friends and O my Enemies, why have the Man and the Woman made that great light in that great Cave, and what harm will it do us?"

Wild Dog lifted up his wild nose and smelled the smell of roast mutton, and said, "I will go up and see and look, and say; for I think it is good. Cat, come with me."

"Nenni!" said the Cat. "I am the Cat who walks by himself, and all places are alike to me. I will not come."

"Then we can never be friends again," said Wild Dog, and he trotted off to the Cave. But when he had gone a little way the Cat said to himself, "All places are alike to me. Why should I not go too and see and look and come away at my own liking." So he slipped after Wild Dog softly, very softly, and hid himself where he could hear everything.

When Wild Dog reached the mouth of the Cave he lifted up the dried horse-skin with his nose and sniffed the beautiful smell of the roast mutton, and the Woman, looking at the blade-bone, heard him, and laughed, and said, "Here comes the first. Wild Thing out of the Wild Woods, what do you want?"

Wild Dog said, "O my Enemy and Wife of my Enemy, what is this that smells so good in the Wild Woods?"

Then the Woman picked up a roasted mutton-bone and threw it to Wild Dog, and said, "Wild Thing out of the Wild Woods, taste and try." Wild Dog gnawed the bone, and it was more delicious than anything he had ever tasted, and he said, "O my Enemy and Wife of my Enemy, give me another."

The Woman said, "Wild Thing out of the Wild Woods, help my Man to hunt through the day and guard this Cave at night, and I will give you as many roast bones as you need."

"Ah!" said the Cat, listening. "This is a very wise Woman, but she is not so wise as I am."

Wild Dog crawled into the Cave and laid his head on the Woman's lap, and said, "O my Friend and Wife of my Friend, I will help your Man to hunt through the day, and at night I will guard your Cave."

"Ah!" said the Cat, listening. "That is a very foolish Dog." And he went back through the Wet Wild Woods waving his wild tail, and walking by his wild lone. But he never told anybody.

When the Man waked up he said, "What is Wild Dog doing here?" And the Woman said, "His name is not Wild Dog any more, but the First Friend, because he will be our friend for always and always and always. Take him with you when you go hunting."

Next night the Woman cut great green armfuls of fresh grass from the water-meadows, and dried it before the fire, so that it smelt like new-mown hay, and she sat at the mouth of the Cave and plaited a halter out of horse-hide, and she looked at the shoulder of mutton-bone—at the big broad blade-bone—and she made a Magic. She made the Second Singing Magic in the world.

Out in the Wild Woods all the wild animals wondered what had happened to Wild Dog, and at last Wild Horse stamped with his foot and said, "I will go and see and say why Wild Dog has not returned. Cat, come with me."

"Nenni!" said the Cat, "I am the Cat who walks by himself, and all places are alike to me. I will not come." But all the same he followed Wild Horse softly, very softly, and hid himself where he could hear everything.

When the Woman heard Wild Horse tripping and stumbling on his long mane, she laughed and said, "Here comes the second. Wild Thing out of the Wild Woods, what do you want?"

Wild Horse said, "O my Enemy and Wife of my Enemy, where is Wild Dog?"

The Woman laughed, and picked up the blade-bone and looked at it, and said, "Wild Thing out of the Wild Woods, you did not come here for Wild Dog, but for the sake of this good grass."

And Wild Horse, tripping and stumbling on his long mane, said, "That is true; give it me to eat."

The Woman said, "Wild Thing out of the Wild Woods, bend your wild head and wear what I give you, and you shall eat the wonderful grass three times a day."

"Ah," said the Cat, listening, "this is a clever Woman, but she is not so clever as I am."

Wild Horse bent his wild head, and the Woman slipped the plaited hide halter over it, and Wild Horse breathed on the Woman's feet and said, "O my Mistress, and Wife of my Master, I will be your servant for the sake of the wonderful grass."

"Ah," said the Cat, listening, "that is a very foolish Horse." And he went back through the Wet Wild Woods, waving his wild tail and walking by his wild lone. But he never told anybody.

When the Man and the Dog came back from hunting, the Man said, "What is Wild Horse doing here?" And the Woman said, "His name is not Wild Horse any more, but the First Servant, because he will carry us from place to place for always and always and always. Ride on his back when you go hunting."

Next day, holding her wild head high that her wild horns should not catch in the wild trees, Wild Cow came up to the Cave, and the Cat followed, and hid himself just the same as before; and everything happened just the same as before; and the Cat said the same things as before, and when Wild Cow had promised to give her milk to the Woman every day in exchange for the wonderful grass, the Cat went back through the Wet Wild Woods waving his wild tail and walking by his wild lone, just the same as before. But he never told anybody. And when the Man and the Horse and the Dog came home from hunting and asked the same questions same as before, the Woman said, "Her name is not Wild Cow any more, but the Giver of Good Food. She will give us the warm white milk for always and always and always, and I will take care of her while you and the First Friend and the First Servant go hunting."

Next day the Cat waited to see if any other Wild thing would go up to the Cave, but no one moved in the Wet Wild Woods, so the Cat walked there by himself; and he saw the Woman milking the Cow, and he saw the light of the fire in the Cave, and he smelt the smell of the warm white milk.

Cat said, "O my Enemy and Wife of my Enemy, where did Wild Cow go?"

The Woman laughed and said, "Wild Thing out of the Wild Woods, go back to the Woods again, for I have braided up my hair, and I have put away the magic blade-bone, and we have no more need of either friends or servants in our Cave."

Cat said, "I am not a friend, and I am not a servant. I am the Cat who walks by himself, and I wish to come into your cave."

Woman said, "Then why did you not come with First Friend on the first night?"

Cat grew very angry and said, "Has Wild Dog told tales of me?"

Then the Woman laughed and said, "You are the Cat who walks by himself, and all places are alike to you. You are neither a friend nor a servant. You have said it yourself. Go away and walk by yourself in all places alike."

Then Cat pretended to be sorry and said, "Must I never come into the Cave? Must I never sit by the warm fire? Must I never drink the warm white milk? You are very wise and very beautiful. You should not be cruel even to a Cat."

Woman said, "I knew I was wise, but I did not know I was beautiful. So I will make a bargain with you. If ever I say one word in your praise you may come into the Cave."

"And if you say two words in my praise?" said the Cat.

"I never shall," said the Woman, "but if I say two words in your praise, you may sit by the fire in the Cave."

"And if you say three words?" said the Cat.

"I never shall," said the Woman, "but if I say three words in your praise, you may drink the warm white milk three times a day for always and always and always."

Then the Cat arched his back and said, "Now let the Curtain at the mouth of the Cave, and the Fire at the back of the Cave, and the Milk-pots that stand beside the Fire, remember what my Enemy and the Wife of my Enemy has said." And he went away through the Wet Wild Woods waving his wild tail and walking by his wild lone.

That night when the Man and the Horse and the Dog came home from hunting, the Woman did not tell them of the bargain that she had made with the Cat, because she was afraid that they might not like it.

Cat went far and far away and hid himself in the Wet Wild Woods by his wild lone for a long time till the Woman forgot all about him. Only the Bat—the little upside-down Bat—that hung inside the Cave, knew where Cat hid; and every evening Bat would fly to Cat with news of what was happening.

One evening Bat said, "There is a Baby in the Cave. He is new and pink and fat and small, and the Woman is very fond of him."

"Ah," said the Cat, listening, "but what is the Baby fond of?"

"He is fond of things that are soft and tickle," said the Bat. "He is fond of warm things to hold in his arms when he goes to sleep. He is fond of being played with. He is fond of all those things."

"Ah," said the Cat, listening, "then my time has come."

Next night Cat walked through the Wet Wild Woods and hid very near the Cave till morning-time, and Man and Dog and Horse went hunting. The Woman was busy cooking that morning, and the Baby cried and interrupted. So she carried him outside the Cave and gave him a handful of pebbles to play with. But still the Baby cried.

Then the Cat put out his paddy paw and patted the Baby on the cheek, and it cooed; and the Cat rubbed against its fat knees and tickled it under its fat chin with his tail. And the Baby laughed and the Woman heard him and smiled.

Then the Bat—the little upside-down Bat—that hung in the mouth of the Cave said, "O my Hostess and Wife of my Host and Mother of my Host's Son, a Wild Thing from the Wild Woods is most beautifully play-ing with your Baby."

"A blessing on that Wild Thing whoever he may be," said the Woman, straightening her back, "for I was a busy woman this morning and he has done me a service."

The very minute and second, Best Beloved, the dried horse-skin Cur-tain that was stretched tail-down at the mouth of the Cave fell down— *woosh!*—because it remembered the bargain she had made with the Cat, and when the Woman went to pick it up—lo and behold!—the Cat was sitting quite comfy inside the Cave.

"O my Enemy and Wife of my Enemy and Mother of my Enemy," said the Cat, "it is I: for you have spoken a word in my praise, and now I can sit within the Cave for always and always and always. But still I am the Cat who walks by himself, and all places are alike to me."

The Woman was very angry, and shut her lips tight and took up her spinning-wheel and began to spin.

But the Baby cried because the Cat had gone away, and the Woman could not hush it, for it struggled and kicked and grew black in the face.

"O my Enemy and Wife of my Enemy and Mother of my Enemy,"
said the Cat, "take a strand of the wire that you are spinning and tie it to
your spinning-whorl and drag it along the floor, and I will show you a
magic that shall make your Baby laugh as loudly as he is now crying."

"I will do so," said the Woman, "because I am at my wits' end; but I
will not thank you for it."

She tied the thread to the little clay spindle-whorl and drew it across
the floor, and the Cat ran after it and patted it with his paws and rolled
head over heels, and tossed it backward over his shoulder and chased it
between his hind-legs and pretended to lose it, and pounced down upon it
again, till the Baby laughed as loudly as it had been crying, and scrambled
after the Cat and frolicked all over the Cave till it grew tired and settled
down to sleep with the Cat in its arms.

"Now," said the Cat, "I will sing the Baby a song that shall keep him
asleep for an hour." And he began to purr, loud and low, low and loud, till
the Baby fell fast asleep. The Woman smiled as she looked down upon the
two of them and said, "That was wonderfully done. No question but you
are very clever, O Cat."

That very minute and second, Best Beloved, the smoke of the fire at
the back of the Cave came down in clouds from the roof—puff!—because
it remembered the bargain she had made with the Cat, and when it had
cleared away—lo and behold!—the Cat was sitting quite comfy close to
the fire.

"O my Enemy and Wife of my Enemy and Mother of my Enemy,"
said the Cat, "it is I, for you have spoken a second word in my praise, and
now I can sit by the warm fire at the back of the Cave for always and
always and always. But still I am the Cat who walks by himself, and all
places are alike to me."

Then the Woman was very very angry, and let down her hair and put
more wood on the fire and brought out the broad blade-bone of the
shoulder of mutton and began to make a Magic that should prevent her
from saying a third word in praise of the Cat. It was not a Singing Magic,
Best Beloved, it was a Still Magic; and by and by the Cave grew so still that
a little wee-wee mouse crept out of a corner and ran across the floor.

"O my Enemy and Wife of my Enemy and Mother of my Enemy,"
said the Cat, "is that little mouse part of your magic?"

"Ouh! Chee! No indeed!" said the Woman, and she dropped the blade-bone and jumped upon the footstool in front of the fire and braided up her hair very quick for fear that the mouse should run up it.

"Ah," said the Cat, watching, "then the mouse will do me no harm if I eat it?"

"No," said the Woman, braiding up her hair, "eat it quickly and I will ever be grateful to you."

Cat made one jump and caught the little mouse, and the Woman said, "A hundred thanks. Even the First Friend is not quick enough to catch little mice as you have done. You must be very wise."

That very moment and second, O Best Beloved, the milk-pot that stood by the fire cracked in two pieces—*ffft*—because it remembered the bargain she had made with the Cat, and when the Woman jumped down from the footstool—lo and behold!—the Cat was lapping up the warm white milk that lay in one of the broken pieces.

"O my Enemy and Wife of my Enemy and Mother of my Enemy," said the Cat, "it is I; for you have spoken three words in my praise, and now I can drink the warm white milk three times a day for always and always and always. But still I am the Cat who walks by himself, and all places are alike to me."

Then the Woman laughed and set the Cat a bowl of the warm white milk and said, "O Cat, you are as clever as a man, but remember that your bargain was not made with the Man or the Dog, and I do not know what they will do when they come home."

"What is that to me?" said the Cat. "If I have my place in the Cave by the fire and my warm white milk three times a day I do not care what the Man or the Dog can do."

That evening when the Man and the Dog came into the Cave, the Woman told them all the story of the bargain while the Cat sat by the fire and smiled. Then the Man said, "Yes, but he has not made a bargain with *me* or with all proper Men after me." Then he took off his two leather boots and he took up his little stone ax (that makes three) and he fetched a piece of wood and a hatchet (that is five altogether), and he set them out in a row and he said, "Now we will make *our* bargain. If you do not catch mice when you are in the Cave for always and always and always, I will throw these five things at you whenever I see you, and so shall all proper Men do after me."

"Ah," said the Woman, listening, "this is a very clever Cat, but he is not so clever as my Man."

The Cat counted the five things (and they looked very knobby) and he said, "I will catch mice when I am in the Cave for always and always and always; but *still* I am the Cat who walks by himself, and all places are alike to me."

"Not when I am near," said the Man. "If you had not said that last I would have put all these things away for always and always and always; but I am now going to throw my two boots and my little stone ax (that makes three) at you whenever I meet you. And so shall all proper Men do after me!"

Then the Dog said, "Wait a minute. He has not made a bargain with *me* or with all proper Dogs after me." And he showed his teeth and said, "If you are not kind to the Baby while I am in the Cave for always and always and always, I will hunt you till I catch you, and when I catch you I will bite you. And so shall all proper Dogs do after me."

"Ah," said the Woman, listening, "this is a very clever Cat, but he is not so clever as the Dog."

Cat counted the Dog's teeth (and they looked very pointed) and he said, "I will be kind to the Baby while I am in the Cave, as long as he does not pull my tail too hard, for always and always and always. But *still* I am the Cat that walks by himself, and all places are alike to me."

"Not when I am near," said the Dog. "If you had not said that last I would have shut my mouth for always and always and always; but *now* I am going to hunt you up a tree whenever I meet you. And so shall all proper Dogs do after me."

Then the Man threw his two boots and his little stone ax (that makes three) at the Cat, and the Cat ran out of the Cave and the Dog chased him up a tree; and from that day to this, Best Beloved, three proper Men out of five will always throw things at a Cat whenever they meet him, and all proper Dogs will chase him up a tree. But the Cat keeps his side of the bargain too. He will kill mice and he will be kind to Babies when he is in the house, just as long as they do not pull his tail too hard. But when he has done that, and between times, and when the moon gets up and night comes, he is the Cat that walks by himself, and all places are alike to him. Then he goes out to the Wet Wild Woods or up the Wet Wild Trees or on the Wet Wild Roofs, waving his wild tail and walking by his wild lone.

Lesser Known
Cat Fairy Tales

SCOTLAND

Scratch Tom

Walter Douglas Campbell wrote this story for his book Beyond the Border, *which was published in 1898.*

It was indeed a dreary November evening, and the wind, herald of the coming winter, swept round the lonely cottage on the moor. Within, a poor old dame sat cowering over the fast-dying embers of a few sticks, the last her feeble strength was able to collect.

It had been a wretched season; the root-crop had failed, her goat had died of disease, and now, without money and without friends—but a half-burnt faggot to warm and a moldy bannock to sustain her—she looked forward to the future with terror and despair. Desolation ruled within, and the wind seemed to moan a dirge without.

Poor old thing! She gave a last stir to the fast-dying embers, placed her wretched bannock on the platter at her side, and drew her thin, faded shawl around her shivering limbs. With a habit born of many a day's task, she stretched out her hand to the old spinning-wheel at her side. Alas! here another disappointment presented itself: there was no wool to spin or flax to card. All had gone, like food and fuel, long ago. Still, she drew it towards her, and moved the treadle with her foot, for its monotonous beat seemed to soothe her, like the voice of an old friend sympathizing, though helpless as herself.

What is that faint cry at the door, accompanied by a dull scratching on the threshold? Can there be another creature more wretched this night than herself, that it seeks for charity at the hand of a poor old dame?

At any rate, the Whatever-it-was had to be admitted, and, opening the door, the kind old woman, forgetful for a moment of her own want in the pity for another's, let in from the darkness something like the shadow of a shade. So thin, so bony, so gaunt was this creature which crept along the floor and squatted down on the hearthstone at her feet, that it seemed but some dried branch blown in by the wind.

Its tail hung down like a frozen cord; its ears, like withered leaves drooped painfully from a seemingly skinless skull; hardly a piece of fur covered its emaciated anatomy; it seemed nought but teeth and claw and eyes. Eyes large as saucers, green as emeralds, these were the only things that revealed it to the old dame as a starving cat.

"Poor creature!" said she; "so there is something worse off than myself at this moment in the world, though I would scarcely have believed that possible. What is your name, creature?" said she.

"Scratch Tom," said the cat.

"I did not ask you what I was to do," said she, "but what your name is, creature."

"Scratch Tom," said the cat.

"Well, if you wish it, I will," said the dame; and she stroked the cat from head to tail, and—would you believe it?—something like the ghost of a purr came from somewhere.

"So there's something more bony than myself," said the dame, as she stroked the cat, "though I scarcely would have thought so."

"And would you like a piece of bannock?" said she. Skulls and cross-bones! What a squeal of assent came from between the teeth of the cat! The wife nearly fell over backward from fright.

So she gave it a piece of cake. There was one snap, and the bit was swallowed; the wife had to draw back her fingers swiftly to prevent them being snapped up too.

"So there's something more hungry in this world than myself," said she, "though I never would have believed that possible."

"Well then, take it all," said the dame; "it may satisfy you, poor thing, and it would only keep starvation from me for a few hours longer at the best."

So she threw the cat the remainder of the bannock. It was stale, and broke into three fragments as it struck the floor.

The cat ate the first bit, and it swelled and grew to the size of the dame's footstool.

The cat ate the second bit, and it swelled and grew to the size of the dame's chair.

The cat ate the third bit, and it swelled and grew to the size of the dame's wooden table. And a more plump and well-furred cat you could not have seen had you searched the town of Kirkcaldy from one end to the other.

"Now," said the cat—for of course you have already perceived it was a fairy cat, not a common one—"you have given me your all, and you took pity on a poor starving cat when in want yourself. You shall have your reward, if you only do as I bid you."

Well, the dame was not slow to promise that, you may be sure.

"Get on my back," said the cat, "and we will seek a fortune in the Caves of Darkness."

"But I shall fall off," said the dame; "for I am weak, and not used to riding."

"Tie your apron under my body," said the cat, "and hold on tight by the strings."

So the wife did as she was bid; she tied her apron under the cat's body, and, seating herself on its back, held tight to the strings.

"Now, off we go," said the cat; "say no more than, but say all that I bid you; do no more than, but do all that I tell you." And the dame promised.

Into the dark night went the cat and his burden, and if the wind blew fierce and wild, it was the cat that won the race and left it shrieking far behind, nor did he draw breath till he arrived at a great rock in the side of a great hill with a great door in the center, studded over with bolts of iron, and hung on hinges of living snakes that curled round and round the granite door-posts on either side.

Here the cat turned, and, bidding the dame dismount, he struck the door with a violent kick, till the great timbers shook and rattled, and the thunder echoed in the mountains.

"Who knocks so loud?" said a voice within.

"The Princess of the Land of Light and her servant, Scratch Tom," said the cat.

"We have heard of neither before, and before I open the gate you must give me the sign," said the voice.

"Put your hand under the door, and I will give you the sign," said the cat.

Then there appeared under the door a long, bony, and hairy arm, like an ape's, with long red and green claws, which shone and glistened in the moonlight.

In a trice the cat had seized the arm between his teeth, and held so fast he drew blood with his fangs.

"Let go!" said the voice. "Let go!"

"Not till you put the key under the gate," said the cat.

So the key was pushed under the gate, and the cat let the arm go.

"Now," said the cat to the dame, "take this key and stand on my back, and turn it in the lock."

So the cat arched its back till it was just so high that the dame, standing on tiptoe, could put the key in the lock.

"Don't let the key go, for your life's sake!" said the cat. So the dame turned the key in the lock, which gave a groan like a dying monster, and then, pulling it out, she hid it under her shawl.

"Now, push," said the cat. So the dame pushed and the cat pushed, and the cat pushed and the dame pushed, till the timbers rattled, and the iron knobs shook, and the snake hinges wriggled again and again, but the door would not open.

"Take three hairs out of my tail," said the cat, "and stroke the nose of the snake-hinge in the center."

The dame did so, and the snake gave so fierce a twist that the great door flew open of its own accord.

"Now, give me my key," said the voice.

"The Princess of the Land of Light takes no service without giving a reward in return," said the cat. "I will whisper to you how the Trolls brew heather beer on Morven."

Now the voice wanted the key back, and also it was anxious to know the secret of heather beer, so it stretched its head down close to the cat's, who swiftly bit it off.

Then they stuffed the voice's body under the gate to prevent it from shutting, and the dame, mounting, took up her apron-strings, and off they went to the Caves of Darkness, where the black east wind ever blows.

Away and away into the gloom went the cat and his burden, and if the wind blew fierce and wild, it was the cat that won the race and left it shrieking far behind.

Suddenly, without giving warning, the cat stopped, so that it almost brought the dame over its ears, and said, "Place your hand behind my left ear, and scratch Tom."

And the dame did so, and oh! it was the brightness of the moon that came from the cat's head, and filled a great space around with dazzling light.

The dame found herself in an immense hall that seemed built of black marble, and round it there were galleries on galleries, one above the other, mounting innumerable to a roof that stretched upward and upward till lost in a black cloudland above. In these galleries were seated in rows, one behind the other, thousands on thousands of strange beings of human shape, but of giant height, clothed in robes of silver scales, with caps on their heads, each cap made of a single ruby, ruddy as blood. Every head was adorned with large yellow parchment ears, tipped with green fur; while under each forehead were enormous eyes like white toadstools, circular and convex, bulging, rolling, and blinking in the unaccustomed glare, while every hairy neck was stretched a yard long into the great space of the hall below.

The King of the Dark Caverns sat at the further end of the hall on a throne of black marble, carved like a shell, and encrusted with golden stars. His robe was of the black swansdown, overlaid with a network of pearls, and his crown was made of one pearl, with a plume above of the feathers of the black sea-cormorant. Beside him sat the Princess, dressed in a garment of gold threads worked crosswise. Her crown was a single diamond, shaped as the crescent moon, and her hands and feet were encased in gloves and shoes studded with lustrous jewels. King, and princess too, had large parchment ears and toadstool eyes, and they both eyed the strangers, and stretched their long hairy necks a full yard towards the dame and Scratch Tom.

"Who are ye?" said the king, in a voice of thunder, "you that dare intrude into the realms of the King of the Dark Caverns?"

"Say 'I am the Princess of the Plains of Light,'" said the cat to the dame, "'and this is my servant Scratch Tom.'"

The dame said so.

"How do you make the bright light?" said the king.

"Say 'That is my secret,'" said the cat.

And the dame said so.

"It's perfectly lovely," said the Princess.

"Perfectly beautiful," echoed the whole assembly.

"Can you make it any brighter?" said the Princess.

"Put your left hand under my chin," said the cat, "and scratch Tom."

And the dame did so, and oh! it was the brightness of the sun that came from the cat's head, and filled the great hall around with dazzling light.

"Too bright, too bright!" shrieked the Princess, and the whole crowd covered their toadstool eyes with their parchment ears, which flapped together on their foreheads with the sound of a million snuff-boxes being shut by a million thumbs, and they drew back their heads behind their shoulders.

"Put your right hand under my chin and scratch Tom," said the cat.

And the dame did so, and oh! it was again as the brightness of the moon.

"That's much better," said the princess. "Much better," shouted the vast crowd, and they lifted their parchment ears from their toadstool eyes, and blinked and rolled them again, and stretched their long hairy necks a full yard towards the dame and Scratch Tom.

"What will you take for your secret?" said the King of the Dark Caverns.

"Say, 'To be your queen,'" said the cat; and the dame said so.

"That cannot be," said the King of the Dark Caverns; but all the crowd were so delighted with the brightness that they clamored and howled, till the King was frightened, and said it should be so. So they prepared a chair of state for the dame beside the King. "Now come and be my queen," said the King of the Dark Caverns.

"Say 'No,'" said the cat, "'not till I have the crown of the single diamond that is on the head of the Princess.'"

And the dame said so.

"That cannot be," said the King of the Dark Caverns; but all the crowd were so delighted with the brightness that they clamored and howled till the King was frightened, and said it should be so.

So they gave the crown made of the single diamond to the dame, and the Princess, when she saw the crown taken away, wept tears of anger which fizzed like molten lead as they fell upon the pavement below the throne. But the dame placed the diamond crown underneath her shawl.

"Put your hand under my right ear," said the cat, "and scratch Tom."

The dame did so, and in one moment the great hall was in complete darkness.

"Now hold on tight," said the cat; and into the darkness went the cat and his burden; and if the wind followed fierce and wild, it was the cat that won the race and left it shrieking far behind.

But the dame was uneasy, what with the crown of a single diamond, and the great key of the gate which she had to keep below her shawl, and in thinking about these she forgot to hold on to the apron strings. To steady herself, she unwittingly laid hold of the cat by the left ear, and in doing so she gave the cat a scratch. It was the least little scratch in the world, but it was quite sufficient for harm, for in an instant there was again the bright light of the moon shining from the cat's head throughout the cavern, and, to her intense horror, she saw behind her the creatures of the cavern, headed by their king, in hot pursuit with scimitars of steel and long forks shod with sharp and barbed fishhooks, and they yelled in triumph as they rushed upon the fugitives.

"Put your left hand under my right ear," said the cat, "and scratch Tom; and be quick about it, or we are lost."

And the dame did so.

Instantly they were plunged into darkness, and the cat and his burden fled into the gloom, till the yells of the pursuers grew fainter and fainter in the distance.

"If you make a mistake like that again we are done for," said the cat.

"Trust me for that," said the dame.

And now they arrived at the door of the cavern, and there, at the cat's bidding, the dame dismounted.

"Pull the body of the voice from under the door," said the cat.

And the dame did so.

"Now, push!" said the cat, "and let us close the door." So the cat pushed and the dame pushed, and the dame pushed and the cat pushed, till the iron knobs shook and the snake-hinges wriggled again and again; but the door would not shut. And the yells of the pursuers grew louder and louder in the distance.

"Take three hairs out of my tail," said the cat, "and strike the nose of the snake-hinge in the center."

Now the dame was so nervous and in such a hurry, that instead of three hairs, she more likely pulled three hundred out from the cat's tail! At any rate, it was quite a handful she applied to the snake's nose, and in consequence the snake-hinge gave such a frantic wriggle that the door flew to before the dame and the cat could get clear of the passage; so, although they themselves managed to get beyond the doorway, the cat's tail and the dame's skirts were firmly wedged between the door and the gate-post.

And the yells of the pursuers grew louder and louder and louder, for they were now at the inner side of the door.

"There's no time to be lost," said the cat, and he turned round and bit his tail off, and tore the dame's dress in two pieces.

"Now," said the cat to the dame, "take the key and get on my back, and turn the key in the lock"; and the cat arched its back till it was just so high that the dame, standing on tiptoe, could put the key in the lock, and the dame turned the key.

"Pull the key out," said the cat.

"I can't," said the dame.

"Then leave it where it is," said the cat; "and quick! get on my back and let us flee!"

For by this time strange things began to crawl underneath the gate, hairy arms with scimitars, and forks shod with fishhooks, that waved about blindly and wildly, striking at their prey.

And the yells of the pursuers grew yet ever louder, and there were scratchings and bitings, and gnawing and kicking, till it seemed as if the gate itself must come down.

But the foolish old dame thought that she would try just once more to get the key out of the lock, and that delay almost cost them their lives; for now bolts began to fly out from the great gate, and the timbers fell cracking and splintering in all directions; the savage yells grew fiercer and fiercer, and the snake-hinges were strained almost to bursting.

So the dame left the key in the lock, and leaped down, for she was in terror at the tumult. But, alas! it was not soon enough, for one of the forks with fishhooks caught her dress; and, as she turned to loosen it, yet another and another fixed itself in her garment, and it was no use for the cat to bite and tear at them, for as soon as he broke one or tore another, more came and encircled the dame in their dreadful grip.

And it was twilight outside the gate, for the sun had not yet risen.

Then with a crash the great gate fell, and the snakes and bolts and timbers burst into a thousand fragments, and there, crowding the mouth of the cavern, the unnumbered hosts of the King of the Dark Caverns stood brandishing their cruel weapons and rolling their toadstool eyes, waiting but for one moment to give a triumphant squall of victory before they rushed in their thousands upon their exhausted and seemingly helpless prey.

With a superhuman effort the cat tore the dame out of the network of fishhooks that held her fast, and seizing her in his teeth, with scarcely a shred of clothing left upon her, he dashed with his burden down the precipice.

But it was of no use. If the cat could leave the wind behind, he could not escape the wild whirlwind of pursuit that fury and vengeance now urged on. Soon the cat found himself hemmed in by the cavern monsters on every side; so escape by flight being impossible, he turned at bay, and placed the dame on the ground and stood above her, lightning flashing from his eyes, and blood and foam dripping from his jaws.

And it was twilight on the battlefield, for the sun had not yet risen.

Like a paladin of old the cat kept up the unequal fight. Forks, fish-hooks, scimitars, claws, arms, eyes, and even heads, that approached too near, were crushed, broken, and bitten off by the jaws and fangs of Scratch Tom. His head seemed to whirl round and be in every direction, no matter from what quarter the attack came; but numbers on numbers pressed from behind to fill the places of those disabled in front, till at last a great rampart of torn bodies and broken weapons made a dreadful circle round the cat and the now unconscious dame.

The sky above seemed a wavy network of quivering swords and whirling hooks. The enemy, gathering themselves for one last tremendous effort, pressed up the sides of the rampart in a wild, frenzied rush of hideous determination and fury. Woe's me for the dame and her defender! Even the magic cat is getting exhausted, for what magic may withstand so overwhelming an onslaught?

And the winter morning twilight still lay dim over the fearful strife.

But just as the surging mass reached the top of the incline, it stood still, for a loud voice, that rang above the tumult, bid them Halt! It was the King of the Dark Caverns himself who gave that order. "To me, and to me alone," he cried, "belongs the task of destroying these robbers; mine is the hand that shall deal the merited vengeance!"

And as he stalked with gigantic strides up the pathway of dead and dying, he waved over his head the tremendous falchion that hung night and day by the side of the black marble throne in the cavern—a sword, indeed, of potent temper, forged in the bosom of volcanoes, whetted on the threshold of the nether-world.

The air whistled as three times he whirled it round his head, and prepared to strike, when . . .

The morning sun rose, and peeped over the hill as if it had been disturbed by the tumult, its bright beams shining straight on the face of the

King of the Dark Caverns. His crown gleamed as white flame in the sun-shine, and the pearls on his sable robe shone like the seven hunters in the heavens when the night is clear.

Then, with a clap as if a million snuff-boxes were being shut by a mil-lion thumbs, the parchment ears of all that vast crowd rang on each fore-head to cover the toadstool eyes from the hated beams. Wild was the rush, anywhere, everywhere; some blindly over the precipice, some into the loch,[1] some into the forest, all attempting to regain the gate of the caverns. Panic-struck and without sight they fell over each other, each treading his fellow-fugitive down in his frantic endeavors.

For one instant the king stood up as if turned to stone; then, with a yell of baffled rage, he flung himself backward on the ground and began scooping out the earth like a superhuman mole, seeking an entrance into the bowels of the mountain, if perchance he might find thus a way to his dominions, and the stones and divots flew up behind him as if discharged from a catapult.

"I'll have that gentleman, at any rate," said the cat, and with one bound he was after the King; but the King in two moments was as many yards into the mountain, and the sable robe of swansdown, into which he had embedded his claws, was all the cat got, in addition to a fearsome crack on the bridge of his snout from an ascending boulder of granite, the parting salute of the vanished potentate.

"It's an ill wind that blows nobody some good," said the cat; "this robe will do to wrap my old dame up in; she must be getting cold by this time."

So he spread the robe out on the hillside, and took the dame and her shawl and the diamond crown, and rolled them all together like a sausage into it. Then, taking the burden up in his teeth, he cantered leisurely homewards.

Now whom should he see at the door of the dame's cottage but an old peddler, with a bag of gold in one pocket and a bag of silver in the other, selling copper saucepans to the neighborhood, a pile of which vessels he carried one on the top of the other above his head.

The cat showed him the crown of a single diamond and the robe of sable feathers, studded with pearls, and the peddler gave the cat the bag of gold for the diamond crown and the bag of silver for the sable robe; and so pleased was he with his bargain that he gave the cat his wallet full of choice

[1] A loch is a Scottish lake.

provisions, and a couple of his best saucepans to cook them into the bargain.

"Now," said the cat, "take three hairs out of my tail, and tickle the nose of this dame with them, for we must get her out of this faint somehow."

But the peddler, after walking round the cat, said he was sorry, but he could not manage to do that anyhow.

"If you don't," said the cat, "I will make collops[2] of you."

"But I can't," whimpered the peddler, for he was frightened at the cat's fierce looks.

"Why not?" said the cat.

"Because, because, your honor has not got a tail to pull the hairs out of," blubbered the peddler.

"Bless me!" said the cat, "I had quite forgotten all about that. Never mind, pull three hairs out of my whiskers; that may perhaps do as well."

The peddler did so, and the dame, feeling her nose tickled, sneezed as if she had tasted mustard; and getting up, she placed her hands at her side to take hold of her skirts to make a curtsy before asking the peddler and the cat to enter her house. But finding no skirts to take hold of, and looking down and seeing how scanty was her costume, she fled into the house without another word, and locked herself up in the cupboard; whereupon the cat told the peddler to go about his business, which he did.

The peddler gone, the cat entered the cottage, and told the dame to come out of the cupboard.

"I won't," said the dame, "as long as that peddler's present."

"Don't be silly," said the cat; "he's gone, and there's only a cat in the house."

So the dame came out of the cupboard.

Then the cat poured out all the gold and the silver and the food on to the floor, and put the saucepan full of water on the hearth to boil. And the dame, when she saw the gold and the silver and all the choice provisions, was so delighted that she rocked backwards and forwards on her chair and smacked herself all over.

As for the cat, he purred so that the embers of the fire were soon in a bright blaze, and before one could say Scissors the breakfast was bubbling and hissing in the saucepans.

[2] Slices of meat.

Then the dame ate and drank, and the cat ate and drank, and everything was cheerful—the sun looked into the window, the robins tapped at the sill, singing a song of welcome home, and the hoodie,[3] looking down the chimney, sniffed the rich food and said, "My certes,[4] how our old dame is enjoying herself!"

"Now," said the dame to the cat, "what am I to do to you in return for all your kindness?"

"Scratch Tom," said the cat.

"That I will do with pleasure," said the dame, and she scratched the cat's back with the toasting-fork till he purred again and again, and the sparks flew up the chimney.

And I'm sure it was not much to do for all his trouble, was it?

[3] The hooded crow.
[4] An old word meaning "certainly" or "truly."

The Lion and the Cat

Andrew Lang, in The Brown Fairy Book *(1904), says this story was adapted from* North American Indian Legends. *I have been unable to locate this book and I have to question whether or not this story actually originated with Native Americans, since it is unlikely that their legends from the nineteenth-century would incorporate lions, pails, and cupboards. Either he cited the wrong source or he did quite a bit of adapting. Whatever the case, this is an amusing and unusual story.*

Far away on the other side of the world there lived, long ago, a lion and his younger brother, the wild cat, who were so fond of each other that they shared the same hut. The lion was much the bigger and stronger of the two—indeed, he was much bigger and stronger than any of the beasts that dwelt in the forest; and, besides, he could jump farther and run faster than all the rest. If strength and swiftness could gain him a dinner he was sure never to be without one, but when it came to cunning, both the grizzly bear and the serpent could get the better of him, and he was forced to call in the help of the wild cat.

Now the young wild cat had a lovely golden ball, so beautiful that you could hardly look at it except through a piece of smoked glass, and he kept it hidden in the thick fur muff that went round his neck. A very large old animal, since dead, had given it to him when he was hardly more than a baby, and had told him never to part with it, for as long as he kept it no harm could ever come near him.

In general the wild cat did not need to use his ball, for the lion was fond of hunting, and could kill all the food that they needed; but now and then his life would have been in danger had it not been for the golden ball.

One day the two brothers started to hunt at daybreak, but as the cat could not run nearly as fast as the lion, he had quite a long start. At least he *thought* it was a long one, but in a very few bounds and springs the lion reached his side.

"There is a bear sitting on that tree," he whispered softly. "He is only waiting for us to pass, to drop down on my back."

"Ah, you are so big that he does not see I am behind you," answered the wild cat. And, touching the ball, he just said: "Bear, die!" And the bear tumbled dead out of the tree, and rolled over just in front of them.

For some time they trotted on without any adventures, till just as they were about to cross a strip of long grass on the edge of the forest, the lion's quick ears detected a faint rustling noise.

"That is a snake," he cried, stopping short, for he was much more afraid of snakes than of bears.

"Oh, it is all right," answered the cat. "Snake, die!" And the snake died, and the two brothers skinned it. They then folded the skin up into a very small parcel, and the cat tucked it into his mane, for snakes' skins can do all sorts of wonderful things, if you are lucky enough to have one of them.

All this time they had had no dinner, for the snake's flesh was not nice, and the lion did not like eating bear—perhaps because he never felt sure that the bear was really dead, and would not jump up alive when his enemy went near him. Most people are afraid of *some* thing, and bears and serpents were the only creatures that caused the lion's heart to tremble. So the two brothers set off again and soon reached the side of a hill where some fine deer were grazing.

"Kill one of those deer for your own dinner," said the boy-brother, "but catch me another alive. I want him."

The lion at once sprang towards them with a loud roar, but the deer bounded away, and they were all three soon lost to sight. The cat waited for a long while, but finding that the lion did not return, went back to the house where they lived.

It was quite dark when the lion came home, where his brother was sitting curled up in one corner.

"Did you catch the deer for me?" asked the boy-brother, springing up.

"Well, no," replied the man-brother. "The fact is, that I did not get up to them till we had run half way across the world and left the wind far behind us. Think what a trouble it would have been to drag it here! So— I just ate them both."

The cat said nothing, but he did not feel that he loved his big brother. He had thought a great deal about that deer, and had meant to get on his back to ride him as a horse, and go to see all the wonderful places the lion talked to him about when he was in a good temper. The more he thought of it the more sulky he grew, and in the morning, when the lion said that it was time for them to start to hunt, the cat told him that he might kill the bear and snake by himself, as he had a headache, and would rather stay at home. The little fellow knew quite well that the lion would not dare to go out without him and his ball for fear of meeting a bear or a snake.

The quarrel went on, and for many days neither of the brothers spoke to each other, and what made them still more cross was that they could get very little to eat, and we know that people are often cross when they are hungry. At last it occurred to the lion that if he could only steal the magic ball he could kill bears and snakes for himself, and then the cat might be as sulky as he liked for anything that it would matter. But how was the stealing to be done? The cat had the ball hung round his neck day and night, and he was such a light sleeper that it was useless to think of taking it while he slept. No! the only thing was to get him to lend it of his own accord, and after some days the lion (who was not at all clever) hit upon a plan that he thought would do.

"Dear me, how dull it is here!" said the lion one afternoon, when the rain was pouring down in such torrents that, however sharp your eyes or your nose might be, you could not spy a single bird or beast among the bushes. "Dear me, how dull, how dreadfully dull I am. Couldn't we have a game of catch with that golden ball of yours?"

"I don't care about playing catch, it does not amuse me," answered the cat, who was as cross as ever; for no cat, even to this day, ever forgets an injury done to him.

"Well, then, lend me the ball for a little, and I will play by myself," replied the lion, stretching out a paw as he spoke.

"You can't play in the rain, and if you did, you would only lose it in the bushes," said the cat.

"Oh, no, I won't; I will play in here. Don't be so ill-natured." And with a very bad grace the cat untied the string and threw the golden ball into the lion's lap, and composed himself to sleep again.

For a long while the lion tossed it up and down gaily, feeling that, however sound asleep the boy-brother might *look,* he was sure to have one eye open; but gradually he began to edge closer to the opening, and at last gave such a toss that the ball went up high into the air, and he could not see what became of it.

"Oh, how stupid of me!" he cried, as the cat sprang up angrily, "let us go at once and search for it. It can't really have fallen very far." But though they searched that day and the next, and the next after that, they never found it, because it never came down.

After the loss of his ball the cat refused to live with the lion any longer, but wandered away to the north, always hoping he might meet with his ball again. But months passed, and years passed, and though he traveled over hundreds of miles, he never saw any traces of it.

At length, when he was getting quite old, he came to a place unlike any that he had ever seen before, where a big river rolled right to the foot of some high mountains. The ground all about the river bank was damp and marshy, and as no cat likes to wet its feet, this one climbed a tree that rose high above the water, and thought sadly of his lost ball, which would have helped him out of this horrible place. Suddenly he saw a beautiful ball, for all the world like his own, dangling from a branch of the tree he was on. He longed to get at it; but was the branch strong enough to bear his weight? It was no use, after all he had done, getting drowned in the water. However, it could do no harm if he was to go a little way; he could always manage to get back somehow.

So he stretched himself at full length upon the branch, and wriggled his body cautiously along. To his delight it seemed thick and stout. Another movement, and, by stretching out his paw, he would be able to draw the string towards him, when the branch gave a loud crack, and the cat made haste to wriggle himself back the way he had come.

But when cats make up their minds to do anything they generally *do* it; and this cat began to look about to see if there was really no way of getting at his ball. Yes! there was, and it was much surer than the other, though rather more difficult. Above the bough where the ball hung was another bough much thicker, which he knew could not break with his weight; and by holding on tight to this with all his four paws he could just manage to touch the ball with his tail. He would thus be able to whisk the ball to and fro till, by-and-by, the string would become quite loose, and it would fall to the ground. It might take some time, but the lion's little brother was patient, like most cats.

Well, it all happened just as the cat intended it should, and when the ball dropped on the ground the cat ran down the tree like lightning, and, picking it up, tucked it away in the snake's skin round his neck. Then he began jumping along the shore of the Big Water from one place to another, trying to find a boat, or even a log of wood, that would take him across. But there was nothing; only, on the other side, he saw two girls cooking, and though he shouted to them at the top of his voice, they were too far off to hear what he said. And, what was worse, the ball suddenly fell out of its snake's skin bag right into the river.

Now, it is not at all an uncommon thing for balls to tumble into rivers, but in that case they generally either fall to the bottom and stay there, or else bob about on the top of the water close to where they first touched it. But this ball, instead of doing either of these things, went straight across to the other side, and there one of the girls saw it when she stooped to dip some water into her pail.

"Oh! what a lovely ball!" cried she, and tried to catch it in her pail; but the ball always kept bobbing just out of her reach.

"Come and help me!" she called to her sister, and after a long while they had the ball safe inside the pail. They were delighted with their new toy, and one or the other held it in her hand till bedtime came, and then it was a long time before they could make up their minds where it would be safest for the night. At last they locked it in a cupboard in one corner of their room, and as there was no hole anywhere the ball could not possibly get out. After that they went to sleep.

In the morning the first thing they both did was to run to the cupboard and unlock it, but when the door opened they started back, for, instead of the ball, there stood a handsome young man.

"Ladies," he said, "how can I thank you for what you have done for me? Long, long ago, I was enchanted by a wicked fairy, and condemned to keep the shape of a ball till I should meet with two maidens, who would take me to their own home. But where was I to meet them? For hundreds of years I have lived in the depths of the forest, where nothing but wild beasts ever came, and it was only when the lion threw me into the sky that I was able to fall to earth near this river. Where there is a river, sooner or later people will come; so, hanging myself on a tree, I watched and waited. For a moment I lost heart when I fell once more into the hands of my old master the wild cat, but my hopes rose again as I saw he was making for the river bank opposite where you were standing. That was my chance, and I took it. And now, ladies, I have only to say that, if ever I can do any-thing to help you, go to the top of that high mountain and knock three times at the iron door at the north side, and I will come to you."

So, with a low bow, he vanished from before them, leaving the maidens weeping at having lost in one moment both the ball and the prince.

IRELAND

Conall Yellowclaw

(Excerpt)

Joseph Jacobs reprints this story in his Celtic Fairy Tales, *which was published in 1892. Unfortunately, he does not say what his original source was. Within this story three other tales are told, only one of which contains a cat. In the main story, the sons of Conall Yellowclaw kill the eldest son of one of the kings of Ireland. In order to spare them, and himself, he must steal a horse from another king. While attempting this, he and his sons are caught and Conall explains his situation to the second king.*

"Now, O Conall," said the king, "were you ever in a harder place than to be seeing your lot of sons hanged tomorrow? But you set it to my goodness and to my grace, and say that it was necessity brought it on you, so I must not hang you. Tell me any case in which you were as hard as this, and if you tell that, you shall get the soul of your youngest son."

"I will tell a case as hard in which I was," said Conall. "I was once a young lad, and my father had much land, and he had parks of year-old cows, and one of them had just calved, and my father told me to bring her home. I found the cow, and took her with us. There fell a shower of snow. We went into the herd's bothy,[1] and we took the cow and the calf in with us, and we were letting the shower pass from us. Who should come in but one cat and ten, and one great one-eyed fox-colored cat as head bard over them. When they came in, in very deed I myself had no liking for their company. 'Strike up with you,' said the head bard, 'why should we be still? and sing a cronan[2] to Conall Yellowclaw.' I was amazed that my name was known to the cats themselves. When they had sung the cronan,

---

[1] A small wooden cottage, usually occupied by servants.
[2] A Gaelic word which means "purr" or "purring."

said the head bard, 'Now, O Conall, pay the reward of the cronan that the cats have sung to thee.' 'Well then,' said I myself, 'I have no reward whatsoever for you, unless you should go down and take that calf.' No sooner said I the word than the two cats and ten went down to attack the calf, and in very deed, he did not last them long. 'Play up with you, why should you be silent? Make a cronan to Conall Yellow,' said the head bard. Certainly I had no liking at all for the cronan, but up came the one cat and ten, and if they did not sing me a cronan then and there! 'Pay them now their reward,' said the great fox-colored cat. 'I am tired myself of yourselves and your rewards,' said I. 'I have no reward for you unless you take that cow down there.' They betook themselves to the cow, and indeed she did not last them long.

"'Why will you be silent? Go up and sing a cronan to Conall Yellowclaw,' said the head bard. And surely, oh, king, I had no care for them or for their cronan, for I began to see that they were not good comrades. When they had sung me the cronan they betook themselves down where the head bard was. 'Pay now their reward, said the head bard; and for sure, oh king, I had no reward for them; and I said to them, 'I have no reward for you.' And surely, oh king, there was caterwauling between them. So I leapt out at a turf window that was at the back of the house. I took myself off as hard as I might into the wood. I was swift enough and strong at that time; and when I felt the rustling toirm[3] of the cats after me I climbed into as high a tree as I saw in the place, and one that was close in the top; and I hid myself as well as I might. The cats began to search for me through the wood, and they could not find me; and when they were tired, each one said to the other that they would turn back. 'But,' said the one-eyed fox-colored cat that was commander-in-chief over them, 'you saw him not with your two eyes, and though I have but one eye, there's the rascal up in the tree.' When he had said that, one of them went up in the tree, and as he was coming where I was, I drew a weapon that I had and I killed him. 'Be this from me!' said the one-eyed one—'I must not be losing my company thus; gather round the root of the tree and dig about it, and let down that villain to earth.' On this they gathered about the tree, and they dug about the root, and the first branching root that they cut, she gave a shiver to fall, and I myself gave a shout, and it was not to be wondered at. There was in the neighborhood of the wood a priest, and he had ten men

[3] Gaelic for "noise," such as the noise of people going through the woods.

with him delving, and he said, 'There is a shout of a man in extremity and I must not be without replying to it.' And the wisest of the men said, 'Let it alone till we hear it again.' The cats began again digging wildly, and they broke the next root; and I myself gave the next shout, and in very deed it was not a weak one. 'Certainly,' said the priest, 'it is a man in extremity— let us move.' They set themselves in order for moving. And the cats arose on the tree, and they broke the third root, and the tree fell on her elbow. Then I gave the third shout. The stalwart men hastened, and when they saw how the cats served the tree, they began at them with the spades; and they themselves and the cats began at each other, till the cats ran away. And surely, oh king, I did not move till I saw the last one of them off. And then I came home. And there's the hardest case in which I ever was; and it seems to me that tearing by the cats were harder than hanging tomorrow by the king of Lochlann."

"Och! Conall," said the king, "you are full of words. You have freed the soul of your son with your tale."

Conall proceeds to tell two more tales and frees his other two sons. In his final tale, he tells of rescuing a mother and child from a giant. The king's mother reveals that he was the child saved by Conall. The king rewards Conall with the horse and a sack filled with gold, silver, and precious gems.

JAPAN

The Story of the Faithful Cat

This story was published in Tales of Old Japan *in 1871 by Lord Redesdale (Algernon Bertram Freeman-Mitford), who was the British attaché to Japan from 1866 to 1870.*

About sixty years ago, in the summer-time, a man went to pay a visit at a certain house at Osaka, and, in the course of conversation, said—

"I have eaten some very extraordinary cakes to-day," and on being asked what he meant, he told the following story:

"I received the cakes from the relatives of a family who were celebrating the hundredth anniversary of the death of a cat that had belonged to their ancestors. When I asked the history of the affair, I was told that, in former days, a young girl of the family, when she was about sixteen years old, used always to be followed about by a tom-cat, who was reared in the house, so much so that the two were never separated for an instant. When her father perceived this, he was very angry, thinking that the tom-cat, forgetting the kindness with which he had been treated for years in the house, had fallen in love with his daughter, and intended to cast a spell upon her; so he determined that he must kill the beast. As he was planning this in secret, the cat overheard him, and that night went to his pillow, and, assuming a human voice, said to him—

"'You suspect me of being in love with your daughter; and although you might well be justified in so thinking, your suspicions are groundless. The fact is this: There is a very large old rat who has been living for many years in your granary. Now it is this old rat who is in love with my young mistress, and this is why I dare not leave her side for a moment, for fear the old rat should carry her off. Therefore I pray you to dispel your suspicions. But as I, by myself, am no match for the rat, there is a famous cat,

130

named Buchi, at the house of Mr. So-and-so, at Ajikawa: if you will borrow that cat, we will soon make an end of the old rat.'

"When the father awoke from his dream, he thought it so wonderful that he told the household of it; and the following day he got up very early and went off to Ajikawa, to inquire for the house which the cat had indicated, and had no difficulty in finding it; so he called upon the master of the house, and told him what his own cat had said, and how he wished to borrow the cat Buchi for a little while.

"'That's a very easy matter to settle,' said the other: 'pray take him with you at once'; and accordingly the father went home with the cat Buchi in charge. That night he put the two cats into the granary; and after a little while, a frightful clatter was heard, and then all was still again; so the people of the house opened the door, and crowded out to see what had happened; and there they beheld the two cats and the rat all locked together, and panting for breath; so they cut the throat of the rat, which was as big as either of the cats: then they attended to the two cats; but, although they gave them ginseng and other restoratives, they both got weaker and weaker, until at last they died. So the rat was thrown into the river; but the two cats were buried with all honors in a neighboring temple."

INDIA
The Cat Who Became a Queen

Reverend J. H. Knowles recorded this story in his book Folk-Tales of Kashmir, *which was published in 1888.*

"Ah me! ah me! What availeth my marriage with all these women? Never a son has the Deity vouchsafed me. Must I die, and my name be altogether forgotten in the land?" Thus soliloquized one of the greatest monarchs that ever reigned in Kashmir, and then went to his *zanána*, and threatened his numerous wives with banishment if they did not bear him a son within the next year. The women prayed most earnestly to the god Shiva to help them to fulfill the king's desire, and waited most anxiously for several months, hoping against hope, till at last they knew that it was all in vain, and that they must dissemble matters if they wished to remain in the royal household. Accordingly, on an appointed time, word was sent to the king that one of his wives was *enciente*, and a little while afterwards the news was spread abroad that a little princess was born. But this, as we have said, was not so. Nothing of the kind had happened. The truth was that a cat had given birth to a lot of kittens, one of which had been appropriated by the king's wives. When His Majesty heard the news he was exceedingly glad, and ordered the child to be brought to him—a very natural request, which the king's wives had anticipated, and therefore were quite prepared with a reply. "Go and tell the king," said they to the messenger, "that the Brahmans have declared that the child must not be seen by her father until she is married." Thus the matter was hushed for a time. Constantly did the king inquire after his daughter, and received wonderful accounts of her beauty and cleverness; so that his joy was great. Of course he would like to have had a son, but since the Deity had not condescended to fulfill his desire, he comforted himself with the thought of marrying his daughter to some person worthy of her, and capable of ruling

132

the country after him. Accordingly, at the proper time he commissioned his counselors to find a suitable match for his daughter. A clever, good, and handsome prince was soon found, and arrangements for the marriage were quickly concluded. What were the king's wives to do now? It was of no use for them to attempt to carry on their deceit any longer. The bridegroom would come and would wish to see his wife, and the king, too, would expect to see her. "Better," said they, "that we send for this prince and reveal everything to him, and take our chance of the rest. Never mind the king. Some answer can be made to satisfy him for a while." So they sent for the prince and told him everything, having previously made him swear that he would keep the secret, and not reveal it even to his father or mother. The marriage was celebrated in grand style, as became such great and wealthy kings, and the king was easily prevailed on to allow the palanquin[1] containing the bride to leave the palace without looking at her. The cat only was in the palanquin, which reached the prince's country in safety. The prince took great care of the animal, which he kept locked up in his own private room, and would not allow anyone, not even his mother, to enter it.

One day, however, while the prince was away, his mother thought that she would go and speak to her daughter-in-law from outside the door. "O daughter-in-law," she cried, "I am very sorry that you are shut up in this room and not permitted to see anybody. It must be very dull for you. However, I am going out today; so you can leave the room without fear of seeing any one. Will you come out?"

The cat understood everything, and wept much, just like a human being. Oh those bitter tears! They pierced the mother's heart, so that she determined to speak very strictly to her son on the matter as soon as he should return. They also reached the ears of Párvatí,[2] who at once went to her lord and entreated him to have mercy on the poor helpless cat. "Tell her," said Shiva, "to rub some oil over her fur, and she will become a beautiful woman. She will find the oil in the room where she now is." Párvatí lost no time in disclosing this glad news to the cat, who quickly rubbed the oil over its body, and was changed into the most lovely woman that ever lived. But she left a little spot on one of her shoulders, which

---

[1] A type of covered carriage, usually for one person, that is carried by poles on the shoulders of two or more men.
[2] Párvatí is the Hindu mountain goddess who is Shiva's wife.

remained covered with cat's fur, lest her husband should suspect some trickery and deny her.

In the evening the prince returned and saw his beautiful wife, and was delighted. Then all anxiety as to what he should reply to his mother's earnest solicitations fled. She had only to see the happy, smiling, beautiful bride to know that her fears were altogether needless.

In a few weeks the prince, accompanied by his wife, visited his father-in-law, who, of course, believed the princess to be his own daughter, and was glad beyond measure. His wives too rejoiced, because their prayer had been heard and their lives saved. In due time the king settled his country on the prince, who eventually ruled over both countries, his father's and his father-in-law's, and thus became the most illustrious and wealthy monarch in the world.

The Two Caskets

Benjamin Thorpe told this story from South Småland in his book Yule-Tide Stories, *published in 1853.*

There was once an ugly, cross woman who had two daughters living with her, one her own daughter and the other her stepchild. The daughter was as cross and ugly as her mother, and spoilt and petted besides, but the stepdaughter was kind, gentle and considerate, and very pretty too, so that she had a good word from everyone and all the neighbors loved her. This love and esteem in which she was held made the other two dislike her more and more, so that their hatred became a frenzy and they determined to get rid of her. So one day the stepmother called the two girls to bring their spinning wheels out to the well and to sit on the edge and spin there. "And be careful what you do," she said, "for the first one that lets her thread break, down into the well she goes." But she did not play fair, for her own daughter got the finest flax to spin, but the other was given mere refuse, all tangled and lumpy and weak, so, careful though she was, her thread was bound to snap soon, and when it did the stepmother rushed out of the house, picked up her legs and shot her down into the well. "Good riddance to bad rubbish!" said the wicked pair, and went laughing into the house. But the good stepdaughter fell and fell, until at the bottom a door seemed to open in the ground, and she fell softly through onto a grassy bed of flowers, with the frightened tears still wet on her cheeks. She found herself in a fair land, with trees and grass and flowers, and the birds singing all about, though there was no sun above her, and a light like early morning. There seemed no way out of the land, and she was afraid of her stepmother's cruelty, so she got up and went to seek her fortune. There was a narrow path leading through the trees and she followed it until it came into the open through a field and she came to a rickety fence, all

135

overgrown with old-man's beard. As she looked along it to find a low place to cross, the fence spoke to her. "Dear little maiden; please do me no harm. I'm am an old fence, so old and decayed." "Don't be afraid, dear fence," said the girl, "Indeed I will do you no harm." She climbed over the fence, very lightly and carefully, so that not a plank moved, and went on her way. And the silver fronds of the old-man's beard waved after her and the fence murmured after her; "All good luck go after you, my considerate child!" The next thing that the girl noticed was an oven that stood close by the path, full of warm, new-baked bread, with a peel lying by it, and she paused, for she was very hungry, and the oven spoke to her. "Dear little maiden, please do me no harm. I am only a poor oven! Take out and eat as much as you want, but take nothing with you and put back what you do not eat." "Indeed I would not hurt you, kind oven," said the girl. She opened the oven door and drew out one loaf on the peel and sat down to eat it. She only needed half, so she put what was left back in the oven and put the peel where she had found it, thanked the oven kindly for its hospitality and went on her way. And the oven wished her good fortune in the world.

After a while the girl came to a meadow where a cow was grazing, with a pail hung on its horn. Her udder was so full that it was plain she needed milking. The cow looked round to her and said: "My dear, good lass, do me no harm. I am only a poor cow. Drink as much of my milk as you want but do not scatter my milk on the ground. Pour what is left over my hoofs, and hang the pail on my horn." "Indeed, dear cow, I would not harm you," said the girl. "It is very kind of you to let me drink your milk." She milked the cow gently and deftly into the pail, took a long drink of the milk, and emptied what was left very carefully over the cow's hoofs. Then she stroked the cow and thanked it and went on her way. And the cow mooed after her, "Good luck go with you, my gentle lass."

The next thing the girl saw was a very old apple tree, whose boughs almost touched the ground, laden with fruit, some green and some red and juicy. And the tree called out to her: "My dear little girl, please do me no harm; I am so old and bent. Gather as many of my ripe fruits as you need, but carry none away with you. Eat what you need and bury the rest at my root. But prop my bending branches before you go." The girl did exactly as he said, propped the bending branches carefully, and went on her way. And the tree called after her; "May all good go with you, my considerate maiden."

After this the road grew wider, and the girl saw a very old woman with long white hair leaning on a gate. The girl came up to her, and said: "Good evening, dear mother!"

The old woman said: "And good evening to you again. Who are you, who greets me so kindly?" "I am only a poor stepchild," said the girl, "and I am seeking service in this world which is strange to me." "If that's so," said the old woman, "You can spare time to wait a little and comb my hair for me. And we can talk while you do it." "Indeed I will," said the girl, and she combed it most carefully. When she had finished the old woman said: "Since you didn't think yourself too good to comb me I will tell you where you can find a service. Be discreet and all will go well with you." She then directed the girl where to go, and gave her much good advice as well. The girl listened most carefully, thanked her and went by the way she had directed. There she found a large farm where they were in need of a serving maid to milk and tend the cows and to sift the corn in the barn. So she was engaged for a year. She was to start on her duties in the morning. That night she had her supper and went to bed.

Early in the morning, as soon as it was light, the young girl started on her work. She went into the cow house and made friends, patting and stroking them and speaking to them gently. Before she milked them she fetched hay and straw, and fed them, swept out the cow house and made all neat and comfortable. Then she fetched the pails and stool and sat down to milk them. They in their turn were as gentle and loving as she was. Each one lowed with pleasure when she came up, and played no tricks on her; not one of them kicked the pail over or lashed about with its tail, but they all stood as quiet as lambs, and let down their milk willingly. Indeed it was a pleasure to see how the little girl set about her duties and how well she and the cows got on together. When the milking was done the girl carried the pails into the dairy next door and strained the milk and collected it into the measure, and as she was doing this a great company of cats came in, a multitude of them, great and small, mewing round her so earnestly that her soft heart was touched, saying:

> "Give us a little milk!
> Give us a little milk!"

The girl looked round and saw a great shallow bowl on the floor, evidently meant for the cats.

"My poor little pusses" she said. "I daresay you are all very hungry and thirsty. Wait, I will give you something to drink." With that she lifted one of the pails and filled the big flat bowl. The cats all took their turn, and as they finished they gathered round the girl, rubbed themselves against her knees, arched their backs and purred with delight, so that it was a pleasure to see how they caressed the little serving maid.

When she had finished her work in the cow-byre the girl went into the big barn to sift the corn, and she worked long and hard, riddling and sifting, till she had made a great pile of the good grain and the chaff was all swept into one corner. As she was still at work a great flight of sparrows came down into the yard and hopped nearer and nearer to the barn, picking what they could from the ground and fluttering nearer to the great barn. At length they hopped on to the high threshold of the door, and began chirping all together:

> "Give us a little corn!
> Give us a little corn!"

"My poor little sparrows!" said the girl. "You have a hard life, I am sure, picking up what little bits you can find. Wait, I'll give you something to eat." And she picked up a few handfuls from the heap, and scattered the grain amongst them, and sparrows came fluttering about her, pecking and fluttering their wings, and were so glad, just as if they would thank the little girl for being so kind to them.

So the time passed, day after day, and every day the little maid cared for the cows and fed and groomed and milked them, so that they grew sleek and plump, and there never was a greater abundance of milk or finer cattle on the farm either before or since. And every day she gave the cats their share of milk and every day the sparrows were given their handfuls of corn and all the farm was happy and prospered.

One day the mistress of the farm sent for the little stepdaughter and said to her: "I have noticed how well you keep the cows and how willingly you do all that you are set to do. Now I want to see what you make of more difficult work. Take that sieve, carry it to the stream and bring it back full to the brim without spilling a single drop."

The girl did not see how she could do that, but it was her business to obey her mistress, so she picked up the sieve and went down to the stream. And a flight of sparrows followed her. The little maid dipped the sieve carefully in the water and lifted it gently up, but the water ran so quickly through every hole that it was all gone by the time the sieve reached shoulder level, and at last, wet and cold, she burst into tears. Suddenly there was a twittering from the boughs that surrounded the pool, where all the sparrows had gradually gathered together. The girl thought they were trying to cheer her, so she dried her eyes to listen to their chirping. But it was words they were singing:

> "Ashes in sieve,
> Then it will hold!
> Ashes in sieve,
> Then it will hold!"

they sang again and again. She thought perhaps they were right, so she jumped up and ran and fetched ashes, and packed the bottom of the sieve carefully with them and when she lowered it gently into shallow water the ashes swelled, and held the water without a drop leaking as she carried it home.

The old woman was amazed, and said: "I never knew you had so much knowledge. Who instructed you in this?" But the girl said nothing, for she was afraid of getting the sparrows into trouble.

Time went on, and one day her mistress called the little stepdaughter again and said: "Here are two skeins of wool, but the black skein is not black enough and the white is not white enough, so take them down to the stream and wash them till the white skein is black and the black skein is white."

There seemed no sense in this to the girl, but she was used to trying to obey her stepmother's commands, however unreasonable, so she took the two skeins down to the stream, and some of the sparrows went after her. The poor girl washed and scrubbed, but the white skein remained white and the black, black, until at last at the thought of disappointing the mistress who had spoken so kindly to her, she burst into tears; but at this there was a great twittering of the sparrows, and when she lifted her head to listen she heard them singing in human words:

> "Take the black,
> Turn to the east!
> Take the black,
> Turn to the east."

She knew they were trying to help her, so she picked up the black skein and waded upstream to the east, until she came to a pool in which she could dip it. She had only dipped it and lifted it out when it turned a dazzling white, and she was going to try washing the white skein when the birds cried out again:

> "Turn to the west!
> Turn to the west!
> Take the white
> And turn to the west!"

So she waded down the stream, and stood looking westward, and after one dip the skein turned a deep rich black; the sparrows flew twittering away, and the girl carried them down joyfully to her mistress, who was absolutely amazed, and asked her again who had helped her, but the girl only smiled and said nothing, for she would not betray the kind little sparrows.

After that all went smoothly, until her mistress called the little step-daughter before her again, and said: "There is one last task for you to do, and then there will be no more. Here are the two skeins that you washed. You must weave them up before the sunset hour, and they must be smooth and even, with no breaks or joins, and when that is done I shall be satisfied."

The girl took the skeins and went to the room where the loom was kept. But when she began to set up the skein her heart sank, for it was like the flax her stepmother had given her. It was all in short pieces, lumpy and uneven. Even to set up a smooth warp was impossible, and when it came to the weft, it was still worse. And this was her last test! She leant forward on her stool and cried bitterly. All at once the door was pushed open and the long procession of cats came into the room. They rubbed themselves against her, purring loudly, and asked her what was the matter. She told them all about it, and showed them the lumpy thread and broken ends. They sat down and purred loudly. Then the leader cried: "Leave this to us, we can easily finish before the sunset hour. You have always been kind and loving to us, and now we have the chance to repay you." With that all the cats jumped up to the loom. They pulled out the lumps or lengthened the short threads, and licked and twisted the broken ends, so that they joined like magic. Then the cats jumped on to the loom and clattered it to and fro, so that in no time at all the yarn was woven, and it was close and fine and even, better than any human hand could do it. The girl ran down with it gladly to her mistress, who was amazed at the workmanship. "I never knew you could do a piece of work like this!" she said. "Who taught you such a craft?" But the girl smiled gently and said nothing, for she did not want to betray her dear friends the cats.

After that all went well until the year came to its end, and then the girl began to feel that she must go into the upper world again, though everyone was kind to her in the under world, and she hated to leave her friends the cats, and the little sparrows and her dear cows. But a longing was on her to see the sun again and to feel the free air of the upper world. So she went to her mistress and asked to be released from her service. Her mistress said, "I am sorry to lose you, but I cannot keep you if you wish to go. You have pleased me in everything, so I should like to give you a reward for your services. Go up to the attic above this room and you will find a number of caskets. Choose any one you like and you may take it home; but do not unlock it until you put it into the place where you mean to remain." The girl thanked her mistress, and climbed up into the attic, and the cats streamed up after her. The attic was filled with caskets, of all sizes, shapes and colors, so that it took quite a time to look at them all. Some of them seemed to the girl too grand to be payment for her work when she had had good food and lodgings, and kindness too from men and beasts. And as she was puzzling over them the cats all called out "Take the black! Take the black!" She looked all round, and in a far corner she found a little, strong black casket with a key hanging from its handle. So she said, "Yes, of course, dear pussies, that's the one for me." And she took it down to show to her mistress, who said: "You have made a wise choice. Good-bye, my girl, good fortune will go with you." The girl thanked her mistress with great gratitude for her beautiful present, and for all her kindness and said good-bye her; and then she said good-bye to her cats and her sparrows and her cows, and that was a sad farewell indeed, for they could hardly bear to lose her, and indeed everyone on the farm was sorry when she went. Her journey back was quicker going than coming, and when she got to the place where the well had been, a door opened in front of her and she went up a steep staircase which came out into the upper world just by the well. So she went into her old home, where her stepmother and stepsister were surprised and angry to see her. "Well," said her stepmother, "I thought you were dead long ago, and your bare bones lying at the bottom of the well. Life is full of disappointments! Where have you been all this long time?" "I went down into the underworld," said the stepdaughter, "and took service for a year. And, look, they gave me this good black box for my wages. May I have a corner where I can keep it?" "What insolence!" said her stepmother. "As if we'd clutter our nice house with you or your dirty black box either. Be off with you!" Then she thought that the neighbors might talk; for they had been rather disagreeable about the disappearance of the girl. So she added—"If you must stay be off into the hen house, and set up your dirty box there." So the girl went off, and she swept and washed and cleaned the hen house, and found a nice corner where she could keep her box. Then she unfastened the key from the handle and unlocked it. Such a light burst out as she lifted the lid that she started back. Shining gold and diamonds and rubies and emeralds flashed out of it, so that the old rickety hen house looked as if it was on fire and all the neighbors round rushed in to the rescue. They saw the jewels before the two wicked ones did, and it was perhaps just as well for the girl, for all the neighborhood came to look until they all knew every jewel in the box, and the stepmother dare not take so much as a brooch or a ring, for it would be recognized. And those two were ill with envy, so that they could not sleep nor eat. They knew most of what had happened to the girl from the talk of the neighbors, and at last they determined that the stepsister would do better, for they were both sure that she was worth twenty of the poor little stepdaughter. So one fine day the stepmother made her daughter sit on the well-curb and thrust her down into the cold deep well. She wasn't sure at the last that she really wanted to go, but when she landed on the bed she was quite reassured and sure that she would make her way and bring back something far handsomer than her sister's box. So she got up and went on her way, but she was disgusted by the rickety old fence that she came across first, and affronted that it had the impertinence to speak to her. She tore up the palings and pulled off the old man's beard, and went on quite triumphant, never hearing that the paling called after her; "You shan't have done this to me for nothing." As she started, so she went on. She tore off the oven door, scattered the loaves and broke the peel. When she had drunken all the milk she wanted she threw what was left over the ground, and broke the pail. She shook all the apples over the ground and broke down the branches. And after her came again and again the muttered curse, "You shan't have done this to me for nothing." It can be imagined how furious she was at being asked to comb the old woman's hair. She thrust past her through the gate, slamming it behind her so fiercely that she nearly knocked the poor old woman down, and the curse that went after her this time concluded "Continue in the same wickedness and you will see how it will go with you in the world."

In spite of this, however, she was engaged as a maid-servant, for they had been without one since her step-sister left them, and she was as cruel and bad as the little maid had been good. The poor cows were half starved, ill-kept and roughly used. They were thin and wretched, and had little milk to give. Sometimes too they kicked over their pails which made matters worse. As for the cats, when they appeared begging for milk, she hit them, threw things at them and drove them away. She threw stones at the sparrows and chivvied them into the wood, so that there was no more merry chirping about the farmyard. But indeed there was not much grain to spare, for the cats dare not come into the barns to keep down the rats and mice. In fact the whole farm suffered from her cruel ways. All the same the mistress kept her on and in course of time set her the same tests as she had set to her stepsister. But there were no sparrows or cats to help her so she failed dismally. When her time came to give her notice the mistress took it willingly and told her that she was the worst maid she had ever had. All the same she allowed her to choose a casket in payment for her year's service. The girl hurried up to the loft and chose the largest and gaudiest casket she could see. She said good-bye to no one, but hurried home with it and was eagerly greeted by her mother who admired the casket as well as she did. They took it up to the best bedroom and eagerly unlocked it, expecting to be dazzled with light cast by the jewels. A light did dazzle them indeed, but it was of a real flame, leaping up, which licked round the walls and set the roof on fire. The neighbors rushed out, but the house burnt like tinder and the wicked mother and daughter were consumed with it. Only the little hen house, standing apart, was safe from the flames, and there the stepchild lived a happy peaceful life, beloved by all her neighbors and kind to all living things. And when she died the box was the heritage of all considerate girls, and by its help they can always keep themselves neat however little they have. And so the story ends.

NORWAY

Lord Peter

This story originally appeared in Peter Christen Asbjörnsen and Jörgen Engel-bretsen Moe's Norske Huldre-Eventyr og Folkesagen *(Norwegian Mythi-cal Tales and Popular Legends),* which was published in two volumes in 1845 and 1848. It was translated by Sir George W. Dasent for his *Popular Tales from the Norse,* which was published in 1858. It contains a mixture of some elements from "Puss in Boots" and "The White Cat."*

Once on a time there was a poor couple, and they had nothing in the world but three sons. What names the two elder had I can't say, but the youngest he was called Peter. So when their father and mother died, the sons were to share what was left, but there was nothing but a porridge-pot, a griddle and a cat.

The eldest, who was to have the first choice, he took the pot; "for," said he, "whenever I lend the pot to any one to boil porridge, I can always get leave to scrape it."

The second took the griddle; "for," said he, "whenever I lend it to any-one, I'll always get a morsel of dough to make a bannock."

But the youngest, he had no choice left him; if he was to choose any-thing it must be the cat.

"Well," said he, "if I lend the cat to anyone I can't get much by that; for if pussy gets a drop of milk, she'll want it all herself. Still, I'd best take her along with me; I shouldn't like her to go about here and starve."

So the brothers went out into the world to try their luck, and each took his own way; but when the youngest had gone a while, the cat said, "Now you shall have a good turn, because you wouldn't let me stay behind in the old cottage and starve. Now, I'm off to the wood to lay hold of a fat head of game, and then you must go up to the king's palace that you see yon-der, and say that you are come with a little present for the king; and when he asks who sends it, you must say, 'Why, who should it be from but Lord Peter?'"

Well, Peter hadn't waited long before back came the cat with a reindeer from the wood; she had jumped upon the reindeer's head, between his horns, and said, "If you don't go straight to the king's palace I'll claw your eyes out."

So the reindeer had to go whether he liked it or no. And when Peter got to the palace he went into the kitchen with the deer, and said, "Here I'm come with a little present for the king, if he won't despise it."

Then the king went into the kitchen, and when he saw the fine plump reindeer, he was very glad.

"But, my dear friend," he said, "who in the world is it who sends me such a fine gift?"

"Oh," said Peter, "who should send it but Lord Peter?"

"Lord Peter! Lord Peter!" said the king. "Pray tell me where he lives"; for he thought it a shame not to know so great a man. But that was just what the lad wouldn't tell him; he dare not do it, he said, because his master had forbidden him.

So the king gave him a good bit of money to drink his health, and bade him be sure and say all kinds of pretty things, and many thanks for the present to his master when he got home.

Next day the cat went again into the wood, jumped on a red deer's head, and sat between his horns, and forced him to go to the palace. Then Peter went again into the kitchen, and said he was come with a little present for the king, if he would be pleased to take it. And the king was still more pleased to get the red deer than he had been to get the reindeer, and asked again who it was that sent so fine a present.

"Why, it's Lord Peter of course," said the lad, but when the king wanted to know where Lord Peter lived, he got the same answer as the day before, and this day, too, he gave Peter a good lump of money to drink his health with.

The third day the cat came with an elk. And so when Peter got into the palace-kitchen, and said he had a little present for the king, if he'd be pleased to take it, the king came out at once into the kitchen; and when he saw the grand big elk, he was so glad he scarce knew which leg to stand on; and this day, too, he gave Peter many more dollars—at least a hundred. He wished now, once for all, to know where the Lord Peter lived, and asked and asked about this thing and that, but the lad said he dare not say, for his master's sake, who had strictly forbidden him to tell.

"Well then," said the king, "beg Lord Peter to come and see me."

Yes, the lad would take that message, but when Peter got out into the yard again and met the cat, he said: "A pretty scrape you've got me into now, for here's the king, who wants me to come and see him, and you know I've nothing to go in but these rags I stand and walk in."

"Oh, don't be afraid about that," said the cat; "in three days you shall have coach and horses, and fine clothes, so fine that the gold falls from them, and then you may go and see the king very well. But mind, whatever you see in the king's palace, you must say you have far better and grander things of your own. Don't forget that."

No, no, Peter would bear that in mind, never fear.

So when three days were over the cat came with a coach and horses, and clothes and all that Peter wanted, and altogether it was as grand as anything you ever set eyes on; so off he set, and the cat ran alongside the coach. The king met him well and graciously; but whatever the king offered him, and whatever he showed him, Peter said it was all very well, but he had much finer and better things in his own house. The king seemed not quite to believe this, but Peter stuck to what he said, and at last the king got so angry, he couldn't bear it any longer.

"Now I'll go home with you," he said, "and see if it be true what you've been telling me, that you have far finer and better things of your own. But if you've been telling a pack of lies, Heaven help you, that's all I say."

"Now you've got me into a fine scrape," said Peter to the cat, "for here's the king coming home with me; but my home, that's not so easy to find, I think."

"Oh! never mind," said the cat; "only do you drive after me as I run before."

So off they set; first Peter, who drove after his cat, and then the king and all his court.

But when they had driven a good bit, they came to a great flock of fine sheep, that had wool so long that it almost touched the ground.

"If you'll only say"; said the cat to the shepherd, "this flock of sheep belongs to Lord Peter, when the king asks you, I'll give you this silver spoon," which she had taken with her from the king's palace.

Yes, he was willing enough to do that. So when the king came up, he said to the lad who watched the sheep, "Well, I never saw so large and fine a flock of sheep in my life! Whose is it, my little lad?"

"Why," said the lad, "whose should it be but Lord Peter's?"

A little further on they came to a great, great herd of fine brindled cattle, who were all so sleek the sun shone from them.

"If you'll only say," said the cat to the neat-herd, "this herd is Lord Peter's, when the king asks you, I'll give you this silver ladle"; and the ladle too she had taken from the king's palace.

"Yes, with all my heart," said the neat-herd.

So when the king came up, he was quite amazed at the fine fat herd, for such a herd he had never seen before, and so he asked the neat-herd who owned those brindled cattle.

"Why, who should own them but Lord Peter?" said the neat-herd.

So they went on a little farther, and came to a great, great drove of horses, the finest you ever saw, six of each color, bay and black and brown and chestnut.

"If you'll only say this drove of horses is Lord Peter's when the king asks you," said the cat, "I'll give you this silver goblet"; and the goblet too she had taken from the palace.

Yes, the lad was willing enough; and so when the king came up, he was quite amazed at the great drove of horses, for the match of those horses he had never yet set eyes on, he said.

So he asked the lad who watched them, whose all these blacks and bays and browns and chestnuts were.

"Whose should they be," said the lad, "but Lord Peter's?"

So when they had gone a good bit farther they came to a castle; first there was a gate of tin, and next a gate of silver, and next a gate of gold. The castle itself was of silver, and so dazzling white that it quite hurt one's eyes to look at the sunbeams which fell on it just as they reached it.

So they went into it, and the cat told Peter to say this was his house. As for the castle inside, it was far finer than it looked outside, for everything was pure gold—chairs, and tables and benches, and all. And when the king had gone all over it, and seen everything high and low, he got quite shameful and downcast.

"Yes," he said at last, "Lord Peter, has everything far finer than I have, there's no gainsaying that." And so he wanted to be off home again.

But Peter begged him to stay to supper, and the king stayed, but he was sour and surly the whole time.

So as they sat at supper, back came the troll who owned the castle, and gave such a great knock at the door.

"WHO'S THIS EATING MY MEAT AND DRINKING ME MEAD LIKE SWINE IN HERE," roared out the troll.

As soon as the cat heard that she ran down to the gate.

"Stop a bit," she said, "and I'll tell you how the farmer set to work to get in his winter rye."

And so she told him such a long story about the winter rye.

"First of all, you see, he plows his field, and then he dungs it, and then he plows it again, and then he harrows it"; and so she went on till the sun rose.

"Oh do look behind you, and there you'll see such a lovely lady," said the cat to the troll.

So the troll turned round, and, of course, as soon as he saw the sun he burst.

"Now all this is yours," said the cat to Lord Peter. "Now you must cut off my head; that's all I ask for what I have done for you."

"Nay, nay," said Lord Peter, "I'll never do any such thing. That's flat."

"If you don't," said the cat, "see if I don't claw your eyes out."

Well, so Lord Peter had to do it, though it was sore against his will. He cut off the cat's head, but there and then she became the loveliest princess you ever set eyes on, and Lord Peter fell in love with her at once.

"Yes, all this greatness was mine first," said the princess, "but a troll bewitched me to be a cat in your father's and mother's cottage. Now you may do as you please, whether you take me to your queen or not, for you are now King over all this realm."

Well, well, there was little doubt Lord Peter would be willing enough to have her as his queen, and so there was a wedding that lasted eight whole days, and a feast besides, and after it was over I stayed no longer with Lord Peter and his lovely queen, and so I can't say anything more about them.

The Cat's Elopement

This story was translated from David Brauns's Japanische Märchen und Sagen (Japanese Fairytales and Stories), *which was published in 1885.*

Once upon a time there lived a cat of marvelous beauty, with a skin as soft and shining as silk, and wise green eyes, that could see even in the dark. His name was Gon, and he belonged to a music teacher, who was so fond and proud of him that he would not have parted with him for anything in the world.

Now not far from the music master's house there dwelt a lady who possessed a most lovely little pussy cat called Koma. She was such a little dear altogether, and blinked her eyes so daintily, and ate her supper so tidily, and when she had finished she licked her pink nose so delicately with her little tongue, that her mistress was never tired of saying, "Koma, Koma, what should I do without you?"

Well, it happened one day that these two, when out for an evening stroll, met under a cherry tree, and in one moment fell madly in love with each other. Gon had long felt that it was time for him to find a wife, for all the ladies in the neighborhood paid him so much attention that it made him quite shy; but he was not easy to please, and did not care about any of them. Now, before he had time to think, Cupid had entangled him in his net, and he was filled with love towards Koma. She fully returned his passion, but, like a woman, she saw the difficulties in the way, and consulted sadly with Gon as to the means of overcoming them. Gon entreated his master to set matters right by buying Koma, but her mistress would not part from her. Then the music master was asked to sell Gon to the lady, but he declined to listen to any such suggestion, so everything remained as before.

At length the love of the couple grew to such a pitch that they determined to please themselves, and to seek their fortunes together. So one
moonlit night they stole away, and ventured out into an unknown world.
All day long they marched bravely on through the sunshine, till they had
left their homes far behind them, and towards evening they found themselves in a large park. The wanderers by this time were very hot and tired,
and the grass looked very soft and inviting, and the trees cast cool deep
shadows, when suddenly an ogre appeared in this Paradise, in the shape of
a big, big dog! He came springing towards them showing all his teeth, and
Koma shrieked, and rushed up a cherry tree. Gon, however, stood his
ground boldly, and prepared to give battle, for he felt that Koma's eyes
were upon him, and that he must not run away. But, alas! his courage
would have availed him nothing had his enemy once touched him, for he
was large and powerful, and very fierce. From her perch in the tree Koma
saw it all, and screamed with all her might, hoping that some one would
hear, and come to help. Luckily a servant of the princess to whom the park
belonged was walking by, and he drove off the dog, and picking up the
trembling Gon in his arms, carried him to his mistress.

So poor little Koma was left alone, while Gon was borne away full of
trouble, not in the least knowing what to do. Even the attention paid him
by the princess, who was delighted with his beauty and pretty ways, did
not console him, but there was no use in fighting against fate, and he
could only wait and see what would turn up.

The princess, Gon's new mistress, was so good and kind that everybody loved her, and she would have led a happy life, had it not been for a
serpent who had fallen in love with her, and was constantly annoying her
by his presence. Her servants had orders to drive him away as often as he
appeared; but as they were careless, and the serpent very sly, it sometimes
happened that he was able to slip past them, and to frighten the princess
by appearing before her. One day she was seated in her room, playing on
her favorite musical instrument, when she felt something gliding up her
sash, and saw her enemy making his way to kiss her cheek. She shrieked
and threw herself backwards, and Gon, who had been curled up on a stool
at her feet, understood her terror, and with one bound seized the snake by
his neck. He gave him one bite and one shake, and flung him on the
ground, where he lay, never to worry the princess any more. Then she
took Gon in her arms, and praised and caressed him, and saw that he had

the nicest bits to eat, and the softest mats to lie on; and he would have had nothing in the world to wish for if only he could have seen Koma again.

Time passed on, and one morning Gon lay before the house door, basking in the sun. He looked lazily at the world stretched out before him, and saw in the distance a big ruffian of a cat tearing and ill-treating quite a little one. He jumped up, full of rage, and chased away the big cat, and then he turned to comfort the little one, when his heart nearly burst with joy to find that it was Koma. At first Koma did not know him again, he had grown so large and stately; but when it dawned upon her who it was, her happiness knew no bounds. And they rubbed their heads and their noses again and again, while their purring might have been heard a mile off.

Paw in paw they appeared before the princess, and told her the story of their life and its sorrows. The princess wept for sympathy, and promised that they should never more be parted, but should live with her to the end of their days. By-and-bye the princess herself got married, and brought a prince to dwell in the palace in the park. And she told him all about her two cats, and how brave Gon had been, and how he had delivered her from her enemy the serpent.

And when the prince heard, he swore they should never leave them, but should go with the princess wherever she went. So it all fell out as the princess wished; and Gon and Koma had many children, and so had the princess, and they all played together, and were friends to the end of their lives.

IRELAND

Owney and Owney-na-peak

*This curious fairy tale comes to us from Gerald Griffin's "Holland-Tide;" or,
Munster Popular Tales, which was published in 1827. After several years as
a writer, and suffering from an unrequited love, Griffin (1804–1840)
became a monk. Two years later he died of typhus at the age of thirty-seven.
The cats in this story play a more sinister role than in the other tales I have
included in this book, in that they have aligned forces with Simon Magus.
Simon Magus was the Biblical wizard who bewitched the people of Sumaria,
as mentioned in Acts 8:9–13. Although the Bible says that he was converted
by the Apostle Philip, Christian tradition maintains that he later broke with
the apostles and continually opposed them (especially Peter) throughout their
missionary travels. Tradition also identifies him as the founder of Gnosticism.
Since the Middle Ages, he has come to be considered a close ally of Satan and
sometimes even "Old Horny" himself in disguise.*

When Ireland had kings of her own—when there was no such thing as
a coat made of red cloth in the country—when there was plenty in men's
houses, and peace and quietness at men's doors (and that is a long time
since)—there lived, in a village not far from the great city of Lumneach,[1]
two young men, cousins: one of them named Owney, a smart, kind-
hearted, handsome youth, with limb of a delicate form, and a very good
understanding. His cousin's name was Owney too, and the neighbors
christened him Owney-na-peak (Owney of the nose), on account of a
long nose he had got—a thing so out of all proportion, that after looking
at one side of his face, it was a smart morning's walk to get round the nose
and take a view of the other (at least, so the people used to say). He was a
stout, able-bodied fellow, as stupid as a beaten hound, and he was, more-

---

[1] Now called Limerick.

over, a cruel tyrant to his young cousin, with whom he lived in a kind of partnership.

Both of them were of a humble station. They were smiths—white-smiths—and they got a good deal of business to do from the lords of the court, and the knights, and all the grand people of the city. But one day young Owney was in town, he saw a great procession of lords, and ladies, and generals, and great people, among whom was the king's daughter of the court—and surely it is not possible for the young rose itself to be so beautiful as she was. His heart fainted at her sight, and he went home desperately in love, and not at all disposed to business.

Money, he was told, was the surest way of getting acquainted with the king, and so he began saving until he had put together a few *hogs*,[2] but Owney-na-peak, finding where he had hid them, seized on the whole, as he used to do on all young Owney's earnings.

One evening young Owney's mother found herself about to die, so she called her son to her bedside and said to him: "You have been a most dutiful good son, and 'tis proper you should be rewarded for it. Take this china cup to the fair—there is a fairy gift upon it—use your own wit, look about you, and let the highest bidder have it—and so, my white-headed boy,[3] God bless you!"

The young man drew his little bed curtain down over his dead mother, and in a few days after, with a heavy heart, he took his china cup, and set off to the fair of Garryowen.

The place was merry enough. The field that is called Gallows Green now was covered with tents. There was plenty of wine (poteen not being known in these days, let alone *parliament)*, a great many handsome girls, and 'tis unknown all the *keoh* that was with the boys and themselves. Poor Owney walked all the day through the fair, wishing to try his luck, but ashamed to offer his china cup among all the fine things that were there for sale. Evening was drawing on at last, and he was thinking of going home, when a strange man tapped him on the shoulder, and said: "My good youth, I have been marking you through the fair the whole day, going about with that cup in your hand, speaking to nobody, and looking as if you would be wanting something or another.'

"I'm for selling it," said Owney.

2 A type of coin.
3 An Irish phrase for the favorite child.

"What is it you're for selling, you say?" said a second man, coming up and looking at the cup.

"Why then," said the first man, "and what's that to you, for a prying meddler? What do you want to know what it is he's for selling?"

"Bad manners to you (and where's the use of my wishing you what you have already?), haven't I a right to ask the price of what's in the fair?"

"E'then, the knowledge o' the price is all you'll have for it," says the first. "Here, my lad, is a golden piece for your cup."

"That cup shall never hold drink or diet in your house, please Heaven," says the second; "here's two gold pieces for the cup, lad."

"Why then, see this now—if I was forced to fill it to the rim with gold before I could call it mine, you shall never hold that cup between your fingers. Here, boy, do you mind me, give me that, once for all, and here's ten gold pieces for it, and say no more."

"Ten gold pieces for a china cup!" said a great lord of the court, who just rode up at that minute, "it must surely be a valuable article. Here, boy, here are twenty pieces for it, and give it to my servant."

"Give it to mine," cried another lord of the party, "and here's my purse, where you will find ten more. And if any man offers another fraction for it to outbid that, I'll spit him on my sword like a snipe."

"I outbid him," said a fair young lady in a veil, by his side, flinging twenty golden pieces more on the ground.

There was no voice to outbid the lady, and young Owney, kneeling, gave the cup into her hands.

"Fifty gold pieces for a china cup," said Owney to himself, as he plodded on home, "that was not worth two! Ah! mother, you knew that vanity had an open hand."

But as he drew near home he determined to hide his money somewhere, knowing, as he well did, that his cousin would not leave him a single cross to bless himself with. So he dug a little pit, and buried all but two pieces, which he brought to the house. His cousin, knowing the business on which he had gone, laughed heartily when he saw him enter, and asked him what luck he had got with his punch-bowl.

"Not so bad, neither," says Owney. "Two pieces of gold is not a bad price for an article of old china."

"Two gold pieces, Owney, honey! Erra, let us see 'em, maybe you would?" He took the cash from Owney's hand, and after opening his eyes in great astonishment at the sight of so much money, he put them into his pocket.

"Well, Owney, I'll keep them safe for you, in my pocket within. But tell us, maybe you would, how come you to get such a *mort* o money for an old cup o' painted chaney, that wasn't worth, maybe, a fi-penny bit?"

"To get into the heart o' the fair, then, free and easy, and to look about me, and to cry old china, and the first man that *come* up, he to ask me, what is it I'd be asking for the cup, and I to say out bold: "A hundred pieces of gold," and he to laugh hearty, and we to huxter together till he beat me down to two and there's the whole way of it all."

Owney-na-peak made as if he took no note of this, but next morning early he took an old china saucer himself had in his cupboard, and off he set, without saying a word to anybody, to the fair. You may easily imagine that it created no small surprise in the place when they heard a great big fellow with a china saucer in his hand crying out: "A raal *chaney* saucer going for a hundred pieces of goold! Raal chaney—who'll be buying?"

"Erra, what's that you're saying, you great gomeril?" says a man, coming up to him, and looking first at the saucer and then in his face. "Is it thinking anybody would go make a *muthaun* of himself to give the like for that saucer?" But Owney-na-peak had no answer to make, only to cry out: "Raal chaney! One hundred pieces of goold!"

A crowd soon collected about him, and finding he would give no account of himself, they fell upon him, beat him within an inch of his life, and after having satisfied themselves upon him, they went their way laughing and shouting. Towards sunset he got up, and crawled home as well as he could, without saucer or money. As soon as Owney saw him, he helped him into the forge, looking very mournful, although, if the truth must be told, it was to revenge himself for former good deeds of his cousin that he set him about this foolish business.

"Come here, Owney, eroo," said his cousin, after he had fastened the forge door and heated two irons in the fire. You child of mischief!" said he, when he had caught him, "you shall never see the fruits of your roguery again, for I will put out your eyes." And so saying he snatched one of the red-hot irons from the fire.

It was all in vain for poor Owney to throw himself on his knees, and ask mercy, and beg and implore forgiveness; he was weak, and Owney-na-peak was strong; he held him fast, and burned out both his eyes. Then taking him, while he was yet fainting from the pain, upon his back, he carried him off to the bleak hill of Knockpatrick,[4] a great distance, and there laid him under a tombstone, and went his ways. In a little time after, Owney came to himself.

"Oh sweet light of day! what is to become of me now?" thought the poor lad, as he lay on his back under the tomb. Is this to be the fruit of that unhappy present? Must I be dark for ever? And am I never more to look upon that sweet countenance, that even in my blindness is not entirely shut out from me? He would have said a great deal more in this way, and perhaps more pathetic still, but just then he heard a great mewing, as if all the cats in the world were coming up the hill together in one faction. He gathered himself up, and drew back under the stone, and remained quite still, expecting what would come next.

In a very short time he heard all the cats purring and mewing about the yard, whisking over the tombstones and playing all sorts of pranks among the graves. He felt the tails of one or two brush his nose; and well for him it was that they did not discover him there, as he afterwards found. At last—

"Silence!" said one of the cats, and they were all as mute as so many mice in an instant. "Now, all you cats of this great country, small and large, gray, red, yellow, black, brown, mottled and white, attend to what I'm going to tell you in the name of your king and the master of all the cats. The sun is down, and the moon is up, and the night is silent, and no mortal hears us, and I may tell you a secret. You know the king of Munster's daughter?"

"O yes, to be sure, and why wouldn't we? Go on with your story," said all the cats together.

"I have heard of her for one," said a little dirty-faced black cat speaking after they had all done, "for I'm the cat that sits upon the hob of Owney and Owney-na-peak, the whitesmiths, and I know many's the time young Owney does be talking of her, when he sits by the fire alone, rubbing me down and planning how he can get into her father's court."

"Whist, you natural!" says the cat that was making the speech, "what do you think we care for your Owney, or Owney-na-peak?"

---

[4] A hill in the west of the County of Limerick on the summit of which are the ruins of an old church and a cemetery. The situation is exceedingly singular and bleak.

"Murther, murther!" thinks Owney to himself, "did anybody ever hear the aiqual of this?"

"Well, gentlemen," says the cat again, "what I have to say is this. The king was last week struck with blindness, and you all know well how blindness may be cured. You know there is no disorder that can ail mortal frame, that may not be removed by praying a round at the well of Barry-gowen[5] yonder, and the king's disorder is such that no other cure whatever can be had for it. Now, beware, don't let the secret pass one o' yer lips, for there's a great-grandson of Simon Magus, that is coming down to try his skill, and he it is that must use the water and marry the princess, who is to be given to any one so fortunate as to heal her father's eyes; and on that day, gentlemen, we are all promised a feast of the fattest mice that ever walked the ground." This speech was wonderfully applauded by all the cats, and presently after, the whole crew scampered off, jumping, and mewing, and purring, down the hill.

Owney, being sensible that they were all gone, came from his hiding-place, and knowing the road to Barrygowen well, he set off, and groped his way out, and shortly knew, by the rolling of the waves,[6] coming in from the point of Foynes, that he was near the place. He got to the well, and making a round like a good Christian, rubbed his eyes with the well-water, and looking up, saw day dawning in the east. Giving thanks, he jumped up on his feet, and you may say that Owney-na-peak was much astonished on opening the door of the forge to find him there, his eyes as well or better than ever, and his face as merry as a dance.

"Well, cousin," said Owney, smiling, "you have done me the greatest service that one man can do another; you put me in the way of getting two pieces of gold," said he, showing two he had taken from his hiding-place. "If you could only bear the pain of suffering me just to put out your eyes, and lay you in the same place as you laid me, who knows what luck you'd have?"

"No, there's no occasion for putting out eyes at all, but could not you lay me, just as I am, tonight, in that place, and let me try my own fortune, if it be a thing you tell thruth; and what else could put the eyes in your head, after I burned them out with irons?"

[5] The practice of praying rounds, with the view of healing diseases, at Barrygowen Well, in the County of Limerick, still continued at the end of the nineteenth century, despite the exertions of the neighboring Catholic priesthood.
[6] Of the River Shannon.

"You'll know all that in time," says Owney, stopping him in his speech, for just at that minute, casting his eye towards the hob, he saw the cat sitting upon it, and looking very hard at him. So he made a sign to Owney-na-peak to be silent, or talk of something else; at which the cat turned away her eyes, and began washing her face, quite simple, with her two paws, looking now and then sideways into Owney's face, just like a Christian. By and by, when she had walked out of the forge, he shut the door after her, and finished what he was going to say, which made Owney-na-peak still more anxious than before to be placed under the tombstone. Owney agreed to it very readily, and just as they were done speaking, cast a glance towards the forge window, where he saw the imp of a cat, just with her nose and one eye peeping in through a broken pane. He said nothing, however, but prepared to carry his cousin to the place; where, towards nightfall, he laid him as he had been laid himself, snug under the tombstone, and went his way down the hill, resting in Shanagolden that night, to see what would come of it in the morning.

Owney-na-peak had not been more than two or three hours or so lying down, when he heard the very same noises coming up the hill that had puzzled Owney the night before. Seeing the cats enter the churchyard, he began to grow very uneasy, and strove to hide himself as well as he could, which was tolerably well too, all being covered by the tombstone excepting part of the nose, which was so long that he could not get it to fit by any means. You may say to yourself that he was not a little surprised when he saw the cats all assemble like a congregation going to hear mass, some sitting, some walking about, and asking one another after the kittens and the like, and more of them stretching themselves upon the tombstones, and waiting the speech of their commander.

Silence was proclaimed at length, and he spoke: "Now all you cats of this great county, small and large, gray, red, yellow, black, brown, mottled, or white, attend—"

"Stay! stay!" said a little cat with a dirty face that just then came running into the yard. "Be silent, for there are mortal ears listening to what you say. I have run hard and fast to say that your words were overheard last night. I am the cat that sits upon the hob of Owney and Owney-na-peak. And I saw a bottle of the water of Barrygowen hanging up over the chimbley this morning in their house."

In an instant all the cats began screaming, and mewing, and flying, as if they were mad, about the yard, searching every corner, and peeping under every tombstone. Poor Owney-na-peak endeavored as well as he could to hide himself from them, and began to thump his breast and cross himself, but it was all in vain, for one of the cats saw the long nose peeping from under the stone, and in a minute they dragged him, roaring and bawling, into the very middle of the churchyard, where they flew upon him all together, and made *smithereens* of him, from the crown of his head to the soles of his feet.

The next morning very early, young Owney came to the churchyard to see what had become of his cousin. He called over and over again upon his name, but there was no answer given. At last, entering the place of tombs, he found his limbs scattered over the earth.

"So that is the way with you, is it?" said he, clasping his hands, and looking down on the bloody fragments; "why then, though you were no great things in the way of kindness to me when your bones were together, that isn't the reason why I'd be glad to see them torn asunder this morning early." So gathering up all the pieces that he could find, he put them into a bag he had with him, and away with him to the well of Barrygowen, where he lost no time in making a round, and throwing them in all in a heap. In an instant, he saw Owney-na-peak as well as ever, scrambling out of the well, and helping him to get up, he asked him how he felt himself.

"Oh is it how I'd feel myself you'd want to know?" said the other; "easy and I'll tell you. Take that for a specimen!" giving him at the same time a blow on the head, which you may say wasn't long in laying Owney sprawling on the ground. Then, without giving him a minute's time to recover, he thrust him into the very bag from which he had been just shaken himself, resolving within himself to drown him in the Shannon at once, and put an end to him for ever.

Growing weary by the way, he stopped at a shebeen house *overright* Robertstown Castle, to refresh himself with a *morning*, before he'd go any farther. Poor Owney did not know what to do when he came to himself, if it might be rightly called coming to himself, and the great bag tied up about him. His wicked cousin shot him down behind the door in the kitchen, and telling him he'd have his life surely if he stirred, he walked in to take something that's good in the little parlor.

Owney could not for the life of him avoid cutting a hole in the bag, to have a peep about the kitchen, and see whether he had no means of escape. He could see only one person, a simple-looking man, who was counting his beads in the chimney-corner, and now and then striking his breast, and looking up as if he was praying greatly.

"Lord" says he, "only give me death, death, and a favorable judgment! I haven't anybody now to look after, nor anybody to look after me. What's a few tinpennies to save a man from want? Only a quiet grave is all I ask."

"Murther, murther!" says Owney to himself, "here's a man wants death and can't have it, and here am I going to have it, and, in troth, I don't want it at all, see." So, after thinking a little what he had best do, he began to sing out very merrily, but lowering his voice, for fear he should be heard in the next room:

> "To him that tied me here,
>   Be thanks and praises given!
> I'll bless him night and day,
>   For packing me to heaven.
> Of all the roads you'll name,
>   He surely will not lag,
> Who takes his way to heaven
>   By traveling in a bag!

"To heaven, *ershishin?*"[7] said the man in the chimney-corner, opening his mouth and his eyes; "why then, you'd be doing a Christian turn, if you'd take a neighbor with you, that's tired of this bad and villainous world."

"You're a fool, you're a fool!" said Owney.

"I know I am, at least so the neighbors always tell me—but what hurt? Maybe I have a Christian soul as well as another; and fool or no fool, in a bag or out of a bag, I'd be glad and happy to go the same road it is you are talking of."

After seeming to make a great favor of it, in order to allure him the more to the bargain, Owney agreed to put him into the bag instead of himself; and cautioning him against saying a word, he was just going to tie him, when he was touched with a little remorse for going to have the innocent man's life taken: and seeing a slip of a pig that was killed the day before, in a corner, hanging up, the thought struck him that it would do just as well to put it in the bag in their place. No sooner said than done, to

---

[7] "Ershishin?" means "Does he say?"

the great surprise of the natural, he popped the pig into the bag and tied it up.

"Now," says he, "my good friend, go home, say nothing, but bless the name in heaven for saving your life; and you were as near losing it this morning as ever man was that didn't know."

They left the house together. Presently out comes Owney-na-peak, very hearty; and being so, he was not able to perceive the difference in the contents of the bag, but hoisting it upon his back, he sallied out of the house. Before he had gone far, he came to the rock of Foynes, from the top of which he flung his burden into the salt waters.

Away he went home, and knocked at the door of the forge, which was opened to him by Owney. You may fancy him to yourself crossing and blessing himself over and over again, when he saw, as he thought, the ghost standing before him. But Owney looked very merry, and told him not to be afraid. "You did many is the good turn in your life," says he, "but the equal of this never." So he up and told him that he found the finest place in the world at the bottom of the waters, and plenty of money. "See these four pieces for a specimen," showing him some he had taken from his own hiding hole: "what do you think of that for a story?"

"Why then that it's a droll one, no less; sorrow bit av I wouldn't have a mind to try my luck in the same way; how did you come home here before me that took the straight road, and didn't stop for so much as my *gusthah*[8] since I left Knockpatrick?"

"Oh, there's a short cut under the waters," said Owney. "Mind and only be civil while you're in Thiernaoge,[9] and you'll make a sight o' money."

Well became Owney, he thrust his cousin into the bag, tied it about him, and putting it into a car that was returning after leaving a load of oats at a corn-store in the city, it was not long before he was at Foynes again. Here he dismounted, and going to the rock, he was, I am afraid, half inclined to start his burden into the wide water, when he saw a small skiff making towards the point. He hailed her, and learned that she was about to board a great vessel from foreign parts that was sailing out of the river. So he went with his bag on board, and making his bargain with the cap-

[8] "Gusthah" literally means "walk in."
[9] One of the Gaelic words for fairyland. More commonly written as "Tír-na-n-Óg," it literally means "the Land of Youth."

tain of the ship, he left Owney-na-peak along with the crew, and never was troubled with him after, from that day to this.

As he was passing by Barrygowen well, he filled a bottle with the water; and going home, he bought a fine suit of clothes with the rest of the money he had buried, and away he set off in the morning to the city of Lumneach. He walked through the town, admiring everything he saw, until he came before the palace of the king. Over the gates of this he saw a number of spikes, with a head of a man stuck upon each, grinning in the sunshine.

Not at all daunted, he knocked very boldly at the gate, which was opened by one of the guards of the palace. "Well! Who are you, friend?"

"I am a great doctor that's come from foreign parts to cure the king's eyesight. Lead me to his presence this minute."

"Fair and softly," said the soldier. "Do you see all those heads that are stuck up there? Yours is very likely to be keeping company by them, if you are so foolish as to come inside these walls. They are the heads of all the doctors in the land who came before you; and that's what makes the town so fine and healthy this time past, praised be Heaven for the same!"

"Don't be talking, you great gomeril," says Owney; "only bring me to the king at once."

He was brought before the king. After being warned of his fate if he should fail to do all that he undertook, the place was made clear of all but a few guards, and Owney was informed once more that if he should restore the king's eyes, he should wed with the princess, and have the crown after her father's death. This put him in great spirits, and after making a round upon his bare knees about the bottle he took a little of the water, and rubbed it into the king's eyes. In a minute he jumped up from his throne and looked about him as well as ever. He ordered Owney to be dressed out like a king's son, and sent word to his daughter that she should receive him that instant for her husband.

You may say to yourself that the princess, glad as she was of her father's recovery, did not like this message. Small blame to her, when it is considered that she never set her eyes upon the man himself. However, her mind was changed wonderfully when he was brought before her, covered with gold and diamonds, and all sorts of grand things. Wishing, however, to know whether he had as good a wit as he had a person, she told him that he should give her, on the next morning, an answer to two questions, otherwise she would not hold him worthy of her hand. Owney bowed, and she put the questions as follows:

"What is that which is the sweetest thing in the world?"

"What are the three most beautiful objects in the creation?"

These were puzzling questions; but Owney, having a small share of brains of his own, was not long in forming an opinion upon the matter. He was very impatient for the morning; but it came just as slow and regular as if he were not in the world. In a short time he was summoned to the courtyard, where all the nobles of the land assembled, with flags waving, and trumpets sounding, and all manner of glorious doings going on. The princess was placed on a throne of gold near her father, and there was a beautiful carpet spread for Owney to stand upon while he answered her questions. After the trumpets were silenced, she put the first, with a clear sweet voice, and he replied:

"It's salt!" says he, very stout, out.

There was a great applause at the answer; and the princess owned, smiling, that he had judged right.

"But now," said she, "for the second. What are the three most beautiful things in the creation?"

"Why," answered the young man, "here they are. A ship in full sail—a field of wheat in ear—and—"

What the third most beautiful thing was, all the people didn't hear; but there was a great blushing and laughing among the ladies, and the princess smiled and nodded at him, quite pleased with his wit. Indeed, many said that the judges of the land themselves could not have answered better, had they been in Owney's place; nor could there be anywhere found a more likely or well-spoken young man. He was brought first to the king, who took him in his arms, and presented him to the princess. She could not help acknowledging to herself that his understanding was quite worthy of his handsome person. Orders being immediately given for the marriage to proceed, they were made one with all speed; and it is said that before another year came round, the fair princess was one of the most beautiful objects in the creation.

NORTHERN AFRICA

The Clever Cat

This story was adapted for Andrew Lang's The Orange Fairy Book *(1906) from* Contes Berbères (Stories of the Berbers). *The Berbers are a people of northern Africa who speak the Berber language. They mainly live in Morocco, Algeria, and Tunisia, with a few in Libya, Mali, Niger, and Mauritania. They were conquered by the Arabs in the seventh century and now most of the Berbers are Muslim, although there are a few who are Jewish.*

Once upon a time there lived an old man who dwelt with his son in a small hut on the edge of the plain. He was very old, and had worked very hard, and when at last he was struck down by illness he felt that he should never rise from his bed again.

So, one day, he bade his wife summon their son, when he came back from his journey to the nearest town, where he had been to buy bread.

"Come hither, my son," said he; "I know myself well to be dying, and I have nothing to leave you but my falcon, my cat and my greyhound; but if you make good use of them you will never lack food. Be good to your mother, as you have been to me. And now farewell!"

Then he turned his face to the wall and died.

There was great mourning in the hut for many days, but at length the son rose up, and calling to his greyhound, his cat and his falcon, he left the house saying that he would bring back something for dinner. Wandering over the plain, he noticed a troop of gazelles, and pointed to his greyhound to give chase. The dog soon brought down a fine fat beast, and slinging it over his shoulders, the young man turned homewards. On the way, however, he passed a pond, and as he approached a cloud of birds flew into the air. Shaking his wrist, the falcon seated on it darted into the air, and swooped down upon the quarry he had marked, which fell dead to the ground. The young man picked it up, and put it in his pouch and then went towards home again.

Near the hut was a small barn in which he kept the produce of the little patch of corn, which grew close to the garden. Here a rat ran out almost under his feet followed by another and another; but quick as thought the cat was upon them and not one escaped her.

When all the rats were killed, the young man left the barn. He took the path leading to the door of the hut, but stopped on feeling a hand laid on his shoulder.

"Young man," said the ogre (for such was the stranger), "you have been a good son, and you deserve the piece of luck which has befallen you this day. Come with me to that shining lake yonder, and fear nothing."

Wondering a little at what might be going to happen to him, the youth did as the ogre bade him, and when they reached the shore of the lake, the ogre turned and said to him:

"Step into the water and shut your eyes! You will find yourself sinking slowly to the bottom; but take courage, all will go well. Only bring up as much silver as you can carry, and we will divide it between us."

So the young man stepped bravely into the lake, and felt himself sinking, sinking, till he reached firm ground at last. In front of him lay four heaps of silver, and in the midst of them a curious white shining stone, marked over with strange characters, such as he had never seen before. He picked it up in order to examine it more closely, and as he held it the stone spoke.

"As long as you hold me, all your wishes will come true," it said. "But hide me in your turban, and then call to the ogre that you are ready to come up."

In a few minutes the young man stood again by the shores of the lake.

"Well, where is the silver?" asked the ogre, who was awaiting him.

"Ah, my father, how can I tell you! So bewildered was I, and so dazzled with the splendors of everything I saw, that I stood like a statue, unable to move. Then, hearing steps approaching, I got frightened, and called to you, as you know."

"You are no better than the rest," cried the ogre, and turned away in a rage.

When he was out of sight the young man took the stone from his turban and looked at it. "I want the finest camel that can be found, and the most splendid garments," said he.

"Shut your eyes then," replied the stone. And he shut them; and when he opened them again the camel that he had wished for was standing before him, while the festal robes of a desert prince hung from his shoulders. Mounting the camel, he whistled the falcon to his wrist, and, followed by his greyhound and his cat, he started homewards.

His mother was sewing at her door when this magnificent stranger rode up, and, filled with surprise, she bowed low before him.

"Don't you know me, mother?" he said with a laugh. And on hearing his voice the good woman nearly fell to the ground with astonishment.

"How have you got that camel and those clothes?" asked she. "Can a son of mine have committed murder in order to possess them?"

"Do not be afraid; they are quite honestly come by," answered the youth. "I will explain all by-and-by; but now you must go to the palace and tell the king I wish to marry his daughter."

At these words the mother thought her son had certainly gone mad, and stared blankly at him. The young man guessed what was in her heart, and replied with a smile:

"Fear nothing. Promise all that he asks; it will be fulfilled somehow."

So she went to the palace, where she found the king sitting in the Hall of Justice listening to the petitions of his people. The woman waited until all had been heard and the hall was empty, and then went up and knelt before the throne.

"My son has sent me to ask for the hand of the princess," said she.

The king looked at her and thought that she was mad; but, instead of ordering his guards to turn her out, he answered gravely:

"Before he can marry the princess he must build me a palace of ice, which can be warmed with fires, and wherein the rarest singing-birds can live!"

"It shall be done, your Majesty," said she, and got up and left the hall.

Her son was anxiously awaiting her outside the palace gates, dressed in the clothes that he wore every day.

"Well, what have I got to do?" he asked impatiently, drawing his mother aside so that no one could overhear them.

"Oh, something quite impossible; and I hope you will put the princess out of your head," she replied.

"Well, but what *is* it?" persisted he.

"Nothing but to build a palace of ice wherein fires can burn that shall keep it so warm that the most delicate singing-birds can live in it!"

"I thought it would be something much harder than that," exclaimed the young man. "I will see about it at once." And leaving his mother, he went into the country and took the stone from his turban.

"I want a palace of ice that can be warmed with fires and filled with the rarest singing-birds!"

"Shut your eyes, then," said the stone; and he shut them, and when he opened them again there was the palace, more beautiful than anything he could have imagined, the fires throwing a soft pink glow over the ice.

"It is fit even for the princess," thought he to himself.

As soon as the king awoke next morning he ran to the window, and there across the plain he beheld the palace.

"That young man must be a great wizard; he may be useful to me." And when the mother came again to tell him that his orders had been fulfilled he received her with great honor, and bade her tell her son that the wedding was fixed for the following day.

The princess was delighted with her new home, and with her husband also; and several days slipped happily by, spent in turning over all the beautiful things that the palace contained. But at length the young man grew tired of always staying inside walls, and he told his wife that the next day he must leave her for a few hours, and go out hunting. "You will not mind?" he asked. And she answered as became a good wife:

"Yes, of course I shall mind; but I will spend the day planning out some new dresses; and then it will be so delightful when you come back, you know!"

So the husband went off to hunt, with the falcon on his wrist, and the greyhound and the cat behind him—for the palace was so warm that even the cat did not mind living in it.

No sooner had he gone, than the ogre who had been watching his chance for many days, knocked at the door of the palace.

"I have just returned from a far country," he said, "and I have some of the largest and most brilliant stones in the world with me. The princess is known to love beautiful things, perhaps she might like to buy some?"

Now the princess had been wondering for many days what trimming she should put on her dresses, so that they should outshine the dresses of the other ladies at the court balls. Nothing that she thought of seemed good enough, so, when the message was brought that the ogre and his wares were below, she at once ordered that he should be brought to her chamber.

Oh! what beautiful stones he laid before her; what lovely rubies, and what rare pearls! No other lady would have jewels like *those*—of that the princess was quite sure; but she cast down her eyes so that the ogre might not see how much she longed for them.

"I fear they are too costly for me," she said carelessly; "and besides, I have hardly need of any more jewels just now."

"I have no particular wish to sell them myself," answered the ogre, with equal indifference. "But I have a necklace of shining stones which was left me by father, and one, the largest, engraven with weird characters, is missing. I have heard that it is in your husband's possession, and if you can get me that stone you shall have any of these jewels that you choose. But you will have to pretend that you want it for yourself; and, above all, do not mention me, for he sets great store by it, and would never part with it to a stranger! Tomorrow I will return with some jewels yet finer than those I have with me today. So, madam, farewell!"

Left alone, the princess began to think of many things, but chiefly as to whether she would persuade her husband to give her the stone or not. At one moment she felt he had already bestowed so much upon her that it was a shame to ask for the only object he had kept back. No, it would be mean; she could not do it! But then, those diamonds, and those strings of pearls! After all, they had only been married a week, and the pleasure of giving it to her ought to be far greater than the pleasure of keeping it for himself. And she was sure it *would* be!

Well, that evening, when the young man had supped off his favorite dishes which the princess took care to have specially prepared for him, she sat down close beside him, and began stroking his hand. For some time she did not speak, but listened attentively to all the adventures that had befallen him that day.

"But I was thinking of you all the time," said he at the end, "and wishing that I could bring you back something you would like. But, alas, what is there that you do not possess already?"

"How good of you not to forget me when you are in the midst of such dangers and hardships," answered she. "Yes, it is true I have many beautiful things; but if you *want* to give me a present—and tomorrow is my birthday—there *is* one thing that I wish for very much."

"And what is that? Of course you shall have it directly!" he asked eagerly.

"It is that bright stone which fell out of the folds of your turban a few days ago," she answered, playing with his finger; "the little stone with all those funny marks upon it. I never saw any stone like it before."

The young man did not answer at first; then he said slowly:

"I have promised, and therefore I must perform. But will you swear never to part from it, and to keep it safely about you always? More I cannot tell you, but I beg you earnestly to take heed to this."

The princess was a little startled by his manner, and began to be sorry that she had ever listened to the ogre. But she did not like to draw back, and pretended to be immensely delighted at her new toy, and kissed and thanked her husband for it.

"After all, I needn't give it to the ogre," thought she as she dropped to sleep.

Unluckily the next morning the young man went hunting again, and the ogre, who was watching, knew this, and did not come till much later than before. At the moment that he knocked at the door of the palace the princess had tired of all her employments, and her attendants were at their wits' end how to amuse her, when a tall negro dressed in scarlet came to announce that the ogre was below, and desired to know if the princess would speak with him.

"Bring him hither at once!" cried she, springing up from her cushions, and forgetting all her resolves of the previous night. In another moment she was bending with rapture over the glittering gems.

"Have you got it?" asked the ogre in a whisper, for the princess's ladies were standing as near as they dared to catch a glimpse of the beautiful jewels.

"Yes, here," she answered, slipping the stone from her sash and placing it among the rest. Then she raised her voice, and began to talk quickly of the prices of the chains and necklaces, and after some bargaining, to deceive the attendants, she declared that she liked one string of pearls better than all the rest, and that the ogre might take away the other things, which were not half so valuable as he supposed.

"As you please, madam," said he, bowing himself out of the palace.

Soon after he had gone a curious thing happened. The princess carelessly touched the wall of her room, which was wont to reflect the warm red light of the fire on the hearth, and found her hand quite wet. She turned round, and—was it her fancy? or did the fire burn more dimly than before? Hurriedly she passed into the picture gallery, where pools of water showed here and there on the floor, and a cold chill ran through her whole body. At that instant her frightened ladies came running down the stairs, crying:

"Madam! madam! what has happened? The palace is disappearing under our eyes!"

"My husband will be home very soon," answered the princess—who, though nearly as much frightened as her ladies, felt that she must set them a good example. "Wait till then, and he will tell us what to do."

So they waited, seated on the highest chairs they could find, wrapped in their warmest garments, and with piles of cushions under their feet, while the poor birds flew with numbed wings hither and thither, till they were so lucky as to discover an open window in some forgotten corner. Through this they vanished, and were seen no more.

At last, when the princess and her ladies had been forced to leave the upper rooms, where the walls and floors had melted away, and to take refuge in the hall, the young man came home. He had ridden back along a winding road from which he did not see the palace till he was close upon it, and stood horrified at the spectacle before him. He knew in an instant that his wife must have betrayed his trust, but he would not reproach her, as she must be suffering enough already. Hurrying on he sprang over all that was left of the palace walls, and the princess gave a cry of relief at the sight of him.

"Come quickly," he said, "or you will be frozen to death!" And a dreary little procession set out for the king's palace, the greyhound and the cat bringing up the rear.

At the gates he left them, though his wife besought him to allow her to enter.

"You have betrayed me and ruined me," he said sternly; "I go to seek my fortune alone." And without another word he turned and left her.

With his falcon on his wrist, and his greyhound and cat behind him, the young man walked a long way, inquiring of everyone he met whether they had seen his enemy the ogre. But nobody had. Then he bade his falcon fly up into the sky—up, up, and up—and try if *his* sharp eyes could discover the old thief. The bird had to go so high that he did not return for some hours; but he told his master that the ogre was lying asleep in a splendid palace in a far country on the shores of the sea. This was delightful news to the young man, who instantly bought some meat for the falcon, bidding him make a good meal.

"Tomorrow," said he, "you will fly to the palace where the ogre lies, and while he is asleep you will search all about him for a stone on which is engraved strange signs; this you will bring to me. In three days I shall expect you back here."

"Well, I must take the cat with me," answered the bird.

The sun had not yet risen before the falcon soared high into the air, the cat seated on his back, with his paws tightly clasping the bird's neck.

"You had better shut your eyes or you may get giddy," said the bird; and the cat, who had never before been off the ground except to climb a tree, did as she was bid.

All that day and all that night they flew, and in the morning they saw the ogre's palace lying beneath them.

"Dear me," said the cat, opening her eyes for the first time, "that looks to me very like a rat city down there, let us go down to it; they may be able to help us." So they alighted in some bushes in the heart of the rat city. The falcon remained where he was, but the cat lay down outside the principal gate, causing terrible excitement among the rats.

At length, seeing she did not move, one bolder than the rest put its head out of an upper window of the castle, and said, in a trembling voice:

"Why have you come here? What do you want? If it is anything in our power, tell us, and we will do it."

"If you would have let me speak to you before, I would have told you that I come as a friend," replied the cat; "and I shall be greatly obliged if you would send four of the strongest and cunningest among you, to do me a service."

"Oh, we shall be delighted," answered the rat, much relieved. "But if you will inform me what it is you wish them to do I shall be better able to judge who is most fitted for the post."

"I thank you," said the cat. "Well, what they have to do is this: Tonight they must burrow under the walls of the castle and go up to the room where an ogre lies asleep. Somewhere about him he has hidden a stone, on which are engraved strange signs. When they have found it they must take it from him without his waking, and bring it to me."

"Your orders shall be obeyed," replied the rat. And he went out to give his instructions.

About midnight the cat, who was still sleeping before the gate, was awakened by some water flung at her by the head rat, who could not make up his mind to open the doors.

"Here is the stone you wanted," said he, when the cat started up with a loud mew; "if you will hold up your paws I will drop it down." And so he did. "And now farewell," continued the rat; "you have a long way to go, and will do well to start before daybreak."

"Your counsel is good," replied the cat, smiling to itself; and putting the stone in her mouth, she went off to seek the falcon.

Now all this time neither the cat nor the falcon had had any food, and the falcon soon got tired carrying such a heavy burden. When night arrived he declared he could go no farther, but would spend it on the banks of a river.

"And it is my turn to take care of the stone," said he, "or it will seem as if you had done everything and I nothing."

"No, I got it, and I will keep it," answered the cat, who was tired and cross; and they began a fine quarrel. But, unluckily, in the midst of it, the cat raised her voice, and the stone fell into the ear of a big fish which happened to be swimming by, and though both the cat and the falcon sprang into the water after it, they were too late.

Half drowned, and more than half choked, the two faithful servants scrambled back to land again. The falcon flew to a tree and spread his wings in the sun to dry, but the cat, after giving herself a good shake, began to scratch up the sandy banks and to throw the bits into the stream.

"What are you doing that for?" asked a little fish. "Do you know that you are making the water quite muddy?"

"That doesn't matter at all to me," answered the cat. "I am going to fill up all the river, so that the fishes may die."

"That is very unkind, as we have never done you any harm," replied the fish. "Why are you so angry with us?"

"Because one of you has got a stone of mine—a stone with strange signs upon it—which dropped into the water. If you will promise to get it back for me, why, perhaps I will leave your river alone."

"I will certainly try," answered the fish in a great hurry; "but you must have a little patience, as it may not be an easy task." And in an instant his scales might be seen flashing quickly along.

The fish swam as fast as he could to the sea, which was not far distant, and calling together all his relations who lived in the neighborhood, he told them of the terrible danger which threatened the dwellers in the river.

"None of us has got it," said the fishes, shaking their heads; "but in the bay yonder there is a tuna who, although he is so old, always goes everywhere. He will be able to tell you about it, if anyone can." So the little fish swam off to the tuna, and again related his story.

"Why *I* was up that river only a few hours ago!" cried the tuna; "and as I was coming back something fell into my ear, and there it is still, for I went to sleep when I got home and forgot all about it. Perhaps it may be what you want." And stretching up his tail he whisked out the stone.

"Yes, I think that must be it," said the fish with joy. And taking the stone in his mouth he carried it to the place where the cat was waiting for him.

"I am much obliged to you," said the cat, as the fish laid the stone on the sand, "and to reward you, I will let your river alone." And she mounted the falcon's back, and they flew to their master.

Ah, how glad he was to see them again with the magic stone in their possession. In a moment he had wished for a palace, but *this* time it was of green marble; and then he wished for the princess and her ladies to occupy it. And there they lived for many years, and when the old king died the princess's husband reigned in his stead.

SCANDINAVIA

Kisa

This story was adapted from Dr. Adeline Rittershaus's 1902 book, Die Neuisländischen Volksmärchen (Scandinavian Folktales), *for* The Brown Fairy
Book, *which was edited by Andrew Lang and published in 1904. Dr. Rittershaus found this story in an 1866 manuscript which is in the Landesbibliothek of Reykjavik, Iceland.*

Once upon a time there lived a queen who had a beautiful cat, the
color of smoke, with china-blue eyes, which she was very fond of. The cat
was constantly with her, and ran after her wherever she went, and even sat
up proudly by her side when she drove out in her fine glass coach.

"Oh, pussy," said the queen one day, "you are happier than I am! For
you have a dear little kitten just like yourself, and I have nobody to play
with but you."

"Don't cry," answered the cat, "laying her paw on her mistress's arm.
Crying never does any good. I will see what can be done."

The cat was as good as her word. As soon as she returned from her
drive she trotted off to the forest to consult a fairy who dwelt there, and
very soon after the queen had a little girl, who seemed made out of snow
and sunbeams. The queen was delighted, and soon the baby began to take
notice of the kitten as she jumped about the room, and would not go to
sleep at all unless the kitten lay curled up beside her.

Two or three months went by, and though the baby was still a baby,
the kitten was fast becoming a cat, and one evening when, as usual, the
nurse came to look for her, to put her in the baby's cot, she was nowhere
to be found. What a hunt there was for that kitten, to be sure! The servants, each anxious to find her, as the queen was certain to reward the
lucky man, searched in the most impossible places. Boxes were opened
that would hardly have held the kitten's paw; books were taken from

174

bookshelves, lest the kitten should have got behind them, drawers were pulled out, for perhaps the kitten might have got shut in. But it was all no use. The kitten had plainly run away, and nobody could tell if it would ever choose to come back.

Years passed away, and one day, when the princess was playing ball in the garden, she happened to throw her ball farther than usual, and it fell into a clump of rose-bushes. The princess of course ran after it at once, and she was stooping down to feel if it was hidden in the long grass, when she heard a voice calling her: "Ingibjorg! Ingibjorg!" it said, "have you forgotten me? I am Kisa, your sister!"

"But I never had a sister," answered Ingibjorg, very much puzzled; for she knew nothing of what had taken place so long ago.

"Don't you remember how I always slept in your cot beside you, and how you cried till I came? But girls have no memories at all! Why, I could find my way straight up to that cot this moment, if I was once inside the palace."

"Why did you go away then?" asked the princess. But before Kisa could answer, Ingibjorg's attendants arrived breathless on the scene, and were so horrified at the sight of a strange cat that Kisa plunged into the bushes and went back to the forest.

The princess was very much vexed with her ladies-in-waiting for frightening away her old playfellow, and told the queen who came to her room every evening to bid her good-night.

"Yes, it is quite true what Kisa said," answered the queen; "I should have liked to see her again. Perhaps, some day, she will return, and then you must bring her to me."

Next morning it was very hot, and the princess declared that she must go and play in the forest, where it was always cool, under the big shady trees. As usual, her attendants let her do anything she pleased, and, sitting down on a mossy bank where a little stream tinkled by, they soon fell sound asleep. The princess saw with delight that they would pay no heed to her, and wandered on and on, expecting every moment to see some fairies dancing round a ring, or some little brown elves peeping at her from behind a tree. But, alas! she met none of these; instead, a horrible giant came out of his cave and ordered her to follow him. The princess felt much afraid, as he was so big and ugly, and began to be sorry that she had not stayed within reach of help; but as there was no use in disobeying the giant, she walked meekly behind.

They went a long way, and Ingibjorg grew very tired, and at length began to cry.

"I don't like girls who make horrid noises," said the giant, turning round. "But if you want to cry, I will give you something to cry for." And drawing an axe from his belt, he cut off both her feet, which he picked up and put in his pocket. Then he went away.

Poor Ingibjorg lay on the grass in terrible pain, and wondering if she should stay there till she died, as no one would know where to look for her. How long it was since she had set out in the morning she could not tell—it seemed years to her, of course; but the sun was still high in the heavens when she heard the sound of wheels, and then, with a great effort, for her throat was parched with fright and pain, she gave a shout.

"I am coming!" was the answer; and in another moment a cart made its way through the trees, driven by Kisa, who used her tail as a whip to urge the horse to go faster. Directly Kisa saw Ingibjorg lying there, she jumped quickly down, and lifting the girl carefully in her two front paws, laid her upon some soft hay, and drove back to her own little hut.

In the corner of the room was a pile of cushions, and these Kisa arranged as a bed. Ingibjorg, who by this time was nearly fainting from all she had gone through, drank greedily some milk, and then sank back on the cushions while Kisa fetched some dried herbs from a cupboard, soaked them in warm water and tied them on the bleeding legs. The pain vanished at once, and Ingibjorg looked up and smiled at Kisa.

"You will go to sleep now," said the cat, "and you will not mind if I leave you for a little while. I will lock the door, and no one can hurt you." But before she had finished the princess was asleep. Then Kisa got into the cart, which was standing at the door, and catching up the reins, drove straight to the giant's cave.

Leaving her cart behind some trees, Kisa crept gently up to the open door, and, crouching down, listened to what the giant was telling his wife, who was at supper with him.

"The first day that I can spare I shall just go back and kill her," he said; "it would never do for people in the forest to know that a mere girl can defy me!" And he and his wife were so busy calling Ingibjorg all sorts of names for her bad behavior, that they never noticed Kisa stealing into a dark corner, and upsetting a whole bag of salt into the great pot before the fire.

"Dear me, how thirsty I am!" cried the giant by-and-by.

"So am I," answered his wife. "I do wish I had not taken that last spoonful of broth; I am sure something was wrong with it."

"If I don't get some water I shall die," went on the giant. And rushing out of the cave, followed by his wife, he ran down the path which led to the river.

Then Kisa entered the hut, and lost no time in searching every hole till she came upon some grass, under which Ingibjorg's feet were hidden, and putting them in her cart, drove back again to her own hut.

Ingibjorg was thankful to see her, for she had lain, too frightened to sleep, trembling at every noise.

"Oh, is it you?" she cried joyfully, as Kisa turned the key. And the cat came in, holding up the two neat little feet in their silver slippers.

"In two minutes they shall be as tight as ever they were!" said Kisa. And taking some strings of the magic grass which the giant had carelessly heaped on them, she bound the feet on to the legs above.

"Of course you won't be able to walk for some time; you must not expect that," she continued. "But if you are very good, perhaps, in about a week, I may carry you home again."

And so she did; and when the cat drove the cart up to the palace gate, lashing the horse furiously with her tail, and the king and queen saw their lost daughter sitting beside her, they declared that no reward could be too great for the person who had brought her out of the giant's hands.

"We will talk about that by-and-by," said the cat, as she made her best bow, and turned her horse's head.

The princess was very unhappy when Kisa left her without even bidding her farewell. She would neither eat nor drink, nor take any notice of all the beautiful dresses her parents bought for her.

"She will die, unless we can make her laugh," one whispered to the other. "Is there anything in the world that we have left untried?"

"Nothing, except marriage," answered the king. And he invited all the handsomest young men he could think of to the palace, and bade the princess choose a husband from among them.

It took her some time to decide which she admired the most, but at last she fixed upon a young prince, whose eyes were like the pools in the forest, and his hair of bright gold. The king and the queen were greatly pleased, as the young man was the son of a neighboring king, and they gave orders that a splendid feast should be got ready.

When the marriage was over, Kisa suddenly stood before them, and Ingibjorg rushed forward and clasped her in her arms.

"I have come to claim my reward," said the cat. "Let me sleep for this night at the foot of your bed."

"Is that *all?*" asked Ingibjorg, much disappointed.

"It is enough," answered the cat. And when the morning dawned, it was no cat that lay upon the bed, but a beautiful princess.

"My mother and I were both enchanted by a spiteful fairy," said she, "and we could not free ourselves till we had done some kindly deed that had never been wrought before. My mother died without ever finding a chance of doing anything new, but I took advantage of the evil act of the giant to make you as whole as ever."

Then they were all more delighted than before, and the princess lived in the court until she, too, married, and went away to govern one of her own.

NETHERLANDS

The Cat and the Cradle

This story is from Dutch Fairy Tales *by William E. Griffis (1843–1928), which was published in 1918. Griffis, a clergyman and the author of numerous books, is chiefly known for his nonfiction books on Japan.*

In the early ages, when our far-off ancestors lived in the woods, ate acorns, slept in caves, and dressed in the skins of wild animals, they had no horses, cows or cats. Their only pets and helpers were dogs. The men and the dogs were more like each other than they are now.

However, they knew about bees. So the women gathered honey and from it they made mead. Not having any sugar, the children enjoyed tasting honey more than anything else, and it was the only sweet thing they had.

By and by, cows were brought into the country and the Dutch soil being good for grass, the cows had plenty to eat. When these animals multiplied, the people drank milk and learned to make cheese and butter. So the Dutch boys and girls grew fat and healthy.

The oxen were so strong that they could pull logs of wood or draw a plow. So, little by little, the forests were cut down and grassy meadows, full of bright colored flowers, took their place. Houses were built and the people were rich and happy.

Yet there were still many cruel men and bad people in the land. Sometimes, too, floods came and drowned the cattle and covered the fields with sand, or salt water. In such times, food was very scarce. Thus it happened that not all the babies born could live, or every little child be fed. The baby girls especially were often left to die, because war was common and only boys, that grew into strong warriors, were wanted.

It grew to be a custom that families would hold a council and decide whether the baby should be raised or not. But if any one should give the infant even a tiny drop of milk, or food of any kind, it was allowed to live and grow up. If no one gave it milk or honey, it died. No matter how much a mother might love her baby, she was not allowed to put milk to its lips if the grandmother or elders forbade it. The young bride coming into her husband's home always had to obey his mother, for she was now as a daughter and one of the family. All lived together in one house, and the grandmother ruled all the women and girls that were under one roof.

This was the way of the world, when our ancestors were pagans, and not always as kind to little babies as our own mothers and fathers are now. Many times was the old grandmother angry, when her son had taken a wife and a girl was born. If the old woman expected a grandson, who should grow up and be a fighter, with sword and spear, and it turned out to be a girl, she was mad as fire. Often the pretty bride, brought into the house, had a hard time of it with her husband's mother, if she did not in time have a baby boy. In those days a "Herman," a "War Man" and "German" were one and the same word.

Now when the good missionaries came into the land of Friesland, one of the first of the families to receive the gospel was one named Altfrid. With his bride, who also became a Christian, Altfrid helped the missionary to build a church. By and by, a sweet little baby was born in the family and the parents were very happy. They loved the little thing sent from God, as fathers and mothers love their children now.

But when some one went and told the pagan grandmother that the new baby was a girl instead of a boy, the old woman flew into a rage and would have gone at once to get hold of the baby and put it to death. Her lameness, however, made her move slowly, and she could not find her crutch; for the midwife, who knew the bad temper of the grandmother, had purposely hid it. The old woman was angry, because she did not want any more females in the big house, where she thought there were already too many mouths to fill. Food was hard to get, and there were not enough war men to defend the tribe. She meant to get to the new baby and throw it to the wolves. The old grandmother was a pagan and still worshipped the cruel gods that loved fighting. She hated the new religion, because it taught gentleness and peace.

But the midwife, who was a neighbor, feared that the old woman was malicious, and so she had hid her crutch. This she did, so that if the baby was a girl, she could save its life. The midwife was a good woman, who had been taught that the Great Creator loves little girls as well as boys.

So when the midwife heard the grandmother storm and rave, while hunting for the crutch, she ran first to the honey jar, dipped her forefinger in it and put some drops of honey on the baby's tongue. Then she passed it out the window to some women friends who were waiting outside. She knew the law, that if a child tasted food, it must be allowed to live.

The kind women took the baby to their home and fed it carefully. A hole was drilled in the small end of a cow's horn and the warm milk, fresh from the cow, was allowed to fall, drop by drop, into the baby's mouth. In a few days the little one was able to suck its breakfast slowly out of the horn, while one of the girls held it. So the baby grew bigger every day. All the time it was carefully hidden.

The foolish old grandmother was foiled, for she could never find out where the baby girl was, which all the time was growing strong and plump. Her father secretly made her a cradle, and he and the babe's mother came often to see their child. Every one called her Honig-jé, or Little Honey.

Now about this time, cats were brought into the country and the children made such pets of them that some of the cows seemed to be jealous of the attentions paid to Pussy and the kittens. These were the days when cows and people all lived under one long roof. The children learned to tell the time of day, whether it was morning, noon, or night by looking into the cat's eyes. These seemed to open and shut, very much as if they had doors.

The fat pussy, which was brought into the house where Honig-jé was, seemed to be very fond of the little girl, and the two, the cat and the child, played much together. It was often said that the cat loved the baby even more than her own kittens. Everyone called the affectionate animal by the nickname of Dub-belt-jé, which means Little Double, because this puss was twice as loving as most cat mothers are. When her own furry little babies were very young, she carried them from one place to another in her mouth. But this way, of holding kittens, she never tried on the baby. She seemed to know better. Indeed, Dub-belt-jé often wondered why human babies were born so naked and helpless; for at an age when her kittens could feed themselves and run about and play with their tails and with each other, Honig-jé was not yet able to crawl.

But other dangers were in store for the little girl. One day, when the men were out hunting, and the women went to the woods to gather nuts and acorns, a great flood came. The waters washed away the houses, so that everything floated into the great river, and then down towards the sea.

What had, what would, become of our baby? So thought the parents of Honig-jé, when they came back to find the houses swept away and no sign of their little daughter. Dub-belt-jé and her kittens, and all the cows, were gone too.

Now it had happened that when the flood came and the house crashed down, baby was sound asleep. The cat, leaving its kittens, that were now pretty well grown up, leaped up and on to the top of the cradle and the two floated off together. Pretty soon they found themselves left alone, with nothing in sight that was familiar, except one funny thing. That was a wooden shoe, in which was a fuzzy little yellow chicken hardly four days old. It had been playing in the shoe, when the floods came and swept it off from under the very beak of the old hen, which, with all her other chicks, was speedily drowned.

On and on, the raging flood bore baby and puss, until dark night came down. For hours more they drifted until, happily, the cradle was swept into an eddy in front of a village. There it spun round and round, and might soon have been borne into the greater flood, which seemed to roar louder as the waters rose.

Now a cat can see sometimes in the night, better even than in the day, for the darker it becomes, the wider open the eyes of puss. In bright sunshine, at noon, the inside doors of the cat's eyes close to a narrow slit, while at night these doors open wide. That is the reason why, in the days before clocks and watches were made, the children could tell about the time of day by looking at the cat's eyes. Sometimes they named their pussy Klok'-oog, which means Clock Eye, or Bell Eye, for bell clocks are older than clocks with a dial, and because in Holland the bells ring out the hours and quarter hours.

Puss looked up and saw the church tower looming up in the dark. At once she began to meouw and caterwaul with all her might. She hoped that someone in one of the houses near the river bank might catch the sound. But none seemed to hear or heed. At last, when Puss was nearly dead with howling, a light appeared at one of the windows. This showed that someone was up and moving. It was a boy, who was named Dirck, after the saint Theodoric, who had first, long ago built a church in the village. Then Puss opened her mouth and lungs again and set up a regular cat-scream. This wakened all her other relatives in the village and every

Tom and Kitty made answer, until there was a cat concert of meouws and caterwauls.

The boy heard, rushed downstairs, and, opening the door, listened. The wind blew out his candle, but the brave lad was guided by the sound which Pussy made. Reaching the bank, the boy threw off his wooden klomps, plunged into the boiling waters, and, seizing the cradle, towed it ashore. Then he woke up his mother and showed her his prize. The way that baby laughed and crowed, and patted the horn of milk, and kicked up its toes in delight over the warm milk, which was brought, was a joy to see. Near the hearth, in the middle of the floor, Dub-belt-jé, the cat, was given some straw for a bed and, after purring joyfully, was soon, like the baby, sound asleep.

Thus the cat warned the boy, and the boy saved the baby, which was quite welcome in a family where there were no girls, but only a boy. When Honig-jé grew up to be a young woman, she looked as lovely as a princess and in the church was married to Dirck! It was the month of April and all the world was waking to flowers, when the wedding procession came out of the church and the air was sweet with the opening of the buds.

Before the next New Year's day arrived, there lay in the same cradle, and put to sleep over the same rockers, a baby boy. When they brought him to the font, the good grandmother named him Luid-i-ger. He grew up to be the great missionary, whose name in Friesland is, even today, after a thousand years, a household word. He it was who drove out bad fairies, vile enchanters, wicked spirits, and terrible diseases. Best of all, he banished "eye-bite," which was the name the people gave to witchcraft. Luid-i-ger, also, made it hard for the naughty elves and spirits that delude men.

After this, it was easy for all the good spirits, which live in kind hearts and noble lives, to multiply and prosper. The wolves were driven away or killed off and became very few, while the cattle and sheep multiplied, until everybody could have a woollen coat, and there was a cow to every person in the land.

But the people still suffered from the floods, which from time to time drowned the cattle and human beings, and the ebb tides, which carried everything out to sea. Then the good missionary taught the men how to build dykes, which kept out the ocean and made the water of the rivers stay between the banks. The floods became fewer and fewer and at last rarely happened. Then Santa Klaas arrived, to keep alive in the hearts of the people the spirit of love and kindness and good cheer forever.

At last, when nearly a hundred years had passed away, Honig-jé, once the girl baby, and then the dear old lady, who was kind to everybody and prepared the way for Santa Klaas, died. Then, also, Dub-belt-jé, the cat, which had nine lives in one, died with her. They buried the old lady under the church floor and stuffed the pussy that everybody—kittens, boys, girls, and people—loved. By and by, when the cat's tail and fur fell to pieces, and ears tumbled off, and its glass eyes dropped out, a skillful artist chiseled a statue of Dub-belt-jé, which stands over the tomb in the church. Every year, on Santa Klaas Day, December sixth, the children put a new collar around the statue's neck and talk about the cat that saved a baby's life.

ITALY

The Colony of Cats

This version of this fairy tale was included in the Andrew Lang's The Crimson Fairy Book, *which was published in 1903. It is interesting to note the similarities between this story from Italy (probably Sicily) and "The Two Caskets," which is from Scandinavia.*

Long, long ago, as far back as the time when animals spoke, there lived a community of cats in a deserted house they had taken possession of not far from a large town. They had everything they could possibly desire for their comfort, they were well fed and well lodged, and if by any chance an unlucky mouse was stupid enough to venture in their way, they caught it, not to eat it, but for the pure pleasure of catching it. The old people of the town related how they had heard their parents speak of a time when the whole country was so overrun with rats and mice that there was not so much as a grain of corn nor an ear of maize to be gathered in the fields; and it might be out of gratitude to the cats who had rid the country of these plagues that their descendants were allowed to live in peace. No one knows where they got the money to pay for everything, nor who paid it, for all this happened so very long ago. But one thing is certain, they were rich enough to keep a servant; for though they lived very happily together, and did not scratch nor fight more than human beings would have done, they were not clever enough to do the housework themselves, and preferred at all events to have someone to cook their meat, which they would have scorned to eat raw. Not only were they very difficult to please about the housework, but most women quickly tired of living alone with only cats for companions, consequently they never kept a servant long; and it had become a saying in the town, when anyone found herself reduced to her last penny: "I will go and live with the cats," and so many a poor woman actually did.

185

Now Lizina was not happy at home, for her mother, who was a widow, was much fonder of her elder daughter; so that often the younger one fared very badly, and had not enough to eat, while the elder could have everything she desired, and if Lizina dared to complain she was certain to have a good beating.

At last the day came when she was at the end of her courage and patience, and exclaimed to her mother and sister:

"As you hate me so much you will be glad to be rid of me, so I am going to live with the cats!"

"Be off with you!" cried her mother, seizing an old broom-handle from behind the door. Poor Lizina did not wait to be told twice, but ran off at once and never stopped till she reached the door of the cats' house. Their cook had left them that very morning, with her face all scratched, the result of such a quarrel with the head of the house that he had very nearly scratched out her eyes. Lizina therefore was warmly welcomed, and she set to work at once to prepare the dinner, not without many misgivings as to the tastes of the cats, and whether she would be able to satisfy them.

Going to and fro about her work, she found herself frequently hindered by a constant succession of cats who appeared one after another in the kitchen to inspect the new servant; she had one in front of her feet, another perched on the back of her chair while she peeled the vegetables, a third sat on the table beside her, and five or six others prowled about among the pots and pans on the shelves against the wall. The air resounded with their purring, which meant that they were pleased with their new maid, but Lizina had not yet learned to understand their language, and often she did not know what they wanted her to do. However, as she was a good, kind-hearted girl, she set to work to pick up the little kittens which tumbled about on the floor, she patched up quarrels, and nursed on her lap a big tabby—the oldest of the community—which had a lame paw. All these kindnesses could hardly fail to make a favorable impression on the cats, and it was even better after a while, when she had had time to grow accustomed to their strange ways. Never had the house been kept so clean, the meats so well served, nor the sick cats so well cared for. After a time they had a visit from an old cat, whom they called their father, who lived by himself in a barn at the top of the hill, and came down from time to time to inspect the little colony. He too was much taken with Lizina, and inquired, on first seeing her: "Are you well served by this nice, black-eyed little person?" and the cats answered with one voice: "Oh, yes, Father Gatto, we have never had so good a servant!"

At each of his visits the answer was always the same; but after a time the old cat, who was very observant, noticed that the little maid had grown to look sadder and sadder. "What is the matter, my child—has anyone been unkind to you?" he asked one day, when he found her crying in her kitchen. She burst into tears and answered between her sobs: "Oh, no! they are all very good to me; but I long for news from home, and I pine to see my mother and my sister."

Old Gatto, being a sensible old cat, understood the little servant's feelings. "You shall go home," he said, "and you shall not come back here unless you please. But first you must be rewarded for all your kind services to my children. Follow me down into the inner cellar, where you have never yet been, for I always keep it locked and carry the key away with me."

Lizina looked round her in astonishment as they went down into the great vaulted cellar underneath the kitchen. Before her stood the big earthenware water jars, one of which contained oil, the other a liquid shining like gold. "In which of these jars shall I dip you?" asked Father Gatto, with a grin that showed all his sharp white teeth, while his moustaches stood out straight on either side of his face. The little maid looked at the two jars from under her long dark lashes: "In the oil jar!" she answered timidly, thinking to herself: "I could not ask to be bathed in gold."

But Father Gatto replied: "No, no; you have deserved something better than that." And seizing her in his strong paws he plunged her into the liquid gold. Wonder of wonders! When Lizina came out of the jar she shone from head to foot like the sun in the heavens on a fine summer's day. Her pretty pink cheeks and long black hair alone kept their natural color, otherwise she had become like a statue of pure gold. Father Gatto purred loudly with satisfaction. "Go home," he said, "and see your mother and sisters; but take care if you hear the cock crow to turn towards it; if on the contrary the ass brays, you must look the other way."

The little maid, having gratefully kissed the white paw of the old cat, set off for home; but just as she got near her mother's house the cock crowed, and quickly she turned towards it. Immediately a beautiful golden star appeared on her forehead, crowning her glossy black hair. At the same time the ass began to bray, but Lizina took care not to look over the fence into the field where the donkey was feeding. Her mother and sister, who were in front of their house, uttered cries of admiration and astonishment when they saw her, and their cries became still louder when Lizina, taking her handkerchief from her pocket, drew out also a handful of gold.

For some days the mother and her two daughters lived very happily together, for Lizina had given them everything she had brought away except her golden clothing, for that would not come off, in spite of all the efforts of her sister who was madly jealous of her good fortune. The golden star, too, could not be removed from her forehead. But all the gold pieces she drew from her pockets had found their way to her mother and sister.

"I will go now and see what I can get out of the cats," said Peppina, the elder girl, one morning, as she took Lizina's basket and fastened her pockets into her own skirt. "I should like some of the cats' gold for myself," she thought, as she left her mother's house before the sun rose.

The cat colony had not yet taken another servant, for they knew they could never get one to replace Lizina, whose loss they had not yet ceased to mourn. When they heard that Peppina was her sister, they all ran to meet her. "She is not the least like her," the kittens whispered among themselves.

"Hush, be quiet!" the older cats said; "all servants cannot be pretty."

No, decidedly she was not at all like Lizina. Even the most reasonable and large-minded of the cats soon acknowledged that.

The very first day she shut the kitchen door in the face of the tom-cats who used to enjoy watching Lizina at her work, and a young and mischievous cat who jumped in by the open kitchen window and alighted on the table got such a blow with the rolling-pin that he squalled for an hour.

With every day that passed the household became more and more aware of its misfortune.

The work was as badly done as the servant was surly and disagreeable; in the corners of the rooms there were collected heaps of dust; spiders' webs hung from the ceilings and in front of the window-panes; the beds were hardly ever made, and the feather beds, so beloved by the old and feeble cats, had never once been shaken since Lizina left the house. At Father Gatto's next visit he found the whole colony in a state of uproar.

"Caesar has one paw so badly swollen that it looks as if it were broken," said one. "Peppina kicked him with her great wooden shoes on. Hector has an abscess in his back where a wooden chair was flung at him; and Agrippina's three little kittens have died of hunger beside their mother, because Peppina forgot them in their basket up in the attic. There is no putting up with the creature—do send her away, Father Gatto! Lizina herself would not be angry with us; she must know very well what her sister is like."

"Come here," said Father Gatto, in his most severe tones to Peppina. And he took her down into the cellar and showed her the same two great jars that he had showed Lizina. "In which of these shall I dip you?" he asked; and she made haste to answer: "In the liquid gold," for she was no more modest than she was good and kind.

Father Gatto's yellow eyes darted fire. "You have not deserved it," he uttered, in a voice like thunder, and seizing her he flung her into the jar of oil, where she was nearly suffocated. When she came to the surface screaming and struggling, the vengeful cat seized her again and rolled her in the ash-heap on the floor; then when she rose, dirty, blinded, and disgusting to behold, he thrust her from the door, saying: "Begone, and when you meet a braying ass be careful to turn your head towards it."

Stumbling and raging, Peppina set off for home, thinking herself fortunate to find a stick by the wayside with which to support herself. She was within sight of her mother's house when she heard in the meadow on the right, the voice of a donkey loudly braying. Quickly she turned her head towards it, and at the same time put her hand up to her forehead, where, waving like a plume, was a donkey's tail. She ran home to her mother at the top of her speed, yelling with rage and despair; and it took Lizina two hours with a big basin of hot water and two cakes of soap to get rid of the layer of ashes with which Father Gatto had adorned her. As for the donkey's tail, it was impossible to get rid of that; it was as firmly fixed on her forehead as was the golden star on Lizina's. Their mother was furious. She first beat Lizina unmercifully with the broom, then she took her to the mouth of the well and lowered her into it, leaving her at the bottom weeping and crying for help.

Before this happened, however, the king's son in passing the mother's house had seen Lizina sitting sewing in the parlor, and had been dazzled by her beauty. After coming back two or three times, he at last ventured to approach the window and to whisper in the softest voice: "Lovely maiden, will you be my bride?" and she had answered: "I will."

Next morning, when the prince arrived to claim his bride, he found her wrapped in a large white veil. "It is so that maidens are received from their parents' hands," said the mother, who hoped to make the king's son marry Peppina in place of her sister, and had fastened the donkey's tail round her head like a lock of hair under the veil. The prince was young and a little timid, so he made no objections, and seated Peppina in the carriage beside him.

Their way led past the old house inhabited by the cats, who were all at the window, for the report had got about that the prince was going to marry the most beautiful maiden in the world, on whose forehead shone a golden star, and they knew that this could only be their adored Lizina. As the carriage slowly passed in front of the old house, where cats from all parts of the world seemed to be gathered, a song burst from every throat:

> Mew, mew, mew!
> Prince, look quick behind you!
> In the well is fair Lizina,
> And you've got nothing but Peppina.

When be heard this the coachman, who understood the cat's language better than the prince, his master, stopped his horses and asked, "Does your highness know what the grimalkins are saying?" And the song broke forth again louder than ever.

With a turn of his hand the prince threw back the veil, and discovered the puffed-up, swollen face of Peppina, with the donkey's tail twisted round her head. "Ah, traitress!" he exclaimed, and ordering the horses to be turned round, he drove the elder daughter, quivering with rage, to the old woman who had sought to deceive him. With his hand on the hilt of his sword he demanded Lizina in so terrific a voice that the mother hastened to the well to draw her prisoner out. Lizina's clothing and her star shone so brilliantly that when the prince led her home to the king, his father, the whole palace was lit up. Next day they were married, and lived happy ever after; and all the cats, headed by old Father Gatto, were present at the wedding.

The Gray Cat

Jane G. Austin (1831–1894) wrote this story, along with five other fairy tales, in her book Fairy Dreams; or, Wanderings in Elf-Land, *which was pub-lished in 1859. She wrote over twenty books, most of which deal with New England history. She lived in Boston, Massachusetts, and was friends with Nathaniel Hawthorne, Ralph Waldo Emerson, and Louisa May Alcott.*

From these and the travelers the youth heard many stories of the great world, its wonders and its pleasures, and several times his visitors had invited him to go with them and see the marvels which they described; but Ernest always shook his head, saying, "No, no, I have no place in this great world of yours; nobody would know or care for me. Here I have friends on every side—the loons, the gulls, the wild geese, and the ospreys know me and like me. I think even the waves feel acquainted with me, and I know that the fish do. No, I will stay."

So the tourists and the sailors went their way, and Ernest remained alone.

At last a whole year went by, and brought no visitors. Autumn, winter, spring, and summer passed, and autumn had come again, without a single word having broken the silence which reigned about the little hut. No voice but the solemn ocean murmur.

At first Ernest liked this, and dreaded the arrival of a stranger; but by-and-by he began to wonder why no one came, and then to look longingly up and down the beach and out to sea, in hopes to see some one, but he looked in vain.

At last, when the pleasant summer was quite gone, and the cold and dreary autumn winds began to blow, lashing the sea into foam and whistling drearily down the chimney of the little hut, Ernest grew very sad and discontented. He roamed uneasily up and down the beach, but never

191

could make up his mind to leave it and turn his steps inland, and always at night he found himself back at his little cabin.

One night, when the winds and the waves together were making such a din and commotion that one could hardly have heard a cannon at a quarter of a mile's distance, Ernest sat gloomily alone brooding over his driftwood fire, which danced and flickered uneasily as the draughts from door or windows fanned it. Ernest had no clock or watch, nor would he have known the use of it if he had; but after sitting quite motionless for a long time staring at the fire, which now was almost out, he began to feel as if it were bedtime, and was wearily rising from his chair to look out once more at the night, when from the window behind him he heard a faint and prolonged

"M-e-w!"

Turning hurriedly about, Ernest ran to the window and threw it open, upon which, with a pleased and grateful purr, a beautiful gray cat stepped upon the table which stood beneath the window, and, looking in the young man's wondering face, remarked again,

"M-e-w!"

"You said that before, but I don't know what it means," said Ernest gaily, who, although he had never seen a real cat, had heard them described and had seen pictures of them, so he at once guessed what his visitor was, and was well pleased that at last he had a companion.

"Let me see; perhaps 'mew' means fish," continued he, going to a shelf in the corner, which served him for a pantry, and taking a wooden platter with the remains of a boiled fish upon it. This he set upon the table in front of the gray cat, who, first rubbing herself with a melodious purr against his hand, applied herself to the fish, and daintily ate some of the best pieces, then drank a little water which Ernest offered her with an apology for having no milk to give, which he said he had heard ladies of her degree were very fond of. "But," as he said, "since I not only have no milk, but never saw it, I am very glad to see that your highness can drink water."

The cat, having finished her meal, leaped softly to the floor, and, after walking slowly round the room, looking attentively at every thing in it, she sprang gracefully into Ernest's arm chair (which was indeed the only chair in the whole house), and, seating herself upright in the middle of the cushion, began to wash her face and paws with her little red tongue.

"That's right, my queen, don't be ceremonious," said Ernest, laughing aloud. "To be sure you have left me nothing to sit on except this log of wood, but then you are company, and should have the best. Pray make yourself entirely at home. I am very sorry I have no fine napkin to offer you to wipe those pretty paws upon now that you have washed them, but perhaps you can dry them by the fire. Let me make it up."

So Ernest threw some more wood upon the fire; and then, seating himself upon a great block in the opposite chimney corner, leaned his elbows upon his knees and took an attentive survey of his visitor, who, having completed her toilet, sat regarding the fire with half-closed eyes, purring softly a little tune of her own composition, and beating time with her long tail.

She was a very pretty cat, with fur of a rich dark gray, except her paws and face, which were pure white, and a crown or circle about her head, of an indescribable glittering appearance. It was this crown-like circle which had induced Ernest to call her highness and queen.

After looking at her a while, the young man reached across the fire, and taking the cat gently up, placed her in his lap and began to smooth her rich fur and fondle her, but in spite of all his endeavors to hold her, Pussy glided from his grasp, and with noiseless leap regained her position in the easy-chair.

"You don't like familiarity—mustn't be handled, eh?" said Ernest. "Your majesty is very unkind, I think; but perhaps when we are better acquainted—"

Ernest stopped thunderstruck. It was just twelve o'clock, although he did not know it; and at the moment when the clock, had there been one, would have struck the hour, a cloud of golden sparks rose from the circlet upon the cat's head and filled the whole room, so that Ernest closed his eyes and covered his face with his hands.

In a moment, however, he looked up and rubbed his eyes. The flaming sparks no longer blinded him, but still he doubted his own sight, for there before him, there where a moment before he had seen the gray cat, he now beheld, seated in his old armchair, as if on a throne, a beautiful and majestic woman, in the first bloom of youth and loveliness.

Her long, wide dress, which flowed upon the ground at each side, was a rich, soft velvet of a beautiful silver-gray color, and from its loose sleeves and beneath its hem peeped the smallest and whitest of hands and feet. The beautiful face was surrounded by long, dark hair, and in a circle about her head was the glittering, crown-like appearance which Ernest had noticed on the cat's head. It did not seem of any substance, like gold, for instance, but merely light and color. The large, light-colored eyes of the beautiful stranger were fixed anxiously upon Ernest, as if waiting for him to speak.

At last he stammered out:

"Are you—can it be—but it was a cat!"

"Yes, it was a cat," replied the sweetest voice in the world, "but it was also me, Ernest. I am the princess Phelia, only daughter of the king of Cat-land. All my race have the privilege of assuming at will the human form or the cat form. The nobility and royalty generally appear as men and women, only assuming the cat form in play or as a disguise; but vast numbers of our subjects of the inferior order retain the cat form altogether, and as such live unsuspected among men.

"As for me, I never was degraded from the human form until in an unhappy hour I wandered from my father's kingdom into that of our neighbor, the Gold King. Here I met his daughter Oriphera, who is an enchantress, and of a very bad disposition. She hated me beside, because she had heard that I was more beautiful than she. So snatching from my head the crown which I always wore as a badge of my rank, she threw some water in my face and said:

"'Take your cat form, you miserable Pussy, and retain it for the rest of your life, except during the half hour between twelve and one o'clock on Halloween. You never shall be released from this spell unless you can find a young man twenty-five years of age, who has never looked on woman's face, although free to go wherever he chooses, and who shall be able to take from me this crown, and replace it on your head before two years from this day.'

"As she finished she threw some more water upon me (I never could bear to be wet), and with a mew of grief and anger I ran away as fast as I could go. Of course I could not present myself at my father's court in such a disguise—I, who had always taken pride in being as un-catlike in my demeanor as possible; and so I wandered uneasily about the world, look-ing for the wonderful youth, who, although at perfect liberty to do so, had never looked upon a woman's face. Fortunately I was not to be mistaken for a common cat. Oriphera, although she stole my crown, could not deprive me of its light, which is my birthright, and by that I have always been recognized among cats as one of the royal family, although no one knew me as the unhappy Phelia.

"You may be sure I never omitted to ask every cat with whom I met if they had ever heard of a young man such as I described, but every one answered no, and I began to despair, for in one month more, the two years will be gone, and after that all aid is vain. But a few weeks ago I fell in with a seafaring cat, just returned from a whaling voyage, and he, in answer to my inquiries turned two somersets backward (which is equivalent among cats to clapping the hands among men), and said, "'I know the very man. My master, who is a sailor, was shipwrecked four years ago, and rescued by the very youth you want to find. I have often heard him speak of him.'

"My friend, the seafaring cat, then proceeded to tell me minutely where to find you; and, not to be tedious, I arrived very tired and discouraged at your window this evening." Here the princess, overcome by her feelings, covered her face with her hands and made a long pause—at last looking up and smiling sweetly upon Ernest, she said, "Now tell me, will you recover my crown from that—Oriphera, and make me the happiest of princesses?"

"Can you ask, revered princess? My life is yours; only tell me how and where to find her," exclaimed Ernest.

"The kingdom of Aura, her father, is in the center of the earth. You will find the entrance in the forest of Gnomes; but you can never get the crown unless you have the flute from the Cave of the Four Winds, to lull the Gnomes to sleep."

"And where is the Cave of the Four Winds, most beautiful of princesses?" asked Ernest, eagerly.

"It is on the top of—m-e-w!" This last word was uttered in a very angry voice, for just as Phelia had said "top of," her half hour of freedom closed and she was suddenly retransformed into a cat, without even power to add the one word which would have directed Ernest to the Cave of the Four Winds.

The young man was as much disappointed as the princess, but consoled himself by promising her that he would use so much diligence and make so many inquiries, that he did not doubt to soon meet with some one who could direct him to the cave where the magic flute was to be found.

To this, however, the cat only shook her head with a melancholy air, and Ernest felt quite discouraged again. Suddenly, as he sat thinking of every possible way in which to gain the desired information, a thought flashed into his head which made him clap his hands for joy.

"I have it, dear Phelia," said he. "The winds themselves shall carry me." He then went on to narrate that several years before he had been visited by an old man of wise and venerable appearance, who appeared to be very much delighted about something, and at last told him that he had traveled the world over to find the place where the Four Winds meet, for there is where they bring every thing that is lost in the world, and heap all up together, so that any man who can find this place may help himself to whatever he pleases. The old man had taken all he wished, which was a parchment containing the secret of a lost art—that of making gold; and he was going away content. He advised Ernest to go and search in this wonderful collection which abounded in wealth, honors, and all that men value. "But," said he, "you must be careful not to be caught there when the Four Winds meet at midnight, for you would be whirled up and carried away to their cave before you knew it."

Ernest had never thought much about the old man's advice till now, as he did not know exactly what he wanted to find, and had never lost any thing; but now he at once determined to go to the place described, and wait till midnight, when the Four Winds should meet to go home together, and would whirl him away with them.

He told his plan to the gray cat, who purred an assent; and then, as morning had broke, he led her out to the sea-shore and showed her a little cove where every evening she would find fish of some kind stranded among the rocks. He advised her to remain in the hut all the time when she was not at the cove, lest something should happen to harm her, and he faithfully promised, that, unless he lost his life in the attempt, she should see him with the missing crown in his hand before many days. Ernest then took leave of the disguised princess, who graciously presented her white paw for him to kiss, and set out upon his lonely travels.

All that day and the next he journeyed among the mountains which lay behind his little hut, but although he followed attentively the directions which the old man had given him, it was not until evening on the second day that he found himself approaching the place where the Four Winds meet.

This was a deep, rocky valley, approached from the north, south, east, and west by a deep, narrow ravine, which was the only means by which the valley was made accessible.

All the surface of the valley was strewn with the lost articles which the winds had swooped up and brought there. It would take a whole book, and a large one too, to tell half the precious things which lay scattered there; so I will only say that every thing which once was possessed, and now is hopelessly lost, was to be seen there, and a wonderful sight it was.

In the middle of the valley, however, was a small space entirely clear of everything, even of the last particle of dust. It was swept clean every night by the Four Winds when they met. Ernest knew in a moment that this must be the case; and when it grew too dark for him to see the curious things which lay scattered about him, he wrapped himself closely in the great cloak which he wore, and seated himself in the center of the clean-swept space.

Presently, overcome by fatigue, he fell asleep; nor did he stir till midnight, when he was awakened by a terrific rushing and roaring sound.

It was the Four Winds, each coming down his own ravine, and making for the common center. As they entered the valley Ernest could hear the lost things which they had brought pattering on the ground all about him as they were dropped; but in another moment the Winds were upon him, and almost senseless with the rapid motion, he found himself whirled round and round, and up and up, and on and on, till it seemed to him that they had flown beyond the stars. Suddenly he found himself dropped softly to the earth, and heard the Winds entering a cave above him with a hollow, rushing sound. Freeing himself with some difficulty from the cloak, which had been wound about him by the rapid, circular motion till it was almost as tight as his skin, Ernest looked about him.

He found himself upon the top of one of the highest mountains in the whole world, entirely inaccessible to man, bird, or beast. All around lay silence and perpetual snow, and it was owing to the soft bed of the latter, upon which he had fallen, that Ernest found himself unhurt. The cave in which dwelt the Four Winds lay above him, on the very crest of the mountain. Creeping softly up to the mouth of the cavern, he peeped cautiously in and, finding himself unheeded by the Winds, who were busy unloading themselves of the material for their suppers which they had brought with them, crept through the narrow entrance and crouched in a dark corner among some little Breezes which were sleeping there, and looked curiously about him.

The cave was divided into four quarters by two deep, narrow cracks or chasms, extending through its whole length and breadth. In each division stood a chair and table, and at each table now sat a Wind eating his supper. The reason of their being thus distinct Ernest perceived was because the temperature in which each one delighted would have been very disagreeable to either of his brothers, and so with the food and drink which stood before them.

The North Wind was voraciously eating a great lump composed of narrow strips of meat wound round and round into a ball, and then thoroughly saturated with melted grease. Before him stood a bucket filled with whale-oil, from which every few moments he drank greedily. His dress was the skin of a polar bear, with the fur outside, which he wrapped about him like a mantle. His face was red and full, his eyes, of a bright, clear blue, sparkled frostily, his long, light hair hung about his shoulders and his bushy, flax-colored beard and moustache were hung full of icicles.

His voice was deep and thunderous; and when he laughed, fragments of the solid rock were shaken off and fell about him.

Next to him sat the West Wind, whose name was Zephyrus, and Ernest at once decided that he was by far the most prepossessing of the four brothers. He was as tall as his neighbor the North, but not nearly so heavy, looking strong, but yet graceful. His hair and curling beard were of a dark brown, his eyes a dark gray, his teeth very white and sound, and he had a particularly fresh and healthy glow shining through the tan upon his cheeks. His voice and laugh were hearty and joyous, but not so deep and rough as that of the North Wind. His table was spread with ears of Indian corn, heads of wheat, a wild turkey, and a large ham. He was drinking from a little cask of Catawba wine.

Next came the South Wind, sometimes called Auster, a slight, dark-skinned youth, with straight, purple-black hair and glowing, dark eyes. He looked pale and languid, and reclined in his chair as if he wished it were a bed; his voice was soft and sighing, and he never laughed.

Upon the table before him were bunches of grapes, oranges, melons, bananas, and sugar-cane. For drink he pressed some orange juice into a jar, and then set one of the Breezes to fill it with snow, remarking at the same time with a sigh, that sherbet was the only luxury which he gained by living in this horribly cold cave with his brothers.

"Ho! ho!" laughed the North Wind. "Nothing could be more comfortable than this cave, if only you will keep at your proper distance, and not be melting me with your hot breath."

"I have to breathe as fast as I can to keep a little circle of air warm around my table," murmured the South. "If I did not, you and East would chill me to death."

"Yes, you always run away when I come," piped East. "How many times I have whistled with delight at seeing how everything would change before me when I come stealing along at noon, after you have been making a fine morning on earth. How the people begin to shiver and shut down the windows and put on their shawls—how the flowers wither up, and droop, and hang their heads—ph-e-w!"

Thus spake Eurus, the East Wind, a thin, sallow, unhappy looking person, with watery blue eyes, a peaked blue nose, and a withered, crooked form. He looked bilious and ill-natured, had a shrill, whining voice, and never laughed, although he whistled a great deal in a very sharp, ill-natured manner. His supper consisted of a little rice, a raw fish, which he had whipped up as he came sweeping over the Atlantic Ocean, and a great bowl of tea which he had brought from China.

Supper ended, the North Wind, whom his brothers addressed as Boreas, stretched himself, and said, "Well, I'm off! I have got some ships jammed up there near the Pole, and I'm going to blow 'em out. I wish these navigators, as they call themselves, would stay away. They come creeping along up there, and you always help them, Auster, which I think is very ill-natured of you; and then I have to get 'em out after they're blocked in, or if I don't come, the sailors plague my life out whistling for me. Pretty soon, too, I shall have to drive down the snow clouds. I have got a nice flock of them waiting up there at the Pole. I am going to make a tremendous winter of it."

"Yes, winter is your time, and spring is mine," said Eurus, the East Wind. "Auster and I, between us, will soon drive you from the field when we set about it. Just now, though, I have got a fine little lot of vessels to attend to on the Atlantic coast. I am going to drive them on the rocks, and then, how I'll whistle through the ropes—ph-e-w! They call some of the ropes shrouds—a capital name when I get hold of 'em. Then I have a good deal to do in China. I suppose they are waiting for me to get their ships out of the river. If I feel good-natured I'll do it; if not, I'll leave 'em just at low tide, and let them pull for themselves. It does me good to plague these mortals."

"It does you good to plague anybody, I believe, Eurus," sighed Auster. "I am sure you are always thwarting me. I am going to visit the tropics tomorrow, and shall leave the northern regions to Boreas, Zephyrus, and you, for several months."

"What route do you take, brother?" asked Zephyrus; "for I don't wish to interfere with you."

I am going through the forest of Gnomes, and then straight down to Quito. I like to see the Gnomes at work, they look so warm. Where are you going, brother?"

"I don't know," said Zephyrus. "I have some whalers to help round Cape Horn, and then I think I shall go and see Boreas. He and I do nicely together, when he is not too savage. Let us each take a turn at the flute, to see if our voices are in tune, and then be off."

So saying, Zephyrus took from a shelf behind him an instrument shaped something like a German flute, and played a piece of spirited martial music upon it, with great taste and execution.

He then passed the flute to the North Wind, who roared through it a stormy Norwegian Berserker song, and then threw it to East, who squealed out a favorite Chinese air, with very high notes and very little variety. Auster, the South, was the next performer, and played a fandango, followed by the tune of a languishing love-song.

The flute was then replaced on its shelf, and as it wanted an hour of sunrise, the usual hour for the brothers to set out upon their day's journey, each composed himself for a little nap.

As soon as the Four Winds and all the Breezes and Zephyrs were sound asleep, Ernest stole softly from his place of concealment, took the flute, disjointed it, and placed it in his breast; then, creeping carefully under the loose mantle of the South Wind, he tied himself firmly to one of his legs (for all the Winds were four or five times as large as common men), and waited anxiously for sunrise, which he knew would awake all four brothers.

The moment at last arrived; Boreas, Zephyrus, and Eurus, one after the other awoke, and left the cave; and last of all, Auster, who, finding himself belated, rushed through the narrow opening with great velocity, without noticing at all in his hurry the passenger whom he was taking with him.

After traversing with the speed of the "winds" many a mile of sea and land, Ernest found that his conductor was pausing in the tops of some high pine trees in the centre of a vast forest.

Peering cautiously down, the young man perceived some little yellow figures running about among the trees, diving suddenly into the earth, and as suddenly reappearing upon its surface. Ernest at once concluded that this must be the forest of the Gnomes, and, hastily untying the scarf with which he had bound himself to the South Wind, he slipped off into the top of a tree and scrambled down the branches, leaving the Wind languidly sighing and moaning before taking a fresh start.

Having reached the lower branch of the tree which he had selected, Ernest looked attentively about him. The little yellow men were still running about as busily as ever, and did not seem to have heard his approach. They seemed to be employed in bringing little scales and particles of gold from beneath the ground and scattering it upon the earth; and Ernest, noticing that the trees and shrubs grew greener and larger as they did so concluded that the Gnomes were watering their garden. Presently he noticed that directly at the foot of the tree where he crouched was one of the holes by which the Gnomes continually emerged and reentered, and, seizing a moment when it was empty, Ernest dropped himself directly into it, and found himself at the top of a long flight of rocky steps. For a moment the Gnomes stood motionless with astonishment at this sudden apparition; but as soon as they perceived the intruder was a man, they rushed toward him, each armed with the little pick-axe which he wore in his belt; and although each Gnome was very small, their numbers made them formidable.

However, the instant he touched ground, Ernest had pulled the flute from his bosom and commenced putting it together. As he did so, he noticed that there were four mouthpieces, each marked with the name of a Wind, and, selecting that of the South as likely to be the most soothing, he began to play as he had seen the Winds do. To his pleasure and surprise—for he knew nothing about music—the flute played the same airs which it had done when the South Wind blew into it, and the Gnomes, dropping their weapons, sunk down upon the ground, and presently fell fast asleep.

As soon as Ernest was sure that they were so, he began to descend the steps, which wound round and round, constantly descending, so that very soon not a ray of light was to be seen. Then he stopped playing, and, indeed, all his breath was no more than sufficient to support him in the close and heavy atmosphere in which he found himself. At last the steps ended in a narrow passage, and Ernest proceeded a long distance through it in total dark and silence, guiding himself by feeling the cold, dripping walls at each side, which seemed hewn out of the solid rock, and was so low and narrow that he was obliged to stoop very low to get through at all.

Suddenly a sound of merry voices broke the silence, and turning a sharp corner, the young man found himself close to an opening, which appeared to conduct into a grotto or cavern, but the only thing which Ernest could distinguish was a heavy curtain whose rich folds lay upon the ground at his feet. It seemed to be of satin; but on putting out his hand to pull it cautiously away, Ernest found to his astonishment that it was made of gold, so pure in its quality and beaten so thin in substance, that it was flexible and delicate as silk. Creeping cautiously along behind this screen, Ernest presently came to a small opening between his curtain and the next one, through which he could see plainly without being himself discovered.

He found that the opening, as he supposed, let into a small grotto, across whose rocky roof ran in every direction veins of purest gold, which sparkled in the brilliant rays of the immense carbuncle hanging from the center of the roof, which was thickly studded with twinkling diamond stars.

All around, the walls were draped with curtains like that which concealed Ernest, and the floor was composed of alternate blocks of gold and silver.

At one side of the cavern was a throne of gold and gems, over which hung by way of canopy an immense orange, the lobes divided and spread apart at the bottom, but united at the top. The peel of this orange was of solid gold, roughened to resemble the natural skin; but the interior or pulp was composed of innumerable little cells, each wrought separately in fine gold, and then placed in their natural position; the seeds were represented by very pale topazes, cut in the exact shape of an orange seed.

Upon this throne sat a young woman about the age of Phelia, whom Ernest at once concluded to be her rival Oriphera; for on her head, which was covered with long golden ringlets, was placed a crown, composed entirely of the gems known as cat's-eyes, held together by gold wire.

This princess was very gorgeously dressed and decorated with a great many jewels, and to most persons would have appeared very beautiful; but, of course, Ernest could not think any thing of the sort, seeing in her as he did, only the enemy and rival of his beloved Phelia.

All around the princess stood her beautiful maids of honor, while behind the throne Ernest perceived a body-guard of Gnomes, each armed, in addition to his pick-axe, with a sling, while in a pouch at his belt he carried a supply of golden bullets. Other Gnomes were constantly appearing from behind the screens and laying at the feet of their princess whatever rare or beautiful gems they had discovered in their mining operations. Some of these Oriphera ordered her treasurer, a little, old, yellow Gnome, to take up and carry away, others she pushed aside with her foot, and they were taken away to be put in the rubbish pit.

Suddenly, as Ernest was looking with all his eyes, he heard a noise behind him, and listening attentively, he found that the Gnomes whom he had left above ground had awakened from their sleep and were pursuing him.

Seizing his flute, Ernest blew a hurried strain with all his force; but, not stopping to select his mouthpiece, he took that belonging to Boreas, the North Wind, and the noise which ensued was so loud and sudden that it cracked the golden curtain from top to bottom, caused several of the diamond stars to fall from the roof, set the great carbuncle swinging like a pendulum, and made the princess and all her attendants fall down as if they had been shot.

Ernest stood for a moment, thunderstruck at the mischief he had wrought; but, quickly recovering himself, he darted forward, seized Phelia's crown from the head of the prostrate Oriphera, filled his pockets with some of the refuse diamonds, rubies, and emeralds, and then, finding the proper mouthpiece, he made the best of his way out of the grotto and up the stairs, playing away as hard as he could at the fandango and love-song of the South Wind. He however found it necessary to go very slowly, not only on account of the darkness, but because on almost every step lay a Gnome stupefied, or rather entranced with the music; and Ernest, who was a very kind-hearted young man, could not bear to hurt one of the little fellows, although they would willingly have killed him.

At length he found himself once more in the open air, and, heaving a great sigh of relief, he hastened on, hoping soon to get out of the wood; but what with constantly losing his way, and what with having to stop every little while to play the Gnomes to sleep (who pursued him furiously), it was many days before he gained the open country, and a great many more before he found himself approaching the beloved hut where he hoped to find Phelia waiting for him. Even then he turned a little out of his way to visit the place where the Four Winds meet, that he might lay the borrowed flute upon the little circle in the center, where the Winds could not fail to see and reclaim it; for, as Ernest said to himself, if they had not the flute, how could they try their voices to see if they were in tune? and if they were obliged to sing false, what would become of the world then?

Finally, toward evening, on the very last day of the month which had been allowed him for his enterprise, Ernest came in sight of his little hut, where almost the first object that met his view was the Gray Cat perched upon the top of the chimney, and anxiously looking in every direction to see if she could catch sight of her deliverer.

No sooner did she see him than, leaping to the ground, she came bounding to meet him; but before she had quite reached him, her dignity as a princess overcame her delight as a cat, and, pausing at the foot of a low rock, she leaped upon it, and seated herself upright with her tail folded closely about her feet, in a very stately and formal manner.

Ernest approached the presence of this little sovereign with all the respect imaginable, and, kneeling upon one knee, laid the recovered crown at her feet.

The cat purred her thanks and approval, but gracefully intimated, by placing her paw upon the crown and then upon her head, that she would thank her gallant knight to complete her transformation by placing the diadem in its proper place.

Ernest understood the silent request, and immediately complied with it. No sooner had he done so than the Gray Cat forever disappeared, and in her place sat the Princess Phelia, who extended her white hand to the young man with the same gracious dignity with which she had given him her paw to kiss when he was setting out upon his journey.

"How can I ever thank you—how can I ever reward you, dearest friend?" said she, softly.

"I will tell you, fairest Phelia," replied Ernest, blushing far more deeply than the princess, brought up in a court, had done.

"You can reward me by giving me this little hand, which I fear but for me would have been but a cat's paw to the end of time."

Phelia, to this proposition—which, perhaps, was not quite unexpected—yielded a gracious assent; and the next day the young couple journeyed together to Catland, where they were immediately married, and, soon succeeding to the throne, lived and reigned many, many happy years; and, for any thing I have ever heard, they do so still.

SWITZERLAND

Spiegel, The Kitten

Gottfried Keller (1819–1890) published "Spiegel, das Kätzchen (Spiegel, the Kitten)" in his book Die Leute von Seldwyla (The People of Seldwyla) *in 1856. After spending several years in poverty in Berlin as a landscape painter, he switched to writing and was much more successful. He became a well-known Swiss novelist and poet.*

When a man from Seldwyla has made a bad bargain or been hoaxed, they say of him, "He's bought the fat off the cat." This surely may be said elsewhere too, but nowhere as frequently as in Seldwyla, perhaps because in this town there exists an old legend on the origin and meaning of the proverb.

Some hundreds of years ago, so the story goes, an elderly female lived at Seldwyla alone, save for a beautiful little gray-and-black cat, who shared her life in all good cheer and prudence and never harmed a body that left him in peace. He had only one passion, the hunt; but satisfied this reasonably and temperately without ever citing in extenuation the facts that the passion also served a useful end and pleased his mistress, or allowing them to tempt him to excessive cruelty. He therefore caught and killed only the most vexatious and brazen mice to be encountered within certain limits of the house, but these with dependable skill. Only seldom would he pursue an especially tricky mouse, which had aroused his ire, beyond these limits, and in any such case he politely asked the neighbors for permission to do a spot of mousing in their homes. It was always willingly granted since he neither touched the milk jars nor leaped upon the hams which might be hanging on the walls, but went about his business quietly and attentively and, having finished, decently withdrew with the mouse in his jaws.

Moreover, this cat was by no means shy and ill-mannered but agreeable to everyone and did not flee from sensible people. On the contrary, from such he could take a good joke and even let them pull his ears a little without scratching. From a sort of stupid folk, on the other hand, whose stupidity he held to be due to an immature and worthless heart, he would stand for no nonsense, and either kept out of their way or rapped them smartly enough over the fingers when they clumsily molested him.

Spiegel (or Mirror), as the little cat was called for his sleek and shiny coat, thus led a cheerful, dainty, and contemplative life in decent affluence and without swagger. He would not sit too often on the shoulder of his kind mistress, snatching morsels off her fork, but waited until he perceived that this jolly game would please her. In the daytime he seldom lay sleeping on his warm cushion behind the stove, but kept himself in trim and rather liked to lie on the narrow banisters on the roof gutter, there to yield to philosophical meditations and the observation of the world.

Only once in each spring and autumn would this tranquil life be interrupted for a week, when the violets bloomed or the mild warmth of St. Martin's summer aped the violet time. Then Spiegel went his own ways in amorous rapture, roaming over the remotest roofs and singing the loveliest songs. Like a real Don Juan he went through the gravest adventures by day and by night, and when he came home on rare occasions he would look so bold and boisterous, indeed so scraggly and disreputable, that his quiet mistress almost indignantly exclaimed, "Why, Spiegel! Aren't you ashamed to lead such a life!"

But it was far from Spiegel to be ashamed. As a man of principle, knowing well what was permissible for a healthy change, he very calmly went to work restoring the gloss of his fur and the innocuous gaiety of his appearance, and he led his moist little paw over his nose as naively as if nothing had happened.

Yet this placid life suddenly took a sad end. Just as Spiegel was in the prime of his years, his mistress died unexpectedly of old age and left the beautiful little cat alone and orphaned. It was the first disaster in his life; with the plaintive noises which so piercingly question the real and just cause of a great sorrow, he accompanied the corpse into the street, and for the rest of the day roamed about the house, and around it, not knowing what to do.

But soon his good nature, common sense, and philosophy told him to compose himself, to bear the unalterable, and to prove his grateful attachment to his late mistress's house by offering to serve her laughing heirs and preparing to aid them in word and deed, to keep checking the mice, and, besides, to tell them many a good thing that the fools would not have spurned had they not been brainless humans. But these people would not let Spiegel say a word, but threw the slippers and the dainty footstool of the dear departed at his head whenever he came in sight, and finally, after a week of quarreling among each other, they went to law and closed up the house for the time being, so that now no one at all could live in it.

Poor Spiegel, sad and forsaken, sat on the stone steps before the gate with no one to let him in. At night, to be sure, he would follow a devious route under the roof of the house, and at the beginning he also spent the greater part of the day in hiding there, trying to sleep off his grief. But soon hunger drove him back to the light and obliged him to appear under the warm sun and among people, to be on hand and present if perchance a mouthful of scant food should show up somewhere. The more rarely this happened, the more vigilant Spiegel became, and all his moral qualities dissolved in this vigilance, so that he soon no longer looked like himself. He made numerous excursions from his doorstep, shyly and fleetingly stealing across the street and returning sometimes with a bad, unappetizing scrap, the like of which he never used to look at, and sometimes with nothing at all.

Besides getting thinner and scragglier by the day, he turned greedy, sneaky, and cowardly; all of his courage, his dainty feline dignity, his common sense and philosophy had vanished. When the boys came home from school he crawled into a hidden corner as soon as he heard them, peering out only to see which of them threw away a crust of bread and memorizing the spot where it fell. When the most wretched cur approached at a distance, Spiegel would scurry off, while formerly he had looked danger calmly in the face and often bravely chastised vicious dogs. Only when a rude and fatuous human came along, of the sort he otherwise had prudently avoided, the poor cat would not move away, although with his rusty knowledge of men he discerned the yokel: his needs forced little Spiegel to deceive himself and to hope that for once the bad man would kindly pet him and hand him a bit of food. And even when he was beaten instead, or his tail pinched, he would not scratch but soundlessly ducked aside and kept looking longingly after the hand which had beaten or pinched him but still smelled of sausage or herring.

One day, when the sage and noble Spiegel had sunk so low and was sitting quite lean and sad on his stone step, blinking into the sun, the Town Sorcerer, Mr. Pineiss, came along, saw the cat, and came to a halt before him. Hoping for a good turn although he knew the uncanny man well enough, little Spiegel humbly sat on his stone and waited for what Mr. Pineiss might do or say. But when he started by remarking, "Well, Cat—shall I buy your fat off you?" Spiegel lost hope, for he thought the Town Sorcerer meant to mock him on account of his leanness. Still, smiling so as not to get in wrong with anyone, he modestly replied, "Oh, Mr. Pineiss is pleased to jest!"

"By no means," cried Pineiss. "I'm in full earnest. I need cat's fat particularly for my sorcery; but it must be ceded to me legally and voluntarily by the esteemed Messrs. Cats, otherwise it is ineffectual. I think if ever an honest pussy was in a spot for a good bargain, you're it. Enter my service; I'll feed you splendidly and make you fat and round with sausages and roast quail. On the immensely tall old roof of my house—which for a cat, by the way, is the most delightful house in the world, full of interesting regions and corners—the finest emerald-green grass grows on the sunniest heights, waving slim and delicate in the breezes and inviting you to bite and relish the tenderest tips when my delicacies upset your digestion. So you will keep in the best of health and in due time provide me with rich, useful fat."

Spiegel had long pricked up his ears and listened with his mouth watering. But the matter was not yet clear to his weakened mind, and so he replied, "So far it does not sound bad, Mr. Pineiss! If I only knew how—since to give you my fat I must give up my life—I may receive the price agreed upon and enjoy it when I am no more?"

"Receive the price?" the sorcerer said, astonished. "The price, of course, is what you will enjoy in the abundant and luxurious victuals with which I'll fatten you; that's self-evident. But I won't force you into the deal." And he began to move off.

But Spiegel hastily and anxiously said, "At least you'll have to allow me a moderate grace beyond the time of my maximum roundness and fatness, so that I must not instantly depart when that agreeable and, alas! so depressing moment has come and been noted!"

"So be it," said Mr. Pineiss with seeming benevolence. "To the next full moon you shall then be free to enjoy your pleasant condition—but no longer! For it must not last into the waning moon, as that would exert a diminishing influence on my well-acquired property."

The tomcat hastened to agree and with his sharp handwriting, his last possession and token of better days, to sign a pact which the sorcerer carried with him for emergencies.

"You can now come to dine with me, Cat," said the sorcerer. "Dinner is at twelve sharp."

"With your permission, I shall take the liberty," said Spiegel and punctually about the noon hour made his appearance at Mr. Pineiss's house. There, for some months, an extremely pleasant life began for the cat. He had nothing to do in the world but to eat the good things set before him, to watch the master practice the black art when possible, and to stroll on the roof. This roof resembled a huge black tricorne or fog-splitter, as the big hats of the Swabian peasants are called; and as such a hat casts its shadow on a brain full of tricks and ruses, this roof covered a large, dark, and angular house full of witchery and hocus-pocus.

Mr. Pineiss was a jack of all trades who served in a hundred little posts. He cured people, exterminated bugs, pulled teeth, and lent money on interest; he was the guardian of all widows and orphans; in his leisure time cut pens,[1] a dozen for a penny, and made fine black ink; he traded in ginger and pepper, in wagon-grease and orange brandy, in copybooks and hobnails; he fixed the steeple clock and annually prepared the almanac with the weather, the peasants' rules, and the bloodletting indices.

He did ten thousand lawful things in bright daylight at reasonable rates, and some unlawful ones only in the dark and out of private passion, or before letting the lawful ones out of his hand he swiftly hung an unlawful little tail on them, as little as a young frog's tail, just for oddity's sake as it were. Besides, he made the weather in difficult times, kept a knowing eye on the witches, and had them burned when they were ripe. As for himself he conducted witchcraft only as a scientific experiment and for home use, just as in drafting and editing the town laws he would privately test and twist them, to explore their durability.

Since the Seldwylers always needed such a citizen who would do all unpleasant little and big things for them, he had been appointed Town Sorcerer and for many years had filled this office with tireless skill and devotion, early and late. Accordingly, his house was stuffed from cellar to attic with all conceivable things and Spiegel had much fun in seeing and sniffing them all.

---

[1] In order to turn a feather into a quill pen, the tip must be cut.

At the start, however, he could pay attention to nothing but the food. He eagerly gulped down whatever Pineiss handed him and hardly could wait from one mealtime to the next. Thus he overloaded his stomach and really had to go up on the roof, to chew on the green grass and cure himself of all sorts of disorders.

The sorcerer, noting this ravenous hunger, was pleased. He thought that the cat would soon grow fat in this manner, and that the more he spent on him now, the more shrewdly he would be acting and saving on the whole. He therefore built a real landscape in his room for Spiegel, growing a little forest of fir trees, raising little hills of rock and moss, and putting in a little lake. The trees he stocked with fragrantly roasted larks, finches, tits, and sparrows, each in season, so that Spiegel always found something to fetch down and nibble at. In artificial mouse holes in the little hills he hid gorgeous mice, carefully fattened on wheat flour and then drawn, larded with tender bacon strips, and roasted. Some of these mice were in reach of Spiegel's paw, while others, to heighten the pleasure, were more deeply buried but tied to a string, by which Spiegel had to pull them out carefully if he wished to enjoy this delightful mock hunt. The bowl of the lake, however, was daily filled by Pineiss with sweet fresh milk for Spiegel to quench his thirst, and swimming therein were fried gudgeon,[2] since Pineiss knew that cats like to fish now and then.

As Spiegel was now leading such a sumptuous life, able to do and omit, eat and drink whatever and whenever he pleased, he visibly prospered in the flesh, his coat again became sleek and shiny, and his eye alert. But at the same time, as his mental powers equally returned, he resumed better manners, his savage greed subsided, and with one sad experience behind him he now became more clever than before. He tempered his desires and ate no more than was good for him, at the same time yielding again to sensible and profound meditations and regaining his acute insight. Thus one day he fetched a pretty little fieldfare[3] down from the branches, and in thoughtfully carving it found its little stomach all round and full of fresh and undigested food. Green, neatly rolled little herbs, black and white seeds and a shining red berry were stuffed so daintily and close together as if a mother had packed her son's bundle for a journey. When Spiegel had slowly devoured the bird and hung up the so gaily filled little stomach on

[2] A small European freshwater fish in the minnow family.
[3] A type of thrush.

his claw to regard it philosophically, he was moved by the fate of the poor fowl which after peacefully accomplished business had been robbed of its life so fast that it could not even digest the packed provisions.

"What did it help him now, poor chap," reflected Spiegel, "feeding so zealously and industriously that this little bag looks like a day's work well done? This red berry was what lured him from the free forest into the fowler's trap. But he, at least, meant to do well by himself and eke out his life with such berries, while I who have just eaten the hapless bird have only eaten myself a step closer to death! Can one sign a more wretched and cowardly contract than to let his life be prolonged for a while at the price of losing it then? Would not a voluntary, speedy death have been preferable for a resolute cat? But I did not think; and now that I can think again, all that I see before me is the fate of this fieldfare. When I am round enough I must depart, for no other reason than that I am round. A fine reason, for a lusty and quick-witted tomcat! Oh to be able to get out of this trap!"

II

He now engaged in considering as to how this might be done; but as the time of danger had not yet arrived, it did not seem clear to him and he could find no way out. Until then, however, as a wise man, he yielded to virtue and self-control, which always is the best way of training and passing the time before a decision. He spurned the soft cushion which Pineiss had spread for him so he might busily sleep and get fat thereon, and preferred to lie on narrow ledges again and in high, dangerous places, when he wished to rest. He also spurned the roasted birds and larded mice; instead, since he now had a lawful hunting ground again, he would rather catch himself a simple live sparrow on the roof, with cunning and agility, or a swift mouse in the attic, and such prey tasted better than the roasted game in Pineiss's artificial preserve, while it did not make him too fat. The exercise and courage, as well as the regained use of virtue and philosophy, also kept him from fattening too quickly, so that Spiegel, while looking healthy and shiny, astonished Pineiss by standing still at a certain stage of corpulence far from that at which the sorcerer was aiming with his kind fattening. For what he had in mind was an animal round as a ball, too heavy to move from its cushion, and consisting of sheer fat. And this was just where his magic had failed, and for all of his cunning he did not know that if you feed an ass it will remain an ass, and if you feed a fox you will get nothing but a fox—for every creature grows only after its own fashion.

When Mr. Pineiss discovered that Spiegel always remained on the same point of a well-fed but trim and agile slenderness, without acquiring a considerable obesity, he suddenly called him to account one evening and gruffly asked, "What does this mean, Spiegel? Why don't you eat the good victuals that I prepare and fix for you with so much care and art? Why don't you catch the roasted birds on the trees, why don't you hunt the tasty mice in the holes in the hills? Why have you stopped fishing in the lake? Why aren't you taking care of yourself? Why don't you sleep on the cushion? Why do you take such strenuous exercise and fail to get fat?"

"Why, Mr. Pineiss," said Spiegel, "because this way I feel better! Am I not to spend my brief period of grace in the manner most agreeable to me?"

"What?" cried Pineiss. "You're to live so you'll get fat and round, and not to hunt yourself silly! I know very well what's in your mind, though. Do you mean to fool me and put me off, so I'll let you run around forever in this intermediate condition? You certainly shall not succeed. It is your duty to eat and drink and take good care of yourself, so that you'll put on weight and get fat! Therefore, renounce immediately this temperance which amounts to trickery and breach of contract, or I'll have a word with you!"

Spiegel interrupted the comfortable purring which he had begun to keep his composure, and said, "I do not know of a word in our contract which would provide for my renouncing temperance and a healthy mode of living. If the Honorable Town Sorcerer has counted on my being a lazy glutton, that isn't my fault. You do a thousand lawful things each day, so let this be added, too, and let both of us stay in good order, for you well know that my fat will serve you only if it has grown to rights."

"See here, you babbler," Pineiss cried irately, "do you mean to instruct me? Let's see how far you've prospered anyway, you lazybones. Perhaps one could finish you soon, after all!" He grabbed the tomcat by the stomach; but Spiegel, feeling unpleasantly tickled thereby, fetched the sorcerer a sharp scratch over the hand. Pineiss looked at it attentively, and then said, "Is that how we stand, you beast? All right, so I herewith solemnly declare you fat enough in the sense of our contract. I am content with the result, and I shall know how to assure myself of it. The moon will be full in five days. Until then you may enjoy your life, as stipulated, and not a minute longer!" With that, he turned his back on Spiegel and left him to his thoughts.

These were now heavy and dark. Was then the hour near, after all, when good Spiegel was to lose his skin? And was nothing more to be done, with all his shrewdness? Sighing, he climbed on the tall roof, the tops of which rose darkly into the sky of a beautiful autumn evening. Then, as the moon rose over the town and cast its light on the black mossy tiles of the old roof, a lovely song rang in Spiegel's ears and a snow-white she-cat shiningly passed over an adjoining rooftop. Instantly Spiegel forgot the prospects of death, and answered the beauty's song of praise with his most beautiful caterwaul. He rushed to join her and soon was engaged in a hot battle with three strange tomcats, whom he bravely and wildly put to flight. Then, with fiery devotion, he courted the lady and spent days and nights with her, without thinking of Pineiss or showing up in his house. He sang like a nightingale throughout the fair moonlit nights, pursued his white beloved over the roofs and through the gardens, and more than once, in violent amorous play or in the struggle with his rivals, rolled down over tall roofs to land in the street—but only to pick himself up, shake his fur, and recommence the wild chase of his passion. Silent and noisy hours, sweet sentiments and angry quarrels, graceful dialogue, witty conversation, tricks and jests of love and jealousy, caresses and scuffles, the power of bliss and the sufferings of misfortune would not let the loving Spiegel come to himself; and when the disk of the moon had grown full, all these passions and excitements had so reduced him that he looked more wretched, thinner, and scragglier than ever. At this very moment Pineiss, from a roof tower, called to him, "Spiegel, dear Spiegel, where are you? Won't you come home for a little while?"

And Spiegel left his white lady-love, who went her way contently and coolly miaowing, and proudly turned to his hangman, who went down to the kitchen, rustled his contract, and said, "Come, Spiegel, come, Spiegel!" And Spiegel followed him, and in the sorcerer's kitchen sat down defiantly before the master, in all his thinness and scraggliness.

When Mr. Pineiss saw how scurvily he had been tricked out of his profit, he jumped up like one possessed and furiously screamed, "What's this I see? You knave, you unscrupulous rascal! What have you done to me?" Beside himself with wrath, he reached for a broom and wanted to hit little Spiegel; but the cat arched his black back, raised up his fur so that a pale gleam sparkled across it, laid back his ears, hissed, and spat so grimly at the oldster that he jumped back three steps, in awe and terror. He began to fear that he might have another sorcerer before him, who was mocking him and whose power exceeded his own. Uncertainly and timidly he said, "Is the honorable Master Spiegel of the trade, perhaps? Should a learned master of wizardry have pleased to assume your external form, since he can command his flesh at his pleasure and become just as corpulent as he deems pleasant, not too little and not too much, or unawares become as lean as a skeleton to escape from death?"

Spiegel calmed down and honestly said, "No, I'm no wizard. It is the sweet power of passion alone which has thus reduced me and, to my pleasure, has removed your fat. By the way, if we will now start our business all over, I'll honestly do my part and eat right heartily. Just put a fine, big fried sausage in front of me. I'm all exhausted and hungry."

At that Pineiss furiously grabbed Spiegel by the neck, locked him in the goose pen, which was always empty, and screamed, "Now see if your sweet power of passion gets you out once more, and if it is stronger than the power of sorcery and of my legal contract! Now it's eat, rascal, and die!" At once he fried a long sausage which smelled so tastily that he could not keep from licking a bit on both ends himself, before pushing it through the wire.

Spiegel ate it up from end to end, and then, comfortably cleaning his moustache and licking his fur, he said to himself, "Upon my soul, love is a beautiful thing. For this time, it has pulled me out of the trap. Now I'll rest up a little and seek to recollect my wits by contemplation and good food. Everything in its time. A little passion today, a little rest and reflection tomorrow—each is good in its way. This prison is not so bad at all, and certainly something useful can be thought up in it."

But Pineiss was doing his best now, and every day, with all his art, he prepared such delicacies of such enticing variety and wholesomeness that the captured Spiegel could not resist—for Pineiss's stock of voluntary and lawful cat's fat was daily diminishing and threatened soon to vanish altogether, and then, without this prime requisite, the sorcerer would be helpless. Yet the good sorcerer always kept feeding Spiegel's mind along with Spiegel's body; there was absolutely no getting rid of this irritating adjunct, wherefore his magic proved here to be deficient.

At last, when Spiegel in his cage seemed fat enough to him, he hesitated no longer but put all utensils in readiness before the very eyes of the watching tomcat and stoked a bright fire in the stove to boil out his long-desired profit. Then he honed a great knife, opened the prison, pulled out little Spiegel after carefully locking the kitchen door, and happily said, "Come on, you ne'er-do-well! We'll cut off your head to begin with, and then pull off your skin. That will furnish a warm cap for me—something I hadn't even thought of yet, fool that I am. Or shall I skin you first and then cut off your head?"

"No, if you please," Spiegel said meekly, "rather cut off the head first."

"You're right, poor chap," said Mr. Pineiss, "we won't torture you uselessly. Always do the right thing."

"How true! How true!" said Spiegel with a pitiful sigh, turning his head resignedly to one side. "If only I had always done the right thing, and not frivolously neglected so weighty a matter, I could now die with an easier conscience. I'd be glad to die, without this wrong to spoil an otherwise so welcome death—for what has life to offer me? Nothing but fear, sorrow, and poverty, and for a change a storm of consuming passion that is even worse than quietly trembling fear."

"Say," Pineiss asked curiously, "what wrong, what weighty matter?"

"Oh, what good is talking now?" Spiegel sighed. "What's done is done, and remorse now comes too late."

"See what a sinner you are, you rapscallion?" said Pineiss. "And how well you deserve to die? But what the dickens is it that you've done? Have you perhaps stolen, removed, destroyed something of mine? Have you done me some crying wrong, you Satan, of which as yet I know, dream, suspect nothing? What a pretty story! Good that I've caught on to it in time. Confess right this instant, or I'll skin and boil you alive. Will you speak up or won't you?"

"Oh, no," said Spiegel, "as far as you are concerned I have nothing to reproach myself with. It concerns the ten thousand guilders[4] of my late mistress—but what good is talking! Although—when I think of it and look at you, perhaps it might not even be too late yet—when I look at you I see you're still quite a handsome and capable man, in the prime of life. Tell me, Mr. Pineiss, haven't you ever felt the urge to wed, honestly and profitably? But what am I gabbing—how should so wise and artful a man harbor such idle thoughts? How should so usefully occupied a master think of foolish women?

---

[4] Any of various gold coins formerly issued by German states.

"Though of course even the worst of them still has something about her which might benefit a man—there's no denying that. And if she is but half worth her salt, a good housewife may be white of body, careful of mind, affectionate of manner, faithful of heart, a thrifty manager but lavish in caring for her husband, entertaining in words and pleasing in action, ingratiating in everything she does. She kisses the man with her lips and strokes his beard; she hugs him with her arms and scratches him behind the ears as he likes it—in short, she does a thousand things not to be sneezed at. She keeps herself quite close to him or at a modest distance, depending upon his mood, and when he goes about his business she does not disturb him, but meanwhile spreads his praise within and without the house, for she won't hear a word against him and praises whatever there is of him.

"But the loveliest part of her is the wonderful quality of her delicate bodily being which Nature, for all seeming human likeness, has made so differently from ours that in a happy marriage it effects a continuous miracle and really hides the trickiest magic within it. But what am I gabbing there like a fool, on the threshold of death! How should a wise man heed such vanities? Forgive me, Mr. Pineiss, and cut off my head."

But Pineiss hotly cried, "Will you stop for a moment, you chatterbox, and tell me: where is such a one, and does she have ten thousand guilders?"

"Ten thousand guilders?" said Spiegel.

"Why, yes," cried Pineiss impatiently, "wasn't that what you were just talking of?"

"No," was the response, "that's another matter. They lie buried some place."

"And what are they doing there? Whose are they?" Pineiss shouted.

"They're nobody's. That's just what is on my conscience, for I was to have disposed of them. They really belong to the man who marries a person like I described. But how to get three such things together in this Godless town: ten thousand guilders, a wise, fine, and good housewife, and a wise and righteous man? So my sin is really not all too great, for the task was beyond a poor cat."

"If you," Pineiss cried, "will not stick to the matter now and tell it comprehensibly and in order, I'll start by cutting off your tail and both ears! Now get going!"

"Since you command, I must needs tell the story," said Spiegel and calmly sat down on his hind legs, "although this delay serves only to add to my sufferings." Pineiss stuck his sharp knife into the floor between Spiegel and himself, and sat curiously upon a keg to listen while Spiegel continued:

III

You must know, Mr. Pineiss, that that good woman, my late mistress, died unmarried, as an old maid who quietly did much good and never harmed a soul. But things about her had not always been so still and quiet, and although she was never of an evil disposition, she nevertheless had done plenty of harm in her day; for in her youth she was the most beautiful damsel for far around, and whatever young gentlemen and bold youths lived in the vicinity or came by the way would fall in love with and insist upon marrying her. As for her, she certainly was very eager to marry and take a handsome, honorable, and clever man for her husband, and she had a full choice, with natives and strangers fighting over her and more than once running their swords through each other so as to gain the advantage.

"There gathered around her suitors bold and timid, shrewd and candid, rich and poor, owners of good and decent businesses and others who daintily lived on their incomes as gentlemen; one with this advantage, the other with that, eloquent or silent, one gay and amiable, while another appeared to be deeper, even though he looked a bit simple—in short, the damsel had as perfect a choice as any marriageable spinster might wish for. Yet besides her beauty she possessed a handsome fortune of many thousand guilders, and these were the cause of her never getting around to making a choice and taking a husband.

"For she managed her estate with excellent care and foresight and set great store by it, and since mankind always judges others by its own inclinations, it happened that whenever an estimable suitor approached and half-way pleased her, she instantly imagined that he desired her only for her property's sake. If one was rich, she believed that he still would not want her if she were not rich, too, and of the poorer ones she assumed for a certainty that they had their eyes on her guilders alone and were looking forward to their enjoyment, and the poor damsel, herself thinking so much of earthly possessions, was unable to tell this love of money and wealth on her suitors' part from their love of her—or, if it might perhaps really exist, to overlook and forgive it.

"Several times she was as good as betrothed and her heart would beat stronger at last; but suddenly she would conclude from some token that the man was betraying her and thinking only of her wealth, and she would instantly break off the affair and sadly but unmercifully withdraw. Those who did not displease her she tested in a hundred ways, so that only the deftest could avoid being trapped; and in the end the only man who could approach with any hope would be an utterly crafty and deceitful one—for which reason alone the choice then got really difficult, because at length such people arouse an eerie disquiet and leave a beauty in the most painful doubts, the craftier and cleverer they are.

"Her principal method of trying out her admirers was to test their unselfishness by daily luring them into great expenditures, rich gifts, and charitable deeds. But however they might act, they never could do the right thing; for if they showed themselves generous and unselfish, if they gave glittering festivities, brought her presents, or entrusted her with considerable sums for the poor, she would suddenly say that all this was done only to catch a salmon with a worm or throw a sausage at the ham, as the saying goes. And she passed on the gifts as well as the entrusted money to convents and beneficent foundations and fed the poor; but as for the disappointed suitors, she mercilessly rejected them. If on the other hand they showed themselves wary, not to say miserly, they were condemned in advance, for she resented that even more and believed that it expressed a base and naked callousness and selfishness.

"So it came about that she who sought a pure heart, devoted only to herself, was in the end surrounded only by deceitful, shrewd, and self-seeking suitors whom she could never make out and who resented her life.

"One day she felt so gloomy and despondent that she turned her whole court out of the house, closed it up, and traveled to Milan where she had a cousin. As she rode across the St. Gotthard[5] on a little donkey, her mood was as black and horrible as the wild rocks towering out of the abyss, and she felt sorely tempted to hurl herself from Devil's Bridge into the raging waters of the Reuss. The guide, and two maids whom she had along and whom I myself knew (although they are long dead now), succeeded only with the greatest effort in calming her and dissuading her from her dark

[5] St. Gotthard Pass runs through the alps between Zurich, Switzerland, and Milan, Italy.

purpose. Yet she was pale and sad on her arrival in the fair land of Italy, and not even its blue skies would brighten her somber thoughts. After a few days with her cousin, however, another melody would unexpectedly sound, and a spring of which thus far she had known little was to dawn in her.

"For in her cousin's house there arrived a young compatriot whom at the very first glance she liked so well that she could be said to be falling in love by herself now, and for the first time. He was a handsome youth, well-bred and nobly mannered, and then neither poor nor rich, for he had nothing but ten thousand guilders inherited from his late parents, with which he desired to start a silk business in Milan. He had learned the merchant's trade and was enterprising and clear-headed and lucky, as is often the way with candid and innocent folk—for the young man was that, too; for all his learning he seemed harmless and innocuous like a child. And although he was a merchant and of such ingenuous disposition, which is already a preciously rare combination, he was nevertheless firm and chivalrous of bearing and carried his sword as boldly on his side as only an experienced warrior may.

"All of this, together with his fresh, handsome youth, conquered the damsel's heart, so that she could barely control herself and showed him the utmost friendliness. She grew merry again, and even when she was sad in between it was in the swift change of love's fears and hopes, which was in any case a nobler and more pleasant feeling than that painful embarrassment of choice which she formerly had felt among her many suitors. Now, the only worry and care she knew was how to please the good and handsome youth, and the lovelier she was, the humbler and less self-assured she became now that for the first time she felt a true affection.

"The young merchant also had never seen such beauty, or at least had never been so close to one, and found such warm and gracious treatment at her hands. And since, as I said, she was not only fair but also kind of heart and refined of manner, it is no wonder that the frank and candid youth, whose heart was still quite free and inexperienced, should likewise fall in love with her, and with all the violence and recklessness corresponding to his whole nature. And yet none might ever have known, if his simple soul had not been encouraged by the damsel's cordiality—which he, ignorant of guile himself, dared with secret fear and trembling to regard as proof that his love was returned. He constrained himself for a few weeks and believed he was concealing the matter; but everybody saw from far off that he was mortally in love, and whenever he came near the damsel or heard her name mentioned it was to be seen at once with whom.

"He was not long in love, however, before he really began to love with all the violence of his youth, so that the damsel became the highest and best in the world for him, to stake his salvation and the whole worth of his own person on, once and for all. This delighted her hugely; for in whatever he said or did his way was different from anything that she had known hitherto, and confirmed and moved her so deeply that she in turn also yielded to the deepest love and there was no further question of any choice.

"The little game was watched by all, and caused some open words and a good deal of banter. The damsel felt highly pleased with it, and, though her heart would burst with anxious expectation, helped a little to involve and string out the romance, so as to taste and relish it to the full. For the young man in his confusion was doing things so precious and boyish as she had never experienced, which for her became more flattering and pleasant all the time. Yet his candor and honesty could not long stand this state of things; with everybody hinting and freely jesting about it, it seemed to him to be turning into a comedy, as the subject of which his beloved was much too good and sacred; and what she liked best was precisely what made him depressed, uncertain, and embarrassed for her sake.

"He also deemed it offensive and deceitful on his part to bear so violent a passion around with him for a long time, and ceaselessly to think of her without her having any idea of it, which was certainly quite improper and not right! So one morning, visibly come to a resolution, he confessed his love to her in a few words, determined to avow it once and never for a second time, unless the first should be successful. For he was unaccustomed to the idea that so fair and well-made a damsel might perhaps not speak her true mind, nor immediately give her irrevocable Yes or No in reply. His heart was as tender as his love was violent, he was as brittle as he was childlike and as proud as he was candid, and everything with him was at once a matter of life and death, of Yes or No, blow for blow.

"At the same instant, however, as the damsel heard his confession which she had so longingly awaited, she was seized by her old distrust and it occurred to her, unfortunately, that her lover was a merchant who might perhaps wish only to secure her money, to expand his enterprises. If he were somewhat in love with her person, besides, this was no special merit in view of her beauty but the more outrageous since it made of her a mere desirable adjunct to her gold.

"So instead of confessing her own love and receiving him well, as she would have liked best to do, she instantly thought of a new ruse to test his devotion. Striking a serious, almost sad mien, she confided being already betrothed at home, to a young man whom she loved cordially. She had been several times on the point of telling that to him, the merchant, because she was very fond of him as a friend, as he might well have discovered from her demeanor, and she trusted him like a brother. But the clumsy jokes which had come up in the company had interfered with a familiar colloquy; however, now that he himself had surprised her by baring his good, noble heart to her, she could thank him no better for his affection than by an equally frank confidence.

"Yes, she went on, she could belong only to the one she had chosen and never would be able to transfer her heart to another; this was graven into her soul with golden fire, and the dear man himself, well as he knew her, was unaware of the greatness of her love. But it stood under an evil star: her betrothed was a merchant but poor as a church mouse, so they had planned on his using her means to go into business; a beginning had been made and everything started for the best; their wedding date had been set when an unforeseen mischance caused all of her funds suddenly to be attached and involved in litigation, possibly to be forever lost, while her poor betrothed soon had to make his first payments to the Milanese and Venetian merchants, with all his credit, honor, and prosperity, not to mention their union and connubial bliss! She had hurried down to Milan where she had wealthy relatives, here to find ways and means; but she had come at the wrong time, for nothing seemed to turn out well and yet time was moving on and unless she could help her beloved, she would have to die of despair. For he was the dearest and best man to be imagined, and surely would become a great merchant if he could be helped, and then to be his wife would be her only happiness on earth.

"Long before she finished this story, the poor handsome youth had lost all color and become as pale as a sheet. He uttered not a complaining sound, however, and no longer spoke a single word of himself and his love but merely sadly inquired how large was the amount of the obligations entered into by the fortunate-unfortunate lover. Ten thousand guilders, she replied even more sadly. The sad young merchant rose, asked the damsel to be of good cheer since a way out was sure to appear, and left without daring to look at her for shame of having thrown an eye upon a lady who so faithfully and passionately loved another. For the poor man took every word of her story for Gospel truth.

"Then, without delay, he went to see his business friends and by much pleading and sacrifice of certain sums prevailed on them to cancel the orders and purchases which he himself, at that very time and with his very own ten thousand guilders, was to have paid for and on which he had staked his whole career; and before six hours had passed, he reappeared before the damsel with his entire fortune and asked her for God's sake to be so good as to accept this aid from him.

"Her eyes shone in happy surprise and her heart beat as with hammers. She asked him where he had obtained this capital and he replied that he had borrowed it on the strength of his reputation and would have no trouble returning it, since his business was turning out well. She could see plainly that he was lying, that it was his only wealth and hope which he was sacrificing to her happiness, but she pretended to believe him. She gave free rein to her joyous feelings and cruelly acted as if they were due to her good fortune in being able now, after all, to save and marry the man of her choice; and she could find no words to express her gratitude.

"But suddenly she bethought herself and declared that she could not accept this magnanimous act save on one condition—that otherwise all pleas would be in vain. Asked what this condition was, she demanded his sacred promise that on a certain day he would come to attend her wedding and become the best friend and protector of her future husband as well as the most loyal friend, protector, and counsel of herself. Blushing, he asked her to desist from this request, but all reasons he cited to dissuade her were in vain. In vain he argued that his affairs would not permit him now to travel back to Switzerland and that such a trip would cause him considerable losses. But she resolutely stood her ground and even pushed his gold back toward him when he would not consent.

"Finally he promised, but he had to shake hands on it and swear it to her by his honor and salvation. She told him the precise day and hour when he should arrive, and all this he had to swear to her by his Christian faith and by his hope for salvation. Not until then would she accept his sacrifice and gaily had the treasure carried into her bedchamber, where she locked it with her own hands in her trunk and hid the key in her bosom.

"Now she tarried no longer in Milan but journeyed back across the St. Gotthard as merrily as she had been melancholy in coming. On Devil's

Bridge, where she had wished to leap to her death, she laughed like a madcap and, with her lovely voice brightly rejoicing, threw a bunch of pomegranate blossoms which she wore on her breast down into the Reuss—in short, her joy was unconfined and hers was the merriest journey that was ever taken. Returned home, she opened and aired her house from top to bottom and decorated it as if she were expecting a prince. At the head of her bed, however, she placed the bag with the ten thousand guilders, and at night laid her head on the hard lump and slept on it as blissfully as if it had been a pillow stuffed with the softest down. She could scarcely await the day when she was sure of his arrival, for she knew that he would not break the simplest promise, much less an oath, though it were to cost his life. But the day came and the beloved did not appear, and when as many more days and weeks passed without word from him she began to tremble in every limb and was seized by the greatest fear and anxiety; she sent letters upon letters to Milan, but no one was able to tell her what had become of him.

"In the end it turned out, by chance, that the young merchant had taken a blood-red piece of satin-damask which he had at home from the beginnings of his business and had already paid for, had himself a battle dress made of it, and joined the Swiss who just then were fighting in the Milanese war as mercenaries for King Francis[6] of France. After the battle of Pavia,[7] where so many Swiss lost their lives, he was found lying on a pile of slain Spaniards, torn by many fatal wounds and with his red satin dress rent and tattered from top to bottom. Before giving up the ghost he commended the following message to the memory of a Seldwyler who lay by his side and had been less badly injured, begging him to convey it if he should get out of there alive:

"'Dearest lady! Although I swore to you upon my honor, by my Christian faith, and by my salvation to appear at your wedding, I have since felt incapable of seeing you again and seeing another enjoy the greatest happiness which could exist for me. I had not felt this until you were gone, not having previously known how strict and uncanny a thing is such a love as I bear you, else I should doubtlessly have taken better care. Now that this is the way of it, I would rather lose my worldly honor and spiritual salva-

[6] Francis I (1494–1547).
[7] In 1525.

tion and be eternally damned as a perjurer than once again appear before you with a fire burning in my breast more strongly and unquenchably than that of hell itself, which I shall scarcely feel beside it. Do not pray for me, fairest lady, for I never can and never shall be blessed without you, be it here or there. And so farewell and greetings!'

"Thus, in the battle after which King Francis said, 'All is lost save honor,'[8] the hapless lover had lost all—hope, honor, life, and eternal salvation—all save the love which consumed him. The Seldwyler luckily got away, and no sooner found himself somewhat recovered and out of danger than he faithfully wrote the dead man's words on his writing tablet, lest he forget them, then journeyed home, presented himself to the hapless damsel, and read the message to her as stiffly and martially as was his habit in reading the roll of a company, for he was a field lieutenant.

"The damsel, however, tore her hair and her clothes and began to scream and weep so loudly that she was heard up and down the street and people came running. She dragged out the ten thousand guilders like a crazy woman, scattered them on the floor, threw herself down full length and kissed the glistening gold pieces. Quite out of her senses, she tried to gather up and embrace the rolling treasure, as if her lost lover were present in it. She lay on the gold day and night, refusing to take either food or drink; incessantly she fondled and kissed the cold metal, until she suddenly rose in the middle of the night, carried the treasure down into the garden, industriously running to and fro, and there, amid bitter tears, threw it into a deep well and pronounced a curse over it, that it never should belong to anyone else."

When Spiegel had come so far in his story, Pineiss said, "And is that beautiful money still lying in the well?"

"Where else should it be?" Spiegel answered, "since I alone can get it out and have not done so to this hour?"

"I see, that's right," said Pineiss; "I had forgotten all about that over your story. You're not bad at telling stories, you rascal, and I'm really beginning to hanker after a little wife who would be so taken with me. She would have to be very beautiful, though. But now tell me quickly how the whole thing really hangs together."

[8] King Francis actually said, "I have lost all save life and honor."

"It took many years," Spiegel said, "for the damsel so far to recover from the bitter torment of her soul that she could begin to turn into the quiet old spinster that I came to know. I can boast of having been her only comfort and the most trusted friend of her lonely life, until her quiet end. When she felt this approaching, however, she once more recalled the time of her distant youth and beauty, and once more, with milder and more resigned thoughts, suffered first the sweet excitements and then the bitter agonies of that time, and she quietly wept through seven days and nights for the love of the youth whose enjoyment she had lost by her suspicions, so that her old eyes grew sightless even before she died.

"Then she rued the curse which she had laid on that treasure, and in entrusting me with this important task she said to me, 'I now direct otherwise, dear Spiegel, and empower you to carry out my will. Look around until you find a beautiful but poor maiden who may lack suitors on account of her poverty. If there should then turn up a sensible, righteous, and handsome man who has a good income and wishes to take the maiden to wife regardless of her poverty, solely moved by her beauty, this man shall bind himself with the strongest vows to be as faithfully, as unselfishly, and invariably devoted to her as my unfortunate lover was to me, and to do this woman's will in all things for the rest of his life. Then give the ten thousand guilders in the well to the bride for a dowry, that she may surprise her bridegroom with them on her wedding morn!'

"Thus spoke the dear departed, and I, due to my untoward fate, have neglected to follow up this matter and now must fear that the poor woman therefore rests uneasy in her grave, which may have no very pleasant consequences for myself, either."

IV

Pineiss looked at Spiegel suspiciously and said, "Might you be in a position, my fellow, to give me some proof of the treasure and make it evident to me?"

"At any time," Spiegel retorted, "but you must know, Mr. Town Sorcerer, that you may not simply fish out the gold, just like that. You would unfailingly have your neck wrung; for there is something uncanny about the well. I have certain indications of that, which certain considerations prevent me from mentioning further."

"Why, who said anything about getting it out?" Pineiss said, somewhat fearfully. "Just lead me there and show me the treasure! Or rather, I'll lead you, by a stout cord so you can't escape me!"

"As you please," said Spiegel. "But take also another long cord along, and a lantern which you can let down into the well, for it is very deep and dark."

Pineiss followed this advice and led the merry little cat to the garden of the deceased spinster. Together they climbed the wall, and Spiegel showed the sorcerer the way to the old well, which was buried under wild-growing shrubbery. There Pineiss let down his lantern, greedily looking after it without relaxing his hold upon Spiegel. And indeed, in the depth he saw the gold sparkle beneath the greenish water, and he cried, "Truly, I see it! it's true! Spiegel, you're a grand fellow!" Then he eagerly peered down again and said, "Are there really ten thousand of them?"

"Well, to that I can't swear," said Spiegel. "I've never been down to count them. It's possible, too, that the lady lost a few pieces on the way, in carrying the treasure over here, because she was in a very excited condition."

"Well, let it be a dozen more or less," said Mr. Pineiss, "I won't let that bother me." He sat down on the edge of the well; Spiegel sat down, too, licking his paw. "Now there we have the treasure," Pineiss said, scratching himself behind the ear, "and here we have the man to go with it; there's nothing lacking but the beautiful woman."

"What?" said Spiegel.

"I mean, we're short only the one who is to get the ten thousand for a dowry, to surprise me with them on our wedding morn, and who has all those agreeable virtues that you mentioned."

"Hm," said Spiegel. "It's not quite the way you put it. The treasure is there, as you rightly perceive; the beautiful woman, to admit it candidly, I have already found, too; but the hitch is with the man who would want to marry her under these difficult circumstances. For nowadays beauty has to be gilded like walnuts on Christmas, and the emptier the men's heads get, the keener they are on filling their emptiness with a dowry so as better to pass their time. Then they inspect a horse or importantly buy a piece of velvet, or order a fine crossbow, with so much ado and running, and the gunsmith is never out of the house.

"Next they say, 'I'll have to bring in my wine and clean my kegs, have my trees trimmed or my roof shingled; I have to send my wife to take the baths, she is ailing and costs me a lot of money; I have to get my wood cut and collect my debts; I've bought a few whippets and exchanged my hunting dog; I've traded my big walnut chest for a fine oaken drop-leaf table; I've cut my beanstalks, fired my gardener, sold my hay, and sown my lettuce'—always mine and mine, from dawn to dusk.

"Some even say, 'I have to do my wash next week, I have to air my beds, I must hire a maid and get a new butcher, since I must get rid of the old one; I've picked up the loveliest waffle iron, by chance, and sold my silver cinnamon box, which was no use to me anyway.' Now all that, be it understood, is the wife's business, and thus such a fellow spends his time and steals the day from our dear Lord in recounting all of these doings without moving a hand. At the outside, if such a rogue has to knuckle under, perhaps he may say, '*Our* cows and *our* hogs,' but—"

Pineiss jerked the string so that Spiegel squealed "Miaow!" and shouted, "Enough, you chatterbox! Tell me instantly: where is the woman you know of?" For the listing of all these wonderful things and doings connected with a dowry had only served to water the arid sorcerer's mouth still more.

Spiegel asked in amazement, "So you really will undertake the matter, Mr. Pineiss?"

"I certainly will! Who else? So out with it: where is she?"

"So you can go there and court her?"

"By all means!"

"Then you must know that the matter goes through my hands only. It's me you have to talk to, if you want money and wife," Spiegel said cold-bloodedly and indifferently, assiduously drawing both paws over his ears after wetting them a little each time.

Pineiss thought carefully, moaned a little, and said, "I notice you want to cancel our contract and save your head."

"Would that seem so unfair and unnatural to you?"

"In the end you may be cheating and lying to me, like a rogue."

"That's possible, too," said Spiegel.

"I tell you: don't you cheat me!" Pineiss cried imperiously.

"All right, so I won't cheat you," said Spiegel.

"If you do—"

"I do."

"Don't torture me, Spiegel," Pineiss said almost tearfully.

And Spiegel, seriously now, replied, "You're a marvelous man, Mr. Pineiss! There you are holding me captive on a string, and keep jerking it so I can hardly breathe. You let the sword of death hang over me for more than two hours—what am I saying, for six months! And now you say, 'Don't torture me!' If you'll permit me, I'll put it to you in a few words: I should be only too glad to fulfill my duty of love to the dead woman after all, and to find a suitable husband for the person in question, and it is true that you seem to be sufficient in every respect; it is no child's play to get a woman properly cared for these days, no matter how easy it may seem, and I say once more: I'm glad you're ready to do it. But I won't do it for nothing. Before I say another word or take another step, before I even open my mouth again, I first want my freedom back and my life assured. So take this string away and put our contract down there on the well, on this stone here, or cut off my head—one or the other!"

"Why, you lunatic and scatterbrain," said Pineiss, "you hothead, you don't really mean that, do you? That will have to be properly discussed, and in any event would call for a new contract!"

Spiegel no longer answered and sat immobile for one, two, three minutes. The master grew anxious; he took out his wallet, picked out the paper with a sigh, read it once again, and hesitantly placed it before Spiegel. The paper scarcely lay there before Spiegel had snapped it up and swallowed it, and although he had to gulp strenuously to get it down, it still seemed to him the best and most wholesome food he had ever enjoyed, and he hoped that it would agree with him for a long time and make him round and merry.

When he had finished this agreeable meal he politely greeted the sorcerer and said, "You will hear from me without fail, Mr. Pineiss, and neither wife nor money shall escape you. On the other hand, get ready to be right loving, so that you can promise and fulfill those conditions of unchanging devotion to the caresses of your wife, who is as good as yours already. And herewith I thank you for now, for board and care, and shall take my leave."

With that Spiegel went his way, delighted over the stupidity of the sorcerer who thought he could deceive himself and everyone else when he would marry the hoped-for bride, not disinterestedly, for sheer love of beauty, but forewarned of the existence of the ten thousand guilders. Meanwhile, he already had his eye on a person he meant to foist off on the stupid sorcerer in return for his roasted fieldfares, sausages, and mice.

V

Opposite Mr. Pineiss's house there was another house, the front of which was most cleanly whitewashed and the windows of which always gleamed freshly scrubbed. The modest curtains always were white as snow and appeared fresh from under the iron, and similarly white were the dress, cap, and neckerchief of an old Beguine[9] who lived in the house. The nun-like wimple over her chest always looked as if it were folded from writing paper and spontaneously made you want to write on it—and on the chest, at least, one might have done so conveniently, it being as flat and hard as a board. Sharp as the white edges and points of her dress were the Beguine's long nose and chin, her tongue, and the evil glance of her eyes; but she did little talking with her tongue and little glancing with her eyes, for she disliked waste and used everything only at the proper time and after due deliberation. She went to church three times daily, and when she crossed the street in her fresh, white, and rustling things and with her white, pointed nose, the children fearfully ran away and even grown-up people liked to step behind the house door if there was still time.

However, she enjoyed a high reputation for her strict piety and seclusion and was especially well esteemed by the clergy, although even the priests would deal with her in writing rather than orally, and when she came to confession the priest always shot out of the confessional, sweating as if straight from an oven. Thus the pious Beguine, who was not one to trifle with, lived in full peace and remained unwed. Nor did she bother with anyone or trouble people, provided they kept out of her way; only her neighbor Pineiss seemed to have aroused her special hatred, for whenever he let himself be seen at his window she shot over an evil glance and instantly drew her white curtains. Pineiss dreaded her like fire and only in the very rear of his house, with everything well locked, would dare to crack a joke about her.

White and bright, however, as the Beguine's house looked from the street, from the rear it looked black and smoky, weird and strange; but there almost no one could see it except the birds in the sky and the cats on the rooftops, because it was built into a dark maze of high, windowless fire walls, where no human face was ever seen. There under the roof hung old

[9] A non-monastic order of nuns founded in the twelfth century.

torn petticoats, baskets, and herb bags; growing on the roof were real little oak trees and thorn bushes, and a great, sooty chimney rose eerily toward the sky. Out of this chimney, however, in the dead of night, a witch not infrequently rode her broom to the heights, young and beautiful and stark naked, as God made women and the Devil likes to see them. Riding out of the chimney she would sniff the fresh night air with the most delicate little nose and with smiling cherry lips, soaring along in the white gleam of her body, while her long raven hair streamed behind her like a flag of night.

In a hole by the chimney sat an old owl, and it was to her that the liberated Spiegel went now, in his jaws a fat mouse he had captured on the way.

"A good evening to you, dear Mrs. Owl! Keenly on the lookout?" he said.

And the owl replied, "Have to! A good evening, too. You haven't been seen around here for a long time, Mr. Spiegel."

"There were reasons that I'll tell you about. Here I've brought you a mouse, nothing special, what the season offers, if you'd care for it. Is the mistress out riding?"

"Not yet. She will only go out for an hour or so toward morning. Thanks for the fine mouse. Always the polite Spiegel! I've got a bad sparrow put aside here that came too close to me this morning; if you please, taste the bird. And how have you been doing?"

"Queerly, rather," Spiegel replied. "They were after my skin. Let me tell you, if you please."

While they enjoyed their supper, Spiegel told the attentive owl everything that had happened to him, and how he had freed himself from Mr. Pineiss's hands.

The owl said, "Well, a thousand congratulations! Now you are your own master again, and you can go wherever you please, after such strange experiences."

"That isn't the end of it yet," said Spiegel. "The man must get his wife and his guilders."

"Are you out of your mind, to do a good turn for the rogue who wanted to skin you?"

"Why, he could have done it legally and according to contract, and since I can pay him back in the same coin, why shouldn't I? Who says I want to do him a good turn? That story was pure invention; my late mistress who now rests in God was a simple person who was never in love in her life, nor ever surrounded by suitors, and that treasure is unjust money which she inherited once upon a time and threw into the well lest it bring her bad luck. 'Cursed be whoever takes it out of there and uses it!' she said. So it won't be too much of a good turn."

"That changes matters, of course. And now, where do you expect to get the suitable wife?"

"Here from this chimney. That's why I've come, to talk a sensible word with you. Wouldn't you like to be free again from the bonds of this witch? Think how we may capture her and marry her off to the old villain."

"Spiegel, you only need to approach and I have good ideas!"

"There, I knew you were wise. I've done my part, and it will be even better if you add something too and put new strength to work. Then we can't fail."

"With everything fitting together so well, I don't have to think long. My plans have long been laid."

"How shall we catch her?"

"With a new woodcock snare made of good strong hemp strands. They must have been twisted by a twenty-year-old hunter who has never looked at a woman, and the night dew must have fallen on it three times without a woodcock having been caught in it. The reason for this, however, must be a threefold good deed. Such a net would be strong enough to catch the witch."

"Now I wonder where you'll find that," said Spiegel, "for I know you would not be prattling idly."

"It's already found—just as if made for us:

"In a forest not far from here sits a hunter's son who is twenty years old and has never looked at a woman, for he was born blind. Therefore he is good for nothing but twisting cord, and a few days ago he made a new and very fine woodcock snare. But when the old hunter wanted to set it for the first time, a woman came along and tried to tempt him to sin, but she was so ugly that the old man fled aghast, and left the net on the ground, so that the dew fell on it without a woodcock having been caught, and the cause of it was a good deed.

"The next day, when he went to set it again, a horseman rode by with a heavy sack behind him; in the sack was a hole, from which a gold coin fell every now and then. And the hunter again left the net lying and ran after the horseman, collecting the coins, until the man on horseback turned around, saw what was going on, and wrathfully aimed his lance at him. Now the hunter bowed in fright, handed up his hat, and said, 'Permit me, sir, you have lost a lot of money, which I have been carefully gathering for you.' This was another good deed, honest finding being one of the most difficult and best; but he had come so far from the woodcock snare that he left it lying in the woods for the second night and took the short way home.

"On the third day, finally, which was yesterday, when he was on the way again, he met a pretty woman who often cajoles the oldster and has received many a rabbit from him as a present. Over her he completely forgot the woodcocks, and in the morning said, 'I've spared their poor little lives; one must be merciful even to animals.' And on account of these three good deeds he found that he was now too good for this world, and took the vows of a monk this very morning. So the snare is still lying unused in the woods and I only need to fetch it."

"Fetch it quickly," said Spiegel, "it will be good for our purpose."

"I'll fetch it," said the owl, "if only you will keep watch for me in this hole, and if by chance my mistress should call up the chimney asking whether the air is clear, you have to imitate my voice and answer, 'No, there is no stink yet in the fencing school!'"

Spiegel posted himself in the niche, and the owl silently flew away over the town, toward the woods. Soon she returned with the woodcock snare and asked, "Did she call yet?"

"Not yet," said Spiegel.

So they stretched the net out over the chimney and sat beside it, quietly and wisely; the air was dark and in the light morning breeze a few stars were twinkling. "You ought to see," whispered the owl, "how cleverly she knows how to breeze up the chimney without blackening her white shoulders!"

"I've never seen her as close as that," replied Spiegel softly. "If only she doesn't catch us."

Then the witch called from below, "Is the air clear?"

"Quite clear," cried the owl; "there's a gorgeous stink in the fencing school," and the witch came riding up forthwith and was caught in the net which the cat and owl hastily pulled tight and tied. "Hold tight," said Spiegel, and, "Tie fast," echoed the owl. The witch struggled and writhed, silently, like a fish in the net; but it availed her nothing and the snare proved itself splendidly. Only the handle of her broom stood out through the meshes. Spiegel wanted to pull it out gently but received such a crack on his nose that he all but fainted and realized that one must not come too close to a lioness even in a net. Eventually the witch held still and said, "What do you want of me, you insane animals?"

"You are to release me from your service and restore my freedom," said the owl.

"So much ado about nothing," said the witch. "You're free. Open this net."

"Not yet," said Spiegel who was still rubbing his nose. "You must promise to marry the Town Sorcerer Pineiss, your neighbor, in the manner which we shall tell you, and never leave him."

At that the witch again began to struggle and to spit like the Devil, and the owl said, "She won't bite."

But Spiegel said, "If you aren't quiet and do whatever we wish, we'll hang this net together with its contents out there on the dragon's head under the eaves, right above the street, so that tomorrow everyone will see you and recognize the witch. Now say: would you rather be roasted under Mr. Pineiss's supervision, or roast him by marrying him?"

Then the witch said with a sigh, "Tell me then, what all this means."

And Spiegel neatly explained everything to her and what she would have to do.

"Well, that can be endured if there's nothing else to be done," she said and yielded, with the strongest formulas that may bind a witch. Then the animals opened the prison and let her out. She immediately mounted her broom, the owl sat on the handle behind her, and Spiegel on the twigs in the rear, holding on tight, and thus they rode to the well into which the witch descended to retrieve the treasure.

In the morning Spiegel appeared at Mr. Pineiss's and reported to him that he might now inspect and court the maid in question; however, she had already become so poor that she was sitting before the gate under a tree, completely forsaken and forlorn and weeping bitterly. At once Mr. Pineiss dressed himself in his shabby old yellow velvet doublet that he only wore on festive occasions, donned his second-best poodle cap and girt on his sword; in his hand he carried an old green glove, a small balsam bottle which once had contained balsam and still smelled faintly, and a paper carnation; thereupon he set out with Spiegel for the gate and courtship. There he met a weeping female seated under a willow tree, of such great beauty as he had never seen; but her garment was so scant and torn that however modest she would act, her white body always gleamed through here or there. Pineiss's eyes bulged; he scarcely could stammer his proposal for stormy delight. The beauty dried her tears, gave him her hand with a sweet smile, thanked him for his generosity in a voice like heavenly bells, and vowed to be eternally true to him. But at the same instant he was filled by such furious jealousy and envy of his bride that he resolved never to have her seen by any human eye. He got an age-old hermit to marry them and celebrated the marriage feast in his house, with no guests other than Spiegel and the owl whom Spiegel had requested permission to bring. The ten thousand guilders stood in a bowl on the table and Pineiss frequently reached in and stirred the gold; then again he would look at the beautiful woman who sat there in a sea-blue velvet gown, her hair woven through a gold net and adorned with flowers, and her white throat ringed with pearls. He constantly wanted to kiss her, but she knew how to keep him off in modesty and shame, yet with a seductive smile, and swore that she would not kiss in front of witnesses and before the fall of night. This only made him the more lovesick and blissful, and Spiegel spiced the feast with charming conversation, which the lovely woman continued with the most pleasant, wittiest, and most ingratiating words, so that the sorcerer did not know for joy what was happening to him.

When darkness fell, however, the owl and the cat took their leave and modestly withdrew. Mr. Pineiss saw them to the door with a light and once again thanked Spiegel, whom he called a fine, polite man, and when he returned to the room, there at the table sat the old Beguine, his neighbor, who glanced at him evilly. Pineiss dropped the light in terror and tremblingly leaned against the wall. His tongue hung out, and his face turned as pale and haggard as that of the Beguine. She, however, got up, approached him, and drove him before her into the nuptial chamber, where her hellish arts subjected him to the worst torture a mortal has endured. So now he was irrevocably wed to the hag, and when the people in town heard of it they said, "Look at that! Still waters run deep. Who would have thought that the pious Beguine and the Town Sorcerer would be joined in holy wedlock? Well, they're an honorable and righteous couple, if not especially amiable."

Mr. Pineiss henceforth led a miserable life; his wife had immediately taken possession of all his secrets and ruled him completely. Not the slightest freedom or rest was allowed him; he had to make magic from morning till night as hard as he could, and whenever Spiegel passed by and saw him he would ask politely, "Always busy, always busy, Mr. Pineiss?"

From that time on they have said at Seldwyla, "He's bought the fat off the cat," especially when someone has got a shrewish and repulsive wife in the bargain.

ENGLAND

Rumpty-Dudget's Tower

This story was written by Julian Hawthorne (1846-1934), the son of Nathaniel Hawthorne who was the author of The Scarlet Letter *and* The House of the Seven Gables. *Like his father, Julian became a professional writer. At various times he lived in England, Italy, and Germany, but he spent most of his life in the United States. In 1913, he was convicted for mail fraud in connection with selling Canadian mining stocks and served a year in prison. This fairy tale was written while he was living in England and it first appeared in serial form in* St. Nicholas *magazine in 1879. A year later he published it in his book* Yellow-Cap, and Other Fairy Stories for Children. *He revised the story in 1924 and published it as an illustrated book. This is the original version from* St. Nicholas *magazine.*

Long ago, before the sun caught fire, before the moon froze up, and before you were born, a Queen had three children, whose names were Princess Hilda, Prince Frank, and Prince Henry. Princess Hilda, who was the eldest, had blue eyes and golden hair; Prince Henry, who was the youngest, had black eyes and black hair; and Prince Frank, who was neither the youngest nor the eldest, had hazel eyes and brown hair. They were the best children in the world, and the prettiest, and the cleverest of their age: they lived in the most beautiful palace ever built, and the garden they played in was the loveliest that ever was seen.

This castle stood on the borders of a great forest, on the other side of which was Fairy Land. But there was only one window in the palace that looked out upon the forest, and that was the round window of the room in which Princess Hilda, Prince Frank, and Prince Henry slept. And since this window was never open except at night, after the three children had been put to bed, they knew very little about how the forest looked, or what kind of flowers grew there, or what kind of birds sang in the branches of the trees. Sometimes, however, as they lay with their heads on their little pillows, and their eyes open, waiting for sleep to come and fasten down the eyelids, they saw stars, white, blue, and red, twinkling in the sky overhead; and below amongst the tree-trunks, other yellow stars, which danced about, and flitted to and fro. These flitting stars were called, by grown-up people, will-o'-the-wisps, jack-o'-lanterns, fire-flies, and such like names; but the children knew them to be the torches carried by the elves as they ran hither and thither about their affairs. They often wished that one of these elves would come through the round window of their chamber, and make them a visit; but if this ever happened, it was not until after the children had fallen asleep, and could know nothing of it.

The garden was on the opposite side of the palace to the forest, and was full of flowers, and birds, and fountains, in the basins of which gold fishes swam. In the center of the garden was a broad green lawn for the children to play on; and on the further edge of this lawn was a high hedge, with only one round opening in the middle of it. But through this opening no one was allowed to pass; for the land on the other side belonged to a dwarf, whose name was Rumpty-Dudget, and whose only pleasure was in doing mischief. He was an ugly little dwarf, about as high as your knee, and all gray from head to foot. He wore a broad-brimmed gray hat, and a gray beard, and a gray cloak, that was so much too long for him that it dragged on the ground as he walked; and on his back was a small gray hump that made him look even shorter than he was. He lived in a gray tower, whose battlements could be seen from the palace windows. In this tower was a room with a thousand and one corners in it. In each of these corners stood a little child, with its face to the wall, and its hands behind its back. They were children that Rumpty-Dudget had caught trespassing on his grounds, and had carried off with him to his tower. In this way he had filled up one corner after another, until only one corner was left unfilled; and if he could catch a child to put in that corner, then Rumpty-Dudget would become master of the whole country, and the beautiful palace would disappear, and the lovely garden would be changed into a desert, covered over with gray stones and brambles. You may be sure, therefore, that Rumpty-Dudget tried very hard to get hold of a child to put in the thousand and first corner; but all the mothers were so careful, and all the children so obedient, that for a long time that thousand and first corner had remained empty.

When Princess Hilda and her two little brothers, Prince Frank and Prince Henry, were still very little, indeed, the Queen, their mother, was obliged to make a long journey to a distant country, and to leave the children behind her. They were not entirely alone, however; for there was their fairy aunt to keep guard over them at night, and a large cat, with yellow eyes and a thick tail, to see that no harm came to them during the day. The cat was named Tom, and was with them from the time they got up in the morning until they went to bed again; but from the time they went to bed until they got up, the cat disappeared and the fairy aunt took his place. The children had never seen their fairy aunt except in dreams, because she only came after sleep had fastened down their eyelids for the night. Then she would fly in through the round window, and sit on the edge of their bed, and whisper in their ears all manner of charming stories about Fairy Land, and the wonderful things that were seen and done there. Then, just before they awoke, she would kiss their eyelids and fly out of the round window again; and the cat, with his yellow eyes and his thick tail, would come purring in at the door.

One day, the unluckiest day in the whole year, Princess Hilda, Prince Frank and Prince Henry were playing together on the broad lawn in the center of the garden. It was Rumpty-Dudget's birthday, and the only day in which he had power to creep through the round hole in the hedge and prowl about the Queen's grounds. As ill-fortune would have it, moreover, the cat was forced to be away on this day from sunrise to sunset; so that during all that time the three children had no one to take care of them. But they did not know there was any danger, for they had never yet heard of Rumpty-Dudget; and they went on playing together very affectionately, for up to this time they had never quarreled. The only thing that troubled them was that Tom, the cat, was not there to play with them; he had been away ever since sunrise, and they all longed to see his yellow eyes and his thick tail, and to stroke his smooth back, and to hear his comfortable purr. However, it was now very near sunset, so he must soon be back. The sun, like a great red ball, hung a little way above the edge of the world, and was taking a parting look at the children before bidding them goodnight.

All at once, Princess Hilda looked up and saw a strange little dwarf standing close beside her, all gray from head to foot. He wore a gray hat and beard, and a long gray cloak that dragged on the ground, and on his back was a little gray hump that made him seem even shorter than he was, though, after all, he was no taller than your knee. Princess Hilda was not frightened, for nobody had ever done her any harm; and besides, this strange little gray man, though he was very ugly, smiled at her from ear to ear, and seemed to be the most good-natured dwarf in the world. So she called to Prince Frank and Prince Henry, and they looked up too, and were no more frightened than Hilda; and as the dwarf kept on smiling from ear to ear, the three children smiled back at him. Meanwhile, the great red ball of the sun was slowly going down, and now his lower edge was just resting on the edge of the world.

Now, you have heard of Rumpty-Dudget before and therefore you know that this strange little gray dwarf was none other than he, and that, although he smiled so good-naturedly from ear to ear, he was really wishing to do the children harm, and even to carry one of them off to his tower, to stand in the thousand and first corner. But he had no power to do this so long as the children stayed on their side of the hedge; he must first tempt them to creep through the round opening, and then he could carry them whither he pleased. So he held out his hand and said:

"Come with me, Princess Hilda, Prince Frank and Prince Henry. I am very fond of little children; and if you will creep through that round opening in the hedge, I will show you something you never saw before."

The three children thought it would be very pleasant to see something they never saw before; for if that part of the world which they had already seen was so beautiful, it was likely that the part they had not seen would be more beautiful still. So they stood up, and Rumpty-Dudget took Prince Frank by one hand, and Prince Henry by the other, and Princess Hilda followed behind, and thus they all set off across the lawn toward the round opening in the hedge. But they could not go very fast, because the children were hardly old enough to walk yet; and, meanwhile, the great red ball of the sun kept going down slowly, and now his lower half was out of sight beneath the edge of the world. However, at last they came to the round opening, and Rumpty-Dudget took hold of Prince Henry to lift him through it.

But just at that moment the last bit of the sun disappeared beneath the edge of the world, and instantly there was a great sound of miauing and spitting, and Tom, the cat, came springing across the lawn, his great yellow eyes flashing, and his back bristling, and every hair upon his tail standing straight out, until it was as big round as your leg. And he flew at Rumpty-Dudget and jumped upon his hump, and bit and scratched him soundly. At that Rumpty-Dudget screamed with pain, and dropped little

Prince Henry, and vanished through the opening of the hedge in the twinkling of an eye.

But from the other side of the hedge he threw a handful of black mud at the three children and a drop of it fell upon the forehead of Princess Hilda, and another upon Prince Frank's nose, and a third upon little Prince Henry's chin; and each drop made a little black spot, which all the washing and scrubbing in the world would not take away. And immediately Princess Hilda, who had till then been the best little girl in the world, began to wish to order everybody about, and make them do what she pleased, whether they liked it or not; and Prince Frank, who till then had been one of the two best little boys in the world, began to want all the good and pretty things that belonged to other people, in addition to what already belonged to him; and Prince Henry, who till then had been the other of the two best little boys in the world, began to wish to do what he was told not to do, and not to do what he was told to do. Such was the effect of the three black drops of mud.

Although the Princess Hilda and her two little brothers were no longer the best children in the world, they were pretty good children as the world goes, and got along tolerably well together on the whole. But whenever the wind blew from the north, where Rumpty-Dudget's tower stood, Princess Hilda ordered her brothers about, and tried to make them do what she pleased, whether they liked it or not; and Prince Frank wanted some of the good and pretty things that belonged to his brother and sister, in addition to what were already his; and Prince Henry would not do what he was told to do, and would do what he was told not to do. And then, too, the spot on Princess Hilda's forehead, and on Prince Frank's nose, and on Prince Henry's chin, became blacker and blacker, and hotter and hotter, until at last the children were ready to cry from pain and vexation. But as soon as the wind blew from the south, where Fairy Land was, the spots began to grow dim, and the heat to lessen, until at last the children hardly felt or noticed them any more. Yet they never disappeared altogether; and neither the cat nor the fairy aunt could do anything to drive them away. But the cat used to warn Princess Hilda and her two brothers that unless they could make the wind blow always from the south, the thousand and first corner in Rumpty-Dudget's tower would be filled at last. And when, at night, their fairy aunt flew in through the round window and sat on their bedside, and whispered stories about Fairy Land into their ears, and they would ask her in their sleep to take them all three in her arms and carry them over the tops of the forest-trees to her beautiful home far away on the other side, she would shake her head and say:

"As long as those spots are on your faces, I cannot carry you to my home, for a part of each of you belongs to Rumpty-Dudget, and he will hold on to it in spite of all I can do. But when Hilda becomes a horse, and Frank a stick of fire-wood, and Henry a violin, then Rumpty-Dudget will lose his power over you, and the spots will vanish, and I will take you all three in my arms, and fly with you over the tops of the trees to Fairy Land, where we will live happily forever after."

When the three children heard this, they were puzzled to know what to do; for how could a little princess become a horse, or two little princes a stick of fire-wood and a violin? But that their fairy aunt would not tell them.

"It can only happen when the wind blows always from the south, as the cat told you," said she.

"But how can we make the wind blow always from the south?" asked they.

At that, the fairy aunt touched each of them on the heart, and smiled, and shook her head; and no other answer would she give; so they were no wiser than before.

Thus time went steadily on, tomorrow going before today, and yesterday following behind, until a year was past and Rumpty-Dudget's birthday came round once more.

"I must leave you alone tomorrow," said the cat the day before, "from sunrise to sunset; but if you are careful to do as I tell you, all will be well. Do not go into the garden; do not touch the black ball that lies on the table in the nursery; and do not jump against the north wind."

Just as he finished saying these things, he sprang out of the room and disappeared.

All the next morning the children remembered what Tom, the cat, had told them; they played quietly in the palace, and did not touch the black ball that lay on the nursery table. But when the afternoon came, Princess Hilda began to be tired of staying shut up so long, when out in the garden it was warm and pleasant, and the wind blew from the south. And Prince Frank began to be tired of his own playthings, and to wish that he might have the pretty, black ball to toss up in the air and catch again. And Prince Henry began to be tired of doing what he was told, and wished the wind would blow from the north, so that he might jump against it. At last they could bear it no longer; so Princess Hilda stood up and said:

"Frank and Henry, I order you to come out with me into the garden!" And out they went; and as they passed through the nursery, Prince Henry knocked the black ball off the table, and Prince Frank picked it up and put it in his pocket. But by the time they got to the broad lawn in the center of the garden, the three spots on their faces were blacker than ink and hotter than pepper; and, strange to say, the wind, which hitherto had blown from the south, now changed about and came from the north, where Rumpty-Dudget's tower stood. Nevertheless, the children ran about the grass, tossing the black ball from one to another, and did not notice that every time it fell to the ground, it struck a little nearer the hedge which divided Rumpty-Dudget's land from the Queen's garden. At last Prince Frank got the ball, and kept tossing it up in the air, and catching it again all by himself, without letting the others take their turns. But they ran after him to get it away, and all three raced to and fro, without noticing that at every turn they were nearer and nearer to the high hedge, and to the round opening that led into Rumpty-Dudget's ground. After a long chase Princess Hilda and Prince Henry caught up with Prince Frank, and would have taken the black ball away from him; but he gave it a great toss upward, and it flew clear over the high hedge and came down bounce upon the other side. Just then the great red ball of the sun dropped out of a gray cloud, and rested on the edge of the world. It wanted three minutes to sunset.

The three children were a good deal frightened when they saw where the ball had gone, and well they might be; for it was Rumpty-Dudget's ball, and Rumpty-Dudget himself was hiding on the other side of the hedge.

"It is your fault," said Princess Hilda to Prince Frank; "you threw it over."

"No, it's your fault," answered Prince Frank; "I shouldn't have thrown it over if you and Henry had not chased me."

"You will be punished when Tom the cat comes home," said Princess Hilda, "and that will be in one minute, when the sun sets." For they had spent one minute in being frightened, and another minute in disputing.

Now, all this time, Prince Henry had been standing directly in front of the round opening in the hedge, looking through it to the other side, where he thought he could see the black ball lying beside a bush. The north wind blew so strongly as almost to take his breath away, and the spot on his chin burnt him so that he was ready to cry with pain and vexation. Still for all that, he longed so much to do what he had been told not to do, that by and by he could stand it no longer; but, just as the last bit of the sun sank out of sight beneath the edge of the world, he jumped through the round opening against the north wind, and ran to pick up the ball. At the same moment, Tom the cat came springing across the lawn, his yellow eyes flashing, his back bristling, and the hairs sticking straight out on his tail until it was as big and round as your leg. But this time he came too late. For, as soon as Prince Henry jumped through the hedge against the north wind and ran to pick up the black ball, out rushed Rumpty-Dudget from behind the bush, and caught him by the chin, and carried him away to the thousand and first corner in the gray tower. As soon as the corner was filled, the north wind rose to a hurricane and blew away the beautiful palace and the lovely garden, and nothing was left but a desert covered with gray stones and brambles. The mischievous Rumpty-Dudget was now master of the whole country.

Meanwhile, Princess Hilda and Prince Frank were sitting on a heap of rubbish, crying as if their hearts would break, and the cat stood beside them wiping its great yellow eyes with its paw and looking very sorrowful.

"Crying will do no good, however," said the cat at last; "we must try to get poor little Henry back again."

"Oh, where is our fairy aunt?" cried Princess Hilda and Prince Frank. "She will tell us how to find him."

"You will not see your fairy aunt," replied Tom, "until you have taken Henry out of the gray tower, where he is standing in the thousand and first corner with his face to the wall and his hands behind his back."

"But how are we to do it," said Princess Hilda and Prince Frank, beginning to cry again, "without our fairy aunt to help us?

"Listen to me," replied the cat, "and do what I tell you, and all may yet be well. But first take hold of my tail, and follow me out of this desert to the borders of the great forest; there we can lay our plans without being disturbed."

With these words, Tom arose and held his tail straight out like the handle of a saucepan; the two children took hold of it, off they all went, and in less time than it takes to tell it, they were on the borders of the great forest, at the foot of an immensely tall pinetree. The cat made Princess Hilda and Prince Frank sit down on the moss that covered the ground, and sat down in front of them with his tail curled around his toes.

"The first thing to be done," said he, "is to get the Golden Ivy-seed and the Diamond Water-drop. After that, the rest is easy."

"But where are the Golden Ivy-seed and the Diamond Water-drop to be found?" asked the two children.

"One of you will have to go down to the kingdom of the Gnomes, in the center of the earth, to find out where the Golden Ivy-seed is," replied the cat; "and up to the kingdom of the Air-Spirits, above the clouds, to find out where the Diamond Water-drop is."

"But how are we to get up to the Air-Spirits, or down to the Gnomes?" asked the children, disconsolately.

"I may be able to help you about that," answered the cat. "But while one of you is gone, the other must stay here and mind the magic fire which I shall kindle before we start; for if the fire goes out, Rumpty-Dudget will take the burnt logs and blacken Henry's face all over with them, and then we should never be able to get him back. Do you two children run about and pick up all the dried sticks you can find, and pile them up in a heap, while I get the touch-wood ready."

In a very few minutes, a large heap of fagots had been gathered together, as high as the top of Princess Hilda's head. Meanwhile, the cat had drawn a large circle on the ground with the tip of his tail, and in the center of the circle was the heap of fagots. It had now become quite dark, but the cat's eyes burned as brightly as if two yellow lamps had been set in his head.

"Come inside the circle, children," said he, "while I light the touch-wood."

In they came accordingly, and the cat put the touch-wood on the ground and sat down in front of it with his nose resting against it, and stared at it with his flaming yellow eyes; and by and by it began to smoke and smolder, and at last it caught fire and burned famously.

"That will do nicely," said the cat; "now put some sticks upon it." So this was done, and the fire was fairly started, and burned blue, red and yellow.

"And now there is no time to be lost," said the cat. "Prince Frank, you will stay beside this fire and keep it burning, until I come back with Princess Hilda from the kingdoms of the Gnomes and Air-Spirits. Remember that if you let it go out, all will be lost; nevertheless, you must on no account go outside the circle to gather more fagots, if those that are already here get used up. You may, perhaps, be tempted to do otherwise; but if you yield to the temptation, all will go wrong; and the only way your brother Henry can be saved will be for you to get into the fire your-self, in place of the fagots."

Though Prince Frank did not much like the idea of being left alone in the woods all night, still, since it was for his brother's sake, he consented; but he made up his mind to be very careful not to use up the fagots too fast, or to go outside the ring. So Princess Hilda and Tom the cat bid him farewell, and then the cat stretched out his tail as straight as the handle of a saucepan. Princess Hilda took hold of it, and away! right up the tall pinetree they went, and were out of sight in the twinkling of an eye.

After climbing upward for a long time, they came at last to the tip-top of the pine tree, which was on a level with the clouds. The cat waited until a large cloud sailed along pretty near them, and then, bidding Princess Hilda hold on tight, they made a spring together, and alighted very clev-erly on the cloud's edge. Off sailed the cloud with them on its back, and soon brought them to the kingdom of the Air-Spirits.

"Now, Princess Hilda," said the cat, "you must go the rest of the way alone. Ask the first Spirit you meet to show you the way to the place where the Queen sits; and when you have found her, ask her where the Diamond Water-drop is. But be careful not to sit down, however much you may be tempted to do so; for if you do, your brother Henry never can be saved."

Though Princess Hilda did not much like the idea of going on alone, still, since it was for her brother's sake, she consented; only she made up her mind on no account to sit down, no matter what happened. So she bid the cat farewell, and walked off. Pretty soon, she met an Air-Spirit, carrying its nose in the air, as all Air-Spirits do.

"Can you tell me the way to the place where the Queen sits?" asked Princess Hilda.

"What do you want of her?" asked the Air-Spirit.

"I want to ask her where the Diamond Water-drop is," answered Princess Hilda.

"She sits on the top of that large star up yonder," said the Air-Spirit; "but unless you can carry your nose more in the air than you do, I don't believe you will get her to tell you anything."

Princess Hilda, however, did not feel so much like carrying her nose in the air as she had felt at any time since the black spot came upon her forehead; and she set out to climb toward the Queen's star very sorrowfully; and all the Spirits who met her said:

"See how she hangs her head! She will never come to anything."

But at last she arrived at the gates of the star, and walked in; and there was the Queen of the Air-Spirits sitting in the midst of it. As soon as she saw Princess Hilda, she said:

"You have come a long way, and you look very tired. Come here and sit down beside me."

"No, your Majesty," replied Princess Hilda, though she was really so tired that she could hardly stand, "there is no time to be lost; where is the Diamond Water-drop?"

"That is a foolish thing to come after," said the Queen. "However, sit down here and let us talk about it. I have been expecting you."

But Princess Hilda shook her head.

"Listen to me," said the Queen. "I know that you like to order people about, and to make them do what you please, whether they like it or not. Now, if you will sit down here, I will let you be Queen of the Air-Spirits instead of me; you shall carry your nose in the air, and everybody shall do what you please, whether they like it or not."

When Princess Hilda heard this, she felt for a moment very much tempted to do as the Queen asked her. But the next moment she remembered her poor little brother Henry, standing in the thousand and first corner of Rumpty-Dudget's tower, with his face to the wall and his hands behind his back. So she cried, and said:

"Oh, Queen of the Air-Spirits, I am so sorry for my little brother that I do not care any longer to carry my nose in the air, or to make people mind me, whether they like it or not; I only want the Diamond Water-drop, so that Henry may be saved from Rumpty-Dudget's tower. Can you tell me where it is?"

Then the Queen smiled upon her, and said:

"It is on your own cheek!"

Princess Hilda was so astonished that she could only look at the Queen without speaking.

"Yes," continued the Queen kindly, "you might have searched throughout all the kingdoms of the earth and air, and yet never have found that precious Drop, had you not loved your little brother Henry more than to be Queen. That tear upon your cheek, which you shed for love of him, is the Diamond Water-drop, Hilda; keep it in this little crystal bottle; be prudent and resolute and sooner or later Henry will be free again."

As she spoke, she held out a little crystal bottle, and the tear from Princess Hilda's cheek fell into it, and the Queen hung it about her neck by a coral chain, and kissed her, and bid her farewell. And as Princess Hilda went away, she fancied she had somewhere heard a voice like this Queen's before; but where or when she could not tell.

It was not long before she arrived at the cloud which had brought her to the kingdom of the Air-Spirits, and there she found Tom the cat awaiting her. He got up and stretched himself as she approached, and when he saw the little crystal bottle hanging round her neck by its coral chain, he said:

"So far, all has gone well; but we have still to find the Golden Ivy-seed. There is no time to be lost, so catch hold of my tail and let us be off."

With that, he stretched out his tail as straight as the handle of a saucepan. Princess Hilda took hold of it; they sprang off the cloud and away! down they went till it seemed to her as if they never would be done falling. At last, however, they alighted softly on the top of a hay-mow, and in another moment were safe on the earth again.

Close beside the hay-mow was a field mouse's hole, and the cat began scratching at it with his two fore-paws, throwing up the dirt in a great heap behind, till in a few minutes a great passage was made through to the center of the earth.

"Keep hold of my tail," said the cat, and into the passage they went.

It was quite dark inside, and if it had not been for the cat's eyes, which shone like two yellow lamps, they might have missed their way. As it was, however, they got along famously, and pretty soon arrived at the center of the earth, where was the kingdom of the Gnomes.

"Now, Princess Hilda," said the cat, "you must go the rest of the way alone. Ask the first Gnome you meet to show you the place where the King works: and when you have found him, ask him where the Golden Ivy-seed is. But be careful to do everything that he bids you, no matter how little you may like it; for, if you do not, your brother Henry never can be saved."

Though Princess Hilda did not much like the idea of going on alone, still, since it was for her brother's sake, she consented; only she made up her mind to do everything the King bade her, whatever happened. Pretty soon she met a Gnome, who was running along on all fours.

"Can you show me the place where the King works?" asked Princess Hilda.

"What do you want with him?" asked the Gnome.

"I want to ask him where the Golden Ivy-seed is," answered Princess Hilda.

"He works in that great field over yonder," said the Gnome: "but unless you can walk on all-fours better than you do, I don't believe he will tell you anything."

Princess Hilda had never walked on all-fours since the black spot came on her forehead; so she went onward just as she was, and all the Gnomes who met her said:

"See how upright she walks! She will never come to anything."

But at last she arrived at the gate of the field, and walked in; and there was the King on all-fours in the midst of it. As soon as he saw Princess Hilda, he said:

"Get down on all-fours this instant! How dare you come into my kingdom walking upright?"

"Oh, your majesty," said Hilda, though she was a good deal frightened at the way the King spoke, "there is no time to be lost; where is the Golden Ivy-seed?"

"The Golden Ivy-seed is not given to people with stiff necks," replied the King. "Get down on all-fours at once, or else go about your business!"

The Princess Hilda remembered what the cat had told her, and got down on all-fours without a word.

"Now listen to me," said the King. "I shall harness you to that plow in the place of my horse, and you must draw it up and down over this field until the whole is plowed, while I follow behind with the whip. Come! There is no time to lose."

When Princess Hilda heard this, she felt tempted for a moment to refuse; but the next moment she remembered her poor little brother Henry standing in the thousand and first corner of Rumpty-Dudget's tower, with his face to the wall and his hands behind his back; so she said:

"O King of the Gnomes! I am so sorry for my little brother that I will do as you bid me, and all I ask in return is that you will give me the Golden Ivy-seed, so that Henry may be saved from Rumpty-Dudget's tower."

The King said nothing, but harnessed Hilda to the plow, and she drew it up and down over the field until the whole was plowed, while he fol-

lowed behind with the whip. Then he freed her from her trappings, and
told her to go about her business.

"But where is the Golden Ivy-seed?" asked she, piteously.

"I have no Golden Ivy-seed," answered the King; "ask yourself where
it is!"

Then poor Princess Hilda's heart was broken, and she sank down on
the ground and sobbed out, quite in despair:

"Oh, what shall I do to save my little brother!"

But at that the King smiled upon her and said:

"Put your hand over your heart, Hilda, and see what you find there."

Princess Hilda was so surprised that she could say nothing; but she put
her hand over her heart, and felt something fall into the palm of her hand,
and when she looked at it, behold! it was the Golden Ivy-seed.

"Yes," said the King, kindly; "you might have searched through all the
kingdoms of the earth and air, and yet never have found that precious
seed, had you not loved your brother so much as to let yourself be driven
like a horse in the plow for his sake. Keep the Golden Ivy-seed in this little pearl box; be humble, gentle and patient, and sooner or later your
brother will be free."

As he spoke, he fastened a little pearl box to her girdle with a jeweled
clasp, and kissed her, and bade her farewell. As Princess Hilda went away,
she fancied she had somewhere heard a voice like this King's before; but
where or when she could not tell.

It was not long before she arrived at the mouth of the passage by which
she had descended to the kingdom of the Gnomes, and there she found
Tom the cat awaiting her. He got up and stretched himself as she
approached, and when he saw the pearl box at her girdle, he said:

"So far, all goes well; but now we must see whether or not Prince Frank
has kept the fire going; there is no time to be lost, so catch hold of my tail
and let us be off."

With that, he stretched out his tail as straight as the handle of a
saucepan; Princess Hilda took hold of it, and away they went back
through the passage again, and were out at the other end in the twinkling
of an eye.

Now, after Prince Frank has seen Princess Hilda and the cat disappear
up the trunk of the tall pine tree, he had sat down rather disconsolately
beside the fire, which blazed away famously, blue, red and yellow. Every
once in a while he took a fagot from the pile and put it in the flame, lest it

should go out; but he was very careful not to step outside the circle which the cat had drawn with the tip of his tail. So things went on for a very long time, and Prince Frank began to get very sleepy, for never before had he sat up so late; but still Princess Hilda and the cat did not return, and he knew that if he were to lie down to take a nap, the fire might go out before he waked up again, and then Rumpty-Dudget would have blackened Henry's face all over with one of the burnt logs, and he never could be saved. He kept on putting fresh fagots in the flame, therefore, though it was all he could do to keep his eyes open; and the fire kept on burning red, blue and yellow.

But after another very long time had gone by, and there were still no Princess Hilda and the cat, Prince Frank, when he went to take a fresh fagot from the pile, found that there was only the one fagot left of all that he and Hilda had gathered together. At this he was very much frightened, and knew not what to do; for when that fagot was burned up, as it soon would be, what was he to do to keep the fire going? There were no more sticks inside the ring, and the cat had told him that if he went outside of it, all would be lost.

In order to make the fagot last as long as possible, he took it apart, and only put one stick in the flame at a time; but after a while, all but the last stick was gone, and when he had put that in, Prince Frank sat down quite in despair, and cried with all his might. Just then, however, he heard a voice calling him, and, looking up, he saw a little gray man standing just outside the circle, with a great bundle of fagots in his arms. Prince Frank's eyes were so full of tears that he did not see that the little gray man was Rumpty-Dudget.

"What are you crying for, my dear little boy?" asked the gray dwarf, smiling from ear to ear.

"Because I have used up all my fagots," answered Prince Frank; "and if the fire goes out, my brother Henry cannot be saved."

"That would be too bad, surely," said the dwarf; "luckily, I have got an armful, and when these are gone, I will get you some more."

"Oh, thank you—how kind you are!" cried Prince Frank, jumping up in great joy, and going to the edge of the circle. "Give them to me, quick, for there is no time to be lost; the fire is just going out."

"I can't bring them in," replied the dwarf; "I have carried them already from the other end of the forest, and that is far enough; surely you can come the rest of the way yourself."

"Oh, but I must not come outside the circle," said Prince Frank; "for the cat told me that if I did, all would go wrong."

"Pshaw! what does the cat know about it?" asked the dwarf. "At all events, your fire will not burn one minute longer; and you know what will happen then."

When Prince Frank heard this, he knew not what to do; but anything seemed better than to let the fire go out; so he put one foot outside of the circle and stretched out his hand for the fagots. But immediately the dwarf gave a loud laugh, and threw the fagots away as far as he could; and rushing into the circle, he began to stamp out with his feet the little of the fire that was left.

Then Prince Frank remembered what the cat had told him; he turned and rushed back also into the circle; and as the last bit of flame flickered at the end of the stick, he laid himself down upon it like a bit of fire-wood. And immediately Rumpty-Dudget gave a loud cry and disappeared; and the fire blazed up famously, yellow, blue and red, with poor little Prince Frank in the midst of it!

Just then, and not one moment too soon, there was a noise of hurrying and scurrying, and along came Tom the cat through the forest, with Princess Hilda holding on to his tail. As soon as they were within the circle, Tom dug a little hole in the ground with his two fore-paws, throwing up the dirt behind, and then said: "Give me the Golden Ivy-seed, Princess Hilda; but make haste; for Frank is burning for Henry's sake!"

So she made haste to give him the Seed; and he planted it quickly in the little hole, and covered the earth over it, and then said: "Give me the Diamond Water-drop; but make haste; for Frank is burning for Henry's sake!"

So she made haste to give him the Drop; and he poured half of it on the fire, and the other half on the place where the Seed was planted. And immediately the fire was put out, and there lay Prince Frank all alive and well; but the mark of Rumpty-Dudget's mud on his nose was burned away, and his hair and eyes, which before had been brown and hazel, were not quite black. So up he jumped, and he and Princess Hilda and Tom all kissed each other heartily; and then Prince Frank said:

"Why, Hilda! the black spot that you had on your forehead has gone away, too."

"Yes," said the cat; "that happened when the King of the Gnomes kissed her. But now make yourselves ready, children; for we are going to take a ride to Rumpty-Dudget's tower!"

The two children were very much surprised when they heard this, and looked about to see what they were to ride on. But behold! the Golden Ivy-seed, watered with the Diamond Water-drop, was already growing and sprouting, and a strong stem with bright golden leaves had pushed itself out of the earth, and was creeping along the ground in the direction of Rumpty-Dudget's tower. The cat put Princess Hilda and Prince Frank on the two largest leaves, and got on the stem himself, and so away they went merrily, and in a very short time the Ivy had carried them to the tower gates.

"Now jump down," said the cat.

Down they all jumped accordingly; but the Golden Ivy kept on, and climbed over the gate, and crept up the stairs, and along the narrow passageway, until, in less time than it takes to write it, the Ivy had reached the room with the thousand and one corners, in the midst of which Rumpty-Dudget was standing; and all around were the poor little children whom he had caught, standing with their faces to the wall and their hands behind their backs. When Rumpty-Dudget saw the Golden Ivy creeping toward him, he was very much frightened, as well he might be, and he tried to run away; but the Ivy caught him, and twined around him, and squeezed him tighter and tighter and tighter, until all the mischief was squeezed out of him; but since Rumpty-Dudget was made of mischief, of course when all the mischief was squeezed out of him, there was no Rumpty-Dudget left. He was gone forever.

Instantly, all the children that he had kept in the thousand and one corners were free, and came racing and shouting out of the gray tower, with Prince Henry at their head. And when he saw his brother and sister, and they saw him, they all three hugged and kissed one another as if they were crazy. At last Princess Hilda said: "Why, Henry, the spot that was on your chin has gone away, too! And your hair and eyes are brown and hazel instead of being black."

"Yes," said a voice, which Hilda fancied she had somewhere heard before; "while he stood in the corner his chin rubbed against the wall, until the spot was gone; so now he no longer wishes to do what he is told not to do, or not to do what he is told to do; and when he is spoken to, he answers sweetly and obediently, as a violin answers to the bow when it touches the strings."

Then the children looked around, and there stood a beautiful lady, with a golden crown on her head, and loving smile in her eyes. It was their fairy aunt, whom they had never seen before except in their dreams.

"Oh," said Princess Hilda, "you look like our mamma, who went away to a distant country, and left us behind. And your voice is like the voice of the Queen of the Air-Spirits; and of—"

"Yes, my darlings," said the beautiful lady, taking the three children in her arms; "I am the Queen, your mother; though, by Rumpty-Dudget's enchantments, I was obliged to leave you, and only be seen by you at night in your dreams. And I was the Queen of the Air-Spirits, Hilda, whose voice you had heard before; and I was the King of the Gnomes, though I seemed so harsh and stern at first. But my love has been with you always, and has followed you everywhere. And now you shall come with me to our home in Fairy Land. Are you all ready?"

"Oh, but where is Tom the cat?" cried all the three children together. "We cannot go and be happy in Fairy Land without him!"

Then the Queen laughed, and kissed them, and said: "I am Tom the cat, too!"

When the children heard this, they were perfectly contented; and they clung about her neck, and she folded her arms around them, and flew with them over the tops of the forest trees to their beautiful home in Fairy Land; and there they are all living happily to this very day. But Princess Hilda's eyes are blue, and her hair is golden, still.

The Cat That Winked

This story was written by Anna McClure Sholl (1866?–1956) for her book
The Faery Tales of Weir, *which was published in 1918. Besides writing a*
number of books, she was also a painter.

Once there was an old woman who lived on the edge of the Dark
Wood in a small cottage all covered with thick thatch, and over the thatch
grew a honey-suckle vine; but at the gable where the chimneys clustered,
the wisteria flung purple flowers in May.

On the topmost chimney was a stork's nest, and there dear grandfather
stork stood on one leg, unless he was wanted to carry a little baby to some
house in the village; when he flapped his wings and flew away over the
tree-tops to the Land of Little Souls.

Now the old woman loved her home, because she had lived there many
years with her husband. She loved the two worn chairs on each side of the
great hearth, and her pewter dishes, and her big china water-pitcher with
flowers shining on it—not for themselves, but for the reason that once
someone had used them and admired them with her.

Into the little latticed windows the roses peeped, and these Mother
Huldah loved too, and tended carefully all through the sweet-smelling
summertime. But perhaps she liked best the long winter evenings when
she spun by the fire and sang little songs like these:

> "My heart as a bird has flown away,
> (Princess, where? Princess, where?)
> Into the land that is always gay,
> Out of the land of care.

> "But no bird flies alone to bliss,
> (Princess, why? Princess, why?)

I have no answer but a kiss,
And then the open sky."

Nobody listened but Tommie, who was an immense black cat, held in great reverence by the villagers, for he had the greenest eyes and the longest whiskers and the heaviest fur of any cat in the kingdom. Moreover, he had hundreds of mice to his credit and no birds, for he was a good and wise grimalkin. Sometimes he talked with his tail and sometimes he opened his pink mouth, and said just as plain as words that he had been stalking through the moonlight and had seen old Egbert go limping home as if he had the rheumatism.

So next day Mother Huldah with her little bag of medicines and ointments would go to old Egbert's hut, and sure enough, find him bedridden; or Tommie would tell her that Charlemagne the Stork had carried a baby to a poor mother who had no clothes for it. Then Mother Huldah would go to her great cedar chest and take out linen that smelled all sweetly of lavender, and carry it with some good food to the poor woman.

Mother Huldah was so kind and generous that everybody got in the habit of taking things from her without sometimes so much as a "thank you," or an inquiry as to her own health. But the little children loved her because she made them pretty cakes; and told them the stories she used to tell her own children, her two fine sons who were now soldiers. These sons sent her the money upon which she lived and out of which she made her little charities, and they wrote her fine brave letters, and every year they came home to see her, bearing beautiful presents from foreign lands, ivory toys and shining silks (which she always gave to some bride) and workboxes of sweet-scented wood richly carved—to show how much they loved her.

One dreadful year a great war broke out, and not long after, Mother Huldah heard that her two sons had been killed, and she herself thought she would follow them from grief. But she lived on and as she grew more sorrowful she went less and less to the village, and people began to forget her. Even the little children stayed away since she had no longer the heart to tell them the tales she had once told her sons; and she must no longer bake the little cakes since every day saw her small hoard of money diminishing.

At last, when the winter tempests were raging, and the sleet was beating upon the thatch, there came a day when no food remained in the cottage;

and Mother Huldah felt too weak and sick to go out in quest of it. Nor did she wish to tell her neighbors that no food remained in the cottage.

So, full of weary dreams and old sad thoughts she sat down in one of the armchairs before the fire, and whether she nodded from drowsiness, or whether Tommie nodded at her she never knew, but he moved his black head and opened his pink mouth, and said he, "Suppose I fetch you a bird just this once."

She was much surprised, for Tommie had never talked to her before, but she did not show how astonished she was; she was always very polite to him. So she replied, "Bless your whiskers! Tommie! But we won't break through our rule. Maybe some neighbor will fetch me a loaf!"

"Maybe they will and perhaps they won't," said Tommie. "They're an ungrateful lot."

"They think I am still rich, my dear," she answered.

"So you are, but not in the way they mean," Tommie said. "And, Mother Huldah, if they neglect you a day longer it won't be your Tommie's fault."

Then Mother Huldah shook her finger at him. "You switch your tail just as if you were going to steal something, Tommie. I brought you up better than that."

"Steal! nonsense!" cried Tommie. "Most of 'em have more than they need, anyway."

"Tommie, I believe you're hungry, or your morals wouldn't be so queer!" Mother Huldah said reprovingly.

"Hungry!" exclaimed Tommie. "I dream of lobster claws and chicken wings and blue saucers full of yellow wrinkled cream, twelve in a row. No wonder my morals are queer!"

Then what happened was that poor Mother Huldah dozed off to sleep and when she awoke there was Tommie staring into the fire, his green eyes like two lanterns and his whiskers standing out very stiff and knowing, and at Mother Huldah's feet was a wicker basket from which issued a most appetizing odor. "Why, Thomas" (she always called him Thomas in solemn moments), "what's this?"

"Your dinner," said Tommie, and yawned like a gentleman who lights a cigarette and says, "Oh, hang it all! What a beastly bore life is."

"Thomas," questioned Mother Huldah solemnly, "where did you get this dinner?" for she had taken the cover off the basket and found a small roast chicken with vegetables and a bread pudding.

"Why, I was strolling down the gray lane when I met a woman carrying that basket and I smelled chicken; so up I stood on my hind legs, and winked at her and I said, 'Thank you, I know you are taking that to Mother Huldah; let me carry it the rest of the way.'"

But Mother Huldah cried, "Maybe the dinner wasn't for me, and you frightened her so she had to give it to you."

Tommie yawned again. "Don't you think that the best thing you can do with a good dinner is to eat it?"

So Mother Huldah ate her dinner, hoping all the while that she was making an honest meal; then, when she had fed Thomas, she asked him if Charlemagne the Stork was on the roof. "Indeed, no!" cried he. "Charlemagne has flown to the war country to fetch you a baby!"

"Alas!" cried Mother Huldah. "I pity the poor babes, but how can I bring up a baby!"

"It is your granddaughter," said Tommie. "Charlemagne told me that a year ago your son Rupert married but he meant to bring his bride home as a surprise to you. Then the war broke out and—"

"Oh, poor little daughter-in-law!" cried Mother Huldah. "Did she break her heart?"

"Yes, and so she followed Rupert to the Country of the Brave souls; but Charlemagne is fetching the baby in a warm woolen napkin tied up at the four corners, and when his wings get tired from flying he puts a bit of sugar and a drop of water in the baby's mouth and leans his feathery breast against its little feet to keep them warm!"

"Yes! yes!" said Mother Huldah, "a baby's feet should be always kept warm—but dear me, dear me, the Sweet One will need milk before long, and the grain of the whole wheat to help her grow! I have no money to buy her food."

Tommie looked very wise. "Mother Huldah," he said, as he drew a black paw knowingly over one ear, "don't you know that wherever a baby comes, help comes? Open the linen chest and get your shining shears and begin to make little shirts and dresses. I think I'll take a look at the weather."

He made the last remark carelessly like a young gentleman who will stroll out and leave the women-folk to their devices.

"Oh, Tommie!" said Mother Huldah, "you are not going to do anything impulsive?"

"Mother Huldah," replied Tommie, "did you ever know a cat to do anything impulsive unless he saw a bird, or a mouse?"

With that he left her, and she watched him walk away down the forest path with the sunlight glistening on his coat and his tail held high and straight. Sometimes he would pause and lift one foot daintily, the toes curling in. Mother Huldah always said that Tommie heard not with his ears but with his whiskers, and perhaps it was true.

Tommie himself was making his own plans as he went along. "If I tell these villagers outright that Mother Huldah is in need, each person will think, 'Oh, well, Neighbor Jude, or Gossip Dorcas has more to spare than I. Someone else will take care of the poor old lady, I am sure.' And it will end in her getting nothing at all. I will not talk about her, but to each person I will talk about myself, for that is the way to get people interested."

At which Tommie smiled, and because his great-grandfather was a Cheshire Cat, his smile gave him a wise and jovial look, as if the Sphinx of Egypt should suddenly see a joke. With a good heart he went daintily on his way, shaking the snow from his paws at times, until he reached the village green. Now in the middle of the green stood the pump, made of wood with a flat top. On this Tommie seated himself, put his paws neatly together, folded his tail about them, made his green eyes perfectly round, and stared straight ahead of him.

Now even a cat when he looks as if he could think for himself will draw people's attention; especially if he seems to enjoy his thoughts. And Tommie, seated on the pump in the bright winter sunshine, looked as if he had something in his mind that pleased him.

"Heigh-O," said one of the passers-by. "Here's a witch-cat!"

"You are mistaken," replied Tommie with a wink. "I belong to Mother Huldah, and she is the best woman in the village."

The man was so astonished that he dropped a parcel of eggs he was carrying, and they were all broken.

"That's what comes," said Tommie, "of imagining evil where none exists."

The man was so angry that he made some snowballs hastily and began to pelt Tommie with them, but Tommie understood the beautiful art of dodging—which some people never learn all their lives—so he didn't get hit. By this time a crowd had gathered about the angry man, and were asking him what was the matter.

"Matter!" he shrieked, "that black object on the pump gave me impudence!"

"Heigh-O!" cried little Elsa. "How could a cat give thee impudence!"

"Ask him then," said the man. "He can talk like any Christian."

At which the crowd all looked at Tommie, who winked at them and said, "Does anybody here want to ask me any questions? I'll tell him what he wants to know in perfect confidence between him and me and the pump. If my answer pleases him, he can give me a silver piece. If my reply makes his heart pit-a-pat with joy, he can give me a gold piece. If he doesn't like my answers, he needn't give me anything. Now that's fair, isn't?"

Then everybody looked at everybody else, and dropped their jaws and rubbed their eyes. Nobody stirred for a minute, then a fine young fellow stepped forward, blushing. This was Carl, the miller's son, who was straight as a birch-tree, and had blue eyes like deep lakes, and he walked right up to the pump, and bowed, then whispered into Tommie's ear, "Does Lucia love me?"

Tommie winked his right eye and smiled. "Carl," he replied, "get up your courage and ask her today, for she loves you better than anyone in the world."

Then Carl felt his heart go pit-a-pat, and all the snow wreaths on the trees seemed to turn to bridal flowers. "Thanks, dear and wise Pussy," he said, and took out his handkerchief and spread it at Tommie's feet and on it he placed not one, but three gold pieces.

When the villagers saw the gold pieces glittering in the sun and beheld the radiant face of Carl, they all began to wonder, and each person wanted to try his own luck. "After all," said each one to himself, "if I don't like what the cat says I needn't pay him anything."

The next person to go up was the village tanner, whose skin was like leather and whose eyes were little like a pig's. Tommie was already acquainted with him, having been kicked out once when on an innocent mousing expedition.

"Say," said the tanner, "will my Uncle Jean leave me his farm?"

"No," answered Tommie, winking his left eye. "That he won't! He knows you are always wishing he would die!"

The tanner was so angry that he snarled: "Don't you ever let me catch you around the tannery again, or I'll make you into a muff for my daughter."

"Black furs are not fashionable this winter," said Tommie. "Next?"

Everybody laughed when they saw that the Tanner hadn't paid money for his information, and so, presumably, didn't like it. But strange enough, instead of discouraging, this led them on to try their luck; and the next person who came to ask Tommie a question was poor old half-blind Henley the miser. He put his mouth close to the cat's ear, so the people behind him wouldn't catch what he said, and in a hoarse voice he asked, "Say, old whiskers, will my fine ship loaded with dates and spices reach Norway safely?"

"Yes, it will," said Tommie, "long before your withered old soul will reach a haven of peace."

Henley was so excited over the first words that he didn't even hear the last ones. He hopped about on one leg, and was rushing off at last when Tommie cried, "Heigh-O, you haven't paid me."

The miser felt in his pockets and drew out a silver coin and laid it on the handkerchief.

"Not at all," said Tommie. "Remember the worth of that cargo! Gold or nothing."

Henley began to whine. "I'm a poor old man, Tommie. I'll leave the cream jug on the doorstep every day and no questions asked!"

"I'm not a thief," answered Tommie. "Mother Huldah brought me up better than that. Come, you don't want to have any quarrel with a black cat."

Whereupon Henley reluctantly drew from his pocket a gold piece, while all the villagers opened their eyes very wide, and wondered what Tommie could have told the old gentleman to make him so liberal.

The next person to come up was a little shy girl named Clara. She had big brown eyes and fair floating hair, and under her white chin and about her little white wrists were soft furs; for her father was a wealthy money-lender. She came close to Tommie and whispered, "Tell me, beautiful Pussy, if I shall ever win the love of Joseph Grange."

Tommie winked his right eye several times and replied, "My dear, I see it coming!"

She flushed with joy. "And what shall I do to hasten it?"

Tommie reflected a moment. "Be pleasant, but not anxious. A lady with an anxious expression has little chance of winning a lover! Don't invite him too often; don't talk too much. Now I haven't hurt your feelings, have I?"

"No, indeed," she said, for she was a young lady of good sense. "And Tommie, dear, will you take these gold pieces to Mother Huldah? She was so good to me when I was a little girl, and because I have been so absorbed in my own affairs I haven't been to see her lately."

"That's the trouble with being in love," said Tommie, "it's apt to make people selfish, and it should make them love and remember everybody. It does when it's the real thing."

Little Clara clasped her hands earnestly. "I will come to see Mother Huldah this afternoon," she said, "and bring her some cakes of my own baking."

After Clara one person and another came up. Some asked foolish questions, some wise. Some paid down money, others didn't, but the pile of gold and silver at Tommie's feet grew steadily.

Now all novelties, even talking cats, soon cease to be novelties, and towards afternoon when the villagers saw how much money of theirs lay at Tommie's feet, some of them began to be discontented. Of these the tanner was the ringleader, and he said to the other grumblers, "If we can get that lying cat off the pump, we can take his money. I have three big rats at the tannery, and I know Tommie is starving hungry by this time. We'll let 'em loose on the ground in front of the pump. When he makes a spring one of you grab the money and run."

Now the tanner had guessed right. Tommie was hungry, but he was determined to keep his post until sundown. After a while no more people came, and he was just thinking he would take up the handkerchief by the four corners and go home, when he espied a group of people approaching. Suddenly, oh, me, oh, my! three dinners were scampering towards him, such rats, such big splendid rats in fine condition. Tommie had never used such self-control in all his nine lives, but he sat tight and though his whiskers showed his agitation he never budged.

The tanner was mad clear through, and he cried out, "He's a wizard; he ought to be killed," because some people can't see others controlling themselves without thinking there's something wrong with them. Then he began to make snowballs and to pelt poor Tommie.

Now Tommie, as has been said, was a good dodger, but nevertheless when it rains snowballs it's hard not to get hit. It might have fared badly with him had not some knights and ladies at that moment appeared on the scene in the train of the beautiful Princess Yolande, one of the fairest princesses in all the realm. She rode a great white horse, and she was robed in cream velvet and white furs, while about her slender waist was a girdle of gold set with sapphires which were as blue as her eyes. By her side rode Lord Mountfalcon. He was all in black for he was mourning a brother who had died in the distant war.

Love as well as grief filled his heart, for his dark eyes were continually upon the beautiful Princess, who now reined in her horse and cried out in a sweet voice, "Shame upon you men to hurt a poor cat!"

"He is a wizard and he belongs to a witch," called out the tanner.

"Oh, what a wicked lie," said Tommie. "I don't care what names you call me, but my mistress is one of the best women in the land. She has come to poverty in her old age. For her sake and to get her a little money, I've sat here all day answering truthfully all questions. Now, dear Princess Yolande, believe me, for I am a true cat."

The Princess was so astonished that she couldn't speak for a moment. At last she turned to Lord Mountfalcon and said: "Truly, we have come to wonderland. I'd rather believe the cat than the people who were pelting him, and I have a mind to test his powers. Let us alight and ask him questions."

Then they all dismounted and with the pages and the ladies and gentlemen in armor the scene was as gay as the stage of an opera. Everybody chatted and laughed, and some of the court ladies stroked Tommie's fur with their pretty white hands; and one took off her bracelet and hung it about his neck.

But when the Princess Yolande went forward to ask her question, everyone fell back. Then with sweet dignity, as became a princess, she stood before Tommie and said, "Tell me if Lord Mountfalcon love me truly."

Tommie didn't wink, for he knew the ways of court, his grandfather having been chief mouser to old King Adelbert; but he purred a warm good purr, like a mill grinding out pure white grain.

> "If the sky in heaven be blue,
> Then Mountfalcon loves you true;
> If the sun sets in the West,
> Lord Mountfalcon loves you best.

"You see," he added, "I'm not much of a poet, but those are the facts."

"Never was bad verse so sweet to me," cried the Princess and she put down a whole bag of gold at Tommie's feet.

After her came Lord Mountfalcon himself with that sad grace of his, and all his spirit shadowed with love and grief. "Sir Puss," he said, "shall I wed ever the Princess Yolande?"

"Before there are violets in the vales of the kingdom," replied Tommie.

"Two saddlebags will not hold the gold I shall give thee," exclaimed the nobleman.

"Bring them to the cottage where Mother Huldah lives," said Tommie. "And I ask this further favor: When you leave this spot will you take me up behind you and give the money to a page to convey; and so bring me safely home with the wealth, for I fear mischief from the tanner."

"Most willingly," said Mountfalcon. "I will present your request to the Princess."

After him all the court came with questions; so when the page advanced to gather up the money the load was almost more than he could carry. Then Tommie jumped down from his perch, and another page lifted him safely on to the big warm back of Lord Mountfalcon's horse, which felt fine and comforting to poor Tommie's feet. He was so tired that he took forty winks after he had told the Princess how to reach the cottage of Mother Huldah.

When he awoke they were all in the dim forest and the Princess Yolande and Lord Mountfalcon were talking in low tones like the whisper of the wind through flowers; and it seemed as if their talk were all of love and dreams and far-away griefs and tears that must fall.

At last they reined in their horses where Mother Huldah stood at her gate peering into the forest. When she saw the beautiful lady and the noble knight and Tommie on the horse's back, she cried out, "Oh, bless you, Sir Knight, for bringing him home."

"And I've brought a fortune with me, Mother Huldah," cried Tommie.

At this Mother Huldah looked troubled. "Gracious Lady," she addressed the Princess, "I hope my cat has not been up to mischief."

"No, bless him," replied the Princess; then she told all that Tommie had done. "And fear not to take the money, Mother," she added, "for those who gave it did so of their free will."

"Alas! I would not take it," sighed Mother Huldah, "had not my Rupert and my Hugh died in the great war; and Rupert's wife went with him to the Kingdom of the Brave Souls; and I expect Charlemagne the Stork tonight with their little baby."

"Rupert? what Rupert?" asked Lord Mountfalcon, leaning down from his horse.

"Rupert Gordon; I am Huldah Gordon, his bereaved mother!"

Then Mountfalcon removed his cap, alighted from his horse and bowed low before Mother Huldah. "He died gloriously. He died trying to remove my poor brother from danger," he said. "Now let me be as a son to you, for sweet memory's sake."

Then they all wept softly, for even to hear of those battles and those Silent Ones in the Kingdom of the Brave Souls was to behold the world through tears. And the Princess Yolande alighted and kissed Mother Huldah's hands and promised to visit her often.

So with many true words they parted at last, and Mother Huldah was left alone with Tommie and the bags of gold and silver, which she took indoors and then returned to scan the sky where now the white stars hung and a thin half-circle of a moon. Tommie romped in the snow for the joy of stretching his legs. After a while he said, "Listen, don't you hear something, Mother Huldah?"

"I would I heard wings!" she cried.

"But I hear wings," said Tommie. "Watch! watch where the North Star burns!"

So Mother Huldah watched, and soon she saw the great outspread wings of Charlemagne and saw his long bill with something hanging from the end of it.

"My word, here's the baby," called out Tommie. "Hello, Charlemagne, you old Grandpa! Have you kept that precious infant warm?"

But Charlemagne alighted on his feet and walked solemnly to Mother Huldah and laid in her arms the softest, sweetest, pinkest little baby that she had ever seen. There was golden down on its head, and its little hands were folded like rosebuds beneath its tiny chin.

Mother Huldah felt its feet to know if they were warm; then she cried and sobbed and held the little thing to her breast, and trembled for love of it.

"Take it before the fire," said Tommie. "We're all tired tonight and it will be good to drowse and dream. Goodnight, Charlemagne. The chimney's warm."

So the stork flew up to the roof, and Mother Huldah took her treasure and held it in her warm, ample lap before the fire; and Tommie winked and dozed and looked at the baby with his great green eyes, while Mother Huldah sang:

"The gold of the world will fade away,
    Baby, sleep! Baby, sleep!
But thou wilt live in my heart alway,
    Sleep, my darling, sleep.

"The gold of the world it comes and goes,
    Baby, sleep! Baby, sleep!
But thou wilt bloom like a summer rose,
    Cease my soul to weep."

The Three White Cats

Although this story comes from Brittany, I have not been able to trace its origin any further.

A king and queen who for years had longed for a daughter finally had one born to them. They were the happiest people on earth except for one thing. A year before the princess was born her birth had been predicted along with a warning by a sorceress. It was the warning that weighed heavily on the hearts of the two monarchs.

"Your daughter will fall dead if she ever gives her hand in marriage to a prince," they had been told. "Heed this advice. Find three pure white cats and let them grow up with your child. Give them balls of two types to play with—balls of gold and balls of linen thread. If they ignore the gold and play with the linen, all will be well, but should they ignore the linen and choose the gold, beware!"

The three cats were duly found and became good friends. Better yet they learned to love their young mistress and she them, and as the months passed and became years the linen balls continued to be the only toys the cats chose to play with. The gold balls would have gathered cobwebs had they not been dusted regularly, and everyone began to forget their original purpose.

When the princess grew old enough to learn how to spin the cats were happy as she was. They leaped at the wheel as it turned and at the thread as the princess made it. She begged them to leave things alone but they paid no attention to her and continued to play gaily. The queen, happy as she was in their continued neglect of the gold balls, laughed and indulged their frolicking.

The princess was now sixteen years old and very beautiful. People came from far and near to see her beauty, and princes continued to ask for her

hand in marriage, but she remained indifferent to all. She seemed perfectly content to continue living as she was with her three beloved cats.

One day, however, a prince arrived who was so good and wise and
handsome in her eyes that she knew she would marry him at once if he
asked. But although he visited the palace often and brought many gifts he
never mentioned the subject of marriage. As he was leaving from one of
his extended visits she finally could bear it no longer and confessed her
love for him, and he, in delighted surprise, expressed his for her.

The cats were in the tower room playing with the linen balls but no
sooner had the prince and princess professed their love for each other,
than they seemed to see the gold balls for the first time in their lives and
gave chase to them. The news spread throughout the palace but it wasn't
the princess who was affected by the switch in balls. The prince became
gravely ill and nothing the physicians tried helped to cure the strange mal-
ady which had struck him down.

In desperation the princess sought the sorceress who had made the
prophecy about the cats and balls. What she learned from her was almost
as bad as knowing nothing. There was only one almost impossible way to
save the prince. Only twenty-seven days remained before Christmas but
in that time she would have to spin ten thousand skeins of pure white
linen thread if her lover, whose thread of life had reached the breaking
point, would live. No hand but hers could spin the ten thousand skeins
and the prince would die at midnight of Christmas night if they weren't
finished by then.

The sadly frightened girl rushed home to her spinning wheel and
worked steadily until dawn. More discouraged than tired she gazed at the
little she had accomplished and burst into tears. Through her sobs she
seemed to hear her cats call to her.

Ready to believe anything she gazed lovingly at them. "If you only
knew what was wrong I know you'd help me if you could," she told them.

"We know what's needed and can and will help you," they replied.
"After all, we don't have hands but paws so we can do the spinning for you
and no one will be able to object. Now please let us get to work. Even for
us the time left is very short."

And so it was that the three cats began to spin, each at a wheel provided for it. And spin they did—rapidly and beautifully. All day the three
wheels hummed and when they were silent as evening came the princess

looked into the room to find her beloved cats sound asleep next to three hundred skeins of thread.

As the days passed and the skeins grew in number the prince's health began to mend and the princess's spirits soared. On Christmas day the ten thousand skeins were ready for the sorceress and the prince was almost well.

The sorceress was more than pleased with the cats' work and told the princess to be sure and show her gratitude to the cats for saving the life of her lover. Such a reminder was unnecessary. The girl had always loved them as much as she thought possible but her gratitude had increased even this great love. She gave them all her jewels which she found they had always greatly admired, and at the wedding feast, decked in these jewels, they sat in a place of honor on magnificent cushions.

As the feast continued the cats curled up contentedly on their cushions and suddenly from all three came a pleasant hum. It was the wonderful, happy sound of purring, the reward, the cats explained to the princess, they had received for their help to her. Strangely enough the sound was very much like the whir and hum of a spinning wheel. And from that day to this cats have continued to purr whenever they feel contented.

BIBLIOGRAPHY

PUSS IN BOOTS

Page 3—"The Eleventh Night, The First Fable"
Giovanni Francesco Straparola, *Le piacevoli notti* (*The Facetious Nights* or *The Delectable Nights*) or *Piacefole notti*, 1550-1553 as translated by W. G. Waters in *The Italian Novelists: The Facetious Nights of Straparola*, Vol. 4, Members of the Society of Bibliophiles, 1901.

Page 8—"Puss in Boots"
Charles Perrault, *Histoires ou contes du temps passé* (*Histories, or Tales of Past Times*), 1697 as translated by Robert Samber in 1729, who called it "The Master Cat: or Puss in Boots."

Page 13—"Gagliuso"
Giambattista Basile, *Il Pentamerone* (*The Five Days*) [originally titled *Lo Cunto de li Cunti* (*The Story of Stories* or *The Tales of Tales*)], 1634 as translated by Sir Richard Burton, *Il Pentamerone or The Tale of Tales*, Horace Liveright Inc., 1893 and 1927.

THE KING OF THE CATS

Page 18—"Beware the Cat" (excerpt)
William Baldwin, *Beware the Cat*, 1553. I modernized the spelling primarily relying on the version edited by William P. Holden, *Beware the Cat and The Funerals of King Edward the Sixth*, Connecticut College Monograph No. 8, Connecticut College, New London, Connecticut, 1963, while consulting the version edited by William A. Ringler, Jr. and Michael Flachmann, *Beware the Cat: The First English Novel*, Huntington Library, San Marino, California, 1988.

Page 22—"Sir Walter Scott's Cat" (not its original title)
Washington Irving, an excerpt from "Abbotsford," 1835, *Irving's Works*, Vol. 8, G. P. Putnam's Sons, New York, 1850.

Page 24—"The King of the Cats"
Folk-Lore Journal, Vol. 2 as reprinted by Edwin Sidney Hartland, *English Fairy and Other Folk Tales*, Walter Scott, London, 1890.

DICK WHITTINGTON AND HIS CAT

Page 26—"The History of Whittington"
As reprinted in Andrew Lang, *The Blue Fairy Book,* Longmans, Green and Co., London, 1889. Original source unknown.

Page 33—"The Origin of Venice" (not its original title)
Albert, *The Chronicle of Albert,* c. 1256 originally appeared as *Chronicon Alberti Abbatis Stadensis à condito orbe usque ad auctoris ætatem, &c.,* Helmæstadii, 1687, and is quoted in Thomas Keightley, *Tales and Popular Fictions,* Whittaker and Co., London, 1834.

Page 34—"The Genoese Merchant" (not its original title)
Author unknown, appeared in *Facezie, Motti, Buffonerie et Burle del Piovano Arlotto,* In Firenze appresso, i Giunti, 1565 as quoted in Thomas Keightley, *Tales and Popular Fictions,* Whittaker and Co., London, 1834.

Page 37—"The Island of Kais" (not its original title)
Wásif (Abdulláh, the son of Fazlulláh), *Events of Ages and Fates of Cities,* thirteenth century as quoted in Sir [William] Gore Ouseley, *Biographical Notices of Persian Poets,* W. H. Allen and Co., London, 1846.

An alternate version of Wásif is quoted in James Morier, *Second Journey through Persia, Armenia, and Asia Minor, to Constantinople, Between the Years 1810 and 1816,* Longman, Hurst, Rees, Orme, and Brown, London, 1818, which in turn appears in Thomas Keightley, *Tales and Popular Fictions,* Whittaker and Co., London, 1834. Keightley also cites Sir William [Gore] Ouseley, *Travels in various Countries of the East: More Particularly Persia,* Vol. 1, Rodwell and Martin, London, 1819-1823.

Page 39—"The Honest Penny"
Peter Christen Asbjörnsen's *Norske Folke-Eventyr* (*Norwegian Folk-Tales*), 1871 as translated by Sir George Webbe Dasent, *Tales from the Fjeld,* Gibbings and Co., London, 1874.

Page 44—"The Cottager and His Cat"
Author unknown, *Isländische Märchen* (*Icelandic Fairytales*) as quoted in Andrew Lang, *The Crimson Fairy Book,* Longmans, Green and Co., London, 1903.

GRIMMS' FAIRY TALES

Page 48—"The Bremen Town Muscians"
Brothers Grimm, *Household Tales,* translated by Lucy Crane, Macmillan and Co., New York, 1886.

Page 52—"The Poor Miller's Boy and the Cat"
Brothers Grimm, *Grimms' Complete Fairy Tales,* Nelson Doubleday, Garden City, New York, n.d.

Page 56—"The Three Children of Fortune"
Brothers Grimm, *Grimms' Complete Fairy Tales,* Nelson Doubleday, Garden City, New York, n.d.

OTHER WELL-KNOWN TALES

Page 59—"The White Cat"
Countess Marie-Catherine d'Aulnoy, *d'Aulnoy's Fairy Tales,* translated by J. R. Planché, David McKay, Publisher, Philadelphia, n.d.

Page 93—"The Boy Who Drew Cats"
Lafcadio Hearn, *Japanese Fairy Tales,* Liveright Publishing, New York, 1902.

Page 97—"The Cat That Walked by Himself"
Rudyard Kipling, *Just So Stories,* Doubleday and Co., New York, 1912.

LESSER KNOWN CAT FAIRY TALES

Page 109—"Scratch Tom"
Walter Douglas Campbell, *Beyond the Border,* A. Constable and Co., Westminster, England, 1898.

Page 121—"The Lion and the Cat"
Adapted from *North American Indian Legends* for Andrew Lang, *The Brown Fairy Book,* Longmans, Green and Co., London, 1904.

Page 127—"Conall Yellowclaw" (excerpt)
Joseph Jacobs, *Celtic Fairy Tales,* G. P. Putnam's Sons, New York, 1892.

Page 130—"The Story of the Faithful Cat"
Lord Redesdale (Algernon Bertram Freeman-Mitford), *Tales of Old Japan,* Macmillan and Co., London, 1871.

Page 132—"The Cat Who Became a Queen"
Rev. J. Hinton Knowles, *Folk-Tales of Kashmir,* Trübner and Co., London, 1888.

Page 135—"The Two Caskets"
Benjamin Thorp, *Yule-Tide Stories,* Bohn Library, London, 1853.

Page 144—"Lord Peter"
Peter Christen Asbjörnsen and Jörgen Engelbretsen Moe, *Norske Huldre-Eventyr og Folke-sagen* (*Norwegian Mythical Tales and Popular Legends*), two volumes, 1845 and 1848 as translated by Sir George Webbe Dasent, *Popular Tales from the Norse,* D. Appleton and Co., New York, 1858.

Page 149—"The Cat's Elopement"
David Brauns, *Japanische Märchen und Sagen,* Wilhelm Friedrich, Leipzig, 1885 as quoted in Andrew Lang, *The Pink Fairy Book,* Longmans, Green and Co., London, 1897.

Page 152—"Owney and Owney-na-peak"
Gerald Griffin, *"Holland-Tide;" or, Munster Popular Tales,* Simpkin and Marshall, London, 1827 as quoted in William Butler Yeats, *Fairy and Folk Tales of the Irish Peasantry,* Walter Scott, London, 1888, which was also published as *Irish Fairy Tales, Irish Fairy and Folk Tales,* and *Fairy and Folk Tales of Ireland.*

Page 164—"The Clever Cat"
Adapted from *Contes Berbères* (*Stories of the Berbers*) for Andrew Lang, *The Orange Fairy Book,* Longmans, Green and Co., London, 1906.

Page 174—"Kisa"
Dr. Adeline Rittershaus, *Die Neuisländischen Volksmärchen* (*Scandinavian Folktales*), Max Niemeyer, Halle, 1902 which cites an 1866 manuscript (Lbs. 423 8vo) that is in the Landesbibliothek of Reykjavik, Iceland. It was adapted in Andrew Lang, *The Brown Fairy Book,* Longmans, Green and Co., London, 1904.

Page 179—"The Cat and the Cradle"
William Elliot Griffis, *Dutch Fairy Tales for Young Folks,* Thomas Y. Crowell Co., New York, 1918.

Page 185—"The Colony of Cats"
Andrew Lang, *The Crimson Fairy Book,* Longmans, Green and Co., London, 1903.

Page 191—"The Gray Cat" (originally "The Gray Cat and the Cave of the Four Winds")
Jane G. Austin, *Fairy Dreams; or, Wanderings in Elf-Land,* J. E. Tilton and Co., Boston,
1859.

Page 205—"Spiegel, The Kitten"
Gottfried Keller, *Die Leute von Seldwyla* (*The People from Seldwyla*), 1856, translated by E.
B. Ashton. It also appears in Hermann Kesten, *The Blue Flower: Best Stories of the Roman-
ticists,* Roy Publishers, 1946 and in Jack Zipes, *Spells of Enchantment,* Viking Press, New
York, 1991.

Page 236—"Rumpty-Dudget's Tower"
Julian Hawthorne, originally appeared in *St. Nicholas* magazine, 1879, then in *Yellow-
Cap, and Other Fairy Stories for Children,* Longmans, Green and Co., London, 1880.

Page 254—"The Cat That Winked"
Anna McClure Sholl, *The Faery Tales of Weir,* E. P. Dutton and Co., New York, 1918.

Page 266—"Three White Cats" (not its original title)
As quoted in Claire Necker, *The Natural History of the Cat,* A. S. Barnes and Co., Cran-
bury, NJ, 1970. It also appears in John Richard Stephens, *The Enchanted Cat,* Prima Publishing and Communications, Rocklin, California, 1990.